The Other... **W9-BLW-163**
"PURE DELIGHT."
—MaryJanice Davidson, *New York Times* bestselling author

PRAISE FOR
Bone Magic

"Erotic and darkly bewitching, *Bone Magic* turns up the heat on the D'Artigo sisters. Galenorn writes another winner in the Otherworld series, a mix of magic and passion sure to captivate readers."
—Jeaniene Frost, *New York Times* bestselling author

Demon Mistress

"As always, [Galenorn] delivers intriguing characters, intricate plot layers, and kick-butt action!" —*Romantic Times* (★★★★)

"The tense fights, frights, and demon-bashing take front and center in this book, and I love that . . . All in all, *Demon Mistress* certainly makes for enjoyable summer-time reading!"
—*Errant Dreams Reviews*

Night Huntress

"Yasmine Galenorn is a hot new star in the world of urban fantasy. The Otherworld series is wonderfully entertaining urban fantasy." —Jayne Ann Krentz, *New York Times* bestselling author

"Yasmine Galenorn is a powerhouse author; a master of the craft, who is taking the industry by storm, and for good reason!" —Maggie Shayne, *New York Times* bestselling author

"Yasmine Galenorn hits the stars with *Night Huntress*. Urban fantasy at its best!"
—Stella Cameron, *New York Times* bestselling author

"A thrilling ride from start to finish."
—*The Romance Readers Connection*

continued . . .

"Fascinating and eminently enjoyable from the first page to the last . . . *Night Huntress* rocks! Don't miss it!"
—*Romance Reviews Today*

"Love and betrayal play large roles in *Night Huntress*, and as the story unfolds, the action will sweep fans along for this fast-moving ride." —*Darque Reviews*

DRAGON WYTCH

"Action and sexy sensuality make this book hot to the touch."
—*Romantic Times* (★★★★)

"Ms. Galenorn has a great gift for spinning a compelling story. The supernatural action is a great blend of both fresh and familiar, the characters are each charming in their own way, the heroine's love life is scorching, and the worlds they all live in are well-defined." —*Darque Reviews*

"This is the kind of series that even those who do not care for the supernatural will find a very good read." —*Affaire de Coeur*

"If you're looking for an out-of-this-world enchanting tale of magic and passion, *Dragon Wytch* is the story for you. I will be recommending this wickedly bewitching tale to everyone I know!" —*Dark Angel Reviews*

DARKLING

"The most fulfilling journey of self-discovery to date in the Otherworld series . . . An eclectic blend that works well."
—*Booklist*

"Galenorn does a remarkable job of delving into the psyches and fears of her characters. As this series matures, so do her heroines. The sex sizzles and the danger fascinates."
—*Romantic Times*

"The story is nonstop action and has deep, dark plots that kept me up reading long past my bedtime. Here be Dark Fantasy with a unique twist. YES!" —*Huntress Book Reviews*

CHANGELING

"The second in Galenorn's D'Artigo sisters series ratchets up the danger and romantic entanglements. Along with the quirky humor and characters readers have come to expect is a moving tale of a woman more comfortable in her cat skin than in her human form, looking to find her place in the world." —*Booklist*

"Galenorn's thrilling supernatural series is gritty and dangerous, but it's the tumultuous relationships between all the various characters that give it depth and heart. Vivid, sexy, and mesmerizing, Galenorn's novel hits the paranormal sweet spot."
—*Romantic Times*

"I absolutely loved it!" —*Fresh Fiction*

"Yasmine Galenorn has created another winner . . . *Changeling* is a can't-miss read destined to hold a special place on your keeper shelf." —*Romance Reviews Today*

WITCHLING

"Reminiscent of Laurell K. Hamilton with a lighter touch . . . a delightful new series that simmers with fun and magic."
—Mary Jo Putney, *New York Times* bestselling author of *Loving a Lost Lord*

"The first in an engrossing new series . . . a whimsical reminder of fantasy's importance in everyday life." —*Publishers Weekly*

"*Witchling* is pure delight . . . a great heroine, designer gear, dead guys, and Seattle precipitation!"
—MaryJanice Davidson, *New York Times* bestselling author of *Undead and Unfinished*

"Galenorn's kick-butt Fae ramp up the action in a wyrd world gone awry . . . I loved it!"
—Patricia Rice, author of *Mystic Warrior*

"A fun read, filled with surprise and enchantment."
—Linda Winstead Jones, author of *Come to Me*

Berkley titles by Yasmine Galenorn

The Otherworld Series

WITCHLING
CHANGELING
DARKLING
DRAGON WYTCH
NIGHT HUNTRESS
DEMON MISTRESS
BONE MAGIC
HARVEST HUNTING
BLOOD WYNE

The Indigo Court Series

NIGHT MYST

Anthologies

INKED
NEVER AFTER

Berkley Prime Crime titles by Yasmine Galenorn

GHOST OF A CHANCE
LEGEND OF THE JADE DRAGON
MURDER UNDER A MYSTIC MOON
A HARVEST OF BONES
ONE HEX OF A WEDDING

Yasmine Galenorn writing as India Ink

SCENT TO HER GRAVE
A BLUSH WITH DEATH
GLOSSED AND FOUND

BLOOD WYNE

YASMINE GALENORN

PAPL
DISCARDED

B

BERKLEY BOOKS, NEW YORK

THE BERKLEY PUBLISHING GROUP
Published by the Penguin Group
Penguin Group (USA) Inc.
375 Hudson Street, New York, New York 10014, USA
Penguin Group (Canada), 90 Eglinton Avenue East, Suite 700, Toronto, Ontario M4P 2Y3, Canada
(a division of Pearson Penguin Canada Inc.)
Penguin Books Ltd., 80 Strand, London WC2R 0RL, England
Penguin Group Ireland, 25 St. Stephen's Green, Dublin 2, Ireland (a division of Penguin Books Ltd.)
Penguin Group (Australia), 250 Camberwell Road, Camberwell, Victoria 3124, Australia
(a division of Pearson Australia Group Pty. Ltd.)
Penguin Books India Pvt. Ltd., 11 Community Centre, Panchsheel Park, New Delhi—110 017, India
Penguin Group (NZ), 67 Apollo Drive, Rosedale, North Shore 0632, New Zealand
(a division of Pearson New Zealand Ltd.)
Penguin Books (South Africa) (Pty.) Ltd., 24 Sturdee Avenue, Rosebank, Johannesburg 2196,
South Africa

Penguin Books Ltd., Registered Offices: 80 Strand, London WC2R 0RL, England

This is a work of fiction. Names, characters, places, and incidents either are the product of the author's imagination or are used fictitiously, and any resemblance to actual persons, living or dead, business establishments, events, or locales is entirely coincidental. The publisher does not have any control over and does not assume any responsibility for author or third-party websites or their content.

BLOOD WYNE

A Berkley Book / published by arrangement with the author

PRINTING HISTORY
Berkley mass-market edition / February 2011

Copyright © 2011 by Yasmine Galenorn.
Excerpt from *Night Veil* by Yasmine Galenorn copyright © by Yasmine Galenorn.
Cover art by Tony Mauro. Cover design by Rita Frangie.

All rights reserved.
No part of this book may be reproduced, scanned, or distributed in any printed or electronic form without permission. Please do not participate in or encourage piracy of copyrighted materials in violation of the author's rights. Purchase only authorized editions.
For information, address: The Berkley Publishing Group,
a division of Penguin Group (USA) Inc.,
375 Hudson Street, New York, New York 10014.

ISBN: 978-0-425-23974-2

BERKLEY®
Berkley Books are published by The Berkley Publishing Group,
a division of Penguin Group (USA) Inc.,
375 Hudson Street, New York, New York 10014.
BERKLEY® is a registered trademark of Penguin Group (USA) Inc.
The "B" design is a trademark of Penguin Group (USA) Inc.

PRINTED IN THE UNITED STATES OF AMERICA

10 9 8 7 6 5 4 3 2 1

If you purchased this book without a cover, you should be aware that this book is stolen property. It was reported as "unsold and destroyed" to the publisher, and neither the author nor the publisher has received any payment for this "stripped book."

Dedicated to
Maura, Jo, and Jenn-A,
who all too often play cheerleader to my decadent behavior.
Kisses and hugs.

ACKNOWLEDGMENTS

Thank you to my beloved Samwise. And my gratitude to my agent, Meredith Bernstein, and to my editor, Kate Seaver—thank you both for helping me stretch my wings and fly. A salute to Tony Mauro, cover artist extraordinaire—you rock, dude. To my assistant and web comic artist, Jennifer Anderson. To my furry little "Galenorn Gurlz," Lolcats in their own right. Most reverent devotion to Ukko, Rauni, Mielikki, and Tapio, my spiritual guardians.

And the biggest thank-you of all—to my readers, both old and new. Your support helps keep the series going. You can find me on the Net at Galenorn En/Visions: www.galenorn.com. For links to social networking sites where you can find me, see my website.

If you write to me snail mail (see website for address or write via the publisher), please enclose a stamped, self-addressed envelope with your letter if you would like a reply. Promo goodies are available—see my site for info.

The Painted Panther
Yasmine Galenorn
February 2011

All houses are haunted. All persons are haunted. Throngs of spirits follow us everywhere. We are never alone.

–BARNEY SARECKY

Men die in despair, while spirits die in ecstasy.

–HONORE DE BALZAC

CHAPTER 1

"I can't believe I need *another* new bartender." I leaned back in my chair and propped my feet on the desk. Luke had left the bar for a good reason, but that didn't mean I had to like it. And his replacement—Shawn, a vampire—hadn't risen to the challenge. I'd fired him after two weeks of inept bartending and questionable customer service. When I caught him trying to put the fang on a couple of my regulars, I lost it and kicked him out. Nobody messed with my regulars, especially in *my* bar.

But that left a void. The Wayfarer was busy, like every other place during the holiday season, and we needed every hand on board. We'd started early with an Other-world Thanksgiving feast from the grill, and then that weekend I'd put up a fake tree in the corner and handed out bonuses so that my employees could shop. Now, nearing the end of the first week of December, the main focus of Winter Solstice was still ahead of us—and Christmas for my clients who celebrated it—and the parties were getting more frantic and raucous every night as people crowded in, exhausted from shopping and coping with holiday chaos.

Nerissa gave me the what-can-you-do gesture with her hands, tossing them up in the air. "What can I say, doll? I'm sorry, but that's the way things go." Standing behind me, she leaned down and slowly trailed a line of kisses down my cheek to my neck. "I'd work for you, if I didn't have the day job."

"You'd make such an awesome bartender, and then I could yank you back here in my office to make love whenever we felt like it."

"We'd never get anything done," she countered.

I laughed, then shrugged. "I know, I know—hiring people is part of owning a bar, but it fucking sucks."

I tipped my head back and she caught me full on the mouth. I savored my golden goddess's lips as she set off a ricochet of desire that shockwaved through my body. All I could think about was how much I wanted her. *Here. Now.* As I reached for her breast, my fingers sliding over the rounded curves of her body, a knock on the door interrupted us.

"Bad timing." I glanced up at her ruefully. "Rain check?"

"Always." She reluctantly stepped back to sit in the chair next to my desk.

A werepuma, Nerissa was a warped Aphrodite, but she was also extremely diplomatic about knowing when I needed to present a professional appearance. She sat primly in the chair, her skirt suit and tawny chignon making her look like a librarian waiting to bust out and go wild. Everybody knew we were together, but it wouldn't do for the boss to be sucking face when the help checked in.

"Come in." I waited as Chrysandra opened the door and peeked her head in. "What's up?"

She glanced at Nerissa, then at me, and grinned. "Sorry to interrupt, boss, but I've got someone out here looking for a job. I'm not sure, but you might want to talk to him."

"Supe?" I had instituted a policy of only hiring members

of the Supernatural Community. The Wayfarer attracted far too many potential problems for me to take a chance on any more full-blooded humans. Chrysandra had gotten the hang of working around Supes of all kinds, but for a bartender, I needed someone who could also act as bouncer when I wasn't around.

Pieder, the giant, did a good job, but he worked days, and I was hiring for the night shift. I probably should hire a second bouncer while I was at it, but since I worked a majority of evenings in the bar, I usually covered the void. Smart people didn't mess with vampires, and most of my regulars had quickly learned not to cross me.

She nodded. "Yeah, but I'm not sure what kind. He has an odd *feel*." The look on her face told me that either he made her nervous or he was just so strange that she didn't know what to make of him. Chrysandra was, I had discovered, fairly psychic for an FBH—full-blooded human— and she picked up on things easily.

"Send him in." I turned to Nerissa. "Sweetie, you mind giving me a little privacy to interview him?"

"No problem. You sure you want to talk to him alone, girl?" She stroked my cheek with her fingers. "I can stay."

"I can tear apart ninety percent of the creatures I meet if they bother me. Don't forget that I'm a vampire, sweetheart. Never, *ever* forget it." I took her hand, holding it for a moment. I loved her dearly, and because of that, I never wanted her to forget I was a dangerous predator. It was my nature and I accepted it and at times—reveled in it.

"I never do," she whispered softly, then followed Chrysandra out of the room, her skirt swishing in a way that drove me crazy. I wanted to slip my hands under the hem, to run them up her golden thighs. For so long, after Dredge had gotten through with me, I'd repressed my sexuality, but Nerissa had woken it up, full steam ahead, and there was no putting the djinn back in the bottle.

I put my feet on the floor and straightened the papers on my desk. Inventory time was heading full throttle toward us; we were coming up on the end of the year, and I needed to do a full accounting of everything in the bar.

I also was preparing to open the Wayfarer to overnight travelers. We'd cleaned out the rooms upstairs, redecorated and sanded and painted, and now I had space for seven guests, with three communal bathrooms.

But opening to overnight guests meant hiring a maid. I'd also have to find someone to run room service, carry bags, and, in general, take care of the needs of our Otherworld patrons. For the most part, that was who I expected to see. I already had decided that I wouldn't rent to goblins, ogres, or anybody likely to cause trouble.

Since the Wayfarer technically belonged to an OW resident—me—it was considered sovereign territory. I could discriminate for whatever reason I wanted. And letting creeps and miscreants stay in the bar wasn't my idea of equal opportunity. Especially not when my sisters and I were waging a demonic war.

The door opened, and a man cleared the archway. As I glanced at him, looking him up and down, I found myself suitably impressed. I had no doubt the man could chuck people out of the bar.

Brawn, he had. That much was clear. He only stood five eight, but his biceps were works of art, and his thighs looked strong enough to crack a skull. His hair, jet black with a white streak, was held back in a thick ponytail, hitting about midshoulder. It set off eyes as green as my sister Delilah's. He looked to be around his midthirties, but if he was Supe, who knew how old he really was?

And that was the second thing: Supe, he was. I could tell right off that he wasn't human. This dude had some seriously powerful energy rolling off him. Even I, about as headblind as you could get for someone half-Fae, could feel it.

"How do you do? I'm Menolly D'Artigo. And you are . . . ?" I stood and walked around the desk. Compared to my five one, he seemed tall. But I could take him out without blinking an eye. One of the perks of being a vampire: exceptional strength that belied any lack of visible force. Motioning him to a chair, I hopped up to sit on the corner of my desk.

"Derrick. Derrick Means." He took the chair and leaned back, eyeing me closely. "You *look* like a vamp," he said.

I blinked. Nobody had ever said that to my face, but what the hell. He didn't sound like he was insulting me.

"Good. Because that's what I am, and anybody that works for me has to not only tolerate it, but actually *accept* the fact. What about you?"

He arched an eyebrow and folded his arms. "I'm one of the Badger People. I'm a friend of Katrina's. She said you might be open to me applying for the job, even though you're a vamp. Said you hired a werewolf before."

Badger People? So they'd moved into the city now, too?

But I understood why he might be wary. Weres and vamps didn't always get along. However, I wasn't just *any* vamp—I was half-Fae as well as half-human. And Katrina was a friend. She was a werewolf who had started to fall for my former bartender before he ended up having to leave Earthside for Otherworld to protect his sister.

I frowned. I'd never met anyone from the badger tribes before and had very little clue what they were like, in general. Though if he matched his namesake creature, Derrick wouldn't have any hesitation about tossing problem people out on their asses.

"Tell me about your past experience. And are you part of a clan or a loner?"

"Used to be in a clan, until I decided to hit the city and see what life here is all about. I like Seattle, but there's not much chance to interact with my family since I moved here. We keep in touch via e-mail, but I don't get to see them much." He let out a long sigh that sounded suspiciously like a huff and relaxed back into the chair.

"And your experience?"

"I've got fifteen years bartending under my belt, I double as a bouncer no problem, and I've never been fired." He handed me a piece of paper. To my surprise, it was a résumé. A detailed résumé. Usually people just came in and asked for a job. Or at best, an application.

"Why do you want to work at the Wayfarer?" I glanced over his CV. Everything seemed in order. No immediate alarm bells going off in my gut.

"Because I need a job. You need a bartender. And I figure you won't get in my face about taking off the nights of the full moon." He leaned forward. "I'm good at what I do, I'm loyal, and I'll be here, sober, whenever you call. I don't hit on the women—at least not on duty. If you want to call some of my references, the numbers are there."

I stared at the list. Applegate's Bar, Wyson's Pub, the Okinofo Lounge . . . not upscale bars but not seedy dives, either. They were solid taverns with good clientele. I let out a long breath and glanced up at him. "Wait out front in one of the booths."

After he nodded and swaggered out of the office, I put in a few calls. Nobody had anything bad to say about him, and several of the bars praised him, though I could feel a definite tension there. But that was easy: I chalked it up to FBHs dealing with Supes. Making my decision, I headed out front.

Derrick was nursing a Diet Coke.

I slid into the seat across from him. "You drink? Do drugs?"

He shook his head. "Drink beer and Scotch occasionally, but never on duty. Drugs and Badger People aren't a good mix. We have a temper, I am the first to admit it. I know my limits."

"Okay, here's the deal." I motioned at the bar. "I need somebody and I need him now. So if you can start this week, preferably tonight, so much the better. Your shift will be four P.M. until two A.M., but you may need to come in to help with inventory at times during the day. You'll need to be on call—there are nights when I have to be gone, and I can't always predict when that's going to be. So far so good?"

He nodded. "I like to work. I don't mind picking up extra shifts. I send what I don't need home to help my mother raise my brothers and sisters."

That made me feel even better about hiring him. "Good man. I can pay you fifteen dollars an hour to start. If you're as experienced as you seem to be, and you last ninety days, I'll raise that to seventeen. The main thing you need to remember: I'm the boss, you do what I say while you're here, and you keep your nose clean. What do you think? Want the job or not?"

He raised his glass in salute. "Here's looking at you, boss."

At least one of my problems was solved. But it didn't take long for another to rear its head. As I was showing Derrick around the bar, watching how he handled the bottles and—suitably impressed—how he handled customers, the door opened and Chase Johnson swaggered in.

My sister Delilah's ex-lover, a cop who was as good as family by now, Chase dressed in Armani and smelled like a perpetual taco stand. He was also one damned fine detective.

After all the arguments we'd been through, I had to give him props. He'd managed to keep it together in situations that would drive the average FBH wacko. Oh yeah. One other little tidbit: Chase also was as good as immortal, at least in human terms. He'd been given the Nectar of Life in order to save his life, and that put him a long leg up on the rest of FBHs.

He glanced at Derrick and nodded, giving me a quizzical look.

"This is Chase Johnson, detective and friend of the business. Close to being family. Treat him right."

Derrick nodded. "Nice to meet you, Detective."

"Chase, this is Derrick—my new bartender. Derrick, give us a few minutes alone. Chase has something to talk to me about. Don't you?"

"Yeah, though I wish this were just a social call." He shook hands with Derrick, then followed me to a booth. "Werewolf?"

"Badger People. Werebadger."

"Sheesh—is there a Were class for every animal on the planet?" Chase snorted and rubbed one perfectly groomed eyebrow.

"Just about. What is it, Johnson?"

"Trouble. You have the time to take a little ride with me to headquarters? Vampire business. I think." He let out a long sigh.

Hell. Vampire business was so *not* what I wanted to hear because when Chase came calling about vampires, it usually meant somebody was dead. Usually murdered. There'd been an upswing in nocturnal activity lately, but since I was no longer privy to the scuttlebutt going around Vampires Anonymous—a support group for vamps new to the life, run by vampire and former friend Wade Stevens— it was harder for me to ferret out secrets. I had to rely on what Sassy Branson told me, but she was growing more erratic every day. I'd been seriously considering taking my "daughter" Erin out of the older vampire's care.

"Let me tell Chrysandra." I hustled over to my waitress and tapped her on the arm. "Keep an eye on Derrick. Help him learn the ropes. Chase needs me."

"No problem, Menolly. But are you sure? It's his first night." She looked a little worried. Normally I'd chalk it up to nerves, but tonight I stopped and looked into her eyes, trying to get a feel for where her jitters were coming from.

"You have a bad feeling about him?" I cocked my head, waiting.

She glanced over at him, then slowly shook her head. "Not at all . . . but . . . there's something about him. I can't put my finger on it. He's more than he appears to be, but I don't sense . . . he's not hostile, but I think he walks with danger."

"Most Supes do, nowadays." I frowned. "Fetch Tavah

from the basement. Tell Riki to take over for her down there. If anything goes wrong, Tavah should be able to take care of matters."

Tavah, another vampire, spent her nights in the basement of the Wayfarer, guarding the portal to Otherworld and keeping track of the guests who came through. She kept the creeps out and let the paying visitors in.

"Okay. Will do." She ran down the steps as I hightailed it over to Derrick. "Listen, Derrick, I've got to go out. Chrysandra will help you out, and while I'm gone she and Tavah are in charge. I'll be back as soon as I can. Okay?"

He nodded, eyes on the drink he was mixing. "Not a problem. Got it."

And with that, as soon as I saw Tavah appear at the top of the stairs, I followed Chase into the icy night.

Winter in Seattle vacillates between mild and nasty, but the past couple of years had been pretty rough. Instead of the incessant rain, we'd actually seen snow—enough to stop the city in its tracks for a few days. Last year it had been the god-giant Loki, with his Fenris wolf, making a run on the city because of my now-dead sire. This year, I had the feeling more natural factors were at play. La Niña had come to town. We were in a colder, wetter spell.

And now, two and a half weeks before Yule, it was cold enough to snow and I'd already considered putting snow tires on my Jag.

The chill didn't bother me, but Chase buttoned his trench as we headed out. He held the door open for me—he was, at heart, a gentleman—and we hustled to his car. I could tell he was cold; the breath puffed out of his mouth like clouds from a steam engine.

The streets were packed with shoppers looking for Christmas bargains. As we edged through traffic, Chase flipped on the radio and Danny Elfman's voice came out of the speakers, blaring "Dead Man's Party."

"Man, I remember dancing to this at one of the local clubs almost fifteen years ago," he said offhandedly. "I was in high school and dating a girl named Glenda. She had hair a mile high and was in full retro mode. All she wanted to wear was glittery spandex and she looked like one of the B-52 girls."

I glanced at him. "Do you miss those days? The days when you didn't know about us or the demons?"

He tapped his fingers on the steering wheel as we waited for traffic to inch forward. "Trick question. No way to answer that truthfully." Giving me a sideways smirk, he added, "Yes, I do, but only because life was much simpler then. Choices were black and white. But I have to say, since you three entered my life, I've never been bored. Scared shitless, yes. Bored? Never."

Snorting, I leaned forward and turned up the music. "You ever want to, you're welcome to come clubbing with Nerissa and me, as long as we aren't hitting a vamp club. We're damned good on the dance floor."

Chase's turn to snicker. "Right. While I'd be the envy of a thousand men, I don't know if that would fit my style anymore. Then again . . . it might be fun. Hell, I have no clue as to what my style is now." He sounded lost, and a little frightened. "Look—Santa."

A sidewalk Santa was ringing his bell for the South Street Mission in front of a small boutique. The winter was chill and cold, and a lot of people were out of work. Gauging from his expression, Santa wasn't gathering many coins for charity.

"Santa's a freak-ass scary dude in reality. Camille met him when she was young." I stared at the pseudo-Santa through the window as we passed by and fell silent. *Santa passing out presents. The Tooth Fairy handing out coins for teeth. The Easter Bunny hiding eggs.* Humans clung to their myths in the hopes that they'd ward off bad luck and evil, that they'd bring prosperity and security. How little they knew about the truth that hid behind their fairy tales, or what monsters were *really* sliding down their chimneys.

I turned up the music as Ladytron replaced Oingo Boingo. A part of me felt sorry for Chase. We'd thrown a monkey wrench into his life and he could never go back to what he'd been, to the life he'd expected to lead. Collateral damage. We were leaving a nasty trail, and there'd be far more by the time this demonic war was over.

It took us another twenty minutes to reach the FH-CSI (Faerie Human Crime Scene Investigation) headquarters. I knew this building all too well. It seemed like my sisters and I were here all the time, especially since the war against Shadow Wing was escalating.

Most of the building was underground—the bottom level was the morgue, in-house laboratory, and archives. Third floor down held the jail cells for the Otherworld magical and strength-enhanced Supes. Second floor down was the arsenal—containing a vast array of interesting weapons viable for use against anything from werewolves to giants. The main floor contained both police headquarters and the medic unit. Delilah had hinted that she thought there was another level below the morgue, but we didn't know what it was or whether it really existed.

Chase led me straight to his office, rather than the morgue. A good sign, I thought. Straight to the morgue was *bad*. Straight to the morgue meant immediate danger, and right now I wasn't in the mood for trouble.

But as I took a seat opposite his desk, I happened to catch a glimpse of the photographs spilling out of a file on his desk. Crap. *Blood and more blood.* Everything was always covered in blood these days.

"That's your trouble, I take it?" I nodded to the pictures.

"Yes, and I wish you could take it as far away from me as possible." He let out a sigh. "I don't know what to make of it. If it looked like simple vampire killings, at least I'd know what I was dealing with, but there's something else going on." He motioned for me to scoot my chair closer and laid out the photos in a line for me to look at.

There were four women, each with obvious puncture wounds in her neck. Vampire activity, all right.

"Looks pretty straightforward to me," I said.

"Yeah, you would think so, wouldn't you? But look again at the women. Look closely. Notice anything odd?" He frowned and leaned back in his chair, crossing his left leg over his right and interlacing his fingers. "I really want your honest opinion because I want to make sure I'm not just barking up a tree that doesn't exist."

I studied the photographs. Women, all pretty, all somewhere in their thirties, looked to be. All . . . wait a minute. *Pattern*. There was a pattern.

"They all have long brown hair, layered. They all have brown eyes, and they all seem to be around 130 pounds. How tall were they?"

"All between five six and five eight. So you see it, too?"

"Yeah. Was there any connection between them? Any other similarity to their deaths?" A nasty thought was forming in my head, and I had the feeling Chase had already come to the same conclusion.

"Obviously they were all exsanguinated, and they were all killed at night. Puncture wounds on the throat, though there's no way to prove for sure that they were killed by a vampire. All the women were murdered within a five-mile radius, in the Greenbelt Park District. All four were hookers." He frowned. "I'm thinking we have a vampire serial killer. If it weren't for the fact that all the girls look alike, I'd just chalk it up to a rogue vampire attack, but they look so much alike, they could be related."

I stared at the pictures. Chase was right. They did look like sisters. And even though he couldn't make the official call, I knew in my gut that it was a vampire—most likely singular—attacking the women.

"Do you have their bodies, still? I can probably verify

vamp attack, seeing that I am one, but I need to look at their wounds."

Damn, damn, damn. If it was a vampire serial killer, we had big trouble on our hands. Ever since Delilah decked him, Andy Gambit—star reporter for the *Seattle Tattler*, a yellow tabloid that fed on the fears and titillation of Seattle residents—had been on a tear, doing his best to smear Fae and Supes of all kinds. He'd been backing Taggart Jones for the City Council position.

Gambit had done such an effective smear job on Nerissa that she'd lost the race, even though she'd started out with a decent margin and all signs pointed to potential victory. Gambit had dragged her through the mud because of her association with me, and it had worked. The surprise, however, had been that Taggart Jones hadn't won, either. A moderate had swept the election.

Now, Gambit would be all over this story. If word of a vampire serial killer got out, we'd be pouring gasoline on the fire.

Chase led me to the elevator. "So, are you guys ready for Yule yet?"

I grinned. "More or less. Delilah hasn't tipped over the tree yet, but then, we anchored it to the ceiling first thing. Camille and Iris have the house looking like a winter wonderland. All we need is snow for it to feel like the holidays."

"Does Otherworld get much snow?" he asked, holding the door open for me.

I swung in behind him. "Depends on where you're at. Y'Elestrial—yes, we get quite a bit of snow there . . ." I fell silent, biting my lip. Our home city was now sacrosanct and off limits to Camille, although she could still go to other parts of Otherworld. And to us, too. "I miss it. The city is beautiful, but now, I wonder if we'll ever see it again."

"Queen Tanaquar and your father still won't relent?" He looked uncertain, like he thought he should pat me on the shoulder or something.

Shrugging, I shook my head. "When Delilah and I demanded they allow Camille to return to her full status, they told us we had two choices: Abide by their decree or suffer the same fate ourselves. So we all went to work for Queen Asteria instead, and the Otherworld Intelligence Agency is history. At least for us. At least for now."

"They aren't talking to me, either," he said. "Ever since your civil war, it's like they've decided that the FH-CSI doesn't need to be kept in the loop."

"Join the club. Father tried to guilt-trip us like crazy, but Delilah and I shut him out. We hated to do so, but he hasn't been by our sides, up to his elbows in demon blood, wondering if Shadow Wing is coming through next. He doesn't know how fucking hard Camille's worked, nor does he understand the decisions she's had to make. How could Delilah and I stand by and just watch them throw her away?"

Chase nodded. "I get it. I really do. And I admire the choice you made. You three—no matter what, no one will ever come between you."

He looked wistful, and I wondered if he missed Delilah. He was actually at our house more often now that they'd broken up, and he seemed far more relaxed and happy. So did Delilah, even though she was still finding her way with Shade, the half dragon, half Stradolan. A part of the Autumn Lord's world, Shade had strode into her life and they were slowly building what looked like it could be the love match of the century. I'd never seen Delilah's heart so free and easy.

"You okay, Johnson?" I tapped him on the arm.

"Yeah," he said softly. "And just in case you're wondering, no—I'm not pining over Delilah. *I'm* the one who decided I couldn't handle a relationship. And frankly, it's a good thing. My moods are swinging like crazy now that my powers are opening up. I'm happy one moment, pissed the next. *Not* good boyfriend material. Sharah's found someone in town who's going to help me learn how to channel the energy."

"Good, because unbridled psychic energy is dangerous for all concerned." I stopped him as we stepped out of the elevator. "Truth time."

"What?" His dark eyes glistened, and I resisted the impulse to reach up and brush back an unruly cowlick—it was so out of place on his meticulously groomed body that it distracted me.

"Are you sure you're okay with my sister seeing someone else? Because if you have any thoughts of a reunion later, you'd better say something now. She's falling, Chase. She's falling for Shade like I've never seen her fall before." I had no intention of letting him put her on the spot later, forcing her to make a choice she thought she'd already made.

He gazed at me, his eyes limpid, his expression torn. Then, slowly, he asked, "She really loves this guy?"

"I think he's the one, Chase."

"Then I'll remain her blood brother, and I won't interfere. Because I honestly don't know what the hell's going to happen in my life." He paused. "Can I ask *you* something, now?"

So relieved by his reply that I would have granted almost any favor, I nodded. "Ask away."

"Do you think someone like Sharah might ever see me in anything but an official capacity?" He sounded hesitant, almost embarrassed to be asking.

I knew full well that Sharah was in love with the detective, but that was her place to answer, not mine. I gave Chase a soft smile. "Listen, you're a catch. You've had your share of screwups, but, Johnson, you're okay, and I think you're going to make somebody happy someday. Could someone like Sharah be interested in you? I don't see why not."

He thought for a moment, then led the way to the morgue. "We've kept the bodies. We still don't have IDs on three of them. The other one, we know who she is but can't find any family to notify. But word is getting around on the streets. I've got to warn the streetwalkers soon. They deserve to know if there's some nutcase out there targeting them."

I stared at the brilliant white walls of the morgue, the shimmering stainless steel of the sinks and tables. This was my domain—the domain of the dead. Had Dredge not brought me back to life, I'd have walked the hallowed halls, crossing over to the Land of the Silver Falls.

Every time I came face-to-face with mortality, I remembered my own immortality and once again had to face the fact that I was a predator. A creature who belonged in the shadows. Never again would I walk under the sun, not until the day I was ready to give it all up and go home to my ancestors. Until then, there was only the moon for me.

Four bodies were laid out on tables, covered with white sheets. Spotless sheets, like freshly fallen snow against a barren background.

"I take it you've watched them for any signs of rising?"

He nodded. "Yeah. Nothing. I think they're truly dead."

I approached the first one and pulled back the sheet. She was unearthly in her silence, in her stillness. Like a statue, or a figure frozen in ice, she lay there, pale from the lack of blood. I leaned down and examined the puncture wounds on her neck. *Vampire.* I could feel him. *Smell* him. The vamp who'd killed this woman was male and fairly young—at least as a *vampire.* That much I could tell. Quickly, I checked the other bodies, startled by the similarity of their looks. They could have been sisters.

In a way they are, I thought. *Sisters in death.* They were killed by the same vampire. I could smell him on them, his breath, his scent, his . . .

Oh crap. I jumped back, trembling. Very little set me off, but this—this was too familiar, still too stark in a memory that I'd never, ever shake.

"Did you check to see if they were raped?" My voice was sharper than I meant it to be, but I couldn't help it.

Chase looked at me, his expression slipping from

neutral to pained. "Yeah, we did. I was hoping I wouldn't have to tell you. I know what that does to you."

"They were, right? You wouldn't find semen, but they were torn and bruised. I can smell it. I can smell the blood-lust . . . not just around the puncture marks." As I felt the room spin, my fangs came down and I began to panic. I had to get out of there. "Chase, I have to get up to the surface. Now."

"Come on." He guided me out but wisely didn't touch me.

When we came to the elevator, I held out my hand. "You'd better not ride up with me. It's too dangerous right now. I'll meet you out front."

He didn't question, just stood back, letting me board the car without him. I punched *M* for the main floor and counted the seconds as they ticked by. The elevator wasn't slow, but by the time it reached the main floor and I managed to haul ass outside, it felt like I'd spent a thousand years locked in the car.

A thousand years of memories, a thousand years of wanting freedom, a thousand years of wondering if we had another Dredge on our hands.

CHAPTER 2

Chase followed me outside. "You okay?"

I slowly looked up at him, letting my fangs show. "No, not totally, but I will be. Just . . . some memories you never shake. Some deeds are never undone. Dredge was a horror beyond anything you can imagine. Karvanak might have come close, but Dredge—he thrived on the pain of others. On humiliation and degradation. He laughed as I screamed, Chase. He laughed like he was watching some stupid sitcom. And then he . . . when he . . ."

I was awash in the sudden memory of his laughing face as he mounted me, raped my bleeding body, tore at the lacerations that he'd spent hours carving into my skin, and for a moment everything shifted beneath my feet. I wanted to hunt, to chase, to kill—but he was dust. I'd already toasted him and there was nothing left I could do to him.

"Menolly, Menolly—snap out of it. Listen to me!" Chase's voice cut through my bloodlust fog like a razor, slicing the veil of hunger so quickly it felt like I'd been ejected from a womb.

Blinking, I shook my head and stared up at him. "How did you do that?"

"Do what?" He looked puzzled. "What did I do?"

"You yanked me out of bloodlust. When I'm in bloodlust, very little can penetrate the hunger, let alone shake the crazies off me. Camille can do it, but she has the force of the Moon Mother behind her. An older vampire can do it—and once in a great while, someone comes along with that ability, but seldom an FBH." I regarded him quietly, wondering just what powers had woken within our detective when he'd been given the Nectar of Life.

"I have no idea how it happened, but I'm glad it worked. I don't carry a straw and I'm not up for being a long cool drink." He frowned. "What happened?"

"Flashback. I still get them once in a while, but it's been far less since we dusted Dredge. Before then, almost every day I relived Dredge's torture in my dreams. And I couldn't stop them—couldn't wake up. But when it happens during the nights, I go into a bloodlust and my predator surfaces, seeking an outlet for the pain of the memories. The past few months, it's only happened a few times."

"That's good, right? Do you think you'll ever be free of it?"

"You can kill the source, but some sins are never washed clean. Whatever Karvanak did to you—can you easily forget that?"

He shook his head. "And that was just my finger and some . . . light torture. What you went through . . . yeah. I get it."

"Let's change the subject. Give me the locations where you found the bodies. We can find out if they're on a ley line, or if they're near any known vampire nests." My head had already cleared from the panic and hunger, and I suspected that Chase had somehow had more to do with it than he realized.

"Come on back in the building. I'll have Yugi get the information for you." He paused at the door. "Thanks,

Menolly. I know you don't have to help out with things like this—and I realize it takes you away from your real work—but you have to know, I appreciate the assistance."

For what was not the first time since we'd met, I looked up at the detective and saw yet another facet of his personality shining through. He was human and fallible, but even the gods had their faults. Johnson had taken more than most FBHs could handle and still walked through with his head held high. He'd undergone demonic torture and managed to come out relatively unscathed. He'd fought alongside the rest of us against demons, ghouls, and zombies, and there was no way we could fault his courage. All in all, his indiscretions aside, Chase was one of the good guys.

I leaned up on my tiptoes and did something I rarely did—even with my sisters. I gave him a peck on the cheek.

He blinked, slowly raising his hand to his cheek. "What was that for?"

"The fact that you have to ask means you earned it, dude. Now shut up and let's get in there. We've got a serial killer to catch."

So—I guess it's roll call time. I'm Menolly D'Artigo, *jian-tu* turned vampire. *Jian-tu* means . . . well, the most equivalent job over Earthside would be ninja without so much assassin attached to it. But I fell—literally—into a nest of vampires. Dredge, the most villainous piece of filth that Otherworld had ever seen, caught me, tortured me, raped me, killed me, and brought me back as a vampire. After that, I spent the next year in rehab learning how *not* to kill my family or friends.

I'm half-Fae, half-human, and along with my sisters Camille, a wicked good witch and priestess of the Moon Mother, and Delilah, a werecat who's also a Death Maiden, I work for the Otherworld Intelligence Agency. Or rather, *worked*. Until a couple weeks ago. You see, last month the queen of our home city-state and her lover—our father—

disowned Camille for traitorous activity. It was a frame-up, not so pure and not so simple. Delilah and I backed her and got ourselves tossed out on our ears, too, so we now all work for Queen Asteria, the monarch of Elqaneve, the elven lands.

We're in the middle of a nasty demonic war, trying to prevent Shadow Wing, the demon lord in control of the Subterranean Realms, from pulling a major coup on Earth and Otherworld. To do so, he needs to gather as many of the spirit seals—parts of an ancient artifact—as he can. We're trying to get to them first, so it's a race. We've managed to keep five away from him. He's got one. Three are up for grabs.

So far, we've kept him and his hordes at bay, but a month ago they trashed our house and so we're doing our best to regroup and strengthen ourselves. There are so many variables in this war by now that we're taking it one day at a time and hoping for the best. But lately *the best* just seems to mean we get beat up a lot. And a few of our friends have learned the hard way that their connection to us can lead to major injury . . . or death. We do what we can, but one day our luck's going to run dry.

The best we can hope is that somehow we'll emerge victorious. The worst is that our end will be as quick and painless as it can be, because frankly, the more mired we get, the less optimistic we are. But until we know which way the pendulum's going to swing, we'll kick all the demon ass we can, and if we go down, we'll take as many of them with us as we can. Because we know we're on the right side. And that's what counts in this cold, heartless world.

As I headed back to the bar, I thought about the meeting with Chase. A vampire serial killer meant major problems. For one thing, I was persona non grata among the vampires who might give a damn, and a villain among those who would cheer the creep on. Which meant that, for all intents and purposes, I was the odd vamp out.

Sassy Branson—the socialite turned vampire who was fostering the one daughter I'd sired—might help me, although Sassy was having problems of her own, and they were growing more marked. I wasn't quite so trusting of her as of late. But Wade, the leader of Vampires Anonymous, and the rest of the pack that followed him had made it clear I wasn't welcome anymore.

The bar was jumping when I returned, but Derrick seemed to be handling the crowd in stride. I waved to him and headed into my office.

Chrysandra poked her head in. "Nerissa said to tell you she's headed out for the night. She'll call you later."

"Thanks, chickadee," I said, mulling over who might be able to help us out in this situation. Delilah was ostensibly a PI, but really that was more for show than anything else, though she was good at ferreting out information. And no way was I sending her out scouting for information on vampires. That was a recipe for disaster. No, we needed help from the undead side of things.

Hesitating, I picked up a cream-colored invitation and stared at it. I hadn't answered yet—at least, not more than a *maybe*. But the man who'd sent this, he might be able to help. Technically, he wasn't just a man. He was a vampire, but I was very cautious about getting anywhere near him.

With a sigh, I picked up the phone and dialed the number.

Both Kitten and Camille were waiting up when I got home. I'd called and asked them to haul ass out of bed because we had a few things we needed to discuss, and I didn't want to wait until tomorrow night.

Camille was sipping a cup of steaming tea. Dressed in a black filmy gown, she had a cozy fleece robe thrown over the top. She was gorgeous. That raven hair of hers seemed to be getting longer, and her curves filled out the nightgown and robe nicely. *Good thing we're sisters, or I might not be able to keep my eyes to myself,* I thought.

Delilah, on the other hand, was wearing a pair of pink flannel pajamas with a kitty on the front, and fuzzy slippers that reminded me of tribbles. She was nursing a glass of warm milk and munching on cookies.

I took off my boots and jacket and sat cross-legged in the big overstuffed chair that Smoky had bought for the living room to replace one of the chairs damaged when the demons trashed our home. Most of the furniture was new, actually, and there were still gouges on some of the walls where the Tregart demons had punched holes through the drywall.

The guys had repaired all of the outside damage and were slowly working their way through the inside of the house now, taking care of the detail work.

"We've got a problem. Chase called me over to HQ tonight. It looks like we have ourselves a vampire serial killer on the loose." I leaned back against the cushions, closing my eyes. It felt good to be home. I loved clubbing, loved hanging out on the dance floor with my girl, or at the bar with my staff, but at the end of the night, I wanted to be home, to play with Maggie, our cute little calico gargoyle, to chill with my sisters and Iris, and just . . . just to be.

"Great. Another Harold, only after vampires instead of Fae?" Camille grimaced. Harold Young still sat uneasy on her mind. All of our minds, actually. He'd been the worst of the monsters, even though he'd been an FBH. In fact, that was what made him so horrible—he *had* been all human by blood. But pure demon into the depths of his soul.

"No—not a serial killer after vampires. A *vampire serial killer.* He's killing young women." I gave them the rundown on what Chase had shown me. "He has to be either a fairly new vampire or new to the area, unless there was a trigger to set off this spree."

The doorbell rang and we all stared at the hallway for a

moment. It was three in the morning. Who the fuck would be at our door at this time?

"Could it be Nerissa?" Delilah stood, but I motioned for her to sit and silently crossed to the door, wishing I hadn't already taken off my boots.

We were all leery ever since the skirmish in late October when Iris had almost gotten killed. We'd inadvertently left our home open to invasion and paid for it. After that, we begged some brawn from the elven goon squad back in Otherworld. They didn't look particularly strong, but the three elves posted outside the house were deadly when it came to martial arts and magic. Trenyth, Queen Asteria's right-hand man, had arranged for them to stay with us for now.

We had two peepholes, one at Iris's level and one at Delilah's. I used Iris's, and, to my surprise, saw my daughter.

"Erin?" What the hell was she doing here, and alone? I didn't like her wandering around without supervision. I might be an overprotective mother, but I knew what risks there were out there, how great the hunger was for a fledgling and just how easy it was to slip.

I yanked open the door.

"Erin, what are you doing here? Is Sassy with you?" I glanced outside, scanning the yard, but there was no sign of the older socialite.

Erin shook her head and dropped to the floor, kneeling in front of me. As her sire, I'd always take on a certain godlike essence to her, and she'd fear my displeasure for a long time. At least until the day her powers grew to the point where she could destroy me. But considering who my sire was, chances were that day would never come.

Dredge had been one of the strongest, deadliest vamps to ever walk either Earthside or Otherworld, and I'd fed directly from his veins. Erin was once removed from him, and she was also human.

I'd turned Erin a little over a year ago, when she was forty-nine years old. She'd always been butch until Sassy took over fostering her. Now she was dressed in Chanel, with a stylish haircut, and her tan had faded into the albino skin that most vamps sported. Erin would never be beautiful, at least not to most eyes. But her heart was pure gold, even in her new state.

I held out my hand for her to kiss, as custom dictated. She pressed her lips against my pale skin, and I motioned for her to stand. "Come in. What's going on? Why are you here? If you needed me, you could have called and I'd have come right over."

I led her into the living room and nodded for Camille and Delilah to leave us. Not good for Erin to be around the living much. Not yet. The temptation to drink was a strong force. Thirst burned in the young.

Erin waved at my sisters, and they waved back as they left the room, Camille with a stricken look on her face. Erin had been her friend, and Dredge had used her as a weapon when he came after me. *Collateral damage.* So far, two of Camille's friends had lost their lives thanks to our enemies.

"We'll be in the kitchen," Delilah said as they slipped into the hallway.

I motioned for Erin to sit next to me. "What's going on? Why are you here?" Vampires didn't usually dillydally with small talk. It was a waste of words.

"I'm worried about Sassy." Erin gazed at me, her pale brown eyes fading into the mist. They were shifting to gray, as most vampire eyes did over time. She drew her hand across her face and pinched her brow. "Mistress, Sassy, she's . . . something's not right."

"What isn't right? Can you be more specific?" I had a sinking feeling I already knew the answer but hoped I was wrong.

"Last night someone came to the house. I don't know who it was, but I know it was another vampire. He brought . . ." She stopped and swallowed, fear clouding her face. "I don't want to get Sassy in trouble. She's done so much for me." As a look of clarity raced through her eyes, I realized that Erin was, indeed, growing and learning.

"Tell me. I know you're afraid, but you can tell me anything." I reached out and slowly stroked her face, running my fingers down her cheek. I'd vowed never to sire a child, but here she was, my daughter forever until one of us walked into the sunlight. How could I not care what happened to her? And her behavior would reflect on me.

Erin shuddered at my touch, raising her hand to cover mine. "I know I can. That's why I came to you. Someone came over last night; a vampire, but I don't know his name. He brought a girl with him. Sassy told me to go to my room and stay there—that she had some business to attend to. I was angry. Earlier we'd had a fight. I wanted to wear my jeans but she wanted me to wear some designer crap. Anyway . . . she and this guy disappeared with the girl as I pretended to do what she told me to. I know I'm supposed to obey her, but something felt wrong."

My stomach sank and I had the nasty feeling I knew how this was going to end. "What happened?"

"I followed them. They took the girl down to Sassy's safe room. I was able to watch without being seen. They savaged her, Menolly. I wanted so bad to go join them, to feed, but I forced myself to remember what you taught me about honor and the path we walk. And I don't think the girl wanted it. They . . . fell on her and . . ." She paled—if vampires can pale—and hung her head, looking sick. "It was bad. It was really bad. I've never seen Sassy so cruel."

"What did she do?" I didn't want to know, and yet I had to.

"She went down on her, then fed from her. *Down there.* The girl started screaming but fell into a stupor. When Sassy finished, the male vamp took his turn. Neither one of them was looking for just food. And then . . . they drained her. I know she was dead," Erin whispered, bloody tears trailing from her eyes. "It made me sick. I ran back to my room and kept my mouth shut. I wanted to come right over, but if they knew I was gone, they'd have come after me. Tonight, Sassy went to a party and left me home, so I slipped out."

I stared at my daughter. What the fuck had I been thinking, leaving her in the care of someone I didn't really know? What the hell had I done? I wanted to punch something but stopped. If I put a hole through the wall, Iris would have my ass.

"What has Janet said about these goings-on?" Janet was Sassy's lifelong companion—a combination older sister/ personal maid. The elder woman was as delightful as Julia Child and as prim as Emily Post. I'd come to love how she looked after Sassy.

"Not much of anything. I don't think she knows. Janet's really sick," Erin said, staring at the floor.

My stomach lurched. Janet had a brain tumor that was slowly eating away at her life. "Is she . . . her tumor?"

"Yeah, I think she's in the last stages. She's been in bed a lot lately. And she's scared, Menolly. Sassy . . . Sassy keeps talking about turning her, and Janet keeps begging her not to."

"Crap. How long do you think Janet has?" I bit my lip, wanting to cry. Janet didn't deserve to be harassed at the end of her life, and the old Sassy would never have even *thought* of turning her best friend.

"A few days at the most, but it could be any time. She's been asking about you."

"I'll go as soon as I can—in the next night or so. I promise. Meanwhile, you're not going back. You will sleep here tomorrow, with me. But you must promise to be on your best behavior. And I'll find a safer place for you to live." I stood up and held out my hands. She took them and smiled at me, bravely. Erin might have been a grown woman when she died, but all vamps revert back into an awkward stage for their first few years after death. In essence, Erin was both a middle-aged woman and a shy teenager.

"Come now. I'm going to take you down to my lair and get you some blood—wait till you taste what Morio makes for me. It's almost as good as being alive again." It wasn't ideal to reference life in a newly minted vamp's presence.

Erin would still be mourning her loss, but with the flavored blood my sister's youkai-kitsune husband prepared for me, Erin would get a little taste of her former life back.

"Come." I led her into the kitchen. Delilah and Camille looked up. "Erin's going to be staying with us for the night. She'll sleep in my lair with me. I'm just going to get her a bottle of blood and settle her in, and then I'll be back."

Camille flashed us a warm smile. "Erin, it's so good to see you again."

Erin stared at her, wistful. "I know. I just wish . . ." Her voice trailed off as I pulled out a bottle of strawberry shake–flavored blood and led her behind the bookcase, into the secret staircase leading to my lair. I settled her in with the television and the blood, then returned upstairs.

Delilah and Camille were waiting. "Trouble. I have big trouble." I told them what Erin had told me.

"Not Sassy!" Delilah's jaw dropped. "What the hell are we going to do? How can we stop her?"

"Sassy told me some months back she felt her predator rising and was having trouble controlling it. Looks like she wasn't lying." I stared at my hands. "In one sense, it's none of my business. Vampires take out people every day and I don't do anything. But six months ago she made me promise that when she lost sight of herself, I'd put an end to it. She didn't want to become like this."

"Does that mean you're planning to kill her?" Camille bit her lip, tears streaking down her cheeks. "Sassy's our friend. Is there anything we can do to help her?"

"I am so torn." I looked up as Iris entered the kitchen, Maggie on her hip. "Hey, Iris—we have company. Don't go into my lair alone, okay? Erin's staying with us for a little while and I think she's safe, but she's so young I don't dare trust her alone around you guys."

Iris blinked, blurry eyed, and nodded. "Sure thing. Care to tell me why we have another vampire staying here?"

"Because Sassy's crossed the line into her predator."

I held out my arms for our calico girl, and Iris handed her to me. "Maggie, baby, how are you tonight? Did you wake up?"

"Melly . . . Melly . . ." Maggie threw her fuzzy arms around my neck and buried her head against my chest, promptly falling into a light snooze. I cuddled her, burying my face in her soft downy fur, clinging to the innocence in my embrace, holding her tight.

Maggie was the only one in our lives untouched by the demons—though even she had started out her life in a demon's lunch bag. Luckily, Camille managed to rescue her. But she was our touchstone to hope, our hearthstone to unconditional love. The baby gargoyle would take a long, long time to grow up—hundreds of years—and we'd be here for her.

Iris started the tea. "I take it we're up for an all-nighter? Tea and cinnamon toast?"

Camille moved to the fridge and pulled out the bread. "Sounds good to me. So you haven't answered yet." She glanced at me. "Do you have to kill Sassy?"

Iris set the kettle down. Hard. "Sassy Branson? You're seriously talking about staking her?"

"I told you, she's crossed into her predator self. There's no coming back once that happens. When the blood-lust takes hold to that degree, it's easier and easier to slip until there is only the hunt and the chase and the frenzy." I pressed my lips together as Maggie began to play with my nose, then tugged on my hair. She was the one creature I'd never felt anger at. Somehow, the baby gargoyle effected a soothing balm on my soul and temper.

As Iris made tea, and Camille and Delilah fixed their toast, I carried Maggie over to the window and peeked out into the winter night. A few snowflakes were falling—the first of the season—and I felt a chill inside so deep it shook my core. Sassy had always been a champion of mine. She'd taken my side when Wade dumped me out of Vampires

Anonymous, and now . . . now would I stand at her door, stake in hand? Would I take her down in a bloody battle and dust her? Would she curse me or thank me?

Either way, I knew the time was coming when I'd have to deal with her. And meanwhile, what about Erin? She couldn't stay here. And then there was the vampire serial killer who was prowling the night.

Feeling bathed in blood, I turned back to my sisters and Iris. "It's snowing," was all I said.

CHAPTER 3

That night was the first night anybody had ever stayed in my lair with me, that I knew of. Sometimes my sisters stashed Maggie down there, or Iris hid there when necessary, but I'd never intentionally invited anybody in for a slumber party.

When I joined Erin, after Camille and Delilah went to bed, she was sitting in the armchair, watching a late-night monster movie—*The Return of Dracula*. She startled as I came in, scrambling to kneel. I let her, then gently laughed and sat on the arm of her chair.

"At ease, Erin. Sit down and watch the movie." I motioned to the screen. "Thank heavens we don't dress the old-school way anymore, huh?"

She blinked, cautiously taking her seat. "I'd look pretty bad in a cape and low-cut dress. Did you call Sassy, Mistress?"

"Not yet. And you can call me Menolly in private." I *really* wanted to pay a visit to Sassy, but first I had to think over what I was going to say. But I knew I'd have to talk to her eventually. As Erin and I settled in to watch the movie, around four thirty the phone rang.

"Menolly! Thank God, you're there. Is Erin with you?" Sassy sounded flustered. "I just checked on her and she's not in her room. I'm so sorry—but I thought you might know where she is. I pray she's not lost."

Either Sassy was fishing to find out what I knew, or she really did believe Erin had taken off somewhere and gotten herself lost. Either way, the longer I kept Sassy in the dark about Erin spilling the beans on her nocturnal blood sports, the better. At least until I decided what to do about the problem.

"Yes, she is. Erin called me from the park. She just went out for a walk and got a little confused. I decided to bring her home with me so we could spend some time together. She's fine. I'll drop by tomorrow night."

Sassy paused. Then, hesitantly, "Are you sure? I can come get her."

"No—don't worry. Erin's going to play slumber party here. I'll call you tomorrow night." Another lie. I was planning on showing up unannounced, without Erin. That ship had sailed and gone. Erin would never spend another night at Sassy's.

"If you're sure . . ." A strain in Sassy's voice caught my attention. A tension that hadn't been there before. I listened to the nuance below it. *She was hungry.* Sassy was hungry and longing to hunt. I knew the feeling all too well, but I kept my hunting within strict perimeters. Sassy had crossed the line.

As I murmured good-bye, I wondered again: Did I have the right to put an end to Sassy's hunting? She was becoming the predator, but did that mean it was my place to play judge, jury, and executioner?

True, she had asked me to end her life if I noticed her slip over the edge. But would she want that now? Would she still be willing to stand there, waiting for the stake? Would she walk into the sun if she realized just how far she'd crossed the line? But the fact remained, from what Erin said, that Sassy was now kidnapping and torturing the innocent. And *that* was unacceptable.

"Menolly?"

I turned back to find Erin staring at me. "Yes?"

"Sassy and I've talked many times about right and wrong . . . good and evil. She didn't want to be a vampire in the first place. She wasn't given a choice. She told me more than once that she doesn't want to wear a black hat, as she put it. She said that as much as she loved me . . ."

Here, Erin hung her head and a bloody tear streaked down her face. I reached out and lifted her chin, nodding for her to go on. "She told me that she doesn't think she has much of a future left. That it's too hard for her to control the desire to hunt."

"I'm sorry, Erin. I'm so sorry." I knew that my daughter and Sassy had formed a romantic bond, even though I'd encouraged them to wait before sealing their relationship— at least until Erin had spent long enough in the *life* to know what she wanted.

Erin shrugged. "I am, too. I came out of the closet to my family about being gay and a vampire and they drove me out of their lives a few months ago. I'm alone in this world and still unsure about myself. Sassy's all I've got."

"No, no she isn't." I put my hands on her shoulders. She was a little taller than I, but looked so unsure and hesitant. "You have me—I'm your Blood-Mother. You have Tim and Camille and Delilah. They all care about you, and Tim's your best friend. We are family. Don't ever forget it."

"Tim's married now. He . . . he belongs in the world of the living, not in our world." She bit her lip, and I realized just how disconnected she was feeling from everything that had ever meant anything to her.

"Tim and you were best friends," I said slowly. "Unfortunately, things *do* change once you cross over the veil and become a vampire, but that doesn't mean that every relationship you had has to vanish or die with your old life.

Tim may have married Jason, but he still cares about you. He misses you. In fact, he's waiting for you to adapt enough so that you *can* be friends again, no matter how the friendship has to evolve."

She considered my words. "I suppose you're right. I guess I expected everything to go on the same, just with me being a vampire. I didn't have time to think it through."

"Are you sorry you asked me to turn you?" I touched her arm, lightly, praying she wouldn't say yes. I'd sworn I'd never sire another vampire and had broken my rule only because Grandmother Coyote had warned me that I needed to break through my own fears for the sake of destiny. Whatever the future held for Erin, I had a feeling it was far more than she dreamed of.

Erin mulled over my words. I liked that she was no longer so eager to please that she'd blurt out anything she thought might make me happy. She was growing into her fangs.

"No, I'm not sorry. I wasn't ready to die, and this was the only choice. I think, to be honest, that living with Sassy has been good for me, but I'm ready to move on. She's making me nervous and I can't do anything without her approval or she throws a fit."

It was my turn to bite my lip. Sassy had lost a daughter, many years ago. Had she pinned all her love—both maternal and romantic—onto Erin's shoulders? She was still protecting Erin from the monster she was becoming, or she wouldn't have sent her out of the room before attacking her victim. But had she also kept her from growing independent?

I decided to lighten the mood and held up a deck of cards. "Want to play a game of gin rummy?" I knew that Sassy and Erin played like fiends, and though the game bored me stiff, I wanted Erin to feel comfortable.

She shook her head. "If you don't mind, I hate that game. I play because Sassy loves it."

Laughing, I pitched the cards into the corner. "Fair

enough. It's not one of my favorites, either. What do you want to do? We have a couple hours till sunrise."

Erin let out a long sigh. "I'd like to go for a walk with you. Get outside, walk through the woods. Sassy doesn't take me out very often, and I miss the sound of the wind in the trees."

I hunted through my closet and pulled on a pair of Doc Martens. "Sounds good to me. Come on, let's go." And leading her up the stairs, I decided right there and then that I'd keep a tight watch over the next home I found for my daughter.

We returned to the house a half hour before sunrise to find my phone ringing. I snatched it up, afraid it might be Sassy again, as Erin contentedly sprawled in the armchair. We'd walked for about a half hour, then did a mad-dash all-out sprint through the woods, skimming the trunks and undergrowth through the freshly fallen snow. I taught Erin how to scale a tree—Sassy had ignored a good share of Erin's physical training, much to my dismay—and by the time we got back, she was looking forward to sunrise and sleep. I never liked the drowsy pull, but for Erin, it seemed to hold no dread.

I picked up the receiver to hear a low voice, almost a growl, on the other end. "Please summon Menolly to the phone."

The accent gave him away. As did the power behind the accent. It didn't matter whether my Caller ID was blocked. I knew who was on the other end.

"Hello, Roman. This is Menolly."

"Ah, the girl remembers my voice. That delights me." He let out a short laugh, and my stomach tied itself in knots. His voice was so rich, so strong, and even through the phone line he beckoned to me, reeling me in. "My maid relayed your message."

Shivering, I forced myself to sit on the bed. Roman scared the hell out of me. He was an ancient vampire whom I'd met once, thanks to Sassy. He could have taken on Dredge and slapped him down with one hand. Calculating he was, and cool, and perfectly at home in his skin. And he wanted me to attend the midwinter Vampire's Ball as his escort.

I hesitated. Roman was Sassy's friend. How was I going to juggle what I wanted to ask him with her meltdown? I had to say something, though—I wasn't about to play head games with the godfather of vampires. *That* would be a losing proposition.

"I need your help, if you're willing to offer it." There. Plain, simple, blunt.

He laughed again, his mirth rich and rolling over me like delicious honey. "And what will you offer me in return, I wonder? But first, you will attend the ball with me as my escort?"

It might sound like a question, but behind the façade, it was a demand. I rolled my eyes and decided what the hell—it couldn't hurt. Nerissa wouldn't be going anyway. It didn't do to take breathers to a vampire soiree.

"Yes, I'd love to. Thank you. I assume formal dress?"

"Lovely, and yes. Pick out whatever you like and send the bill to me. I would be happy to buy your dress for you. A fur, if you like."

Whoa. Dresses and fur coats on the first date? I started to say something, then bit my words back. Again, the whole power struggle thing was not something I wanted to get into. *Yet.* He could wipe me out with the blink of an eye, even though I had Dredge's blood in me.

"Um . . . thank you, but I have dresses."

"The offer stands. Now, what do you need my *help* with?"

I could hear the smirk behind the words and it ticked me off, but I kept my temper at bay. "We have a problem. I think we have a vampire serial killer at work in the city. I need to put an end to it."

A pause. Then, "And just what do you want me to do? Such matters don't interest me. You will find him, or you won't. Chances are, sooner or later, you will track him down and kill him. You're too good at your job not to. And then it will be over, for the time being, and you will move on to another case."

Somehow his confidence in me didn't make me feel better. "Have you heard anything out of the ordinary? Someone new to the life who's gone off balance?"

"A lot of vampires lose their way when they're turned. They walk into the shadows and lose their sense of reason. Those of us who make it to an ancient age must repress our consciences while maintaining logic and reason."

Something about the way he said that gave me the shivers. "I see. You do realize, this vampire is going to make life hard for all of us."

"Agreed. While I don't care about the humans on whom he feeds, he will give us a bad name. We live by the treaty to avoid all-out war, but not all vampires have agreed to it. Until the Regencies are set up, we won't have an *official* ruling class approved by the government to enforce sanctions against aberrant behavior. Which brings me directly to a topic *I* wish to discuss: your friend Wade."

Uh-oh. Wade was running for Regent against Terrance from the Fangtabula. Was Roman backing Terrance? I hoped not; it would tell me a lot more about him than I wanted to know. Though I'd wiped Wade off my radar after he kicked me out of Vampires Anonymous, truth was, I hoped he'd win. At least he'd be a *sane* choice for the job. Terrance was trouble incarnate.

Roman cleared his throat and I could hear a whistle. He must be smoking one of his cigars. Roman might be a hedonist, but he also refused to allow his passions to rule his life. He was in control with a capital *C*.

"This matter directly impacts you. I have a job for you, Menolly."

Great. Another person yanking on my coattails, and one whom I couldn't afford to ignore. "What do you want us to do?" I glanced over at Erin. She was happily absorbed in another movie, oblivious to my conversation. I had the feeling Sassy limited her television.

"*Us?* Not *us* if you're referring to your sisters, though if you need their help, I won't object. This is a serious task. But I trust that you will succeed. You are the only one I *will* trust for this matter, precisely because you aren't part of the vampire politics swirling through the town right now." He sobered, and behind the strength, I could hear a tinge of worry.

"What's going on, Roman?" I blinked. Vampire politics was so not on my plate right now. We had enough worries now with Stacia Bonecrusher—a demon general—dead. When Shadow Wing realized she'd vanished like her predecessors, he'd send someone bigger and badder after us.

"The phone is no place to discuss this matter. Come to my place. Eight thirty tonight. We'll dine on the richest blood you'll ever taste—voluntarily harvested from my stable of beauties. And I will tell you what I want of you."

His voice lingered over the words as his energy coiled through the phone to trail around me, caress my shoulders, and gently coax me in. Roman didn't just want my *help.* I could feel it, and the thought scared me shitless. He was the godfather of vampires, someone you just didn't say no to. He was no Dredge, but I had the feeling he could be far worse if he wanted to.

"Roman . . . I'm not sure what you're asking—"

"Eight thirty. My driver will pick you up."

"No, I'll drive. I've been there before." I refused to be at the mercy of anyone else's transportation.

"Very well, as you wish. But come alone. We have several matters to go over, so plan on staying late." And then silence as he hung up.

I stared at the receiver, then slowly replaced it on the cradle. The drowsy pull of dawn beckoned, and I tapped Erin on the shoulder. She startled out of her fixation on the screen, and as she looked up at me, I could see the tinge in her eyes that marked her as a vampire. She was beginning to develop her glamour—all vampires did, at some point during their early years. Even with her rather plain looks, Erin would be gloriously magnetic in a year or so, and humans would have a hard time resisting her.

"It's nearing sunrise," I said. "Time to sleep."

"I can't sleep on the bed with you. It's not proper. I'll sleep on the floor." She motioned to the bottom of the bed. "This will be fine."

"Wait." I ran upstairs and brought down a spare sleeping bag from the closet. Spreading it out, I tossed on a couple pillows and a lace throw. "There, that should work for you. Sleep now, my daughter."

Holding out my hand for her kiss, I watched as she knelt and pressed her lips to my fingers. Then she silently crawled into the folds of the sleeping bag and—as I made myself comfortable in the bed—she had already sunk into that darkness that claims every vampire with the rising sun.

We walk the world in our sleep, walk through air and shadow, through dream and projection. Before I'd staked Dredge, I'd relived my torture and turning nearly every night, unable to break free from the horror.

But more and more, my dreams carried me out on a wave across the ocean, to wade through the depths of Earth, to spiral out into space and watch the turning of the world. Each time I returned and woke to the night, there was a little part of me that regretted coming back, because my dreams had gone from nightmares to visions of beauty, and they never seemed long enough.

I found myself in a long, narrow room and knew I was dreaming, but my surroundings were so vivid and brilliant that I paused to look around. The walls were heavy, Old World paneling and paper; the floors marbled white with veins of gray. Heavy walnut furniture was arranged in a precise manner, and my instinct told me I could sit and relax. It wasn't that I was tired, but the room invited visitors to rest a spell, and as I took my place on a velveteen sofa, the strains of a harpsichord filtered through the air, like spun glass pipes or chimes in the wind.

Not sure what I was here for, I decided to wait. After all, the sun burned high in the sky and there was no waking for me till she sank beneath the horizon. It wasn't like I was going anywhere in a hurry.

As I passed the time examining the patterns on the wallpaper—the king stag was fighting a hunter, and it looked like he was winning—the door at the far end of the room opened and a figure glided through.

Roman. It was Roman.

I slowly rose and waited for him. The ancient vampire looked barely thirty-five, but power rolled in waves from him, almost knocking me off my feet.

He slowly waved his hand. In that instant, my jeans and jacket vanished and I realized I was wearing a long dress, crimson with rubies awash across the satin material, and a pair of four-inch stiletto pumps. It was a simple sheath, low cut, and my scars showed. Feeling terribly exposed, I glanced over my shoulder, hoping to find my jacket to cover my arms and chest.

"Menolly . . . do not hide who you are. Your lover appreciates the view . . . as do I." And with that, he was by my side, silent as the depths of the ocean. He reached forward and I slid into his arms and we were dancing; his embrace a fortress both trapping and protecting me. He leaned forward, his eyes glowing with hoarfrost. Roman's hair was long and shining, sleeked back into a brunette ponytail, and a goatee graced his chin.

"Roman, is this a dream? Or are you really here?" We

whirled around the room to the music as it rose and shifted from harpsichord to acoustic guitar.

"Oh, I am here, my dear. Make no mistake about that." And then he let go of my hand and with a wave, the walls of the room fell away and we were dancing under the velvet night, the swirl of my skirt a shimmering flutter.

"What do you want with me?" I whispered, staring up at a starry horizon that seemed to stretch forever.

"Have you ever wanted to be a queen, Menolly? Have you ever wanted to rule by the side of someone who can give you more power than you've ever dreamed of?"

Before I could answer, before I could even process the thought, he leaned down and kissed me, and all thought was lost in a blur of passion and longing.

CHAPTER 4

I woke before Erin did—the older the vampire, the quicker the waking.

As I bolted up in bed, remembering where I was and who I was, the dream stuck with me. Roman, the dancing . . . *"Have you ever wanted to be a queen, Menolly? Have you ever wanted to rule by the side of someone who can give you more power than you've ever dreamed of?"*

What had he meant? Had it just been wish fulfillment? Not likely, considering I'd never aspired to be the consort of any king, be he vampire or Fae.

Shaking off the dream, I turned my thoughts to my daughter. What the hell was I going to do with her for now? She couldn't stay here. And I most definitely was *not* going to return her to Sassy. But I couldn't leave her with any of our human friends. *Roman?* No way. Especially after that dream. I thought of Wade and cringed. I couldn't call him.

And then it hit me. Tavah. I trusted her to watch over the portal in the bar. I could trust her to watch Erin. I grabbed the phone and punched in Tavah's cell number. She answered on the third ring.

"Tavah, I have something to ask you. Can you please drop by my house right away? As in the next half hour?"

"Sure thing, boss. What's up?"

"I'll tell you when you get here," I muttered. "Can't talk right now, but it's important. I have a job for you and I really need your help."

As I hung up, it occurred to me that Erin could stay at the bar, in the hidden chamber down in the basement. The panic room was created to keep magic and intruders *out*, and anything up to a demon *in*. No daylight filtered in; no hunters could intrude, stakes in hand. I could tuck Erin in during the day and she would be safe, with no one being the wiser.

"Erin? You awake?" I gave her a few minutes to come out of her stupor. As she sat up, it occurred to me she had no clothes except what she'd been wearing. If there was one thing I didn't appreciate, it was a vampire who dressed in smelly, messy clothing. It was bad enough we fed on blood; we didn't have to look the part. She didn't like Chanel, anyway, and I wasn't going to force it on her like Sassy had. Erin was a grown woman; she could wear what she wanted.

She blinked, then pushed herself to her elbows. "I'm awake. It takes me a while—Sassy says that will change. Is she right?"

"As you age into your new life, yes, you will wake easier and with more clarity. Some of the ancient vampires can last against sunrise for an extra half hour or so, and can wake up even as the sun is starting to dip below the horizon. As long as they aren't directly in its path. Listen, I've got work to do. Important work. I want you to stay with Tavah this evening. She'll take you clothes shopping and then to the bar. I'll meet you there later."

Erin nodded, a hopeful look crossing her face. "Can I

help you out? Please?" And then her words spilled out in a rush. "Menolly, I'm bored. I loved running my shop. I hate just sitting around at Sassy's and playing games or watching TV. Put me to work, and I promise: I won't let you down."

I blinked. The thought of putting Erin to work had never occurred to me. Most vampires I knew were content to run around without a job to impede them. "You're serious? You wouldn't mind working in the bar at night?"

Erin flashed me a grateful smile and her eyes lit up in a way I hadn't seen in a long time. "I'd love it! I miss being busy. I miss . . . being needed. With my store, my clients needed me. Now . . ."

"Sassy needs you." I tried to make her feel better, but that opened up a whole new can of worms.

"I know Sassy needs me, but I feel like her pet." She glanced over at me. "You think we're in love, don't you?"

I slowly nodded. "Sassy gave me that impression, yes."

Erin shifted, obviously uncomfortable. "Sassy is in love with me. But . . ."

"But you're not in love with her?" Understanding began to pound its way into my brain. Why, oh why hadn't I talked this over with Erin before? I'd taken Sassy's word for everything. Feeling every inch the neglectful parent, I asked, "What do you really think of her?"

"I am grateful," Erin said with a shrug. "She's taken me in and makes sure I'm safe and fed and comfortable. I care about her. Maybe I could love her if we were equals, but we aren't. She's my foster mother. She's a good fifteen years older than me, which wouldn't matter if I were really attracted to her in that way. But the whole affair gives me the creeps. I know what she wants and I don't want to give it to her. Truth is, I'm not that interested in a relationship with anybody. I've got too much to learn about myself now."

I sat there dumbfounded. Erin made perfect sense. I kept forgetting that full-blooded humans were more prone to focusing on age than the Fae or half-Fae, or vampires who had been in the life for a long time. Because humans age so quickly, fifteen years could signify a lifetime to some people.

Leaning forward, I propped my elbows on my knees and shook my head. "I'm so sorry, Erin. I never would have left you there if I'd known about this. I should have asked you earlier how you felt."

"I wanted to say something, but I didn't want to displease you." Once again, Erin flashed back to the nervous daughter.

"How's your inner predator?" I asked, cautiously watching her.

"Hungry, but oddly enough—I don't feel the urge to hunt. I'm thirsty, but usually I'm just as good with the bottles of blood as I am with a host. I was a pacifist in life, you know. And somehow . . . that seems to have rubbed off on me in death. *Undeath?*" She laughed then, and I saw a little of the old Erin in the twinkle of her eyes. "I think I can control it, but I guess I should be watched a while longer to make sure."

Completely at a loss for words, I dropped onto the bed beside her. After a moment, I shrugged. "Okay, if you want to work, I'll put you to work. You can sleep at the bar during the day, in the safe room unless we need to use it. Nobody will find you there. I'll teach you how to hunt so you don't go over the edge if your instinct does flare up. I stick to the lowlifes, the scum. Or, if I have to choose an innocent, I curtail how much I drink and leave the person with very good memories and the desire for a thick steak."

Erin grinned at me, her fangs barely showing. "Thank you. I've been so worried about how I was going to make it through the next year—let alone the next hundred years. I need to be busy. I've always worked, ever since I was eighteen. I didn't have a chance to go to college and my parents kicked me out of the house, so I got a job and learned how to take care of myself. I scrimped and saved to open the Scarlet Harlot, and it about killed me to sell it to Tim, though I know he'll do a great job with it."

"Why did your parents kick you out?" I'd never really asked Erin about her background. I knew that her parents were both dead, but her sister and brother were alive. Apparently they didn't like the thought of having a gay member of the family. Or a vampire.

"My parents were fanatics—very right-wing religious types. I wouldn't join their church—it was more a cult than a church, actually. So they kicked me out when I graduated from high school. I stayed with a friend until I got a job and saved up enough for a studio apartment."

Wincing, I couldn't help but think that in some ways, Sephreh, our father, was just as bad. He was a bigot, too, hating Trillian, angry enough at Camille to kick her out.

"I'm sorry it came to that. But I'm your family now. And my sisters, and Tim and Jason. We're here for you."

She smiled shyly. "Thank you, Mis—Menolly."

"So here's what I need: someone to clean the upstairs guest rooms, to keep track of inventory, to sweep and mop the floors after we close. You willing to do that? I'll pay you what I would pay anybody for the job." I knew it was below Erin's level of expertise, but it was all I could offer at the moment.

She, however, seemed thrilled. "I'd love it. Can I rent my own place again? Now that I don't have to go back to Sassy's?"

"No, you don't have to go back to Sassy's, but as far as getting your own place, I think you should live at the bar for a while. But I promise that you'll have more freedom. We'll fix up one of the guest rooms upstairs for you at night. You can watch television and read, play on the computer— I'll buy you a laptop. And you'll sleep in the panic room."

If we needed the safe room to hold another demon or some such creature, I could bring Erin back to the house.

She smiled, looking content. "I'm thirsty," she said, her voice rustling.

I gazed into her eyes. Erin might think she had her predator under control, but she still had a ways to go. But for now, there was blood in the fridge and it tasted like beef stew.

"Listen to me, Erin. I'm going to do my best to help you grow into your new life. But if you ever, ever raise a fang against my family—anyone on this property or who belongs to my family—I will stake you. Do you understand?"

She nodded. "I don't ever want to become like Sassy has. Promise me that?"

"I promise, if you do, I'll put a stop to it." Falling silent for a moment, I gazed at her. My daughter. I'd birthed a monster, but she was also a caring, vibrant person. Trying to lighten the mood, I added, "Come on. You're in for a treat."

As I led her upstairs, I wondered how things were going to shake out with Sassy. But after Erin's disclosure, I wasn't going to worry myself over the socialite's reaction. She had bigger problems than losing a houseguest.

Iris was in the kitchen, putting the finishing touches on dinner. Morio was helping her. The smell of roast beef permeated the air, along with mashed potatoes and gravy and a Dutch apple pie. I glanced at Erin, who was eyeing the food wistfully.

"I have a treat for you," I said, pulling two bottles of the magically enhanced blood out of the refrigerator and popping them in the microwave. "Wait till you taste our dinner."

The doorbell rang and Camille called out, "It's Tavah."

"I'll be right there," I called, then turned to Morio. "When the blood's ready, can you pour a goblet for Erin?"

He grinned. "My pleasure. Does she know about the spell?"

I nodded. "Yes, but I don't think she's fully realized how extensive a selection we have thanks to you."

"Okay. For dessert, I prepared a few bottles that taste like cinnamon applesauce."

"Thank you. You're all right, you know that?" I grinned at my brother-in-law and then headed out to the porch, where Tavah was sitting on the swing. I slipped outside and closed the door behind me. As much as I liked her, I would never invite her in. Too much danger.

Myth and legend were right—to a point. Vampires needed an invitation to enter a private dwelling. *Unless* the building was like the frat house our enemy Harold Young had owned, which had technically been an arm of the university. Or a home-based business. Or a store or bar or other public venue. I wasn't quite clear on how it all worked yet and somehow doubted I'd ever be fully savvy.

The temperature had settled somewhere in the low thirties and promised to plummet even colder. The sky glimmered with that silvery sheen, and it was snowing again. The hours I'd spent in sleep had provided for a soft coating lining the tree branches and a scattering barely covering the grass. Now, by the looks of things, by morning we'd have a blanket of white stretching across the lawn.

"I need you to promise me confidentiality on this. It concerns another vampire. No gossiping, no telling tales to friends, no talking about this outside my earshot."

Tavah was officially employed by Queen Asteria now, too. She'd been paid as an Earthside vamp by the OIA, but after we got our butts kicked out last month, she'd offered to move over to the Elfin Queen's camp with us. So we took her up on it. She nodded her head.

"Of course. What's going on?"

I outlined the basic problem. "I need you to act as Erin's new foster mother when I'm not around, at least for now, till I can get matters settled. I'll take over her training, but I want to make sure she has someone to run to if she gets afraid or if something happens."

Tavah let out a little *hmm* and cocked her head to the

side. She was tall and lean like Delilah, with shoulder-length blond hair that tumbled down her back in a ponytail. She wore scant makeup and kept to herself a good deal. She was a bookworm, albeit dressed in jeans and cashmere. I'd learned enough about her to trust her, but I had the feeling she'd never let anybody in enough to be a good friend.

"I can do that," she said after a moment. "It's a lot of responsibility, but . . . yes, I'll be happy to help. You said you wanted me to take her shopping?"

I nodded. "She hates the things Sassy forces her to wear. Get her a few comfortable, neat outfits and for the sake of the gods, let *her* choose them. Then take her back to the bar and show her what needs to be done in terms of cleaning up. Also, pick up a twenty-five-inch TV, or something close, for one of the rooms upstairs, and an inexpensive laptop. Use the store credit card. Erin might as well start working tonight—show her where to find the cleaning supplies and what to do. I'm going to be late. If there are any problems, call my cell phone."

Standing, I summoned my daughter. All I had to do was reach out with my mind and call her, she was still so freshly turned—and she came running.

"Tavah's taking you shopping, then back to the bar. She's an older vampire, so she'll be able to help you if something happens." Tavah was at least one hundred years old, that much I knew. "I'll see you there when I'm finished with my business."

"Yes, Mistress." Erin automatically bent to kiss my hand, and I reluctantly allowed it. I'd never aspired to sire another vampire; I'd never aspired to control others, only to have power over my own life. Now, it seemed the responsibilities were growing and there was no turning my back on them.

As Tavah led her down the path toward the driveway, I watched them go. My daughter. How odd it felt on my tongue, especially when my daughter had been in her late forties at her death. But I was her sire, and she was my responsibility, and we would be forever linked, no matter what happened in the future.

Roman lived in a fabulous house behind a gated drive, and his staff was scared shitless of him. The one time I'd been here before, the maid had warned me that few who entered the building ever left. I had thought then I'd never come back, but here I was, staring up at the four-story white elephant, the gleaming white columns that marched along the front porch shimmering like marble pillars of light. What would it be like to live in a house like this? Full of artifacts and antiques, luxuriant to the point of excess, with a stable of bloodwhores on the premises? The house reeked of decadence, and yet it was not overripe.

I slid out of my car and slowly approached the front door.

A maid answered—not the same one as I'd met before, but a vampire nonetheless. I didn't ask about the other woman. I didn't want to know.

"Menolly D'Artigo, here to meet Roman. I have an appointment at eight thirty." As she stepped back, motioning me in, I was unaccountably glad I'd worn jeans and a turtleneck and my bad-ass black leather jacket. My stiletto boots tapped on the tile floor, which gleamed—polished to such a sheen that I could see my reflection in it.

She silently led me into the parlor—the one room into which I'd ventured before. An oppressive sense of time rested in knickknacks, in opulent upholstered furniture, in hangings woven by hand from centuries past.

Roman was a very wealthy vampire, and though he had exquisite taste, I felt claustrophobic around him. There was just too much . . . too many vases, and too many roses scenting the air, too many paintings covering the walls, too many throws covering the chairs and love seat and sofa.

"The Master will be with you in time," the doe-eyed young woman whispered. She was a young vampire, of that I was certain, but old enough to pause, give me a long look, and then smile suggestively before she slipped out of the room.

I knew the drill. Roman would let me wait a little past my comfort zone, then suddenly appear at my side. He was so old that he made no noise, moving faster than any vampire I'd ever met. He was older than Dracula, and older than Dredge had been.

"Thinking of anything in particular?" A soft voice echoed from the corner of the room, and I whirled to find myself staring at two gleaming eyes in the darkness. As he emerged from the shadows, I froze, once again feeling like a deer in the headlights.

Roman was as he'd been in my dream. I hadn't forgotten his looks, apparently. He was around five eleven, trim but muscled, and he wore a black smoking jacket and what looked like designer trousers. His hair was slicked back in a ponytail, a rich chocolate brown, and his eyes were almost white—the longer a vampire lived, the more pale his or her eyes became. Mine were already turning gray. His were nearly opaque, but a sparkle delineated the iris, and a faint slit of black reminded me of a cat's pupil.

Roman held out his hand. Sapphire cufflinks set in gold adorned the cuffs of his velvet jacket. A matching pendant hung from a ribbon of gold chain encircling his neck.

"Menolly, so good of you to come." He motioned for me to sit and I did, choosing a chair where he could not sit directly beside me. I didn't trust him. Any vampire that old had to have lost a good share of his humanity.

"You wanted my help, and yet I summon you here to assign you a task." His voice was low, smooth, silken cream, and he smiled. "You will assist me."

His manner had roped me in, but it was common sense that made me nod. When a vampire this old invited you to his home and asked for a favor, you said yes. At least until you could get away and decide how to back out of the obligation.

"What do you want?"

Roman leaned back, pulled out a miniature cigar, and lit it, not inhaling but gathering the smoke in his mouth and forming delicate, perfect rings with it, the tips of his fangs peeking out at me. I stared at his mouth, at the perfect O, and found myself licking my lips. Oh, he was honey and I felt like Winnie the Pooh. After a moment, he set his cigarillo in an ashtray.

"What do I want? I want you to stop a murder."

"Who's in danger?" I yanked my attention out of the gutter and tried to focus on what he was saying, praying it wasn't my sisters or me at risk.

"Wade Stevens. Your friend."

Wade! Wade, the vampire who had been instrumental in introducing me to the vampire scene in Seattle, then turned his back on me? My temper flared.

"Wade and I aren't on speaking terms." And then, because I couldn't help it, I asked, "Who wants to murder him, anyway? Terrance?"

"No," Roman said softly. "But if he doesn't withdraw from the election, I will stake him myself. Or send someone to do the job for me."

What the fuck? I stared at him a minute, waiting for a crack of laughter or anything to indicate he was joking, but none came.

"You can't kill Wade. He's one of the good guys," came racing out of my mouth before I could stop myself.

"I can, and I shall, if he doesn't listen to reason and withdraw from the election. Make him see reason. That's why I called you over here, or at least, one of the reasons." He leaned forward and gazed into my eyes, and I felt myself falling forward, falling into those ancient orbs of frost. "Menolly, persuade Wade to withdraw without telling him why, or I will kill him. It's that simple."

And then, before I could respond, he reached out and took my hand and a shiver raced up my back—and I, who could not feel cold, felt chilled to the bone.

Something inside—the part of me that remembered Dredge—screamed, *No, don't touch me*, but another part begged to be set free.

I forced down my panic. "What happens if I can't? What happens if he won't listen to me?"

"That . . . is not my problem," Roman said, his voice so low I could barely hear him. He drew me close, pulled me out of my chair, and before I realized what was happening, I was sitting in his lap, staring into his eyes. He reached up and caressed my face gently, without any sense of force.

"I have my reasons, Menolly. I could have just ignored everything and ordered him killed. But I knew—even though you two are on the outs—that he was your friend, and so I give you this chance to save him. Will you take it?"

"But why—what could be so wrong about him running in the election? Surely Terrance can't be a better choice. He'll destroy all we've worked to build up, all of the treaties with the breathers and the Fae."

Up close, I could see his face so much more clearly, and I realized Roman was a beautiful man. His hair shimmered under the dim lights from the chandeliers. And his eyes . . . his eyes reminded me of illuminated, mist-shrouded globes of light. I wondered how many moths had been drawn in by the gentle lure. Thoughts of his stable sprang to mind. Were they all human? Were they all women? Did he just feed on them, or were they also his concubines?

Roman's face was mere inches from mine. "Terrance will never hold the position of Regent, rest assured."

"You can't mean for me to talk to Terrance, too. He's out for my blood. And I'm out for his." I shook my head. The owner of the Fangtabula was as good as dead in my opinion—or he would be if I ever managed to catch him alone. He was the worst kind of vampire—totally given over to his predator side. Terrance was a sadist, a Dredge in the making.

"I'm not asking you to talk to him. I can handle Terrance. But young Wade, he has a good idea with his

Vampires Anonymous group. I will spare him if you persuade him to withdraw. But this must be done with discretion and finesse—you cannot tell him outright why you're asking him to walk away from the election. And rest assured, there will be other duties for you, in the future."

He seemed convinced I was going to agree. Of course, considering who he was, he had every reason to assume my cooperation.

"What are you planning to do about Terrance?"

"I'm planning on shutting down the Fangtabula and executing all of its primary players. They feed on the unwilling; they threaten to unbalance our negotiations with the breathers."

Roman gently slid me off his lap and stood up, a crackle of energy racing around him as he drew on his power. Instinctively, I pulled back. If I'd had a pulse to pound, it would be racing with fear.

"Terrance dares to challenge my authority. Menolly, do you know exactly who I am?" He gave me a cold, calculating smile.

I shook my head, slowly, listening to the ivory beads in my cornrows jingling. "Just that you're Roman . . . and that you have considerably more power than I first thought."

"Oh, Menolly," he said softly. "My dear Menolly. I am Roman, Lord of the Vampire Nation, eldest son of Blood Wyne—she who is Queen Mother of the Crimson Veil. And I'm heir to the throne." And then he began to laugh.

CHAPTER 5

"Blood Wyne?" This time, a chill did race down my spine—the kind of chill that doesn't need temperature to back it up. I'd heard rumors of Blood Wyne, the infamous, horrific vampire queen whose name stretched back into obscurity. Whether vampirism started with her, or she was just the one to bring it to notice, Blood Wyne was the first vampire whose name had instilled terror throughout the living and undead alike.

Long before the Great Divide, she had been known across the lands, but after the worlds ripped apart and the Fae split into factions, as humans began to claim the world for their own, Blood Wyne slipped into the shadows.

She was known still, but had retreated into the corner like a spider, watching to see how the next few centuries would fall out. I'd heard of her, but like most of the vampires I'd met, I assumed she'd taken her place in the underworld. But the world had changed. Her people were coming out of the coffin. And apparently, the Queen of the Crimson Veil walked the halls of the living dead once more.

"Your sire is Blood Wyne?" I stared at Roman. No wonder he was so powerful and ancient. He was old past counting. And living in Seattle. In a palatial estate. There was only so much my mind could take in during one conversation, and I had the feeling I'd almost reached my limit.

"Yes—and more. My *mother* is Blood Wyne. She only became my sire when she was turned. And she then turned all of her children. There are eight of us scattered throughout the world. I am the eldest." He rubbed the arm of the chair he was sitting in. "The *Vampyr* are truly the sons and daughters of Blood Wyne, in all imaginable ways."

I slowly inched back into my chair. She'd turned her own children? A sick feeling hit the pit of my stomach. "Were you in danger? Or did she just decide to turn all of you into vampires with her?"

Roman picked up his cigarillo, considered it for a moment, then pinched it out. "Blood Wyne was . . . a *possessive* mother. After her transformation, she waited very little time before attacking us. All eight of us—she ordered the guards to hold us down and then fed on us until we were near death. Of course, at that point she forced us to drink from her veins. I'm lucky. I was the oldest. But my sister and brother, twins . . . they were only twelve years old."

He sounded almost sad, and a mist covered his eyes. "They live forever locked in prepuberty. They turned on her, ran away together. I last heard of them five hundred years ago, when they terrorized and destroyed a village in France."

"Why? Why would she do that to her own children?" I couldn't imagine someone loving her children and deciding to turn them into monsters.

"She wanted to build an empire that would last an eternity. She wanted to keep us with her forever, and for all intents and purposes, she managed to accomplish her mission. At least in terms of life span. But we left home, instead of helping her create the kingdom she desired. Others took care of that desire—vampires who craved the same sense of power. Over the years, she accrued a kingdom, and her children . . . we eventually went back to her, but only on our terms."

"All of you?"

He paused, then said, "Two of my brothers now hang on her skirts. If we'd stayed together from the beginning, we'd rule the world by now. The rest of us agreed to be her emissaries, to help her rule but not from the heart of the throne. She was angry, but finally agreed. She wanted her rule to be visible, but she had to settle for a more sinister existence, ruling from the shadows, letting the mortals go about their business."

"You chose to forgo letting people know about you."

A nod. "We knew that if we allowed her desire to rule logic and reason, a war would be waged against all vampires. The times were not so progressive as they are now. We would be destroyed unless we rampaged across the land and ruled by terror. I'd had enough rampaging while I still lived. I'd rather not repeat the experience. There are times when conquerors are necessary for the world, but I am no longer a warrior, save for when I must take up arms again. I prefer to strike a balance between ends of the spectrum."

I gazed at him. Aligning myself with Roman was a smart move in many ways. On the other hand, I'd certainly draw more attention to myself, and some vampires were not going to like it. Wade, in particular. But he was as good as dead if I didn't do what Roman wanted me to. As angry as he'd made me, I couldn't just let him die.

And, I had to admit: The thought of Terrance being permanently removed from the picture dangled like a juicy, bloody carrot. He was crazed, dangerous, and I had a personal grudge against the man.

Roman possessed enormous power, and it said something for his nature that he hadn't used it to terrorize the city. He outclassed Dredge by far, but Dredge had used his power like a hammer. Roman wore it like a cloak.

I licked my lips. My fangs had descended when he

pulled me onto his lap and they had stayed down. Roman was delicious, and deadly, and all of those wonderful things that made power seductive. In the end, I made my decision based on instinct.

"I'll help you as long as it doesn't interfere with what my sisters and I are doing. Our work always takes priority."

I wasn't about to tell him about the demons, but I had a feeling he already knew. Vampires were cagey, and one as old as Roman didn't make it this long without holding info over the powerful and influential members of society.

I also knew that, at least Earthside, as vampires aged the territory battles increased. Like lions, only one king could rule over a defined area without a fight breaking out. Which explained why Roman's brothers and sisters had spread throughout the world, except for the two still living with Blood Wyne. But with Roman around here, it meant that he'd be the oldest and most powerful in the area.

He inclined his head, his gaze beckoning me. "As you will, my lady." He paused. "Do you dance?"

I nodded, thinking about my dream.

He stood and held out his hand. I took it and he pulled me to my feet. I said nothing as he led me to a door on the left. With a faint smile, Roman drew me through and I gasped as we entered the long chamber that had been in my dream. I wasn't wearing a fancy dress, but everything else seemed the same.

Roman placed his hands on my shoulders and slowly slid my jacket off, tossing it to the side where it fell against the floor.

With a snap of his fingers, music filled the chamber— wild and free. A piercing ululation gave way to thundering drums, and a woman's sultry voice swept in to enshroud us in its rhythm.

And then we were dancing, spinning and turning, a combination of tango and waltz. Faster we went, our feet barely skimming the ground, and I found myself laughing at the pure joy of movement. Roman's eyes flashed, sparkling, as he tightened his grip around my waist and his right hand grasped my own. He broke into a smile that reminded me of a triumphant wolf as he whirled me around the room.

As the song faded, he tumbled onto a backless divan, pulling me down on his lap. I was still laughing, but as I met his gaze, desire flared, sparking off a hunger in me that I hadn't felt for a man since I'd been on the back of Smoky, getting hot and heavy with Vanzir.

Vanzir had promised a wild ride, free of fear that I might hurt my partner, but somehow, we'd never followed through to the actual act. Rozurial had been a delightful lover, but he was too gentle in spirit, even more gentle than my Nerissa.

With Nerissa, I had passion and love and I never minded holding back, making certain I didn't lose it and attack her in a fit of blurred hunger and excitement.

But male lovers? I wasn't looking for emotional attachments. With men, I wanted a no-holds-barred fuckfest where I could let my inner predator out without fear. And Roman smelled like pure, unadulterated sex.

The music shifted to Gary Numan's "Strange Charm" and I stopped laughing. I leaned forward, straddling Roman's legs, and crawled up him as he lay back, our gazes locking.

On my hands and knees, staring down at him, the music was the only sound filling the room. And then, before anything else happened, I whispered, "I can't be anything for you but this. I am in love with the most beautiful woman in the world, and my heart belongs to her, but we have given each other permission to play with the boys."

He reached up and his fingers traced my face, cupping my chin as he pushed himself to a sitting position so that I was straddling his lap, staring into his face. "I will never ask you for love. There is no place in my heart for such emotion. But Menolly, I desire you. I want you and I have enough respect for you not to force the issue. If you choose to grace me with your body, then I will be a most willing and attentive playmate."

That was all the encouragement I needed. I leaned forward and his lips caught mine, and then we were standing, his hands under my ass, holding me as I wrapped my legs around his waist. I pushed the memory of Dredge out of my thoughts—he was the only other vampire I'd ever fucked, and only because he'd raped and tortured me, so I'd had no choice.

But Roman . . . Roman's hands were surprisingly gentle as he carried me over to a thick rug in front of a fireplace and laid me down on the floor. I reached for my jeans, but he stopped me.

"Let me undress you."

"I need to tell you something about myself," I said, stopping his hand. Closing my eyes, I paused. Then the words tumbled out in a rush. "I'm heavily scarred . . ."

He stopped, pulling me to a sitting position. "Dredge, correct? That was the Scourge's preferred method."

I nodded, biting back the flare of anger that rose at the mention of my sire's name. "He raped me. He tortured me, scarring me all over my body before he killed and turned me. The scars remained."

"Your lover, she has no qualms, does she?" He reached out a lazy finger and traced circles on the denim of my jeans, over my knee.

With a shake of the head, I smiled. "No. She taught me to love myself, despite the scars. But they can be disconcerting, and I don't want you freaking out when I show you my body."

"Battle scars, my dear." Roman tipped my chin up with one finger. "Be fiercely proud of them—reclaim them and change them from what they were first intended to do. Take them for your own. They make you the vampire you are. And vampires—we are predators, we are top of the food chain. We walk among the Immortals."

His eyes, so gray and full of mist, frosted over as he

straightened his shoulders. "Your scars no more diminish your beauty than the red of your hair, or the curve of your lips. Your passion, your beauty, reside in your soul, and that you possess intact and for yourself only, no matter what your looks. But trust me, you are a beauty in form as well as spirit."

I let his words settle, then raised my arms. He eased my turtleneck over my head, gently tossing it to the side, baring my breasts. Slowly, Roman leaned forward, his eyes flickering up at me, and took one nipple in his mouth.

A fire sparked somewhere low, rumbling in my belly, and I let out a little moan. He wrapped his arms around me and laid me back, stretching out beside me, his mouth still working my breast. I gasped as the sensations began to spread through my body, setting off explosions down my spine, toward my thighs.

With one hand, Roman unbuckled my belt and I reached up to help him, but he pushed my hands away and then unzipped me. I lifted my ass and slid the jeans down and somewhere between his lips on my nipple and his lips on my neck, my jeans were off and I was exposed in the dim light that filtered down from the chandeliers on the ceiling.

Roman rose up, kneeling beside me as he slid off his jacket, baring a muscled chest. A thatch of chest hair matched the rich brown of his ponytail, thinning as it trailed in a V toward his abs. His arms were strong, well muscled, and scars laced his wrists and chest—not deliberate, like the scars tattooing my body, but marks left by a whip or a crop. I reached forward and traced one that ran the length of his chest. It had to be thousands of years old, preserved in the flesh, a living fossil of a torture long gone.

"I fought many battles before I was turned," he whispered. "My mother was a queen even then. We ruled a small country of nomadic warriors. I waged war by her side, with my brothers and sisters, as we conquered neighboring villages and eventually small territories. I nearly died five times."

"Show me." My gaze lingered on the scars, taking in the scope of what he was telling me. He might even have existed before the Great Divide, when the worlds were ripped apart.

Roman stood and slid out of his trousers, carefully draping them over a nearby chair. He turned to me, strong, hard, ready. But rather than jump me, he motioned toward a long scar that graced his thigh.

"A wooden spear almost killed me. I recovered, though. I was strong and healthy and the magic of our shamans was strong." He pointed toward another scar that marred his left side. "Obsidian arrow. Came close to my heart but missed by just enough to spare me."

He turned and lifted his ponytail. His back was laced with scars from a whip. "When I was caught by an enemy. He tried to whip me to death. Instead, he vanished into the grave and I walked away, bleeding and in pain but triumphant."

Roman drew his shoulders back, standing so regally that I almost forgot he was naked. The power, the elegance rolled off him in a wave and swept me forward. I rose to my knees and leaned forward, pressing my lips to the scar on his thigh. Following it across his stomach to the scar on his side, I left a trail of soft kisses, nibbling, barely nipping him as he shuddered and his erection hardened.

"Oh my beautiful girl, you are such a wild spirit," he murmured, his hand gently holding the back of my head as I slid around and began kissing my way up the lacerations that crisscrossed his flesh. He was cold—unlike my Nerissa—but the chill was familiar, matching my own body temperature, and as I pressed my naked length along his back, a hunger began to build.

Hunger for blood, hunger for sex.

I slid my arms around his waist. "I've never been with a vampire before, except when . . ."

"Sshh . . . don't sully this moment with his name. Not here. Not now." Roman turned around and gathered me in his arms, crushing his lips against mine. He let out a low hiss. "There are so many things we can do," he murmured. "I long to taste you, to feed on you. Will you exchange blood with me?"

I found myself nodding, eager to taste him, eager to feel the rush of cool blood in my mouth. The blood that remained in our bodies was nowhere near normal temperature, but it still flowed, still circulated at an almost unbearably slow rhythm, giving no pulse, no fire to the body.

He lowered his lips to my neck. "Let me drink from you, then drink from me, my beauty, and taste my power." As his fangs touched my flesh, neatly puncturing my neck, a wave of euphoria slid over me and I closed my eyes, spiraling into a river of passion. It flowed, pulling me deep, sucking me under like the fingers of a riptide.

Let me drown forever, let me swim out and never come back. My thoughts were clouded in shades of honey and amber, of incense and sweet perfume. A rush of images raced through my mind—an ancient riverbed, dry as the moon, carving its way through a series of dunes. The thunder of hooves as a group of warriors rode by under the sun, their leader as glorious as the sun that beat down on them. *Roman. Astride the lead horse, and the look in his eyes one of victory.*

And the scenes changed, a sensual collage of people and places but always, always Roman was there, leading the rush, laughing atop a pile of dead bodies, in the middle of battle, his eyes flashing with life as he staked his claim, and then slowly, the euphoric rush began to fade, just enough for me to disentangle my thoughts, as he gently pulled away.

"And now," he whispered, baring his neck. "Come on, baby. Bite me. Suck me. Drink me."

And I did, plunging my fangs into him, feeling the spurt of blood in my mouth as I coaxed the drops to the surface. They were sweet, like sherry or port or flaming liqueur, and as I drove my fangs deeper, I straddled his cock and languorously slid down his length as he thrust up to meet me. He moaned as I licked the wound, willing the blood to fill my mouth. I began to rock my hips against his, reveling in the feel of him inside me, and he encircled my waist with one hand to balance me as he stood, my legs wrapped around him.

The world was a haze of blood and desire, of hunger and touch, and everything dissolved together in a whirl of sensation. And then we were moving—a blur in the night.

Suddenly, I looked up and found that we were standing under the stars. Crystalline clear, they sparkled in the chill of the night, but the cold of the night didn't bother me as the stiff breeze gusted around us, howling like a Bean Sidhe.

I pulled away from his neck, the blood trickling down my chin as he strode across the yard, carrying me through the snow, until we were in the middle of a private grove of cedar and fir. In the center of the clearing was a dais, black marble, and he carried me to the platform and laid me down, then straddled me. I stared up at the stars, remembering another night when the stars were the last beautiful, untainted thing I would remember seeing. Bloody tears began to pour down my cheeks as I began to whimper.

Roman seemed to understand what was happening. He gently brushed my cheek with his hand. "I am not going to hurt you, Menolly. I'll stop any time you want. I am not your sire, and you are no longer the vulnerable girl you were. Look at the beauty of the stars, for they mirror the beauty I see lying beneath me."

"But . . . but . . . the stars are so pure and we are . . ." I struggled to find the words, surprised that these feelings of self-loathing still lurked within me.

He pressed his finger to my lips. "Our lives may be steeped in blood and death, but there is such a beauty to the carnal, to the grave—the beauty of dissolution, the beauty of reintegration with the elements. How can you not believe in your own beauty? In your place in the scheme of things?"

He leaned down and began to kiss me, and his kiss was so caring, so gentle that it opened me up like a flower. And I began to believe again.

Nerissa loved me. She knew *what* I was and *she loved me*. And I could love her without destroying her. My sisters loved me, and I could love them without losing them.

At that moment I realized that I'd been so afraid of having everything I cared about stripped away from me that I'd been holding myself back. Yes, I was a predator, and I was deadly and dangerous. But I still owned my soul. Dredge had taken my life, but he couldn't touch my soul.

I shuddered, my face streaked with the trail of bloodred tears staining my cheeks. "Roman, make love to me. Fuck me. Take me down, into the darkness, and show me the beauty of the grave."

He smiled, icy and chill, his eyes mirroring the snow around us, and slowly entered me, his hips thrusting slowly at first and then harder and faster. As the gentleness fled, we became stag and deer in rut; we thrashed, moaning and grunting in the night, as the wind howled around us and then, under the wailing darkened moon, I fastened my fangs in his neck and drank the life force of the dead.

After a long shower in a bath off a guest room filled with perfume bottles and fancy clothes and antique dolls, I dressed in my clothes and rejoined Roman in the parlor. He was perfectly at ease, his hair wet and slicked back, and he was wearing a black velvet jacket and a pair of indigo-wash jeans.

He rose silently as I entered the room and held out his arms. Back in control of myself, I hesitated but then let him pull me in. He placed a kiss on my forehead, then a gentle kiss on my lips, then stepped back and gazed into my eyes.

"Tonight, you will talk to your friend Wade?"

I nodded, slowly. Talking to my "friend" Wade was still on my *Really-Do-Not-Want* list, but I'd given my word. "Yes, I will."

"Then perhaps this will help you. The vampire killer you seek? There are several newly minted vampires in the area. My servants have mentioned problematic incidents dealing with someone new to the life who refuses to answer when called, who seems to have run amok from his sire. Or if he's still under the influence of his sire, then we have twin problems."

"What do they know about him?" I slowly returned to my seat and flipped out a notebook. Delilah had gotten both Camille and me in the habit of carrying pocket-sized notepads and pens.

Roman considered the question. "Not much. We know that it's a male, and he can't have been in the life longer than six months, but my guess is we're talking younger than that. Reports of vampire sightings have increased around the Greenbelt Park District, and none of the regulars in the area claim territory there."

The Greenbelt Park District. Crap. That was the area where we'd found our victims. And now that I thought about it, the Greenbelt Park District was also known for being haunted, although I rather doubted the veracity of all the reports. Some of the oldest buildings in aboveground Seattle were there, including several bed-and-breakfasts that played on their haunted nature to attract tourists. Most of the buildings were the original stone and masonry work, and the houses in the area were owned by old-money families or young, rich couples looking to renovate. The area wasn't considered *wealthy*, but it was considered historical.

"I know vampires don't congregate around there, but I haven't had the time to find out why. Tell me—why hasn't anybody claimed it as territory?"

Roman glanced at me, then shook his head. "The ghosts. They're very active."

"Then they're real?" I frowned. I'd assumed that most of the sightings were contrived to attract the tourists. "Why are vampires afraid, though? What can the ghosts do to them?"

"The ghosts are very real and very dangerous," Roman said. "To humans, to Fae, and to vampires. There's something there that empowers them—some energy, some force. At least one vampire died from spiritual activity. A ghost staked her."

"A *ghost* staked her? You're kidding?" If ghosts were playing Buffy, then we were in trouble.

"Yes. I was there. I saw the ghostly figure and then a stake rose in the air and went zooming through Elizabetta. She died in a flurry of dust, and we ran and never went back." He moved closer and brushed my braids back with his hand. "If you investigate there, my dear, please, please be very careful. And tell your sisters to do the same."

CHAPTER 6

As I left Roman's, I decided to take a drive up toward the Greenbelt Park District and look around. I appreciated his warning, but I was capable of taking care of myself, and cautious enough not to be stupid. I'd refrain from entering any buildings and just get a feel for the area before bringing my sisters into potential danger. I was a lot more resilient than they were.

As I entered the neighborhood—a short jaunt from the Belles-Faire District in which we lived—the city gave way to more greenery. Fir and cedar soared into the sky along the sides of the street, covered with lacy black moss streaming down like spiderwebs. The buildings shifted from old brick to old stonework and masonry, brooding and heavy. They fit right in with the shroud of trees that surrounded the area.

I pulled alongside a large community park near where the dead girls had been found and jumped out of my car. A strange tang to the air caught my attention, though I couldn't pinpoint whether it was the storm or something else. Granted, it was snowing and that always brought its own sense of magic, but there was something unsettled here. And if I could feel it, then it had to be strong.

Pocketing my keys, I silently moved to the park entrance and easily leaped over the wrought-iron gates, the heels of my boots lightly tapping on the sidewalk as I landed again. The beads clicking in my hair were about the only sound I made now that I was a vampire, and at times I deliberately wore clothing with buckles and heels and chains so that I'd feel a little more . . . *alive*.

The park lights were on, even though the gates were locked. I followed the cobblestone path through the maze of trees and benches and picnic tables. Every now and then a shift in the light took on the shape of a moving shadow, stopping me. I noticed a dark spot over in the midst of a thicket of cedars, near a picnic table, and I headed off the path, my heels leaving soft impressions in several inches of snow that had piled up.

As I wound my way through the poorly manicured ferns and bushes, I smelled something. There was only one thing in the world that smelled so wonderful—*blood*. Crap.

Following my nose, I traced the scent through the undergrowth, hoping I was wrong. But no matter how much you prepare yourself, there's no good way to find a body. And find it I did: a young woman lying stark against the snow, her skirt pushed up and her panties missing. Her legs were spread, and blood trickled down from her inner thigh.

Dizzy, I dropped back on the ground, sitting beside the pale victim. One glance confirmed that the girl fit the pattern we'd noticed. Probably five six, one thirty-five, looked somewhere between twenty and thirty. Raped. And by the pale look of her skin, exsanguinated. She was freshly dead—no rigor yet.

I looked away, listening to the sounds around me. *A rustle in the bushes, and the snuffle of the stray dog causing it. The sound of snow falling muffled against the ground. The light whistle of the breeze ruffling through the firs.*

Glancing back at the girl, I grimaced. Whoever had done this had left her in disarray, without respect, splayed for anybody to find. I wanted to cover her genitals, rearrange her so she could reclaim her dignity, but I had to wait for Chase and his team to get here.

Sighing, I pulled out my cell phone and punched in his number. While I waited for him to pick up, something struck me about the girl. Something off. Her forehead— what—?

"Johnson here."

"Chase, it's Menolly. I found another victim."

"Crap. Where are you?"

I told him where I was and how I'd come to be here, and he said he'd be down with a team within ten minutes. Pocketing the phone again, I leaned down to look at the girl's brow. Her eyes were staring up at me, glassy and vacant.

"I'm sorry. I wish I could close them," I whispered. "I don't know who you are, and until Chase comes, I can't look to find out. I don't know if you're still around here in spirit—that's my sister Camille's territory—but I'm sorry. I'm sorry he did this to you. I'm sorry he left you here alone. I'm sorry I can't do anything for you except sit beside you and keep the animals at bay."

I didn't want to look at her, but as I leaned over her delicate, blank face, I saw it again—something on her forehead. I pulled out a pen flashlight and flipped it on, leaning closer. There, something wet. Something faint against her skin. It could have been snow falling on her and melting, but when I leaned in close, it looked like nothing less than a cross, drawn in water, on her brow.

Frowning, I leaned back. Most vampires didn't hold any truck with religious symbology—it was a nonissue for them. I had little to do with the gods. They hadn't been there for me when I was screaming for them, as Dredge ripped into me. And now, I didn't need them. As far as I was concerned, the gods could fuck themselves.

So why had the killer drawn a cross on her forehead

after he killed her? Or had someone else been here and gone between the time she was murdered and the time I found her?

Pondering the answers, I looked up at the snow falling. In the distance, I could hear the faint shouts of Chase's men as they came racing down the path. They skidded to a halt about ten feet from me, as Chase and Sharah lightly crossed to my side.

"You should get some crime scene tape up. You'll want evidence. Even if this is another vampire slaying, and it is, you need to follow protocol." I stood up. "I haven't touched her, though I sat beside her before I thought about what I might be disturbing."

Chase shook his head and motioned for me to move to the side with him as Sharah took over, leading the team into action. "She human?"

"As the sun is bright." I glanced back, again wincing as they began taking photographs and processing the area. "Do they have to photograph her like that? It's so undignified."

"I know," he said, lightly touching my elbow to turn me away from the scene. "I'm sorry, but we need the photos for evidence." He glanced back at the body. "I'm sorry you had to find this."

"I know something about our killer. Or at least I think I do." I kicked the snow with my boot. "I think he was religious in life. Or he's superstitious. He's not remorseful—he doesn't leave the bodies in a dignified manner. But he drew a cross on her forehead. I saw it, though it's probably dried by now."

Chase frowned, pursing his lip. "Vampires wouldn't do that, would they?"

"Not most of the ones I know. But I can smell the scent of the undead on her. I know a vampire did this." The scent was all over her, dank and fresh as the grave.

"Do you think he may be working with humans? Someone who might have decided to draw the cross afterward?"

He tapped his notebook with his pen and glanced at me, waiting.

My turn to frown. Would a vampire work with humans? "I suppose it's possible, though not likely. But he might have his stable with him, if he has one, or people under his glamour. Regardless of how deadly, or even how grotesque, all vampires have an innate charm. Whatever footprints were here are covered up by now. The snow . . . it's falling hard."

"The weather's been getting pretty freaky the past few years. Must be global warming." Chase pushed back his sleeve to look at his watch. "It's near to four in the morning. What were you doing out here?"

I shrugged. "Got a lead on our serial killer." I laid out what Roman had told me about the area. "I wanted to look around before putting anybody else in danger. It's not safe in this area of the city for people. Or vampires. Except our murderer, apparently."

Chase glanced around at the tree-shrouded park. "We do get a lot of reports of injuries from this district, and there have been several unexplained deaths over the years around here. I can believe it's haunted. There were a lot of fights here in the old days. A lot of skirmishes between different factions—some racial, others political."

"Any of those unexplained deaths happen to be murders like our girls?"

He shook his head. "No. Unexplained as in the victims shouldn't be dead and the causes were never explained. I can believe this part of the city teems with ghosts. I never come out here unless I can't help it."

A distant expression washed over him, one I'd seen on Camille's face when she was listening into the energy, and after a moment, he startled out of it. "There are entities here—ugly, old things. I don't know if they're spirits or what . . . but they aren't friendly."

"Chase, how long have you been able to suss energy like that?"

With a shrug, he flipped his notebook shut and stuck it in his pocket. "You know how long—ever since I woke up in the hospital. It's been two months and I feel like I'm walking in Never-Neverland. Everything seems so different. I don't know how you girls do it—walking in two worlds at once. It's driving me nuts."

"Talk to Sharah, she'll help you." I hesitantly reached out, then patted him on the arm. "Dude, you have to learn to live with this because it's yours. For a long, long, long time to come. I know what it's like. Look at me, Chase. Look at what happened to me, and I didn't just get *stabbed* by a demon. I went through hell . . . I remember what happened to me. Every nuance, every cut of the blade, every touch of him on me and inside me."

Chase dipped his head, blushing. "Yeah, and I know I sound like a baby next to you. I'm sorry. I forget sometimes, just what happened to you. I shouldn't complain about my own problems. They're a drop in the bucket."

"You know that's not what I meant. I'm just saying, I understand what it's like to have your life suddenly changed on you, to have everything you ever expected stripped away and replaced with something different."

"Thanks." Laughing then, he motioned toward the walk. "Let's go."

"What about her?" I jerked my head toward the body, not wanting to leave until they got her out of here.

"They'll bring her when they finish with the crime scene."

I glanced over my shoulder, feeling the urge to cry. "Tell them to be careful. It's dangerous to leave them here alone. Let me know when you find out who she was. You're going to have to break the cause of death to the newspapers soon. You can't wait much longer."

Chase let out a long, slow breath, and I could feel the pulsing of his heart from where I stood. This one made him nervous.

"I know. I'll do it tomorrow. But the fallout's going to be hell."

Unfortunately, I knew he was right.

I wandered back to my car. The bar was closed, but I needed to check in on Erin. As I unlocked the door, it occurred to me that once Chase leaked the story about the vampire serial killer to the press, I'd better have safeguards already in place. Like maybe a steel gate in front of the door. It was well known that a vampire owned the Wayfarer, and frankly, I didn't want to have to go apeshit on any miscreants. I stopped in my office and dropped an e-mail to Lisel, my bookkeeper and part-time assistant, to call about starting the process as soon as she got into her office.

As I locked the door behind me, I could hear noise coming from upstairs and headed up to see Erin. She was there, alone. Tavah was in the basement watching the portal.

"Hey, Erin. Everything okay?" I glanced around. Tavah had taken her charge seriously. The guest room was sporting a new TV, a DVD player, an Xbox, and a computer, and I knew that if I checked the mini-fridge I'd find bottles of blood. "Looks like you've got quite the setup here."

Erin paused the DVD she was watching and broke into a beaming smile as she turned. She dropped to submission and I held out my hand for her to kiss.

"Menolly, thank you. And look what else we got." She motioned to a small bookshelf in the corner that was now stuffed with books. There must have been a good forty or fifty paperbacks sitting there on the shelves.

I laughed, feeling the stress of the night ebb away. "I can see that my credit card got in a good workout."

Erin blinked. "I'm sorry—did I spend too much?"

"No, not at all." I'd be paying on the haul for months, but Erin looked happy and that was what counted. She was also back in a pair of nice jeans and a button-down shirt, neither of which Sassy would let her wear, and looked more her old self than since she'd been turned. I sighed. I'd better go talk to Sassy soon, before she showed up here. But there was another phone call that was even more important for me to make.

"Let me go make a call, then I'll come back and we'll talk for a while, okay?" I headed toward the door.

"Sure thing. And again, thank you. I feel like I'm me again. At least as far as I can be 'me.'"

I scurried downstairs to my office and dropped into my chair, staring at the phone. Finally, I decided it wasn't going to make the call itself and pulled my Rolodex toward me, flipping through the cards. Stevens . . . Stevens . . . there it was. Wade Stevens.

My hand on the receiver, I swallowed a bitter taste in the back of my throat. I so did not want to call Wade. He'd pissed me off so badly I'd wanted to stake him when we'd argued. Now, I had no choice. I'd promised Roman. And truth be told, if I was honest with myself, I'd worked out my fury at the idiot—I didn't feel much of anything.

That's not true, either, a voice inside me whispered. *You know you don't want Terrance to become Regent. You know Wade would be a better choice.*

Blinking, I shook off the voice and punched in his number. After three rings, he picked up. "Menolly?"

"You must have Caller ID."

"Yeah, I do." He sounded suspicious, but beneath it I caught a nuance of hope. Yeah, *that* would last a long time once he found out I wanted him to drop out of the running. "What's up?"

"Let me say up front, this is not my idea, but I promised I'd talk to you about it and I have to keep that promise." In a rush, the words raced out of my mouth. "You need to come here, to the bar. I have to talk to you about the election. It's important, Wade, or I wouldn't bother you."

"I can't make it over there now." He paused, then said, "What about if I meet you at the bar tomorrow night? Will that be soon enough?"

"Yeah." I never felt tongue-tied, but this was an awkward situation. I'd be damned if I was going to apologize for kicking him out of my life after the stunt he'd pulled, but I couldn't just leave everything on a sour note, either.

"Listen, on an entirely different subject, we've got trouble in the vampire community. Tomorrow, Chase is going to break news that will put all of us at risk."

"What are you talking about?"

"We've got a vampire serial killer on the loose, and Chase can't hold it from the public any longer. You'd better tell the group at Vampires Anonymous to watch their backs." The mention of the group still stung. I'd been making friends there when Wade kicked me out. But I wanted to warn them. "I have a feeling the backlash won't be pretty. Five women dead so far, all human, and all raped."

Wade's voice dropped an octave. "You're kidding. Please tell me you're kidding."

"No, we've got a fruitcake on the loose and it's going to get worse before it gets better. I'm looking for him, so if you or your . . . friends . . . know of any newly minted vampires around who are wacked enough to pull this sort of stunt, you'd better get that info to me ASAP. He likes to hunt in the Greenbelt Park District."

"I'll see what I can find out," Wade said, any arrogance gone. "I'll see you first thing after sunset at the bar. Until then . . . take care, Menolly. I . . . I've missed you."

"Yeah . . . see you." I sat there, receiver in my hand, listening to the dial tone. *You've missed me so much you haven't bothered to try to contact me, or apologize. Right, dude.*

Slowly, I replaced the phone in the cradle and headed back upstairs, my mind racing over everything that had happened in the past twenty-four hours. The vampire serial killer . . . Erin . . . Roman . . . and now Wade. Couldn't a vamp girl catch a break?

Arriving home shortly before five thirty, I first slipped into Camille's room. She was lying in the huge new bed Smoky had bought for them. Trillian snuggled on her right side, his arm draped around her. Smoky was on her left, his hair lightly playing across her arm in his sleep. Morio was curled up on the bottom of the bed in fox-form. They looked like a perfectly formed jigsaw puzzle, with all the pieces in place. As I slipped over to the bed to wake her, both Smoky and Trillian woke, eyeing me with sleepy frowns.

"I need to talk to Camille," I said aloud, seeing that they were both awake.

Smoky gently poked her in the arm till she woke up. Blurry eyed, she sat up and yawned. "What?"

"I need to talk to you and Delilah, downstairs. Won't take long, but it's important. I need you two to do me a favor before the day's out."

As she clambered across Trillian, her naked body brushing against him, I grinned. Both he and Smoky were staring at her, hunger rife in their expressions. Morio was still asleep—or doing a good job of pretending.

"I'll have her back up here for you guys in a few minutes," I said as she slid into her robe.

Smoky coughed. "We'll be . . . up. Camille, you might want to down a shot of espresso before you return to bed."

Trillian laughed. "Two, even."

She stuck her tongue out at them. "You think you're getting nookie this early, then you're going to owe me a long, luxurious back rub in return."

"Deal." Both men spoke at once.

She pushed me toward the door. "Now see what you've done? Created a couple horny monsters in my bed."

Laughing, I held up my hands. "Hey, I wasn't the one who let them through the door. I have to get Delilah. Why don't you go down and see about waking up Iris, too."

While Camille headed down the stairs, I took off for the third floor to wake Delilah. As I eased into her room, I had to laugh. There, sprawled buck naked and gorgeous on her bed, was Shade, her lover. Our other reptilian resident, he was half dragon, half Stradolan—a shadow walker.

If he hadn't been Delilah's, I might have found him

appealing. He had the same shadowy, Netherworld energy to him that all undead were cloaked in, but he was vibrant and alive and filled with fire. I smiled softly as I saw the golden tabby curled near him on the bed.

My sister. She often slept in her cat form, finding it more comfortable, and we loved her all the more for it. I slid in through the door, not wanting to startle Shade, but the minute I set foot inside the room, he was sitting up, alert, a dagger suddenly in his hand. Where it came from, I had no idea, but there was nothing wrong with his reflexes, that was for sure.

As he saw it was me, he relaxed. "Menolly, I'm sorry—I didn't mean to draw steel on you. Sheer reflex." He lowered the dagger and glanced down, smoothly pulling the sheet over his lap. "Is there something wrong?"

"I can't wait to see you in battle," I blurted out. "You're one hell of a fighter, aren't you?"

Shade laughed, his voice rich and thick. His skin was the color of warm toffee, and his hair flowed over his broad shoulders, honey and amber highlighting the wheat strands. A scar marred his face, but it synchronized with his personality.

"Yes, my vampire friend, I am no stranger to battle."

Remembering why I was there, I leaned down and petted Delilah awake. "Yo, Kitten. Wake up. I need to talk to you downstairs."

The cat languorously stretched, looking totally in bliss. Then she shimmered and began to transform. I stepped back as Shade slipped from under the covers and pulled on his robe. Within a couple of minutes, Delilah appeared on the bed, Hello Kitty PJs and all. So that was why her collar had been pink instead of blue.

"Come on, Kitten. Down to the kitchen and I'll fill you in on all that's happened since you went to bed. I've had a busy night."

She padded over to Shade and slid into his arms. He encircled her waist gently—she was still having some pain from the broken ribs Stacia Bonecrusher had given her a month ago—and his lips touched hers. A spark flared between them, and I watched as they kissed, deep and long, soulful, bound together by an invisible connection. Delilah had never had that with anybody—and I was grateful that now she did.

After a moment, I cleared my throat. "I'll send her back up in a few minutes. You just park yourself, dude."

Shade laughed again and winked at me. "Mistress Menolly, you are a harsh and cruel woman to take my Delilah from me, but I will be good and wait."

As he slid back into bed, Delilah and I headed down the stairs.

"You've got a good man there. He reeks of loyalty." I said it playfully but meant every word. He was entranced by my sister, and though he was always polite to both Camille and me, it was obvious he had placed his heart in our sister's hands.

"He's . . . easy. Easy to be with. Easy to talk to. Easy to lean on when I'm feeling nervous. We laugh together, a lot. I feel safe around him—I don't have to think about it. We can just *be*. I've never known anything like this. I think . . ."

She paused, then shrugged. "I think this is truly what love is. With Chase, it was like being a teenager. I needed to test out what love meant to me, to try on the feeling for practice. But something was missing. Something I don't think I ever would have found with him. I love Chase, but I don't think I was ever *in* love with him."

"How's Zachary taking it?" We didn't bring up the werepuma much. Both Delilah and Chase still felt guilty over Zach's injuries, from when he'd saved Chase's life and taken a nasty blow that had left him paralyzed. At first they thought it would be temporary, but now he'd been moved to a rehab center and the doctors were thinking he would be in a wheelchair forever.

"He still won't talk to me. Nerissa told me he's taken to

spending more and more time in puma form. Something changes when he shifts over and he's free from the pain and able to move again. The healers don't know what the difference is, but in puma form—he's free."

I heard something in her voice. "You think he's going to permanently choose to . . . ?"

A tear trickled down her face and she nodded. "I think, yes, one day Zach will change into puma form and run off and we'll never see him again. I think he'll go into the mountains, live as a lone male. And how can I say he's wrong? In puma form, he can run and hunt and move . . . but in human form, he's seen as a weak member of his Pride. The Rainier Puma Pride is harsh, in many ways, and he's been relegated to a position of lesser status since the accident."

"Why? Just because of his injuries?"

She shook her head, the tips of her fangs poking out. Delilah's fangs were nonretractable. "No," she said, anger washing across her face. "If he'd been protecting the Pride, he'd be considered a hero. No, it's because he was protecting Chase and me. Me, especially. You know how the Rainier Puma Pride feels about us, even though we helped them defeat Kyoka and the werespiders."

"I know. I don't talk about it much, but Nerissa gets flak from her Pride-mates because of her relationship with me. I've had it up to here with the Puma Pride and to be honest, I hope that she leaves them."

Delilah gave me a thoughtful nod. "They aren't as set in their ways as some werewolf packs, but they can be terribly cruel in their assessment of outsiders."

Placing a hand on her shoulder as we entered the kitchen, I whispered, "What will be, will be. Let thoughts of Zach go for now, Kitten. There's nothing you can do."

Camille and Iris were waiting at the table with tea in hand and cookies on a plate. As I sat down, I suddenly realized that this was our pattern. The three of us, with Iris, strategizing in the middle of the night. It had become so routine it was almost comforting. With a soft smile, I sat back and began to lay out everything that had happened since they went to bed.

CHAPTER 7

"Good gods, how can you get in so much trouble in one night?" Camille stared at me, her mouth open. "We leave you alone to get some sleep and you end up involved with Blood Wyne's son?"

"*Son* implies youth, and Roman, while he doesn't look a day over thirty-five, isn't youthful by any stretch of the imagination." I glanced around. The kitchen was almost back together after the demons invaded our home, but there were still deep gouges in a few of the walls and the tile needed to be replaced. The guys had pulled together, and in one month they had cleared out all the debris and repaired a good deal of the damage. New appliances gleamed in the dim light.

"What do you need us to do?" Delilah asked.

"Can you run down as much information on the Greenbelt Park District as you can find—especially regarding ghosts and haunting? And anything you might happen to hear about vampiric activity there."

"Sure. Not a problem." Delilah bobbed her head and I

smiled. The new do suited her so well; it was choppy and spiky and gave her an edgy look that rocked. She'd given in, once it was cut, and tried to dye it back to her normal golden color. For the most part, the calico mess that had come through had abated, though it still showed through here and there.

I looked at Camille. "Now to the problematic. Today Chase is breaking the news of the vampire serial killer. I've got my bookkeeper working on a gate for the Wayfarer, but Camille, you'd better take extra precautions at the Indigo Crescent. I'm afraid the backlash could reach your shop, too."

Her shop had been rebuilt and was open again, this time with Giselle, a demon, as the general manager. But that didn't preclude an attack by the Buffy wannabes.

She jotted down a note for herself. "Will do. Anything else for now?"

I shrugged. "I get to go shopping for a dress, and if I want it, a fur coat, thanks to Roman. Why do I feel a little like I've stumbled into the movie set of *Pretty Woman*? Only I'm no whore and Richard Gere doesn't hold a candle to Roman." Memories of his fangs on my neck rose up and I closed my eyes, reveling once again in being able to let myself go, totally, without fear of hurting anyone. A rush of power surged through me and I jerked my head up, eyes wide, feeling like I could take on Shadow Wing himself.

Camille coughed. "What the fuck did Roman do to you? I've never seen that look on your face before, and I'm not sure what to think."

The energy rolled through me and I shook my head. "I have no idea ... unless ... his blood—we exchanged blood and that means I am connected to his power. The effects will last for a while, given his age and strength. I never thought about this possibility."

"And because he drank from you, he's got Dredge's power in him?"

I nodded. "Yes, but he's more powerful than either

Dredge or me, so it shouldn't have much of an effect on him."

The phone rang. It was Tavah. "I just locked Erin in the safe room and I'm heading out to my lair. Lucius just came in to watch for the day." Lucius was Fae and he watched over the portal on weekdays. Kendra, an elf, took the weekends.

"Sounds good. I've asked my accountant to set up a gate system. Before you head out tonight, watch the news. You might want to double-check the security on your lair."

I hung up, sighing. How many vampires were going to be targeted after Chase broke it to the press that we had a serial killer with fangs on the loose?

Standing up, I glanced at the clock. Enough time for a quick shower and then into the dark slumber. I blew kisses to my sisters. As I headed downstairs, I had the sneaking suspicion my dreams were going to be full of dark vampires and the flow of delicious, ancient blood.

"Menolly! Menolly! We need you awake. *Now*." Camille was standing far enough away to avoid my backlash as I sat up in bed, startled awake at the first moment of sunset.

I blinked. "What? I'm awake, I'm awake." As I pulled out of the long day of walking between worlds—and I'd had some incredible dreams of both Roman and Nerissa—I noticed that she was dressed in a heavy spidersilk skirt and a leather bustier over a pale lavender shirt, and she had on her granny boots. That could mean only one thing.

"Who the hell are we fighting?"

"How'd you guess?" She laughed, then sobered quickly. "Seriously, there's trouble over in the Greenbelt Park District. The news broke about the vampire serial killer, and some reporter also managed to scare up the rumors of ghostly activity. A group of wannabe vampire hunters and ghost hunters decided to join forces and exorcise the area. In the course of two hours, they've managed to rile up the spirits. Chase needs our help to see if we can figure out what to do about the ghosts that have come out of the woodwork."

"*Fuck*. Fuck me *hard*. Why the hell do people pull this shit? They have no clue of what they're doing and yet they go in and hold a little séance or fuck around with a Ouija board and before they know it, they've got a bunch of pissed-off spirits on their ass. Any chance we can keep the posers out while we clean up their mess?" I leaped out of bed and yanked on a pair of jeans and a turtleneck.

"Chase has put up a blockade, but a group of them are trapped in the basement of an old building with a group of angry spirits and can't get out."

I stopped. "Shit, I'm supposed to meet Wade at the bar. Let me make a quick call." I dialed Derrick and asked him to tell Wade I'd be there as soon as I could. "Okay, let's head out and see what we can do."

On the way upstairs, Camille glanced over her shoulder at me. "You be careful. The city's gone apeshit, and being a vampire is not a Good Thing right now. Seriously, it's brought out every loco from the Eastside up to Shoreline and down to Renton. And not just the ones who want to turn you into a pile of dust mites. We're talking seriously ill FBHs. For some reason, the news sparked off that fringe element, and Seattle's turned into loony-tunes town today. There's an anti-Supe rally going on down by the courthouse and a new organization calling itself the "Earthborn Onlies" is holding some sort of vigil in front of the Supe-Urban Café. Marion has hired guards to keep watch, although the cops are doing a pretty good job of holding the nutjobs in check."

Great. Just great. That was all we needed. *This* was why we weren't telling people about Shadow Wing and the demons trying to break through. If news of a vampire serial killer could do this, what would people do when they got wind of an impending demonic invasion?

Everybody was waiting in the living room for us.

Except Delilah, that is. She was still confined to home care. Her ribs were almost healed, but she was off any strenuous activity until the end of the year. But Shade, her lover, was there, as were Camille's three men, and the Demon Twins, as Iris called Rozurial and Vanzir.

"Are the guards posted outside?"

Rozurial nodded. "They are. And your girlfriend's here, but she's taking a nap right now. Nerissa and I are going to stay with Delilah and Iris until you get back. Vanzir's more effective around ghosts than I am."

That meant it came down to Camille and me, Smoky, Trillian, Morio, Vanzir, and Shade. Camille and Morio would probably be our most effective weapons against the spirits, considering the death magic they were able to cook up between them.

"Okay, then. Let's get a move on. Shade, you and Vanzir can ride with me. Camille, we'll meet you guys there. Address?"

"Sent to your cell phone," she said.

And so we headed out, into the night, to rescue a group of FBHs who wanted nothing more than to see me turn to dust. Just one of life's little ironies.

The city streets sped by, a blur of lights, and the wheels of my Jag silently ate up the miles. We lived out in Belles-Faire, but it wouldn't take us long to speed over to the Greenbelt Park District. The snow was softly falling, muting the sounds of traffic, and my windshield wipers kept time with the music as it thundered through the car. Camille was up ahead, adeptly skirting the patches of ice marbling the road.

Finally, she swung a left turn at Daybreak Loop and I followed. Another right and then straight and we entered the Greenbelt Park District. Camille slowed and I knew she was looking for street names. Another five minutes and she signaled a right turn, and I did the same. Halfway down the block we could see several police cruisers, and I slipped into a parking space right behind Camille and her men. As they leaped out of the Lexus, Vanzir, Shade, and I slid out of my Jag and strode over to meet them. Silently, as a group, we headed in Chase's direction.

Chase had cordoned off the road in the opposite direction, and behind the police barricades we could see a small group of people, all screaming and shouting. Several of them carried camcorders, and a few had other assorted electronics draped around their necks. I immediately recognized them as gadgets for ghost hunting. Oh yeah, this was going to be fun.

"Let us in—"

"I can feel them—they need to be released!"

"Freedom of the press! You're trampling on my First Amendment rights!"

I glanced at the group as Chase hurried over to us. "Troublemakers?"

"They wouldn't be if they weren't so cocky." He let out a little growl and shook his head. For a moment his eyes shone in the darkness. *Eye shine, like a cat.* But he didn't seem to realize it and I decided to leave that little conversation for later, when we weren't facing big bad ghosties.

"What's the situation?" I glanced over at the building in front of which we were standing. A simple one-story building, it looked like it had once been a bar or a small diner. "Hostages in there?"

He nodded. "Yeah, in the basement. At least that's the last message we got from one of the women trapped down there. Five people are down there. The last we heard, the ghosts were tearing up the joint—full-on poltergeist activity, swiping passes at the ghost hunters, including claw marks. And we aren't talking *Casper the Friendly* here."

I glanced over at Camille. "What do you and Morio think?"

She shrugged, looking around. Morio had already gone into a trance, looking for all the world like he was stoned out of his mind. But even I knew that he was off on the astral, feeling out the situation.

"Chase, is there anything else you can tell us? Do you know what this place was? Were there any murders here? This is hardcore Earthside supernatural activity, so something brutal must have gone down around here."

"I've got Yugi running a check on it," he said, then stopped. "Just a minute." He pressed his hand against his ear, and I realized he was wearing a Bluetooth earpiece. "It's him. Give me five."

Camille held out her hand and jumped. "I can feel it from out here. You can't tell me that something horrible didn't happen here."

Morio snapped out of his trance at that point. "This entire area is a beacon for Netherworld activity. The energy reads like a cloud of gaseous green pain. I don't know why, but I think this district has become the gathering place for malcontented spirits all around the city."

"We can't take them all on—not at once." Camille pointed toward the building. "We'll have to focus on the ones in there."

"Did you bring the Black Unicorn horn?" I was hoping she'd say yes, but once again, wishes don't always play into reality.

"No, tonight's the new moon and it needs to finish charging. It took a long time to recover after my night with the Hunt." A haunted look crossed her face, and I knew she was remembering. When you sacrifice an Immortal, even if he's to be reincarnated and chose you as his executioner, you don't just forget it and go along your merry way. Camille had been emotionally scarred by the experience, even though it had earned her the mantle of priestess. "You're going to have to make do with Moon and death magic."

"Better the death magic," I mumbled. Camille's Moon magic went astray all too often. Although now that she was working under the dark of the moon more, she seemed to be doing a little better. She'd been assigned the wrong phase since childhood, and it had caused her powers to short-circuit, perhaps more so than her half-human heritage. We weren't sure yet.

I motioned to the others. "Fall in behind me. Shade, you can walk in the shadows. Will you slip up ahead and find out what's going on?"

He nodded—once—and seemed to vanish right before our eyes. Actually, it wasn't like a light going out, or like he'd turned invisible, but more a slow fade till he was translucent. Then he just went *poof* in a quiet way and was gone.

"I'd like to know more about the Stradolan," Morio said. "I can't find any mention of them in any of the books."

"You won't, either." Smoky shook his head. "The Stradolan inhabit the Netherworlds, and they partner with the black dragons to create a unified team. My guess is that somewhere, a linked pair fell in love or lust or something, and boom, Shade was born. His mother would have to be the dragon, though, and his father the Stradolan, or he wouldn't walk in physical form at all."

We all turned to him. "Why did you never tell us this before?" Camille frowned and smacked him on the arm.

He arched his eyebrow. "No one seemed particularly interested."

"I think Delilah will be," I said.

"He's probably told her. I'm pleasantly surprised by how honorable he's turned out to be. Of course, as you know, we dragons are a cagey lot, so I advise keeping watch on him for a while. He's probably listening to every word we say, by the way." Smoky let out a long huff. "I suggest we get in there if you hope to rescue the humans in one piece."

I'd been hoping Shade would come back first, armed with information, but Smoky had a point. The longer we waited, the more dangerous the situation was becoming. "Okay, let's head in. Shade will find us."

I swung toward the building, motioning for Vanzir to move up front with me. Morio and Camille were next, with

Trillian and Smoky taking up the back. We were about to head in when Chase came running over.

"Okay, I've got some info for you. Place used to be a diner, but before that it was a small tavern and card room. Real hole in the wall, and a hangout for thugs. This was back in the 1940s. The owner, one Randy Smith, found out his wife was leaving him for his brother and that they'd been having sex in the basement while he was out running errands. Randy didn't let on he knew, just sneaked back to the bar when one of his buddies gave him the heads-up they were both here, and he caught them. Guy went apeshit. Tied and gagged them both, then closed the bar early, after which he returned to the basement, where he made his wife watch while he bludgeoned his brother to death."

I had a nasty feeling the tale didn't end there.

"He had something extra special planned for his wife. Left her tied up, rubbed some of his brother's blood on her, then brought in a pack of rats and set them loose. They swarmed her and ate her alive." He grimaced. "Yugi saw the photos of what was left. Not pretty."

"So, we have at least two angry spirits." One spirit—trouble. Two—a hornet's nest.

"Not so fast," Chase said. "I'm not done yet. The guy then killed himself by rigging a sawed-off shotgun to shoot his brains out. Nobody found them for three days. Bar was sold to an older mom-and-pop pair who turned it into a diner. Couple who'd been together forty years, happy as clams."

"Why does my gut tell me this is going to get worse?" Camille said.

"Because it does." Chase consulted his notebook. "Within a year, the old guy went nuts and pushed his wife down the basement stairs. She hit her head and died. He must have realized what he'd just done, because he called the cops to turn himself in. By the time they got here, he'd hanged himself right over her fallen body."

"Is that the end of the body count?" I glanced at his face.

He shook his head, his expression grim. "No. The diner sold twice more and there were five more unexplained deaths. No more couples, but odd accidents that never fully added up. Never enough evidence to call them homicide. The building was last vacated in 1981 and has stood empty ever since."

We stared at each other. So, a mob of angry spirits. Violence to the point of nausea. Camille bit her lip and glanced over at the building.

"Are there things . . . remember the goshanti devil on the land where Harold Young's house stood? The land Carter now owns? Remember how it was created by the souls of all the murdered women?"

Morio slowly nodded. "I see what you're getting at, and yes, there are demonic entities—astral beasties—that can be formed by an excess of violence all within a small area. Whether we're dealing with something like that here, I don't know. But we'd better keep it in mind." He looked at me. "Do you think our serial vamp is hanging out here?"

I shook my head. "I don't think so, but you never know. For one thing, if these ghosts can kill vampires like Roman said, it's not a safe place for any of us. For another, I just have a feeling the whole area is tainted and our vampire is just one cog in the spooky wheel."

"I suppose we'd better go in." Camille turned to Chase. "You stay here—the fewer targets we have the better. Have your men keep a tight rein on that little congregation out there." She nodded to the shouting mob just beyond the barricades. "The last thing we need is for them to interfere."

"She's right," I said, looking at the detective. "The damage could be a whole lot worse if they got through."

"Gotcha." He motioned to one of the nearby officers and whispered to him. The guy looked half-elf, but it was hard to say for sure. Whatever his heritage, he nodded and headed back to the crowd control cops.

Chase cleared his throat and shoved his hands into his pockets, stamping from one foot to the other as snow fluttered down to chill the silent world. "I've told them to use tear gas if necessary, and I've called for more backup. But you'd better get moving. Things like this can turn ugly really fast, and they don't seem to realize that a group of ghosts can be as dangerous as a bunch of armed robbers holding hostages in a bank."

I motioned to the others. "Let's go see what we're dealing with." Leading the way with Vanzir by my side, we headed into Spook Central, ready for a fight.

CHAPTER 8

As we approached the building, I noticed that the diner had been boarded shut, but somebody had pried off the plywood—recently, by the smell of splintered wood—and entered through the front door.

Vanzir and I stepped over the threshold, into darkness. I paused, to let my eyes adjust, and glanced around. The room was barely discernible in the glow of the streetlamp from outside. There was a noise and then a light as Smoky and Trillian pulled out flashlights that attached to their belts.

We'd gotten wise after enough fights in the dark—we'd raided the hardware stores in search of any gadgets that might make life easier and wouldn't interfere with Camille's magic. A lot of electronics went wonky around all of us— thanks to our Fae wiring—so we had to be choosy. But we'd found flashlights that could be clipped on the belt and gave off a diffuse light that wouldn't blind us, but still illuminated the corners of a small room. Also, penlights, small and easy to carry, that could be hooked on a keychain.

The room was large, though, so the corners were out of sight in the gloom. But we could see the counter covered with a thick layer of dust, and the door into what was likely the kitchen. The room still had several old Formica-covered tables and vinyl sundae chairs scattered around. A faded Norman Rockwell print hung on a nearby wall.

But as inviting as the diner once must have been, the energy was thick and dank, and the hairs on my arms stood up. Camille let out a little gasp, and Morio stepped closer and took her hand.

"Bad," she said. "This place has bad juju. The energy is like a live wire, and while I don't feel Demonkin, whatever's here is evil. Malignant, like a cancer growing in the very air."

As she spoke, the print on the wall crashed to the ground. I whirled, looking for anybody or anything that might have jarred it down, but there was no one in sight.

"The temperature just dropped," Morio said.

Camille nodded, her teeth chattering. A puff of white escaped from her mouth as she breathed. "By about twenty degrees, I'd say. Spirit activity for sure."

I didn't notice much difference—cold and heat were fairly innocuous to me and neither one caught my attention until it was at an extreme. "What's that mean? Are you talking normal drop or—"

"I'm talking supernatural drop. The temperature just plunged twenty degrees in less than a minute." Morio barely got the words out before a dusty soda glass from behind the counter went flying across the room to smash against the opposite wall, almost hitting Vanzir.

"What the fuck?" Vanzir jumped, whirling around. "Who did that?"

"Poltergeist maybe, but I'm guessing the spirits here are a lot more dangerous than mere poltergeists." Morio warily glanced around. "I'm not sure where to begin. We'd better find the FBHs who are trapped. Where's the basement? Want to make a bet that's where they were headed?"

I glanced around, then saw an opening leading into the back. "Probably over there."

As we headed in the direction of the door, something tapped me on the shoulder. "What?" I glanced back, expecting to see Smoky or Trillian, but they were too far behind me. "Who tapped me on the shoulder?"

Smoky's face was paler than usual. "I saw a black shadow." He shook his head. "One minute I was looking at your back, then a shadow appeared and vanished before I could say a word."

"Not funny." I growled under my breath. "Nobody messes with me, be they human, spirit, or vampire. We have to do something. Morio—Camille—is there something we can rig up here to keep them from bothering us while we investigate—"

I was cut off by another loud crash behind me. We turned in unison, just in time to see a chair sailing through the air toward us. Smoky leaped in front of Trillian, who was about to get hammered by the wooden seat, and met it with upraised arms. He sent it careening to the floor, where it smashed into pieces.

Trillian met his eyes. "Thanks, bro. You saved me from a nasty crack on the head."

"No problem," Smoky said. "Camille would have been pissed if I'd let you get hurt." Even though he tried for a joke, his voice was clearly rattled.

Camille looked at Morio. "We need some sort of protection. I say we weave a moving pentagram to keep the beasties at bay."

Morio nodded. "I think you're right. It will mean another five minutes' delay, but we're not going to be very effective if we have to stop every minute to ward off an unseen attacker."

"What about Shade?" I asked, looking around.

"He'll be along," Smoky said. "He's probably off ahead somewhere, scoping out the situation."

They motioned for the rest of us to draw near, then

clasped hands and closed their eyes. "Don't let anybody jostle us until we finish," said Camille.

Vanzir, Trillian, Smoky, and I formed a circle around them, facing out so that we could see anything coming our way. Morio and Camille began to whisper. I couldn't see what they were doing, but the energy began to filter through the area, so strong that even I could feel it. A pale purple light encircled us, like tracers or quick, neon flashes in long narrow lines. I'd seen them work together enough; I knew this was one of the signature colors of their death magic.

> *"Weave the circle, tightly sewn,*
> *Let nothing evil or unknown*
> *Enter within. Stay without*
> *On pain of death, we cast you out."*

Their voices blended as they slid into a call-and-response chant, with Camille leading and Morio responding.

> *"Ghostly creatures hear me . . ."*
> *"Heart of the night, deep in the dark . . ."*
> *"You of the Nether realms heed me . . ."*
> *"Heart of the night, deep in the dark . . ."*
> *"We weave this spell against your land . . ."*
> *"Heart of the night, deep in the dark . . ."*
> *"We build this circle to stay thy hands . . ."*
> *"Heart of the night, deep in the dark . . ."*
> *"A star of five points, the elements we call . . ."*
> *"Heart of the night, deep in the dark . . ."*
> *"A circle round star, to bind them all . . ."*
> *"Heart of the night, deep in the dark . . ."*
> *"Flaming light blooms from karmic flower . . ."*
> *"Heart of the night, deep in the dark . . ."*
> *"Bind this spell till the Witching Hour . . ."*
> *"Heart of the night, deep in the dark . . ."*

As their voices fell away, a faint shimmer caught my eye. We were standing inside a misty purple vapor, and when I traced the pattern, I realized we were inside a pentagram—a star within a circle, sacred space created by their spellwork.

They took the forefront again. Camille glanced at us. "Stay within the circle of mist and we should have some protection. It won't last once we begin physical combat—if we come to that—but we should be able to make it to the basement. I figure Morio and I might be able to protect the hostages long enough to bring them out using the spell."

We moved forward, with my sister and her youkai-kitsune at the helm. Things began to fly off the walls and tables. In fact, one of the tables came skidding our way. Camille and Morio didn't flinch, and the rest of us managed to hold our ground. As the pot, vase, pitchers, and table met the edges of the misty circle, they were repelled, rebounding off to the side.

Whatever Camille and Morio were doing, they were doing it right. We made it to the door leading into the back and slowly filed through, crowding together to keep within the confines of the circle.

"Stairs to the right," Camille whispered. "We're going to start down. Again—stay inside the circle or you might get hurt. The energy is so thick I could slice it up and serve it on toast."

Slowly, she and Morio led the way, their palms facing forward as they pushed the energy of the moving penta-gram before them. We kept up, walking slowly, in unison. As I stared at their backs, I began to notice a weaving of faint violet light between them—faint, almost impercep-tible, like hair-thin threads joining their auras in a cross-hatch pattern.

Only one person could descend the stairs at a time, so Camille took the lead and, whispering something beneath her breath in rhythm with Morio, slowly stepped on the first stair. Morio followed, then me, then Vanzir. Trillian and Smoky brought up the rear. The stairwell was narrow and the sides dark and dank. Mold grew along the wall, and I could see evidence of termites and rats.

As we entered the basement, the flashlights at Smoky's and Trillian's belts cast out faint shadows, barely to the edge of the circle in front of Camille and Morio. Three steps down and something crashed at the bottom of the stairs, loud and with the sound of breaking glass. A scream rang out, and the panicked sound of a woman's voice.

"Jack, are you hurt? Jack? Oh my God, he's been hit with a shard of glass. Stop it—whoever you are, stop it, please. Just let us go!"

"Who's down there? We've come to help. How many of you are down there?" I called out. "Is anyone seriously hurt?"

There was a pause, and then the same woman's weeping voice echoed up. "Thank God someone's come! There are five of us, but I think Lance is dead. Jack's hurt, and so is Teri. I'm still okay and Mocha seems to be, but she's unconscious."

"We're partway down the stairs. Where are you?"

"When you get to the bottom, turn right and then left at the door. We're in the back room and we can't get out. There are . . . things in the room with us and every time we move, they come toward us."

"Don't move. Keep quiet and we'll be there as soon as we can," Morio said. He turned back to us. "Keep the talking to a minimum. The spirits here are volatile and will do whatever they can to interfere."

Even as he spoke, the stair beneath Camille's feet splintered with a groan and she fell forward into the darkness. Morio immediately grabbed for her and caught her by the wrist, yanking her up onto his stair. The pentagram of protection flickered and vanished.

Breathing heavily, she glanced over her shoulder at me, her eyes wide. But the next minute, she was back in control and, using Morio's hand to brace herself, she stepped over the broken step to the next one below, testing it cautiously before putting her full weight on it. Morio kept hold of her until she'd taken another step down, and then he followed. I nimbly avoided the broken step but thought that a fall down into the darkness could have been deadly. At the very least, painful.

We slowly progressed, Camille testing every step along the way, until we were at last at the bottom of the stairs. The minute Camille stepped onto the floor, she gasped.

"What is it?" I whispered, keeping my voice low.

"Something just passed by me, brushed against me." She glanced around, then moved to the left so the rest of us could exit the stairs.

"It was me," Shade said, appearing out of the shadows. Everybody jumped, but the looks of relief were obvious. "I've had a look around—or tried to. The shadows here are so thick they're hard to pierce. I found several areas that are filled with spirit activity. Up ahead, where the hostages are, is one of them."

Camille exhaled, deeply. "You scared the fuck out of me, but I'm so glad it's you. What do you think about our ghosts? You've spent time in the Netherworld."

"They are no longer merely ghosts. I don't know exactly what they are, but they've become far more dangerous than the typical spirit."

"Great." As I stepped onto the cement floor, a flash of lightning split the air—*en miniature*, to be sure, but lightning it was. A low rumble followed.

"Crap," Trillian said. "What the fuck was that?"

"Apparently, lightning." A squirrely feeling raced over me, like unwelcome fingers across my skin.

"Lightning. Inside. Not a good sign." Shade glanced around. "Camille, Morio, can you feel it? The energy of the Netherworld is thick here. There's a tremendous amount of spirit activity concentrated in this basement. Whoa!" He sucked in a deep breath.

"What?" I'd barely managed to yelp when something

knocked against me and I heard a low growl. A hand grabbed my arm, the grip far stronger than any human could manage. Fangs coming down, I let out a hiss and swiped toward it. My hand went through a semisolid amorphous mass, but the moment I came into contact with it, the creature—or whatever it was—disappeared, along with the pressure on my arm. "The ghosts are trying to mind-fuck us."

Camille sidled toward me. "Death magic deals with creatures from the Netherworld and shades and revenants, but not so much ghosts, though there is a connection. I'm not sure what to do. What do you think?" She glanced at Morio.

He shook his head. "Whatever this is, we can't just wave our magic wands and say, "Go away," and expect it to obey. I suppose we can try an exorcism?"

With a slow nod, she said, "Maybe, but first we have to get the people out of here. Look."

She pointed toward the nearest wall, and Trillian flashed his light to follow. The basement wall, a grungy cream color, was oozing some sort of liquid from a crack. The liquid looked suspiciously familiar and I crept close, inhaling the scent. Hell. *Blood.*

"Don't look now, but we've got an Amityville situation on our hands. That's blood."

"Amityville was a hoax. This isn't." Camille let out a long breath. "Come on, let's find the ghost hunters and get them out of here." She reached in her pocket and pulled out her own flashlight, switching it on as she began to stride forward. As her light splashed through the area, we saw the opposite wall. A door leading into yet another room stood open.

"They must be in there," she whispered.

We started toward the opening, but before we could take more than a half dozen steps, the door slammed closed and a piercing scream came from the other side. One of the women.

"Damn it, I've had enough of this." I raced full tilt at the door and grabbed the knob, yanking on it, but something was holding it closed from the other side. Whatever it was, it was just as strong as I was, and I had a feeling that an icy chill was seeping through the door like a thick fog.

Smoky reached my side and motioned for me to stand aside. I did, and he stepped back, then gave one tremendous kick to the door, splintering it to shreds. The look on his face was grim, and he motioned for Morio and Camille.

"You two—do something."

Morio put his hands on Camille's shoulders and she spread her arms wide. *"Mordente vanis, mordente konkor, mordente vanis en shau te Netherworld."*

Camille dropped her head back, her eyes rolling up in her head. As the faint purple light began to filter between them again, there was another crash as yet another lightning bolt splintered the air and she suddenly swung around, her eyes bloodred and the look on her face murderous.

"No, you shall not pass!" As she thrust one arm forward, a bolt of lightning forked from her hand, hitting me directly in the shoulder. The electrified tuning rod knocked me off my feet, singeing my shirt, but it did no more than stun me. Five inches to the southwest and it would have struck me in the heart and quite possibly dusted me.

As I shook my head, struggling to regain my footing, Morio smacked Camille across the face. Hard. Hard enough to drop her. She screamed as a dark fog lifted from her shoulders, out of her eyes and mouth, then slumped to the floor.

Smoky roared but managed to restrain himself from attacking Morio. Trillian raced to Camille's side while Shade helped me to my feet.

"Will someone tell me what the fuck just happened?" I shook my head to clear the ringing in my ears.

"Some entity just tried to take over Camille—it sent the bolt at you, not her." Morio shook his head. "We don't dare use any aggressive magic in here—not now that we know it can possess her. If it had taken hold of me, you might have had to kill me because I'm one hell of a lot stronger than she is."

I pushed past them and through the door. "The fuck with this—where are those people?"

"We're here!" The cry came from the right, and I turned toward the voice. There, at the end of the hall, huddled a group of five people. Four were on the ground, two of them conscious. The woman we'd been talking to was crouching behind them, the look on her face one of sheer terror.

I raced down the hall, ignoring the invisible hands that reached for me from the walls, and crouched beside her. She looked up at me and cringed.

"You're a vampire!"

"Yeah, and you're not. I'm here to help you, so either deal with it or we'll pack up and leave." I quickly examined the three figures who were dead to the world. One really was—dead, that is. One was hurt and unconscious; the other appeared to be fine but her eyes were closed. A fifth figure—a woman—sat propped against one of the walls with a jacket draped over her. By the odd way her leg stuck out, it was obvious that she'd broken it.

"What's your name?" I glanced at the woman who'd led us here. She looked relatively unhurt. But the haunted expression in her eyes told me she'd never be the same after this experience. I recognized that look—the look of trauma and nightmares and flashbacks.

"Leia. Don't laugh," she said in a hoarse voice. "My parents were *Star Wars* freaks." She shifted. "I think Lance is dead."

I checked the pale young man's pulse. Nothing. "Yeah, I'm afraid he is. Who's this?" I motioned toward the other woman with the broken leg.

"Teri. She broke her leg trying to get away from . . . whatever that creature is . . ." Leia gently patted Teri's arm. "She's in shock from the pain, I think. I put my jacket over her to keep her warm. The other woman is Mocha."

"Good thinking." At that moment, Shade appeared by my side, stepping out of a shadow. Startled, I jerked back. "Dude! You freak me out when you do that."

"The others can't get through the energy that fills this hall. Smoky and Vanzir are going to try, but Camille, Morio, and Trillian can't wade through it. I came by shadow." He eyed the huddle of figures. "I can take them back one by one, but you'll have to protect the others. I have the feeling the minute I move one of them, you're going to get hit with one hell of a ghostly punch. The energy in here is like a dark forest, dripping with vines and tentacles."

Delightful. Tentacles, I could do without. Reminded me too much of the Karsetii demons we'd faced. Just then, Smoky and Vanzir stepped out of the Ionyc Sea.

"You made it. Good—we have to get these people out of here."

Smoky looked at them. "I can take two at a time. Vanzir—you can carry one. Shade, I assume you can walk one through the shadow?"

Shade frowned. "I can, but it's more dangerous than what you do. I'll carry the boy who is dead. That way no one will be hurt."

"I'll return for the other one and you," Smoky said to me. "Do you think you can protect her while we're gone? We're going to take them up top—to Chase."

I nodded, not at all sure I could protect the one who was left with me. "Leave Mocha—the unconscious girl—she appears to be okay except for being out like a light. The man needs medical help." My reasoning was that if something happened, better she be the one left. She couldn't feel terror right now—or at least I hoped she couldn't.

Leia protested, but Smoky ignored her and made her hang onto his arm, tight, and then Shade gathered up Jack and placed him in Smoky's arms. Before I could blink, the dragon had vanished. From the moment he had touched them, the hairs on the nape of my neck stood up and I shivered as a gust of wind flew past. Vanzir gathered Teri in his arms, and she let out a cry that was echoed with a vicious howl from somewhere in the darkness. He vanished.

Shade gazed at me. "I'd rather take you—I don't want to leave you here, even for a moment."

"Just go, dude."

He nodded, silently picking up Lance's body. Stepping into a shadow, he was gone.

The second he was gone, I looked up to see a wooden stake hurtling toward me from the opposite side of the room. A shriek followed as I dove to the side and the stake clattered against the wall with a solid thud, dropping to the ground. Before anything could make it move again, I grabbed it and splintered it into toothpicks.

There was another howl and I found myself flattened against the wall, arms and legs splayed as if I were about to be crucified, by an unseen force. I struggled to break free, growling as my fangs came down and I began to see red. It felt as though something were trying to creep inside my brain, but I fought it off, refusing to allow it, and it retreated even as a fist of energy slammed into my stomach. I would have been doubled over if I'd been able to free my arms, but I could do nothing except let out a loud groan.

The next moment, Vanzir and Shade appeared again. "Smoky's gone to take Camille and Morio out the easy way," the dream-chaser demon said, then stopped as he stared at me, pressed against the wall.

"Enough!" Vanzir strode toward the hall and held out his hands. I could see vague energy lines emanating from them—in reality they were tentacles leading into the astral realm, but I couldn't figure out what the hell he was trying to attach to.

A keening went up through the hall as a puke-green light began to fill the space. Vanzir laughed, leaning back, his eyes a spinning vortex of unnamable colors as his hands shook. He dropped his head back and let out a howl, and was met in return by a ghostly wail.

"Feed on this, you cocksucker!" With another hoarse

laugh, he did something and I could see a pale pink energy feeding into the green from his hands. A shudder raced through the hall, and a piece of the ceiling crashed to the floor opposite us.

Vanzir ignored it, continuing to inject his energy into the nebulous creatures surrounding us, and as he continued, his form began to change. Within a few minutes, he was standing there, vaguely bipedal, but now we could see the tentacles emanating from his hands. He was no longer human-looking but a swirl of lights and sparkles, mesmerizing, and yet the energy of Demonkin rode him like a shroud.

Shade sucked in a deep breath. "He's trying to overload it," he whispered.

"Are you sure he won't bring down the building on us? Maybe you should take Mocha out of here." I was getting nervous now. Vanzir was caught up in a private war against whatever this was, and we were likely to be caught in the crossfire. "Vanzir—stop! Now." I put all the force I could into my voice, and he jerked his head around.

"No, please! I've almost got it!"

"You can't kill it this way. You'll take down the building and us with it." I shook my head.

"Fuck you, bitch!" He glowered, but then was back to himself as he ripped his energy out of the rolling green mass of clouds that were headed our way. But the look on his face was one of obedience. He grabbed up Mocha as Shade pulled me into his arms and, just before the ghostly vapor reached us, we flickered into the ether.

CHAPTER 9

Traveling through shadow was far different from moving through the Ionyc Sea. With Smoky and Vanzir, it was like we were in a protected bubble, but with Shade, I felt as though my body melded into the shadow, became smoke and mirrors, filtering through the hidden cloak brought about by light.

I'm dissolving, losing form, losing myself . . . a sweep of panic ran through me and I clutched onto Shade harder, but we were drifting. *What's my name? What am I?* Another shot of fear raced through me as I realized I had no idea of how long I'd been like this, of what *this* really was.

As we landed next to the police cruisers, stepping out of a nearby shadow, I found myself shaking. The ride had been rough, and I kept touching my arms, my stomach to make sure I was all back together. Shade gave me an odd glance, but smiled.

"Mistress Menolly, you are intact. Never fear. I wouldn't expose you to harm. My journeys can be dangerous for the living at times, but for the dead—and the undead—they hold no threat." He backed away as Camille ran up to me. She looked tired, beyond weary, and I realized that she and Morio must have expended a tremendous amount of energy trying to protect us.

"Are you okay?" I drew her to the side.

She grabbed my hands. "Oh, Menolly, when that thing took possession of me, I almost killed you. That was too close, and I'm not sure how it happened. One minute we were focusing on a spell to drive the spirits back and the next, *boom*, I was standing there like a ventriloquist's dummy with a ghost's hand up my butt."

"It's okay. I wasn't hurt. The only damage left is to my shirt."

"You could have been, though. And what if that had been Delilah, instead? I could have killed her with that lightning bolt. I have to find a way to protect myself from that happening again, so I don't accidentally let someone take over who can hurt you guys." Pensive, she shook her head and turned to Chase, who was walking our way.

I wanted to lighten the mood, but there wasn't much I could say. She was spot-on in her concerns. The lightning bolt would have fried Delilah to a crisp. So I turned to the detective. "Hey, Chase, how are they doing?"

He shook his head. "Lance Carver is dead. We can't figure out what killed him—probably a heart attack the kid shouldn't have had. Mocha Jervis is still in a coma. There doesn't appear to be anything wrong with her, not physically, but she's walled herself off inside her mind. Sharah is trying to figure out what's going on with her."

That wasn't good. Walled off inside her mind probably meant that whatever the ghosts had done, it had been as bad as or worse than what we'd been through with them.

"Teri has a broken leg, two broken ribs, and a fractured pelvis. Leia managed to get away with some scratches and cuts, but she's traumatized and can't handle being

alone—every shadow freaks her out. And Jack Riley's suf-
fering from internal injuries and swelling in the brain, as
well as a fractured skull. He's still unconscious, too, and
we don't know the extent of his brain damage."

"What the hell were they thinking?" I kicked the
ground. "Out hunting for vampires and ghosts, not knowing what the fuck they were doing—not thinking about the
ramifications. And we had to go clean up their mess."

"Except we couldn't clean it up." Camille's lips were
pursed. "We have a building filled with angry, volatile
spirits, and there's nothing we can do to stop them. I don't
even know who to call to deal with this. But evil can spread
like a disease."

"We need an exorcist, someone who's used to dealing
with ghosts. Wilbur's bound to know someone." Or Roman,
I thought. Roman probably knew everybody who was anybody. "Let me ask Roman first. He might be able to help us."
I moved off to the side, well aware of how tired Camille was.

Roman answered on the first ring. "Menolly . . . have
you spoken to Wade?"

"I'm headed there after I finish up here. But we have a
problem and I wondered if you could give us any help. I
need someone specializing in ghost removal."

He let out a snort. "You're looking for the Ghost-
busters?"

"No, I'm looking for somebody who can bust the balls
off some evil spirits that have been stirred up. You know as
well as I do that they won't go back to sleep once they've
been roused." I quickly ran down what had happened.

Roman was silent for a moment, then cleared his throat.
"I know someone who can help you. But you must tell
your sister to go home and cast a protection spell before
she heads into the field again. Camille's magic leaves her
open to possession, and Earthside spirits who are soil-
bound work differently than those in your homeland. She's
in danger every second she's near the building until she
invokes protection."

I pressed my lips together. Great. Just what we needed. "Yeah, okay. So what should I do?"

"I am going to give you the phone number for Ivana Krask. She's a gifted . . . psychic. She can take care of angry ghosts." He rattled off a number and I repeated it, then motioned for Chase to give me a paper and pen because I wasn't sure I trusted my memory.

"I'll call her. Who is she?"

"As I said, she's a gifted psychic. She is not human, but do not ask her what she is. That isn't a question she's prone to answer. If anybody can take the spirits down, she can. But she will demand payment. Don't have any kittens or dogs or children near you at the time. Offer her ten pounds of steak. Make sure it's a *prime* cut. She will help you for this, but she will argue at first. Ignore her counteroffers and just state again that you will pay her ten pounds of steak and no more. The third time, she will accept the deal. Whatever you do, do *not* say thank you at any time."

I stared at my phone. What the fuck kind of creature was she? But I knew I wouldn't get the answer out of Roman. "I'll call her and set it up for tomorrow night—"

"Then call her tomorrow. You must complete the deal *on the day* you contract it—so call before midnight and meet her there early, or call right after midnight and meet her before dawn. Trust me on this: You do not want to break the terms of her contract, or I won't be able to help you."

"Okay, will do." I frowned, wondering just what kind of deal I'd be making. I wasn't into playing Faust. But if she could clear out the lot of evil spirits, then it might be worth it.

"Call me after you talk to Stevens. I will be waiting." Roman hung up abruptly.

I slowly put my phone away, thinking that the night just kept getting stranger and stranger. Chase lightly touched my arm.

"Well?"

"Roman told me who to call in, but leave it to me. From

what little he told me, you aren't going to want to meet the person . . . or creature. I'll get in touch with her tomorrow night and we'll come clear out the area. I need ten pounds prime-grade steak for this—and it better not be cheap meat. No cutting corners on this."

"Steak? Ten pounds of steak? What the hell are you getting yourself into?" Chase looked skeptical.

I gazed up at him, not smiling. "Don't ask. You don't want to know."

He inclined his head. "I believe you. I guess we just mark this a crime scene and post guards to keep people out. The crowd down the block has dwindled, but this isn't the last we're going to hear out of them."

That was the truth. I could feel it in my gut.

After Camille and the men headed for home, I took off for the bar. Not only did I have to check on Erin, but Wade was—hopefully—still waiting for me. I hustled through the door, noticing that the gate had been installed as I'd asked. At least we'd have some measure of protection from vandals during the off-hours.

Stripping off my jacket—I wore it only for the fashion, I didn't need it for the cold—I lightly jumped over the counter to land behind the bar. Derrick was adeptly filling orders. He gave me a two-fingered salute without missing a beat, catching the bottle he'd sent flying into the air before it could spill a drop.

"How's it going?" I gave him the once-over. He looked at ease, comfortable, like he'd been here for months instead of just a couple of days.

"I like it. Much more my style than working an FBH bar. People here all are quirky—or out to see quirky." With a soft smile, he quickly maneuvered five drinks onto Chrysandra's tray and called, "Order up, Chryssie."

She hustled over and picked up the tray, stopping to

point toward one of the back booths. "Wade. He's still here."

I nodded, thinking I should clean up a little. I was covered with dust and cobwebs from the basement jaunt down the Hallway of Hell. But vanity took second place to thinking that if I didn't get over there, Wade wouldn't get Roman's message and might just end up on the wrong side of a stake.

He was sitting in the booth, reading a book, wearing black leather pants, only this time they were real leather—not PVC. And the glasses were gone, but they'd been for show only. His shirt was a neat button-down crimson number, and his hair was shocking platinum and feathered in an edgy cut. Kind of reminded me of Delilah's new do, actually, except hers was back to golden instead of white-gold.

"Wade." I stood beside the booth for a moment as he jerked his nose out of the book and stared at me. I couldn't tell whether he was scowling or whether it was bewilderment. Either way, I couldn't just stand here all night. I slid into the booth and leaned back, gauging his reaction.

He dog-eared the corner of the book, folding it precisely, before he closed the paperback and slid it back into his bag. "What do you need, Menolly?" His voice was smooth, no longer the happy-go-lucky vampire—if any vamp can be called that—I'd first met at Vampires Anonymous.

"I've got a message for you. I wouldn't bother you—I know what your opinion of me is right now—but this is important. Bear in mind, I could have ignored it. I could have just walked away and let nature take its course." I propped my elbows on the table, resting my chin on my hands.

"Okay, you've made your point. You're doing me a favor. What is it?"

"If you don't withdraw from the elections, there'll be a big red bull's-eye painted on your heart and a stake following through to dust you."

All sound fell away as Wade's eyes grew red and his fangs began to descend. "Are you threatening me?"

I shook my head, the beads in my hair making a faint clicking sound, like bones rattling. "Get real. I haven't got the time or the desire to start a personal little war. And I'm not involved in the elections anymore, am I? Thanks to you, I have no place in the current race. No, Wade, this comes from higher up than me. From higher up than you."

With a sullen look, he asked, "Are you working for Terrance?"

The question hit me like gasoline on flame. "Are you a *fucking idiot*? I'm the one who wanted you to take Terrance down, to dust him. But no . . . you refused. Or you couldn't. Believe me, I want to see Terrance out of the gene pool, too, and he will be if things work out right. But if you stay in the race, I guarantee that you're going to meet the sharp end of a long stick and I won't be able to help you then. It will be out of my hands. I've been given a chance to warn you. I didn't have to do it."

Wade's eyes lingered on my face. "I believe you. You wouldn't work for Terrance. And you don't want to run for the office yourself. Who's pulling your strings? It's got to be somebody higher up."

"I can't tell you, but I am telling you that if you want to save your fucking life, you'll withdraw from the election. Believe me, what you think you're fighting for isn't what you're really fighting for. Honestly." I leaned back in the booth and crossed my arms. The ball was in his court.

Wade wasn't stupid. He cocked his head to one side. "It wasn't Sassy that put you up to this. It has to be someone with power. Someone with enough power to make you jump. Who could that be . . ." He began to run over names in his head—I could see the wheels turning—and then stopped. "No. Not *him*."

I kept my mouth shut. Roman hadn't given me permission to drop his name. And name-dropping with vampires wasn't just tacky, it could be deadly. "I promise you, Terrance won't gain the position."

Pulling a couple packets of sugar from the tray on the table, Wade played with them, snapping them together as if he were going to pour them in a cup of coffee. After another moment, he said, "I'll let you know. I'll call you tomorrow night with my answer. Now, you said we have a vampire serial killer on the loose? I saw the reports on the news. Bad scene, if it's real."

"Oh, it's real all right. I've seen the victims, and I found one of them. Hey"—I pointed to his hand—"put the sugar down unless you're planning on eating it, and since I know just how sick you'd get, please don't. I don't need you vomiting blood all over my bar."

He tossed the packets at me. "This is bad. For all of us. What are the details?"

"He—and it *is* a *he*—targets young women, FBHs, under thirty-five, with long brown hair. They're all average build, a little curvy, and average height. Hair is straight, bone structure delicate. The victims could be related by looks. All exsanguinated. Raped. I found a cross drawn on the forehead in water on one of them. We're thinking he's a newly coined vampire, either that or something triggered him off a couple weeks ago."

As I ticked off the salient points, it occurred to me that Wade had lived in Seattle all his life. "What do you know about the Greenbelt Park District?"

"Stay away from there. Bad energy. Lots of reported hauntings. When I was around twelve, I rode my bike too far from home and ended up near there. It was late afternoon and rainy. I ducked into one of the abandoned buildings for cover and was hiding from the rain until I saw a shadow move against the opposite wall. There was nothing to make the shadow—that I could see clearly enough—and it was coming toward me. I ran out of there so fast I tripped and broke a tooth. My mother found out where I'd been and freaked. She'd heard the stories."

I suppressed a grin. His mother was a piece of work and one of the main reasons I'd given up on dating him. She was also a vampire, and she hung around his neck like an albatross. Think George Costanza's mother off *Seinfeld* combined with Fran's mother off *The Nanny*, and you have Belinda Stevens. Oh yeah, she was a piece of work, all right.

"How *is* your mother?" I couldn't help it. The words just slipped out.

He arched one eyebrow and then broke into a short laugh. "Luckily, she's currently obsessed with putting together a moonlight garden club, no less, of matronly vampire women. Not many takers, especially since it's winter, but she's managed to find a few members. They currently play bridge every Thursday night and cultivate night-blooming indoor plants, I guess."

Snorting, I gave him a shrug. Things almost felt back to normal between us. "At least it's a hobby."

"Yeah, I guess. So what do you need to catch this freak?"

"Any information you have on vampires around the Greenbelt Park District. Any info on new vamps to the area. Or someone in the life who had a traumatic event happen a couple weeks ago that could have triggered their behavior." Suddenly feeling conciliatory, I reached out one hand. "Wade, I miss you as a friend. I miss the VA. I'm still terribly hurt by what you did."

He stared at my hand then slowly took it, his skin cool against my own. "I'm sorry," he whispered. "I've wanted this so much—the Regency. But if you're telling me the truth—and I believe you are—then there's no way I'll live to ascend to the position. I just don't want Terrance to win. He would hurt our standing with the breathers so badly."

"I know he would, but he isn't going to make it. Trust me. I'm . . . I'm involved in making sure he doesn't." That was as much as I could say, but Wade squeezed my hand and then softly let go.

"As I said, I need to think about it, but I'll have an answer for you tomorrow." He paused, then asked, "Are you happy? Do you have . . . someone?"

I broke out in a wide grin. "The best girlfriend I ever could have. See?" Holding up my hand, I flashed the gold promise ring. "We're bound. And . . . it looks like I've got another playmate on the side, but I can't talk about that right now."

Wade nodded. "I know who you're talking about. I won't ask." He was sliding out of the booth, about to head toward the door, when it occurred to me I should talk to him about Sassy.

"One more thing. We have a problem with Sassy." I quickly ran down what Erin had told me.

Wade's soft smile turned to a dark frown. "Oh no, not Sassy. But it doesn't surprise me. She quit the VA, you know, when I kicked you out. But even before then, I was starting to sense an edge to her. I'm afraid we've lost her."

"She made me promise that if she ever slipped into her predator . . ." I left the thought unfinished, but Wade picked up the thread.

Bloody tears formed at the corners of his eyes and he squeezed them shut. "Oh, Menolly. Did you promise?"

I nodded.

"Then you have to follow through. Sassy wouldn't like her memory to be sullied with the blood of the innocent. If she were in her right mind . . ." He said no more, but his look told me all I needed to know. I pressed my lips together, raised one hand in farewell, and watched him walk out of the bar.

It was too late to call Ivana, so I made sure Erin was doing okay—she was busy dusting and mopping floors and seemed bright-eyed and happy—and then decided it was time to face Sassy.

Seeking out Chrysandra, I told her, "I'll be back in a

while, but probably not before we close. I've got one other pressing errand to run. Keep an eye on things and if you need help, Tavah's in the basement."

As I dashed out to my Jag, it occurred to me that I missed spending more time behind the counter of the bar. It suited me, and I felt at home serving customers and listening to sad tales, even though most of the time I was rolling my eyes when they couldn't see me. But right now, I had darker matters to attend to. I pulled out of my parking space and headed over to Sassy's house, trying not to think about the coming confrontation.

Sassy Branson. Socialite. Old money inherited from her beloved husband's death. Out-of-the-closet lesbian. Vampire. And until recently, a staunch supporter of Vampires Anonymous.

Oh, we all had our own version of what *innocent victim* meant, but until recently, Sassy had fed exclusively on volunteers and blood bank blood. Now, she'd crossed the line.

A memory flashed through my mind, of a conversation from some months back when I was sitting in her living room, talking with her.

"Why haven't you gone hunting?"

Sassy cleared her throat. I looked up at her. She held my gaze.

"I've started to enjoy it too much. I'm slipping. Just a little, Menolly, but it scares me silly. That's why Erin's good for me. She reminds me of how important training is. Helping her helps me." She hesitated, then continued. "I want you to promise me something. I don't have any family, so consider it payment for helping Erin. Down the line."

I knew what she was going to ask, because I'd made Camille promise me the same thing. "If the time comes, I promise you. I'll be quick. You won't suffer, and you won't make anybody else suffer."

Shutting out the memory of my promise, I swung into the driveway, stopping at the gated entrance. Sassy's mansion was in the Green Lake area—far from the shadowy Greenbelt Park District—and it was truly a mansion.

I opened my window and reached out to press the intercom button. After a moment, Sassy herself answered, which was unusual. Janet, Sassy's lifelong maid and assistant, always manned the intercom.

"Yes? Who is it?" She sounded suspicious, but that could just be me projecting my worries on her.

"Menolly. I need to talk to you, Sassy."

After what seemed like an age, the gate clicked and slowly swung open. I silently drove through, staring at the lights gleaming out of the huge house set back on two acres. As I approached, I thought I saw a figure running from the house, into the woods, but I could have been mistaken. I jumped out of the car and fished around in the trunk for something I'd hoped I'd never have to use. Cautiously, I slid the stake into my boot.

Sassy answered the door—also usually Janet's duty. But if Janet was bedridden, then perhaps Sassy hadn't bothered to find someone to step in for her. I slipped inside, glancing around automatically. The foyer was as tidy as ever . . . well, no. Not quite. There were spots on the floor that looked like dried blood—small ones, drips. And the console table was dusty; the plants looked like they were drooping from lack of water.

I gazed at Sassy. She'd dyed her hair jet black, and a little stream of the dye had stained her temple. That wouldn't come off—dye a vamp's skin with permanent hair dye and it stayed that way. Her clothing was still designer but was stained with blood and what looked like lipstick. The smell of unwashed silk and linen rose to envelop her. But most telling were her eyes—the intensity was too bright, too glittering. And her fangs were down. She looked hungry, ready to hunt.

I hadn't seen her for a couple of months, and now was

shocked to see just how far she'd slipped. I could see it in her eyes, in her movements, in the way she licked her lips when she looked at me.

"Where's Janet?" I motioned for Sassy to follow me into the parlor. She did, no longer graceful in her movements.

My question seemed to bring her back to herself, for a couple of minutes at least. "She's upstairs," she said, her eyes blurring with bloody tears. "Follow me."

I didn't ask, just followed her up the stairs to the second floor, where she led me into a large bedroom. There, in a cushioned bed under a flowered comforter, rested Janet. Her eyes were wandering, but when she saw me she startled and tried to sit up.

Glancing at Sassy, I mouthed, *The tumor?*

Sassy nodded, then, pressing her hand to her mouth, left the room. I turned back to Janet. Inoperable, the brain tumor had been diagnosed six months ago. Erin was right. Time had finally caught up with Janet and was rapidly running out.

Gently, I sat on the side of the bed and took one of Janet's hands. "Hey, Janet . . . so . . ."

She focused on me, though I could tell it was taking her some work to do so. "Miss Menolly. I'm sorry I couldn't be downstairs to greet you . . ."

"Hush." I patted her hand. "Don't worry about that. Erin told me you were sick." As I sought for something comforting to say, Janet clutched my fingers.

"Promise me something . . ."

"If I can, of course. What is it?"

She held tight to my hand and in a fevered plea, she begged, "Don't let her turn me. She's been in here the past few nights, talking about bringing me over. I don't want that. I'm an old, sick woman and I've lived a good life. I don't want to become . . ." Her voice trailed off and she winced. "I'm sorry, but I don't want to be one of you."

I let out a small laugh. "Oh, Janet—I didn't want to be

a vampire, either. I don't think many of us *choose* the life. But yes, I promise you—I won't let her turn you. You say she's been talking about it?"

"Too much. She always promised me she wouldn't, but Miss Menolly, Miss Sassy's not herself. I'm afraid of her now. I don't want to die in fear." Janet was weeping, and I noticed one eye dilated larger than the other. The tumor really had caught up to her.

"Did you drink any of her blood?"

"No," Janet said. "She offered, but I refused."

"Then you will go to your ancestors unharmed. Rest, now. I'm here to make things better. I can't save you, Janet, but I'll save you from becoming one of the undead. And I'll make sure Sassy's taken care of. I promised her six months ago that I would. And now . . . I've come to fulfill that promise."

As she slowly let go of my hand, Janet shuddered. "Thank you. You're one of the good ones, Miss Menolly. You're one of the rare ones." And then she let out a long breath, shuddered, and her head fell to the side. I closed her eyes, gently, and examined her for bite marks to make sure Sassy hadn't already started the process. I was furious when I found numerous punctures—all fresh—on Janet's chest and wrists, but if she hadn't drunk Sassy's blood, she wouldn't turn into a vampire.

"Poor woman, you were betrayed in the end by the one you cared for all of your life. *Sassy, how could you . . .*" Whispering, I rearranged Janet's covers and pulled out a couple coins from my pocket, laying them on her eyes, and then kissed her forehead. "For the boatman. Easy journeys, Janet. Go to your ancestors and be at peace."

As I left the room, I glanced back at Janet's body one last time. Another reason why I had to complete my promise. Another sign that Sassy Branson had freed her inner predator and was losing all sense of reason. She'd loved Janet, had promised time and again she'd never sire another vampire, and yet Janet bore the scars of Sassy's fangs. Yet, she had not given in. In the face of death, she'd chosen to sleep. As I headed down the stairs, I steeled myself for the coming battle.

CHAPTER 10

Sassy was waiting for me in the foyer. She gave me a curious look.

"Janet's dead. She's with her ancestors now, at peace."

"Damn you! You let her die without calling me. You didn't give me a chance." Sassy let out a snarl.

Struggling to take in the changes that had happened to my friend, I crossed my arms and faced her down. "Janet went quietly, just as she wanted to. Thank the gods—and I never thank them lightly." Frustrated, I held out my hands. "How could you bite her, after all these years? How *dare* you bite her? She was helpless and couldn't fight back. You *know* she didn't want to be a vampire, but *still* you drank her blood. Janet was your best friend, your staunchest ally all through your life, and you betrayed her at the end. You made her afraid of you!"

A flash and I saw the old Sassy peering at me through the reddened eyes. "Oh, Menolly. Oh my God, what did I do? No, my sweet, poor Janet. Is she . . . I didn't . . ."

"No, you didn't force her to drink. But you drank

from her when she was at her most vulnerable. Oh, Sassy, you're slipping. Erin told me about the girl. *What have you become?*" I didn't have much truck with the gods—they'd never done much for me—but I prayed. To the Moon Mother, to Bast, asking them for the same strength they gave my sisters.

"I hurt her . . . didn't I?" Remorse filled the elderly woman's face and she covered her eyes with her hands, bloody tears streaking down her cheeks onto the Chanel suit. The old Sassy would never have allowed such an expensive faux pas, but this Sassy didn't even notice.

"You made me promise you something . . . six months ago, you forced me to promise you that I'd stop you from becoming one of the monsters you hate." I spoke softly, in an attempt not to spook her.

Sassy lowered her hands, staring at me. "I'm not ready. I'm not ready . . . but . . ." Helplessly, she glanced at the stairs, looking up toward Janet's room. "I hurt my best friend, my oldest friend . . ."

"You're slipping into your predator, Sassy. Pretty soon you won't care that you hurt people. It's not easy to control, and you don't seem to have the ability to contain or channel the hunger." I watched her face as it convulsed from remorse to anger.

She slowly began to circle me, studying my face, her expression slipping into an ugly cunning. "Suppose I've changed my mind? You took Erin away from me, didn't you? You don't want her with me."

"Not when you're like this. She doesn't love you the way you thought. She saw you with that girl."

"She does too love me!" Sassy blinked. "Why didn't she join me?" A low hiss escaped her throat. "I wanted her there."

"Yeah, I'll bet you did. But it's not going to happen. Erin isn't like you, Sassy. She'd rather learn to control her instincts. I thought you could help her, but you've lost your way. And I don't think you can find the path back."

Sassy tilted her head to the side, eyeing me like an owl might eye its prey. Her fangs were down and her eyes were bloodred. On one level, she looked like my old friend, but when I stood back, distance allowed me to see her as she had become: a traitor to friends, betraying even her beloved Janet.

I knew then it was over. She was ready for a fight and she wasn't going down easy. I glanced around the room. We were in close quarters. We'd trash the place, but I didn't have time to quibble. Sassy was strong, but I had Dredge's blood on my side, and my Fae heritage. Sassy, on the other hand, had the strength of being firmly in her predator.

"Bring it on, Fae-girl. Pretty little girl who has no qualms taking down the bad guys. Well, let me tell you this: Most mortals *are* bad guys. Humans have trashed the planet and each other since the dawn of time, and I was no exception. Have you looked on the Internet lately, Red? Have you seen how much little boys and girls are going for—and not to the vamps. No, but to other humans. Predators, all. Do you know you can buy a twelve-year-old to fuck and beat up in Thailand for five bucks, if that? *Humans* do that, Menolly, not the vampires."

"I know the kind of scum that are out there." I side-stepped to the left, mirroring her movements as we circled one another. "That doesn't mean it's okay to unleash our own predators—not without knowing who our targets are. We are far more powerful than most of the breathers. They can't fight back against us."

"Do I really care? I spent so many nights repressing my urges, trying to believe in Wade's cause. But now . . . it's so simple. All you have to do is let go, Menolly. All you have to do is give in to the voice inside. *This is what we are: Predators. Violent, vicious, predators.* We are top of the food chain. We could own the world if we wanted to."

And any glimpse of reason in her face was gone.

To win, I'd have to let go of Sassy as a friend. Of Sassy as the cultured, funny woman I remembered. I let the floodgates open, just a little, and welcomed my hunger. Sassy's snarl spurred me on, and the image of who she was faded as she loomed large—my opponent, my enemy.

I let her make the first move. As she leaped toward me, I danced to the side and she came down hard, shaking the floor with her impact. I whirled to face her and my feet made contact, knocking her forward as I flipped over her head and came down, rebounding off her back. I landed in a crouch and immediately leaped to my feet and turned.

I'd knocked her back against a china cabinet and winced as delicate cups shattered, jarred by the impact.

Sassy snarled and raced headlong for me, head-butting me before I could duck out of the way. I landed against her sofa with an *oomph*, knocking it over. Somersaulting backward to my feet, I grabbed the nearest chair—an eighteenth-century reproduction—and smashed it over her head, immediately following it up with a lamp off the nearby table.

She shook off the broken glass and grabbed the coat rack, aiming it like a spear. Crap, that would make the world's biggest stake! I jumped out of the way as she sent it sailing through the air toward me. It went skidding into the wall, leaving a crack to slowly filter down the wall.

"I'm stick-a-fork-in-me done with this," I whispered, pulling out the stake from my boot. Racing for her, headlong, I realized I could run faster than she could, thanks to my Fae background. I skimmed over the furniture, lightly leaping from the back of a chair to a tabletop to the floor as she raced out of the room, fear in her face now.

She headed for the front door and I followed. The minute we were outside, she turned to the right and headed off toward the trees surrounding her house, and I sped up. The violent night was alive as the snow fell silently to the ground, burying it in a shroud of white.

I was gaining on her and, before I realized it, had caught up. Grabbing her by the arm, I whirled her around to face me. She snarled. My enemy. My friend. The mirror of what I could become.

"Oh Sassy, I'm so sorry. But I promised. You'd hate who you've become, if you were still in there." And even as she clawed at me, leaving one long scratch down my face, I brought the stake down on her heart, piercing the Chanel suit, piercing the flesh, driving it deep into her. What started as a bloodstain was followed in seconds by dust and ashes as she let out one long shriek and vanished before my eyes into a small brown stain against the snow. I knelt beside the pile of ashes.

"What was life has crumbled. What was form, now falls away. Mortal chains unbind and the soul is lifted free. May you find your way to the ancestors. May you find your path to the gods. May your bravery and courage be remembered in song and story. May your parents be proud, and may your children carry your birthright. Sleep, and wander no more."

Our prayer for the dead. We'd had to say it far more than we ever wanted to the past year. But now Sassy was with her ancestors, and, hopefully, her daughter, whom she'd mourned all these years. Tears slid down my cheeks, and I dashed them away. The Sassy I knew would have handed me one of her crimson handkerchiefs to dry my eyes and not make a mess on my clothing. The Sassy I knew would have . . .

"Thank you, Menolly . . ." The voice trailed on the wind as it crossed past me. I whirled to find myself facing a faint figure, translucent against the snow.

"What . . . Sassy?" She was there, large as life, but pale and misty. I noticed that her hair was a brilliant blond, and she looked younger. A little girl stood by her side, holding her hand, and on the girl's other side, Janet—as a young woman, vibrant and smiling. The child had Sassy's nose and eyes.

"Oh, Sassy . . . you found them both."

Sassy tilted her head to the side. "Thank you," she said again, her voice a whisper on the breeze. "I can go now. I can leave. And look—" She opened her mouth to smile. No fangs. The vampire within her was gone, destroyed by death.

Smiling through my tears, I pushed to my feet and raised my fingers to my lips, blowing her a kiss. She caught it, then slowly turned and, hand in hand with Janet and her little girl, walked away, vanishing into oblivion. Where she'd been standing lay a neatly folded linen handkerchief, crimson red, with a bloodred rose across it.

I picked both up, pressing the handkerchief to my lips. "I'm sorry," I whispered, and tucked it in my pocket.

I silently returned to the house and tidied up, tossing the broken furniture. Then, flipping through the address book on her writing desk, I looked up the name of her lawyer. He knew she was a vampire, and—like most of us who kept property—she'd provided for the possibility of her being staked.

I put in a quick call to him, filled him in on the circumstances, and asked him to see that Janet was given a decent burial, and if he would call me when it was scheduled. It wasn't against the law for a vampire to kill another vampire, so I had nothing to worry about concerning Sassy's death. Her name would be stricken from the vampire rosters the government kept, if she had registered, and that would be that.

He thanked me, took my number, and hung up.

Looking around one last time, I let out a long breath and then softly locked the door and drove back to the bar. It was done. I'd killed a friend. I'd also killed a monster primed to take on the world. As far as nights go, this one ranked right up there on the suckometer.

I entered the bar through the back. I was covered with dust and blood and still had a few wounds from the fight with

Sassy that were healing up. They'd vanish soon, unlike the scars Dredge had left on me before I died.

Heading for my office, I intended to wash up and then change before heading out to see how Derrick was doing. What with the early rising thanks to the sun setting earlier, even though I'd been through the haunting, talked to Wade, and staked Sassy, it was still only a few minutes past eleven and the bar wouldn't close until two A.M. But as I opened the back door, I heard a commotion out front. The gates wouldn't help when we were open.

With a groan—couldn't I have one moment without incident tonight?—I pushed along the hall and entered the main bar. Derrick was standing there with the shotgun out, pointed at a group of about five leather-clad bikers. Chrysandra had the telephone in hand, eyeing Viper, one of the bikers who had been a customer off and on over the past year. He was pointing a Natchez bowie knife at her heart, barely touching her chest. The blade itself was over eleven inches long and it gleamed, sharp and ready to pierce.

"I see we have a standoff," I said, coming up beside Derrick. No doubt they had a few stakes in their packs, just waiting for the likes of me. "Whatcha doing, Viper? Why are you threatening my waitress?"

His gaze flickered toward me. "Menolly . . . It's you we want. Come along quietly and everyone else earns a get-out-of-jail-free card."

Oh joy, just what I needed. A Buffy-wannabe in a biker suit.

"Can't we have a civil conversation? I haven't done a damned thing to bother you. You've sat at my counter, drinking booze and talking to me, and yet tonight you come into my bar and threaten me, my staff, and my patrons? What's wrong with this picture, dude?"

He gave me a once-over, and I saw exactly what he thought of vampires. At least *now*. Good ol' boys were transparent as hell, whether they wore overalls or leather and chains. Viper and his buddies had no doubt heard the news and decided to help the cops by killing every vampire in the area.

"How many of us are you planning on dusting? How many do you think you can possibly get through before we get to you? You can get away with murdering us, but when we hurt you, at least self-defense will play into our trial. You have no excuse. Here I am, running a legitimate business that's bringing in money for the city, and you boys just can't wait to spoil things."

I leaped up to land on the bar. Staring them down, I gave Chrysandra a faint shake of the head. *Stand still, don't try anything.* I hoped she caught my meaning. "What happened? You just hear the news that there's a vampire serial killer out there—a male, I might add—and decide that every vamp has to pay?"

He shuffled his feet, and color began to rise in his cheeks.

"You're a regular reader of the *Seattle Tattler*, too. Am I right? You hooked up with Andy Gambit and Taggart Jones?"

Mr. Bowie Knife blinked. "Those freaks? No. They don't like us, either."

"I see. So you haven't run away and joined the Earthborn Brethren? Or Freedom's Angels? Or one of the numerous other hate groups?" If they weren't part of the movement against the Fae, I might be able to reason him off his high horse. I turned on my glamour. Hell, I'd use every trick in the book to protect Chrysandra and my bar.

Viper blinked again. "Um . . . no. What's that got to do with anything?"

I let out a long breath, for effect, and a loud one. "How many times do the cops come by and harass your group? How often do you guys get thrown in jail just for hanging around the wrong side of town? After all, aren't *all* bikers troublemakers and lawbreakers?"

He stared at me for a moment and I saw the knife waver. I was making an inroad. I crossed my arms and stared him down, willing him to lower the knife. As he slowly acceded—he was easy enough to take on once I'd gotten his attention—I leaped lightly off the bar and walked toward him, holding out my hand.

"Put the knife in my hand, slowly, hilt first."

"Viper, what are you doing, man?" One of his buddies started forward, but I gave him a look and motioned toward Derrick with my head. "Move and he blows you out of the water, dude. And Humpty won't even be able to *find* all of the pieces, let alone put himself together again."

He froze, and Viper slowly handed over the knife. I examined it. Nice blade. "Now the sheath." He obeyed, and I strapped it to my belt, then slid the bowie knife in and snapped it shut. "Good boy."

Chrysandra lithely stepped out of the way, and I put my finger on Viper's chest. "Snap out of it. Now."

As he blinked and saw me standing there, wearing his knife, with Derrick aiming for his chest, Viper sucked in a deep breath. "Oh shit."

"*Oh shit* is right." I smacked him across the face. Hard. "What the fuck do you think you're doing, dude? You want to help out in the investigation, you don't do it that way, you idiot."

Frowning now, he cocked his head. "Are you looking for the killer?"

"Hell yes! He's giving a bad name to all vamps. Just look: I put a gate on my bar and I never had to think about it before. And you come in here, bent on killing me? You think we don't want him caught for all the trouble he's causing? You're all jacked up the wrong way, bro."

Viper blushed again and stared at his feet, looking for all the world like a giant teddy bear. "I'm sorry, Menolly. I didn't think . . ."

"No. You didn't. You reacted instead, and that's usually a bad idea. In this case, you were lucky. Do you really think that I couldn't stop you from hurting my waitress? And if you'd tried, I would have ripped your throat out. You got it? You don't bother me or mine. You leave the vampire hunting to me, and you make sure word gets through to your eager-beaver brethren before some idiot gets himself fanged to death. Because I'm more patient than most vampires. Got it?"

He nodded, thoroughly shamed. "I'm sorry . . ."

"Apologize to my waitress, and to Derrick. Poor man's finger's had to keep the trigger from sending a nice little blast into your gut for so long I bet he has a cramp. Then get the hell out of my bar and go do something useful. Make sure the Toys for Tots motorcycle ride goes smoothly, or something helpful like that."

As Viper hastened to obey, and his followers took note and followed his example, I strode toward the back and grabbed a spare set of clothes. I'd take a shower upstairs. I found Erin cleaning one of the guest rooms. She did a quick drop to the knee, then back up again.

"Just getting the dust. Tavah said that there has been some interest in booking the rooms. She told me word's getting around."

"Erin." I wasn't sure how to break the news but knew I'd better before she heard it from somebody else. "Let's sit down for a moment. I've got something to tell you, and it's not pleasant."

She dropped the cloth on the desk and promptly sat on the bed. I smiled at her obedience, but decided I'd work on severing the cords as soon as possible. It was time to wean her. I wanted her to be able to think on her own in case anything happened to me.

I sat beside her and took one of her hands. Vampires weren't a touchy-feely group, but I thought this news would go down better sugar-coated. Erin might not have been in love with Sassy, but she liked her.

"I went to see Sassy . . ." I let the words drift.

Erin blinked and shifted in her seat. "Do I have to go back?"

"No. No, you don't. In fact, you can't. Janet died while I was there."

She dropped her head and a tear trickled down one cheek. I squeezed her hand. "Janet was always nice to me. She stood as a buffer when Sassy got too eager. Janet held Sassy back from her predator nature until a few months ago. But when her brain tumor started catching up with her, she couldn't muster enough strength to help Sassy keep herself in check. Janet took to her bed over a month ago, and I knew it wasn't going to be long."

"At least I managed to keep her from turning Janet. I was with her at the end, and she went peacefully. But Sassy was feeding on her. Did you know *that*?"

"No," Erin said, and I heard the ring of truth in her voice. She couldn't lie to me, not at this point in her development. "I didn't know, or I would have called you sooner." She paused, then looked up at me. "You killed Sassy, didn't you?"

I bit my lip, then gave her a short nod. "I had no choice, Erin. I promised her, some months back, that I wouldn't let her become a monster. And that's what was happening. When you let your predator take over from the reasoning side of yourself, you forever lose control. There's no coming back. Some vampires live for thousands of years without losing control," I said, thinking of Roman. "Some don't." Dredge had totally given in to his predator and embraced the fury and terror he spread.

"Did you . . . was it by stake?" Her voice was very small now, and she looked afraid. I nodded. "Did it hurt?"

"I can tell you this: After she died, her spirit came back and thanked me. She's with her little girl now, and they've gone to their ancestors."

We sat there for a while, hand in hand, thinking about Sassy. After a while, Erin stood up and kissed my hand, then went back to work. I wished her a good night and headed downstairs. It was time to go home. Derrick and Chrysandra could take care of the bar for the last hour or so.

I needed to see my sisters, to hold Maggie, to push the memory of killing someone who'd once been a friend out of my mind. For the first time in a long while, I mourned not being able to sit out under the light of day, to bask in the healing rays of the sun. The moon gave pale comfort, and the new moon—none at all.

CHAPTER 11

When I got home, Chase was there, Nerissa was there, and it seemed that everybody else was up and active. I kissed Nerissa, then glanced around.

"What's going on?"

"Quite a bit, apparently." Chase leaned back in his chair. He was staring at Delilah, a soft smile on his face as he watched Shade softly stroke her arm. "You guys go first. My news is important, but not immediate."

Smoky gave me a grim look. "I wish I could stay to help, but I received word this evening from my mother. She has an emergency on her hands and needs my help. I'm the oldest son, so I must attend her."

Camille clutched his hand. The two of them were on constant watch for any sign of Smoky's father, Hyto, who had it in for them. The thought that the emergency involved the lecher of a white dragon crossed my mind, and I knew they must be thinking the same thing.

Hyto had been excommunicated from the Dragon realms

and banished from the upper reaches of the Northlands for breathing flame on sacred grounds and for going up against the Wing-Liege. He'd blamed everything on Camille and Smoky's marriage and had vowed to get revenge.

"Did she tell you what's wrong?"

"No, but I must attend her and make certain she's all right. I'll return as soon as I can, and send word to you if I can, once I find out what's wrong." He paused, then added, "I'm taking Rozurial with me. He knows the Northlands, and I can use the company."

Camille let out a little huff and glared at him. "I offered to go."

"Of course you did, wife." His eyes luminous, he leaned down and kissed her cheek. "And I refused. I will not drag you into danger. Here, I have no choice but to allow you to engage monsters. But I won't willingly put you in danger because of my family. I love you too much."

Trillian arched his eyebrows. "Fox-Boy and I will take care of her." Then, his voice belying his carefree look, he added, "Go, but return as soon as you can. We don't want Camille to pine too much. And you're . . . useful around here." He nodded to Morio, who let out what sounded like a growl of agreement.

"Then we'll be off, and return as soon as we can." Smoky stood and Camille jumped up, throwing her arms around him and kissing him deeply before standing back, her face aflame.

"Come back to me. I mean it." She raised one hand and Smoky pressed his palm against it, and then he and Rozurial faded out of sight into the Ionyc Sea.

Camille let out a long sigh and took her seat again, Trillian and Morio flanking her. Iris entered the room, carrying a tea tray, and Trillian quickly leaped up to take it from her and slide it onto the coffee table. He pressed a cup of hot tea into Camille's hands as Morio snaked one arm around her waist and gave her a gentle squeeze.

I decided the best way to distract her was to press on with business as usual. I turned to Nerissa. "Love, what brings you here?"

Nerissa let out a long sigh. "I was fired today."

"What?" We all stared at her. I leaned forward and took her hands, stroking them lightly. "Are you joking?"

"No. Andy Gambit's story about me in the *Seattle Tattler* stirred up sentiment against me at work. Today my supervisor called me into his office. He said my performance hasn't been up to par and then fired me. I'd take them to court, but I recognize a frame-up when I see it." Nerissa was a government worker for the Department of Social and Health Services.

"I thought working for the State of Washington would protect you under the Were Discrimination Act."

"Yeah, so did I. Apparently they've found ways to get around it."

She looked so bereft I wanted to rip the guy's throat out, but that wouldn't do any good. "I'm sorry. Great Mother, it's been one hell of a day all the way around, hasn't it?"

"That's just wrong," Delilah said. "I can organize a strike of government workers in the Supe Community if you like."

Nerissa shook her head. "No. I'm tired of fighting, I'm tired of campaigning. I'm ready for a change. I just wasn't expecting it to happen this way or this soon. But that isn't my only news. I'm leaving the Rainier Puma Pride."

That little announcement stopped everyone cold. Even Chase gave her a stare of disbelief.

I cleared my throat. "Are you sure you want to take that step, especially now, without a job?"

She nodded. "I've thought this through. I was planning on making the break, anyway. Now seems like the right time. As an unmarried female, I'm low on the totem pole, only above unmarried males. Without Venus the Moon Child around, I might as well be stuck in the fifties as far as my rights go. Not to mention, my lover is vampire and female."

Delilah cleared her throat. "Yeah, that could cause some problems, all right."

Nerissa snorted. "Oh, the Pride's open to bisexual shamans, but they aren't fond of the concept when it trickles down into the main population, and you guys know what they think about you three. I get snide comments every day, and I'm sick and tired of it. This afternoon, I went back for a final look at a condo that caught my eye earlier this month. I've had it inspected, and it passed, so it looks like I'm buying my own place not two miles from here."

Again, a shocker.

"How will you afford the mortgage?" Delilah was prone to asking blunt questions, and I was glad she'd asked, not me. I wanted to support my girlfriend in any way I could but was worried she was making a mistake, maybe getting in over her head.

Nerissa flashed her a sly smile. "That's right, you don't know. I'm so used to keeping this a secret that I don't tell many people."

"What? You an heiress?" Chase said, laughing.

"You might say that." Nerissa laughed back at him. "Two years ago, I inherited a tidy sum of money from my mother's aunt. Great-Aunt Lucy was an FBH—she married into the Pride, but they lived in town. But she was definitely Were-friendly."

I stared at her. "You mean I've got myself a rich girlfriend?" Giving her a fangy smile, I leaned back, thinking that at least Nerissa could take care of herself if need be. No wonder she'd thrown herself into a job that paid a fraction of what she was worth—she could afford to follow her passion.

"Well, hardly anybody knows. I didn't want the guys in the Pride trying to marry me just for money, and plenty of them would think of that. And I didn't want the Council of Elders trying to arrange a marriage for me in order to get hold of my savings. With Venus gone and with Zach out of the picture, I have very few supporters left there."

I sat back, shaking my head. Changes, changes everywhere. Then, laughing, I jumped up and planted a long kiss on her. "Now we won't have anybody breathing down our necks about our relationship, and we'll be able to see each other more often." I hadn't yet told her about Roman. With luck, that wouldn't put a crimp in things.

"You know," Chase said, eyeing her closely, "I have an opening for a civilian victims' rights counselor on the FH-CSI. Duties involve helping victims of violent crimes find out what their rights are, counseling them after they've been assaulted—that sort of thing. Seems like it might be right up your alley. I have leeway to appoint someone. Drop me a résumé tomorrow if you like."

Nerissa clapped her hands. "That would be such a welcome change of pace. Maybe for once I would feel like I'm actually making a difference. I hate being part of the bureaucracy where I'm just one more cog in the wheel, pushing paper and never really making an impact on anybody."

"Then come by tomorrow and we'll talk." Chase winked at me. "Your girlfriend is the kind of material the FH-CSI needs."

I found myself smiling at him. For once, the detective had outdone himself. I also realized that I liked him a lot more since he and Delilah called it quits. It was as if both of them had calmed down and quit trying to force a square peg into a round hole.

"So, Chase, what's your offering on the table tonight? I figure something had to bring you out this late."

He shifted, the uncomfortable look returning. "I have a couple important tidbits. First: I asked Sharah to inspect the other victims' foreheads before we release the bodies to the families. She did, and we found thumbprints on each. The same print, smudged in a cross formation. But there isn't any record of the dude's fingerprints in the system. Whoever he was, he didn't enter the judicial system via being arrested."

"Cross formations. Why would he be doing this?"

Camille frowned. "Maybe he feels remorse for the killings."

"Nope," Chase said. "If he did, he wouldn't have left their bodies displayed in such undignified postures. And he also rapes them—it's not like he's just a vampire experiencing angst over the drinking-blood thing."

"Cross indicates Christian. Could be a religious psycho with a split personality who maintained it even into death? Whatever the case, we need to figure it out."

"Well, we can work on that all we want, but let me tell you the other part of the news. This is a bit better. I received a tip on the hotline tonight. Someone saw a vampire traveling via the sewer system in the Greenbelt Park District. They gave me the location of the manhole they saw him slip down. We have a lead to follow up on." He leaned back, a smug look on his face.

"Why didn't you tell me this when I first came home?" I sent a rubber band zinging his way.

He laughed. "Because I am not going down there tonight. I'm exhausted. I'm tired and going to sleep. We can explore tomorrow night. I know that we should now, but the fact is, the sun will rise within a few hours, the vampire will have to sleep, and I'd rather not rush this matter."

I glanced at the clock. It was nearing three thirty. Camille and Delilah looked exhausted. Chase was falling asleep where he sat. "Okay, I get your point. Tomorrow night, first thing after sunset, I'll meet you there. Send over directions tomorrow."

Turning to Nerissa, I nodded. "Come on. Let's go spend some quality time alone." I wanted nothing more than to strip off her clothes and cover her body with kisses.

As we headed toward the parlor, Camille snorted. "We all know what that's a euphemism for. Have fun. Meanwhile, I and my two darlings will retire up to the bedroom for actual sleep." Even though she was joking, I could tell she was worried about Smoky—and why he'd left.

Delilah and Shade pushed to their feet. "We're heading up to bed, too." She winced. "My ribs are still sore, but they're healing."

Chase yawned, and it occurred to me he shouldn't be on the road. "Listen, Johnson. Sprawl on the sofa. Iris will wake you in the morning, won't you?"

Iris, blurry eyed herself, nodded. "I'll bring you a blanket. We don't want you causing some accident because you're too tired to drive."

As we headed in our different directions, it occurred to me that we probably had one of the closest families ever.

When we were alone in the parlor, I flipped on the stereo. David Bowie came blaring out with "Sister Midnight" and, sliding into the beat, I turned to Nerissa. "Are you tired? I really, really want to fuck you. Now."

She let out a low growl. "Never too tired for that, my love." As she moved toward me, I held up my hand.

"First, I have to tell you something. Do you remember me talking about Roman?" As she nodded, I spilled out everything that had happened. "So, I slept with him, and I have a feeling that will happen in the future. But . . . he's . . ."

"A man. And not me." She softly traced her finger over my lips. "Sometimes I need a man, too, and sometimes he needs to be a Were. But that doesn't mean he could ever replace you. I get it. You and I are on the same page. I honestly don't think I could ever fall in love with a man."

"Except for Venus the Moon Child . . ." I gave her a soft smile.

"I can't imagine *not* loving Venus . . . but that's a whole different ball of wax. I love you, Menolly, and I love how our relationship works. That's what matters—that our arrangement works *for us*. And if Roman said he won't interfere with us, then what the hell? *I* hold your heart in my hands. He doesn't."

I pressed her hand to my heart. "That you do, my love. That you do."

Nerissa pressed her lips to mine, crushing against me with her round breasts, with her soft curves. I circled her waist with my arms and floated up just far enough off the floor to meet her gaze. As we kissed, I closed my eyes, melting into the flow of energy. The scent of her perfume hung heavy in the air. Nerissa wore Warm Vanilla Sugar by Bath & Body Works, and it was a rich, carnal fragrance that made me both hungry and horny.

She suddenly forced my feet back to the ground, turning me around so I leaned back against her breasts. As her hands slid up my stomach, she lowered her lips to my neck. I let out a little cry as she found her way under my blouse and the smooth touch of her fingers met my skin, running lightly over the scars up to cup my breast.

Her other hand slid down toward my jeans and I quickly unbuttoned them and slid the zipper down, with her fingers following. Shoving the denim down to the floor, I kicked my way out of them.

"I love that you go commando," she whispered. "Every time I see you, I keep thinking that you're naked under those jeans, that your pussy's just waiting for me to slip my tongue inside."

"You drive me nuts when you talk like that." My fangs were descending, and I had to force them up. "I want to throw you down and slide up your body."

She held tight to me. Nerissa loved to touch me from behind and I loved being touched by her. With my werepuma goddess, I could push away my nature long enough to let her be the strong one, even though we both knew it was a façade. As her fingers slid down to lightly caress my clit, I covered her hand with my own, feeling her strength as she stroked me alive.

Nerissa's lips moved lower, to suck on my neck, and once again, I felt my fangs descend and forced them back up. Memories of exchanging blood with Roman flashed through my mind, but that was him and this was Nerissa and I would never steal blood from my love.

A moment later, I couldn't stand it and whirled out of her embrace, walking her back to the sofa where she gasped at the sight of my eyes, now bloodred with passion and fire.

Silently, I undid the zipper on her skirt, and it dropped to the floor. She was wearing a thin pair of lacy panties, and I slid two fingers beneath both sides and slowly lowered them, getting down on my knees as I did so. Her pubes, tawny hair neatly trimmed, were in front of my face and I found myself hungry for her taste, aching to plunge my tongue against her and watch her squirm.

I reached up and pushed her back onto the sofa, spreading her legs as I did so. As she let out a delicate moan, I lowered my lips to her clit and the soft, musky scent of her sex filtered through my brain. Laughing with delight, my tongue forked out and met her flesh, circling the nub of her passion, licking and nibbling as I pressed harder against her.

Nerissa clinched her knees against my sides and reached down to hold my head as I ate her out and licked her raw. She was crying out now; the harder I tongued her the louder she got, bucking against my mouth. I reached up and grabbed her waist, holding her steady so she couldn't pull away. And then, as she let out a bark of pleasure, I pulled back and slid inside her, circling her pussy with my questioning fingers, delighting as she thrashed against me.

I dragged her fully down to lie flat on the sofa and slid a box out from beneath the divan. This was our place, and we kept our toys firmly tucked out of sight under the dust ruffle. Nerissa saw the box and let out another moan.

"You want it tonight?" I whispered, drawing out a large toy that was the color of amethyst, lined with ridges.

Her eyes went wide and she nodded, so I lowered my mouth to suck her nipple, feeling my own arousal heighten as I watched her body welcome in the length and girth of the dildo.

"Oh my Gods, that feels so damned good." Her voice was hoarse but the pleasure was evident in her eyes, in the upturned corners of her mouth as she dropped her head back and slid her tongue between her teeth.

"You want it hard, baby?"

"Harder, faster... please... I need you to fuck me hard."

I went to work, driving in and out, pressing my breasts against hers as I slid my arm beneath her shoulders, holding her close to my body. Her hips ground against my thrusts, and then she suddenly stiffened and cried out and I slid my thumb up to once again flick her clit and she screamed again, followed by a short, sharp burst of laughter as she crumbled into the orgasm.

A moment later, when she could breathe again, Nerissa sat up. She was glowing, vibrant, and she turned to me. "Now, my love, let me see how loud I can make you scream."

And I, the willing lamb, put myself in her hands.

After we were both satiated, I leaned back in her arms, curled on the sofa with the afghan lightly tossed over us. The snow was still falling outside and we were in for a cold morning. I pressed my head against her heart as she embraced me and sighed with contentment.

"Hey," I said after a moment. "What about you move in here, with us? I can't have you in my lair, but suppose we fix up a room for you out in the studio? Camille and Delilah won't mind, and that way we could be together as much as possible."

She brushed one of my braids back from my face. "Oh,

sweetness, I thank you for that, but I think I need my own place. I've always lived in a compound, always lived by others' rules, and I need a space that is mine alone. At least as far as setting the rules and decorating . . ." With a small sigh, she added, "It's not that I don't love you or want to be with you, but . . ."

"But you need your lair, just like I have mine." I gazed up at her. "I get it." And I did. Nerissa needed to stretch her wings and see how far she could fly sans the Pride. I was along for the ride, so I wasn't going to complain about her wanting a space that she could mark as her own territory.

"I do have something I want to ask you, though. We've been together what . . . almost a year?" She tenderly trailed her hand down my arm.

I nodded. "Yeah, about that."

"What say we turn these promise rings into something a bit more . . . official? I don't think either one of us is ready for marriage, but let's have a promise ceremony. Give it another year and a day and see where we're at? Maybe by then I'll be ready to move in. Maybe by then the demons will have broken through. Maybe by then . . . who knows?" She sat up abruptly, and I had no choice but to sit up with her. "Let's do it. Something small—for family and close friends only?"

I stared at her. I'd given up ever thinking to promise myself to someone. Marriage, a family, even something like a promise ceremony had seemed out of reach once I had been turned. We'd given each other rings, but that had been that, I thought.

Now . . . was I willing to honor a year and a day? Was I ready to commit to a specified length of time? Of course, if it got bad, we'd go our separate ways, but this was a test. A test to see if I was ready for more than just lip service.

I took her hand, kissed the ring on her finger. "Nerissa, you are the only one in the world that I would say yes to. Yes—let's have a promise ceremony. I have no idea what the future will be like, or if there will even be a future, but yes." And with that, we were off making plans, until the approaching dawn drove me down into my lair, into satisfied slumber.

CHAPTER 12

The next night, Nerissa was there when I woke up. She'd gone during the day to apply for the position with Chase, and he'd hired her on the spot. We celebrated and—during the early dinner Iris had fixed—sprang the news of our promise ceremony. We opted to hold it on the Vernal Equinox, during the spring festival of new growth, when life springs forth from the soil and the balance of the year once again hangs forefront. This would give us enough time to find outfits and really hammer out what this meant for us. Nerissa would be in her new condo by then and we could spend time truly alone.

Camille had immediately launched into a fashion discussion with Nerissa about dresses and makeup, while Delilah used the news as an excuse to talk Iris into making cookies, even though I couldn't eat any.

Iris stopped by my chair—I'd vacated my usual place near the ceiling for once—and gave me a tight hug. "Menolly, you deserve this. You deserve so much, and she's a wonderful woman."

Touched, I squeezed her hand gently, then let go as she headed over to the stove. Trillian rushed to help her put dinner on the table—they were having fried chicken and mashed potatoes.

Morio winked at me. "Taking the plunge, are you? About time."

I shook my head at him. "We aren't getting married, dude, but thanks. And I'm happy about it. She's my girl, she is."

Nerissa giggled and blew me a kiss. "I'd better be your *only* girl."

"No doubt about that."

As Trillian passed by with a tray of food, I moved out of the way. The smell of food had been torture until Morio had come up with the enchanted blood for me, but it still wasn't easy.

Morio motioned toward the fridge. "Bottle of chicken soup–flavored blood in the refrigerator, and one that tastes like rhubarb pie."

I cocked my head. "Weird mix, but sounds good." I wasn't going to complain; anything was better than the taste—day after day—of blood.

As I contemplated floating up toward the ceiling, it occurred to me that first, I should call Tavah at the bar to ask how Erin was doing. The phone rang at that moment and Delilah answered. She turned around, hand over the mouthpiece.

"Tavah."

Speak of the devil . . . I took the phone and moved into the hall.

"What's up? Everything okay?"

"Yeah, I just thought I'd check in with you. Listen, Erin is happy as a clam to be working again. It's all we can do to find enough work for her. She genuinely seems content." There was an undercurrent of tension in her words.

"I hear a *but* in there."

"Yeah . . . just that . . . I hate locking her in the safe

room during the day. I know she's safe there, but after I leave at night, that leaves her alone for several hours. She's able to talk to people in the bar, but she hasn't been socialized much over the past year, boss. I think she really needs to meet more vampires and learn how to interact with breathers."

There was one place where she could do that, and I knew it. "Let me call Wade. He was supposed to let me know about his decision anyway."

"Decision?"

"Never mind. I'll see what I can do. Meanwhile, thanks for looking after her. I'll try to be in tonight, but we have an emergency and I'm not sure if I'll be able to get there before the bar closes. Ask Chrysandra to watch Derrick, and tell Erin good night for me, please." As I hung up, I was already dialing Wade's number.

He answered on the second ring. "Dude, we need to talk. I need your answer and I need to ask you a big favor."

"You killed Sassy," he said softly.

"I had no choice." I didn't bother to ask him how he found out but ran over my meeting with her. "She lost it, Wade. She lost it in a big way. I had to keep my promise."

"Yeah, I understand. Listen, nobody else knows. I only know because her lawyer contacted me. Sassy left her mansion to the VA. There's so much we can do with it—we can run a hotel and have a full meeting space."

"You mean *you* can. *I'm* not part of the group, remember?" I couldn't help myself. My voice was bitter. I was still pissed over the situation.

"I wanted to talk to you about that. I was wrong, Menolly. I'm sorry. Please, come back to the group. I'll smooth out any hard feelings there. And, I thought about what you said. I'll step down—as long as you promise Terrance won't win the position."

"That, I can promise. Ro—my . . . source . . . has no desire for Terrance to be in charge."

"Then color me cooperative." Wade paused, then added,

"Menolly . . . I know we don't have a chance of dating again. Too much water under the bridge. But I really miss our friendship. If I promise never to screw up again, will you give me another chance?"

I stared at the phone, then let out a sigh he could hear.

"Whatever you say is gonna be serious . . . you never breathe unless you have to." He tried to laugh, but I could hear the uncertainty in his voice.

"Wade, I hardly ever give second chances. But . . . one more chance. Screw up again and we're forever on the outs. You owe me big for saving your life. Normally I don't keep score, but this time, I am. And I'm going to start calling in my markers now."

"What do you need?"

"Erin needs a mentor. I am so bogged down with . . . well . . . you don't want to know what, but it's terribly dangerous. Erin needs a place to stay, she needs to learn how to interact with both other vampires and breathers. That's what Vampires Anonymous is all about. You give me your word you'll help me with her. I've given her a job that she likes, but she needs more than that in her life."

I waited. Wade was silent for a moment, and then he laughed. "Is that it? I thought you were going to ask for one of my fingers or something. Yeah, I'd be glad to help, Menolly. You're right, that's what the VA is all about. I'll drop in at the bar tonight and have a chat with her, if that's okay."

"Thanks, Wade. I'll call and let them know you're on the way. Now, I have to run. We have a serial killer to catch." As I hung up the phone, it felt like two big weights had lifted off my shoulders. Being on the outs with Wade had bothered me, and I'd missed the VA more than I wanted to admit.

And now, Erin would meet others in the life and learn how to interact with the living without losing control. I thought for a moment about Roman and sent him a brief mental kiss. Without him, Wade and I would still be fighting, and Erin wouldn't have much more of a life than she had with Sassy. Maybe this was all going to work out after all.

After dinner, Trillian, Shade, and Nerissa stayed with Delilah and Iris. Camille and Morio headed out in her car, Vanzir and I in mine. We met up with Chase down in the Greenbelt Park District, in a deserted street near a manhole cover. The snow had let up for the time being and the streets had been plowed, but there was a thin layer of black ice spotting the city, and twice on the way, I swerved and almost lost control of the car.

Vanzir coughed. "Babe, I know you'd survive a crash and I probably would, too, but damn it—I have no desire to get hurt."

"Chill. We'll make it in one piece."

And we did. I parked without further incident and climbed out of the car into the night. Chase headed over in our direction as Camille parked a few spaces up the street. His breath came in little puffs of white, and he was wearing a parka over his suit. I looked up at the overhanging trees that lined the street. Their bare branches were whipping in the wind, and with the clear sky, the temperature was dropping rapidly.

He blew on his hands, rubbing them together, then pulled out a pair of gloves. "You sure you're going to be warm enough?"

I stared at him and snorted. "Johnson, when will you learn that I don't need a coat? I wear them for fashion or when I want to pass, but tonight it would just hold me up. Camille—*she* needs the coat."

At that moment, my sister and Morio wandered over from her car. She had dressed in a heavy spidersilk skirt and top but wore no gloves. They interfered with her magic. Morio had cast a spell against possession on her, and we had to hope it worked, because we needed her with us.

"I really wish your unicorn horn were charged up," I said.

"I wish it were, too. In a day or so it will be ready to go again, but I don't like to touch it so soon after recharging." She looked around. "Quiet here for this time of day."

"Yeah." It was barely six and the streets in the Greenbelt Park District were, for the most part, empty. Nobody on the sidewalks, nobody driving past. I nodded to the manhole cover in the center of the street. "That the one?"

Chase shrugged. "Apparently. I figure what's the worst that can happen? We'll get down there and find nothing."

But as he led the way over to pry the cover up, a voice ran through my mind whispering that the worst that could happen would be that we *would* find something. Something big, something bad, something we couldn't fight.

"Let me go first." I pushed ahead of him. "If our vampire *is* down there, I'm the best one to take him on."

Chase nodded. "Good point. Vanzir, how about if you go next, I'll follow, then Camille and Morio to watch our backs?"

Vanzir clapped him on the shoulder. "You're learning, dude. You're learning."

I sat down on the edge of the hole and attached a flashlight to my belt, then felt for the rung ladder with my foot. It was best if we saved any lights until we were down in the sewer. Within seconds, a metal rod met my foot, but when I swung down and grabbed hold, there was a hissing sound and pain registered through my palms. I yanked myself back up again. Quickly.

"Iron. The bars must be wrought iron. That makes no sense—wouldn't it rust in the weather?"

Chase frowned. "This part of the town hasn't been renovated in years. It could be one of the original sewers, back when they used iron for everything."

"Well, I'll need gloves, and Camille damned well will."

Chase held up his hand, ran back to his car, and returned with several pairs of nylon gloves. "Always keep spares. I lose a lot of gloves due to this job. They get filthy when I'm rooting around crime scenes. I save my leather ones for business and keep a few of these in the car."

The gloves were far too large for Camille and me, but they would work until we got down into the sewer tunnel. I pulled on a pale blue pair and swung back over the side. The gloves cushioned my skin from the iron. Since I'd become a vampire, wrought and cast iron bothered me a lot less, but it could still do major damage to Camille and Delilah. Iron blends and steel weren't nearly as much of a problem, given our mother's heritage, but sometimes a piece of metal would trigger the response when we least expected it.

The ladder led down a long ways, far longer than I expected it to, and by the time I found myself standing down below on a walkway, I had just about given up hope of it ever ending. I quickly stepped to the side and switched on my flashlight, scanning the area. Nothing in sight, though I did see a pile of rat droppings. The tunnel didn't look like a sewer tunnel, though, and it occurred to me that we'd been off about our assessment of the area. For one thing, the floor was cobblestone in some areas, wood in another.

Once the others were down, I lowered my voice and said, "This is no sewer. No wonder it was an iron ladder. What is this place?"

Chase flashed his light around. The walkway ran both right and left, and there was an alcove right across from us. In the alcove were crumbling boxes, an old wooden chair, and a small table. A row of shelves lined one wall of the niche.

"Crap. I don't believe this." Chase stepped over the crumbling wall that exposed the cubbyhole. "I know where we are."

"Where?"

"It's part of the underground Seattle tunnel system that was abandoned when it began caving in."

In the early days of Seattle, the city had originally been built a lot lower than now. After a horrendous fire in 1889, the city streets had been rebuilt one to two stories above the original streets. For a time, customers would climb up and down ladders between the original buildings and the newer sections of the city, but eventually, all of Seattle sprawled across the higher levels, and although the subterranean network remained hidden and unused, it was still a viable network of passages beneath the city.

"I thought the Underground Tour stopped a number of blocks away," I said.

Chase shook his head. "It does. The tour only covers a small portion of what was the original underground city. There actually used to be a series of nightclubs down here—not in this area in particular, but running the length of the tunnels. But they closed up one after another as the structural integrity of this area weakened, and eventually most of the areas were abandoned, forgotten and hard to get to. I had no idea the tunnels ran all the way into the Greenbelt Park District, but that makes perfect sense."

A chill ran up my spine. This city was getting spookier by the second. Memories of *The Night Stalker* flashed through my head. Delilah loved Darrin McGavin, and I'd had to break it to her that he was dead.

"So what's that cubbyhole? That's too small to be a nightclub."

"Some of the shops had basements that became part of the whole underground scene. My guess is that it once belonged to a shop now buried. We're on a lower level than the regular underground Seattle. We're in the sub-basement area. I really had no clue the tunnels spread out this far, or this far belowground."

I looked right and left. "Which way should we go?"

"Which way leads into the heart of the Greenbelt Park District?" Camille asked, pulling off her gloves and tucking them in a side pocket of her skirt. "Since we think the killer is nesting there, it only makes sense to go in that direction."

"True. Let me see . . ." I glanced around. "If this tunnel runs north-south, then we want to go north, which would be . . ." Turning to the right, I nodded. "This way. Let's go. Marching order same as when we descended the ladder. Camille and Morio, keep a good watch on our backs."

As we headed down the walkway, Camille coughed. "The air's dank here."

"Is it breathable? Are you going to have trouble?" I wouldn't have to worry, but the rest of them would.

"Yes, we can breathe, but there's a lot of mold down here, I can tell that right away. Watch for viro-mortis slimes. This would be the prime place to find them."

As if on cue, my light caught something clinging to the wall to my right. I jumped back as we saw an indigo patch of ooze sliding along parallel to us. The creature sparkled in a pretty, jellylike fashion, but that was as good as it got. The indigo viro-mortis slime was deadly.

"It can sense our body heat," Camille said, wrinkling her nose. "Just don't touch it or we'll all be in trouble."

Sometime back, Delilah had gotten a green viro-mortis slime attached to her hand and we had to have Smoky freeze it off. He wasn't with us now, and the indigo varieties were far more poisonous. The creatures acted a lot like the Blob—growing as they enveloped and assimilated their victims. Being digested alive by a living pile of snot was not my idea of a good time.

"Just leave it be, and watch what you touch."

As we headed along the tunnel, I kept my flashlight sweeping from side to side. The fact that there were viro-mortis slimes around meant that we probably had to watch out for other nasty creatures. All sorts of denizens hung around in the dark, waiting for the next unwary traveler to come along: ripe pickings for dinner.

More boxes and another cubbyhole to the right. I briefly

shone my light in the niche, checking it out, but once again it looked like a long-abandoned basement. A thick layer of dust covered everything, and in some spots moisture had worked its way down the walls to leave trails of mold—the regular kind—and mildew.

"The city should come down here and clean this crap up," I muttered.

"Who's going to pay for it?" Chase said. "Seattle is having budget woes as it is. No, I have the feeling most of the city doesn't even know this place exists. It isn't common knowledge that the underground sections comprise more than just what's shown to tourists on the little jaunt that's offered."

The soft cadence of water flowing caught my attention. "Sewer?" I asked after a moment. The others listened, and then Chase shook his head.

"No, sewer wouldn't make that kind of noise. Underground stream, perhaps." He paused. "What's that? Over there?"

I turned my flashlight to the direction in which he pointed. Another cubby, but this one had something else in it. A cleft in the rocks that made up the sides of the tunnel beckoned.

"I don't know. Let's take a look." As I crept over to the alcove, I motioned for everyone to be silent. The cleft wasn't as wide as a passage, but definitely wide enough to go single file. I flashed my light down the blackened passage but couldn't see a thing. "Shall we try it? Just be very careful not to brush against the sides, which means try not to trip or stumble."

As I entered the narrow passage, I hoped it wouldn't go on for too far. I didn't want to get lost in a maze beneath the city streets. Camille hated close quarters, and I knew this wasn't easy on her.

The darkness closed in around us as we continued on, and the only spots of light were the muted beams of our flashlights. I kicked the floor ahead of me as I stepped, scooting loose pebbles to the side so the others wouldn't twist their ankles on them.

"The air here is thick," Camille said from the back. "How much farther, can you tell?"

I squinted in the dim light, trying to gauge how far we had to go. "I don't know, but—wait . . ." Up ahead, the cleft ended in a turn to the left. I peeked around the corner. The opening led to a large room. "You're in luck."

As I stepped into the brick chamber, I immediately began scoping out the area. The others filed in as I took in the man-made cavern. It was a good fifteen feet tall, and as wide as our house, it looked like. There were dark maws opening at regular intervals around the periphery of the walls, and I began to realize this was just a hub in a large tunnel system.

"Damn, look at this. We could so easily get lost down here. What the fuck went on in this freak city?"

"As I said, there was a fire back in the late 1880s. It destroyed over twenty-five blocks of the city. What you see down here are the remains of the original city streets and buildings—" Chase ducked. "Shit! Spider! Crap," he said, brushing something off and stamping on it.

We spread out in the room.

"What do you suppose this was? An intersection?" Morio flickered his light at his feet. Wooden slats, broken and rotted through in places, lined the floor.

"Probably a little market square or something," I said, as a sudden gust blew by. "There's no wind down here, is there?"

"Not that I would think," Vanzir said. "Why?"

"Because if it wasn't a breeze, then something just flew by me and jostled my elbow." I was about to explore one of the side tunnels when another gust hit into me, only this time it was square in the back and hard, like hands shoving me forward. "Who the hell is that?" I whirled around.

Camille shrieked and went sprawling to the floor. "Fuck! Somebody just knocked me down." She scrambled to her feet.

"Quick! Back to back!" I rushed over to her side and the five of us formed a circle, covering our backs. "Who's there? What do you want?"

But there was just a loud echo as laughter ricocheted off the walls. And then, our flashlights went out and we were plunged into darkness.

CHAPTER 13

"Motherfucking pus bucket! What the hell—" Vanzir's voice echoed in the darkness as our unseen assailant took a swipe at me.

Camille let out another yelp. "Something scratched me and man, it stings."

"Enough of this." Morio let out a growl and began to grow into his full demonic form—eight feet of youkai-kitsune, a cross between gorgeous man and dangerous fox with claws that could eviscerate a buffalo. As he shifted, he muttered something under his breath and there was a loud flash in the room and then, slowly, in the inky void, I began to see shapes around us.

Discorporate figures, black silhouettes surrounded by a faint green aura, filled the room. There must have been ten or eleven, circling us, no features showing—just shadow men, darting around us.

"What are they? Ghosts?" Camille breathed slowly, but I could still hear the tremor of her voice.

"Not ghosts," Morio said. "I don't really know what they are."

Chase let out a low sigh. "I can see into them. They're . . . they're little bits of evil, incarnate in shadow form. They have no real consciousness, but they're hungry for our life force." His voice was distant, as if he were a million miles away.

"Chase?" I felt Camille shift as she turned in his direction. "How do you know that?"

"I don't know, but I just do," he whispered, sounding afraid of his own voice. "We need some light."

Morio mumbled and foxfire lit the room with a neon glow. The effect was eerie—the shadow men circling us, a globe of green light hovering over us.

"So, what do we do about them?" I stared at our opponents. They could obviously hurt us, if they'd knocked Camille to the ground and managed to almost shove me off my feet. And now, in the light of the foxfire, I could see that Camille was bleeding from a long scratch down her arm. "You okay?"

She glanced down at it and shrugged. "Yeah, unless it turns out to be poisoned. I've been hurt so many times that I feel like I'm constantly wearing a big red bull's-eye on my back. Let me try a blast of Moon magic."

"Shit, just don't backfire. We don't want to spread too far apart here."

With a nod, she raised her hands and closed her eyes, focusing. I surreptitiously stepped to the side. Although the death magic she performed with Morio usually went right, her Moon Mother magic still backfired a good share of the time. One backlash was all it took.

As she summoned her power, one of the shadow men suddenly let loose and raced for me. I raised my arm to block his high kick and was surprised when he slammed into me hard enough to knock me off my feet.

"They're tough!" I somersaulted backward, rolling easily to my feet. As I came up in a crouch, the shadow closed in on me, and I could hear a faint snarl on the wind. It slashed out with one darkened hand and hit me in the gut, a razor-sharp slice cutting me deep above the belly button. I jumped back and it kept on going, tumbling over itself as I threw it off balance.

As it went down, I decided to see just how corporeal it was and stomped on its back, landing dead center. My boot met solid flesh. "These things have to take form to attack us!" I jumped on its back with both feet, landing as hard as I could. The creature let out a huff and flattened to the floor. Then, before I could do anything, it vanished.

Camille held out her hands toward four of them that were congregating around her. "Eat this, suckers!"

Maybe not the most elegant of spells, but a brilliant flash came forking from her fingers, the lightning striking all four, branching out in the cavern with a concussion that shook the walls and floor. The creatures vanished, sizzling.

Morio raced forward and two of the shadow men engaged him. They swiped at him and blood trickled down his side. He caught them in his massive hands and the next thing I knew, they were howling and trying to get away, but he began to squeeze the shadows together and their screaming grew louder. There was a loud slurping sound and they vanished like bubbles popping.

Stepping out in front of us, Vanzir held out his hands. "Let's see if these motherfuckers have anything to feed on." He closed his eyes, and pale snakelike tentacles emerged from his palms to barb themselves into the shadow men. Vanzir could feed on life energy. If these creatures *had* any form of life.

It occurred to me that whatever spell Morio had cast was allowing us to see into the astral—which made sense if we could see the auras of our enemies. Vanzir's tentacles weren't visible in the physical realm.

Vanzir let out a throaty laugh, reveling in his hold on the creatures. In a way, I felt sorry for him. He had tried to walk away from his nature but we had forced him back into it, the same as Karvanak—his previous owner—had. But at least we were fighting the bad guys.

As his head dropped back, a look of pure lust stole over his face and he opened his eyes. Like pinwheels, unfathomable colors flickered through Vanzir's eyes. His gaze was scintillating. Camille stared at him, mesmerized, and started forward.

"Get away," he said hoarsely, motioning her back. "I can't control myself when I feed, even if my life depends on it. If I didn't snag you in with my feeders, I'd end up tearing your clothes off and fucking you raw."

Camille shook her head, blinking, as Morio yanked her out of the way.

I turned at a scuffling noise behind me and saw Chase wrestling with one of the shadow creatures. I poised myself to leap on it and help him when he let out a shout and the thing rebounded back. I couldn't see what he'd done to it, but the thing went *poof* and vanished.

"Are you okay?" I ran to his side and yanked him to his feet as he raised his hand for help.

"Yeah, I think so." Chase dusted off his suit and nodded toward Vanzir. "He's got the last of them, it looks like."

"Yeah, he does. I think."

Just then, Vanzir drained the shadow men dry, and they vanished. Panting, he turned around to stare hungrily at Camille, and she took a step back. He stepped forward, then stopped himself.

"Don't ever get near me again when I'm feeding." He gave her a stark look. "You have too much life energy and stand out like a lollipop in the middle of a bunch of broccoli. I don't think I could help myself."

Morio let out a low growl, but Camille put her hand on his arm. "Stop. He can't help it—it's his nature." She nodded at Vanzir. "Understood. I'll try to keep my distance when we're in a fight."

He gave her a bleak smile. "Babe, you'd better."

"Now what?" Chase asked.

"I think the question should be, what did you do to that creature?" I stared at him. "You couldn't just knock it out with a punch to the kisser."

Chase looked at me, bewildered. "I don't know, to be honest. I just . . . I reached out and pushed. I remember thinking, *Get off me*, and I . . . shoved and it vanished."

"Shoved . . . do you know if you touched it physically or with your mind?" Camille swung around, eyeing the detective.

He shook his head. "Don't know. I really don't remember."

I gave Camille a warning shake of the head. Chase was obviously opening up in his abilities, but what they were, and what they would become, we didn't have time to find out standing here below the streets of Seattle. "Well, whatever you did, it worked. As to what next . . . hell, I don't know. We could explore each of those passages, but I'm afraid we might get lost."

"Why don't we head back to the main tunnel and see where it leads?" Vanzir nodded back toward the way we'd come. "This area seems too dangerous right now." He seemed antsy.

I stared at him. "What's up with you?"

He blinked. "Nothing. I just don't want anybody hurt."

Camille shrugged. "He may be right."

"Okay," I said. "The tunnels leading out of this chamber look too dark and too narrow anyway. And our flashlights aren't working in here." I led them back through the narrow passage, hurrying to get us back out to the main tunnel. Once we were there, our lights came back on.

"I don't like it down here," Camille said. She drew close to Morio. He put his arm around her shoulder. "I hate being underground."

"I know. Let's get a move on."

We fell back in formation again. We'd been traversing the passage for another ten minutes when I stopped and looked up. Slivers of dim light filtered down.

"Wait here," I said, then slid my gloves back on and headed up the iron-rung ladder again. As I came to the top and cautiously slid the manhole cover aside, I blinked, surprised to find myself smack in the middle of the park in which I'd found the girl's body. About ten yards from where I'd found her body, to be exact. That meant our serial killer was probably using this tunnel system to come and go. If I was right, he had built himself a nest down here somewhere.

I scrambled back down the ladder. As I jumped the last five feet and turned to tell them what I'd found out, there was a loud shriek and a laugh, and one of the broken slats from the wooden floor sailed into the air, directly at me. Morio was standing nearest and he leaped to push me out of the way, but as he did so, the splintered end of the board lodged into his side. *Deep.* Blood began to flow heavily from the wound and he groaned, sinking to the floor.

"Crap!" I leaped to his side. Camille was already there, kneeling by him as Vanzir and Chase looked in vain for the attacker. The next moment, a hail of pebbles rained down on all of us, including a few stones as big as my fist. They hit hard, and we were all under attack.

"What do we do?" Chase yelled, trying to shield Camille and Morio.

Vanzir pushed Chase out of the way. "Get the kitsune above ground," he said. "I can't take him. If I tried to move him through the astral, it might worsen that wound."

"I can do it," I said, prying Camille's hands off Morio. She was sobbing, trying to wake him up. Morio had fainted—probably from the pain. Demon or not, a large wooden stake in the side had to hurt. I gathered him in my arms and slowly began to rise toward the manhole, floating up. Carrying someone made it doubly hard to control the power—passengers were always problematic, but we didn't have a choice. I'd done it a few times and I could do it again. My main goal was to get him up topside before the ghost decided to attack us while we were airborne. I bit my lip, concentrating on keeping us afloat.

Vanzir pushed Chase toward the rungs. "Get the fuck up there, Johnson. Menolly will need your help once she's topside with Morio." He turned back to the direction the stones had pelted us from.

Camille raced to his side, calling up the Moon Mother's energy. As I neared the manhole cover, I heard Vanzir shout something, and then he laughed in that deep, terrifying throaty way he had.

Crap. What was going on? But I couldn't go back to check. Morio's skin was clammy. He'd gone into shock and the scent of his blood was driving me nuts. As I came to the manhole cover, I knocked it away, driving straight into it with the top of my head. Sometimes, vampire strength rocked.

I hovered up and out of the tunnels, coming to rest on the street next to the manhole. Quickly, I darted to the lawn next to the sidewalk and laid Morio down on the snow-covered grass. Fuck. We needed something to cover him with. I could strip off my turtleneck, but that wouldn't do much good. Willing Chase to hurry up, I examined Morio's wound.

We were under a streetlamp, thank gods, and I could see the long, narrow board. Oh hell. It had driven itself a good five inches into his side. The good news was that it hadn't been near his heart. The bad news was that he was bleeding far too much and the scent was so strong and sweet that my fangs had descended. I willed them up, pushed back the hunger, and pressed my hands against the wound, trying not to jostle the stake until we knew what was going on.

Chase climbed over the side of the manhole and yanked out his cell phone, yelling on it as he raced over to my side.

"Sharah, get a team out here now. *Fuck*, where is here?" He stopped to glance around, then caught sight of the street signs. "Cross streets: Greenbelt Drive and Vader Way East.

Morio's been severely injured. He's losing blood." He paused. "I have no idea what blood type a youkai-kitsune takes. And Camille's still . . . hell, Camille and Vanzir are still down there with that thing. Just get here *stat*!" He stuck the phone in his pocket and joined me.

"I've got compression going, but damn, Chase, this is bad. He's in shock. Can you cover him with your coat?"

Chase yanked off his parka and covered Morio with it, then took off his suit coat and balled it up, stuffing it under Morio's head. "He's pale . . . far too pale."

"He's lost a lot of blood. I'm not sure what to do. I have no clue about the physiology of a nature demon." I glanced over at the manhole. Still no Vanzir or Camille. "Where the hell are they? I've got to go check on them. Chase, can you sit with Morio?"

He shook his head. "I can't watch for Sharah and keep compression on his wound, too. You have to stay here with me until the team gets here."

"We may be too late. I have to go see what's going on with my sister." Frantic, I smacked the ground next to me, and the thud ran in a roll beneath our feet. The blood from Morio's wound started again, and I hustled to press my hands to the gash. The scent of the blood was also driving me nuts, and I prayed we didn't have any unwelcome visitors drop out of the woodwork, like our vampire serial killer.

But it wasn't another vampire that showed up. No, we couldn't be that lucky. I heard a noise and glanced over at the nearest tree. There, in a ghostly fog, was a stark figure cloaked in the wreaths of mist. Holy crap, another ghost!

"What the fuck is this? Spook central?" I nodded to the ghost. "Chase, we can't stay here, that thing could—" But before I could get the rest of my sentence out, the spirit hurtled itself our way with a shriek.

I threw myself over Morio's prone body, keeping one hand pressed against the bloody fountain, as Chase paled.

He was half-kneeling, half-standing, and the spirit flew right through him, knocking him to the ground.

With a groan, he hit the pavement, rolling away to come up in a crouch, a look of sheer terror masking his face. He held out his hands as the spirit wheeled and came in for another round, and this time the thing had a face—or rather it *was* a face. Like a giant skull, with mouth shrieking wide, it descended on Chase. I could do nothing, unless I wanted to expose Morio to more danger, except watch as the spirit engulfed the detective.

"Camille! Vanzir!" I screamed as loud as I could, hoping they could hear me, hoping they were all right. "We need you!"

Just then, Chase shuddered and a sparkle of colors began to surround him. The spirit seemed to pull back, and with a massive convulsion, Chase threw it off. The ghostly mist paused, and in that pause, the sound of sirens began to blare up the road. Sharah and her men screeched to a halt in the middle of the road and leaped out of the ambulance. The spirit seemed to think the better of confronting so many and vanished into the night, a puff of fog on the wind.

Chase shook his head and turned, staring at me. "What did I do? How did I keep it from hurting me? I could feel it trying to get into my mind."

"I don't know," I said slowly. That was twice tonight he'd done something to repel our attackers. It occurred to me we needed to run him through a battery of some kind of tests, though I had no clue how or what.

As Sharah and her men came over to help with Morio, the evening took on a surreal feel. The snow started again and I stumbled back, toward the manhole, terrified that if I went down I'd discover Vanzir and Camille, dead. But I had to find out. In the silent night, surrounded by the soft fall of the snow, I stumbled toward the tunnels, my hands slick and bloody. I stared at the drops of red, bringing my fingers to my nose, where I inhaled deeply. The musk of Morio's scent was also clinging to me, and I felt a sudden wash of fear. What if he died? What would happen to Camille? What if she was . . .

Pushing the thought away, I closed myself to the fear and raced over to the manhole. I leaped over the side without a thought to what might be waiting below, and hurtled to the ground. As I landed, I flashed on my light and looked around, praying that they were okay.

I caught sight of Vanzir first. He was standing there, arms hanging down, staring bleakly at the wall, shaking his head.

"What? What's wrong? Where's Camille?" I grabbed him by the arm and swung him around. His eyes were spinning and I could tell he'd been feeding. "No . . . please don't tell me . . . Camille! Where are you?"

"I'm right here." Camille's voice cut through the darkness as she stepped away from a pile of broken wood. Her expression was bleak, too. "Morio?" Her voice hung in the air, and I stared at her. Her dress was ripped in several places and her face was covered with dirt.

"Morio's alive, but seriously wounded. Sharah's up there with him now. Chase and I had to protect him against a ghost or I would have . . . are you okay?" Something in her demeanor was guarded and I couldn't read her, for once.

A dark cloud passed over her face, but she nodded. "Yeah. I'm all right. Just roughed up. We managed to hold that thing at bay. But I want to get the fuck out of here. I need to be with Morio." She headed for the ladder, passing by Vanzir without a word, her lips pressed together.

I watched as she began to reach for the rungs with bare fingers. "Stop! Use these." Mutely, she allowed me to slide my gloves on her hands, then silently started up the ladder.

Turning back to Vanzir, I said, "What happened? Tell me what happened down here! We heard an explosion and Camille's shriek . . . and you . . . laughed."

"Camille set off one fucking hell of a spell. That I can tell you. And I fed." He said nothing more, just stared at me. I found myself wanting to go to him, but shook myself out of it.

"Did anything else happen? Anything I should know about?" I watched his face, but he was careful not to reveal anything.

"We were fighting for our lives. Ask Camille if you want to know more," he said abruptly, then headed for the ladder.

I glanced back at the tunnels. We hadn't found our killer's nest, but we'd discovered too much down here. Chase's powers were emerging. The spirits of Seattle were growing strong and dangerous. And something else had happened . . . but just what, I wasn't sure.

As I scrambled up the ladder, jumping out right behind Vanzir, it was just in time to see the ambulance go shrieking off, lights blazing. Camille was racing toward her car, tears pouring down her face.

"Camille—Morio, is he—?"

She stopped, fumbling to open the door. "He's alive, but in critical condition. I'm headed to the hospital." Pausing, she stared at Vanzir, who headed over to her car.

"I'm going with you," he said.

She flashed him a dark look, then shrugged as he leaped in the front seat.

"I'll meet you there," I said, heading toward my Jag. Yes, something had happened, and I wanted to know what. But nobody was talking. I threw the car into gear and screeched away from the street, Chase following me.

I decided that I had to contact Ivana Krask as soon as I'd cleaned up and ask for her help. If she could take care of some of the spirits in the Greenbelt Park District, I'd buy her a whole fucking side of beef, if she wanted.

CHAPTER 14

~❧~

The FH-CSI building was always lit up. As I pulled in, I
saw Camille's car, but neither Camille nor Vanzir was in
sight. She'd sped down the road like a bat from hell. Chase
leaped out of his car, right next to me. He met up with me
and we silently jogged to the building.

As we headed toward the medic unit, I glanced at him.
He wasn't panting as much; he was having an easier time.
I had set my pace briskly but held back so that he'd be able
to keep up. Usually Chase struggled, but he was breathing
easily at this point. But right now, Chase's changes weren't
my main focus.

As we burst through the ER doors, I could hear shouts
from one of the emergency rooms and saw two of the
nurses, both elves, preventing Camille from bursting
through the doors. Vanzir was sitting on one of the sofas,
his head down, elbows propped on his knees.

I hurried over to my sister. "What? What have they
said?"

"Only that he's alive. He's hurt so badly, Menolly. A

splinter from the stake hit his liver or something bad like that. I know he can heal fast, but he has to stay out of danger long enough for the process to begin." Her face was streaked with tears, the mascara leaving long trails along her cheeks. She looked stunned, like a deer caught in the headlights.

She's in shock, I thought, *and nobody has bothered to notice*. With Morio's life-threatening injuries, it was no wonder, but . . . I motioned to one of the nurses. "My sister's in shock, I think. Can you get her a blanket?"

She nodded. "Be right back. Meanwhile, some food would probably help her."

"She's insane. How can I eat right now?" Camille shook her head, but Vanzir was on his feet, heading for the door. He was pulling out some change for the vending machines.

Chase joined us after peeking into the ER. "He's alive. They've taken the stake out of his side and are working on his injuries. Sharah and Mallen will do everything possible to help him. Please, trust them."

Camille sniffled and Chase handed her his handkerchief. She dabbed at her tears and blew her nose. A nurse came rushing back and wrapped a blanket around her shoulders, leading her over to a chair.

"Sit here and if you feel faint, let us know. We're all working on your husband right now, but ask at the front desk if you need help." She scurried away, a worried look in her eye.

Vanzir returned and handed her both a couple of Reese's peanut butter cups and a package of cashews. "I couldn't find a Milky Way . . . sorry. But these should help. I'm going to find some coffee for you."

Camille gave him a long look, then accepted them and ripped open the candy, forcing herself to eat. "I do trust them—I've trusted Sharah with my life before. But . . . but . . . he was hurt *so* badly . . ."

Pausing, she let out a low, bleak sigh. "I don't understand. How did the ghosts grow so powerful? Death magic won't work on them, that much I can tell you. They seem supercharged."

"I'm not sure what's going on. I'm not an expert on spirits. Do you think they're over a ley line?" I frowned. Where was Delilah when we needed her and her super-duper computer? *Crap, Delilah!* I hadn't even thought to call and let them know how we were.

I held up my hand and moved to one side, punching speed dial for home on my phone. Delilah answered.

"We've been wondering what the hell's going on. Are you guys okay? I've been antsy all evening. I've had the feeling something went terribly wrong."

"It's bad." I lowered my voice to keep Camille from overhearing. All of us had super-sized hearing. "Morio's in surgery. He was seriously injured when a spirit tried to stake me and ended up running it through his liver."

"Holy fuck." Delilah fell silent for a moment, then asked, "Will he live? Is anybody else hurt?"

"He's in surgery now. We just have to hope we got help soon enough. As far as everyone else . . . Chase did some pretty spectacular tricks down there and we're going to have to get him tested. Something's changed inside him—he's developing an ability to repel spirits out of his aura. And . . . I know something weird went down between Vanzir and Camille, but neither is talking and both look shaken."

"I knew I should have come with you—"

"Nonsense. Your ribs still need a couple of weeks to finish knitting. We may heal quickly but you were really fucked up, Kitten. Sharah told you to rest and she meant it. Stacia Bonecrusher almost gave you a ten-inch waist there."

The demon general had taken her natural form as a giant anaconda with the torso of a woman, and she'd caught Delilah with her tail and begun to constrict, breaking a number of ribs and doing more muscle damage than we'd first thought.

"When will you be home?"

"I don't know. I don't want to leave Camille here alone . . . just in case. I'm going to send Vanzir home, though."

"Sounds good. Have him stop and pick up snacks on the way." A pause, then a sudden, "Oh my gods, I sound so heartless. I'm sorry—please never tell Camille I was thinking about my stomach while Morio is lying on the operating table." She sounded so contrite I wanted to hug her.

"I know, I know. It's okay. I won't say anything." I hung up and crossed over to Vanzir, tapping him on the shoulder. "Come with me, dude."

He followed me down the hall a ways. "What's up?"

"You go home. Stop on the way to get Delilah some of her favorite treats, would you? Take Camille's car, but for the sake of the gods, don't wreck it."

Vanzir had just gotten his license two weeks ago. He knew how to drive but had never bothered to learn the rules of the road. After a perilous race to hide our werewolf friend Amber and one of the spirit seals at Grandmother Coyote's portal a couple months ago, we made him both apply for a Supe Alien Visa and then get his license. We'd told the authorities that he was a shifter—a lie, but it would work and prevent them from knowing there were demons running around. Most Supes of questionable heritage used that ruse, and so far the government hadn't caught on to it.

He shook his head. "I should stay with your sister."

"Look," I lowered my voice to a whisper, leaned in, and tapped his chest. "I don't know what went on between you two, and I have the feeling I'm not going to like whatever it is, but I need you to do what I ask. Camille's in mild shock, her husband is lying on the operating-room table, and if you did something to exacerbate that shock, then I'm going to . . . come to think about it, if you did do something, why aren't you dead? She could kill you with a thought." Maybe I'd been wrong. But the look on Vanzir's face told me I wasn't far off the mark.

"Your sister has more empathy than I deserve." He shook his head and grabbed my keys out of my hand. "I'll do as you say. See that she gets plenty of food. The shock from . . . the tunnels will wear away and she'll be okay. I just hope Morio survives."

As Vanzir headed out, I couldn't help but feel that something had been put into motion that wasn't going to end well. Not at all.

I headed back to Camille but stopped short. She was waiting for Sharah, who was walking down the hallway toward her. As I watched her stiffen, waiting for whatever news the elf had, I was almost afraid to join her. Silently, I crossed to her side and felt for her hand. Everything around us seemed to slow, and I closed my eyes, the strains of Cat Power's "Werewolf" echoing through my mind in a haunting refrain.

Camille said nothing, just stood, shoulders back, blanket on the chair behind her. She didn't run forward, didn't step back, just planted herself in the middle of the hall. Her hand trembled, and I could hear the rustle of her breath as she struggled to control herself.

Sharah seemed to be walking through water, her pace slow and deliberate. She was in scrubs, covered with blood, spatters even dotting her flaxen hair. She looked . . . unreadable, as so many of the elves were.

She approached us and stopped, holding up a chart.

Camille waited, unwilling to be the first to talk.

"How is he?" I asked for her.

Sharah consulted her notes. "Alive. But he's been seriously wounded. He lost a lot of blood and half of his liver. An inch higher and the stake would have left almost nothing of it. The liver regenerates, but this is serious."

"Will he live?" Camille whispered.

"If he makes it through the rest of the surgery, he'll

have a chance. Mallen is working on him now—repairing delicate tears so fine I can barely see them. Once he's off the operating table, the next twenty-four hours will tell the tale." Sharah pressed her lips together, then let out a slow sigh.

"What are his chances?" My sister's voice was strained raw; she was barely keeping it together.

"I'd give him a sixty percent chance. Mallen's a talented surgeon and can work miracles, but there was so much damage, it's hard to find everything that needs repair. We may have to go in for a second surgery tomorrow." Brushing a weary hand against her hair, she motioned to the chairs. "Please sit down. You don't look so good, Camille."

"It's not about me," Camille whispered. "It's not about me." But she slid back into the chair and wrapped her blanket around her, staring at the wall. "Trillian should be here," she added after a moment.

"I'll call him." I motioned to Sharah and walked her back toward the operating room. "Are you serious about his chances? He's not worse off and you're trying to prepare Camille for bad news?"

Sharah shook her head. "Only the next twenty-four hours will tell the story. My instinct tells me he'll make it, but he's not going anywhere for a while. If he'd been human, or Fae or elf, he'd be dead now."

"Or vampire," I whispered. She gave me a questioning look. "He saved my life. He pushed me out of the way. The stake was aimed at me and he took the hit. If he dies, it's because of me." I looked back at Camille, wondering if that thought had registered with her yet.

"He did what you all do—looked out for the others. He saw you were in danger and he acted to save you. You'd do the same for him. *Any* of you guys would have done the same thing if it had been him the stake was aiming for."

"Be that as it may, this has to stop. Listen, I'm going to get someone out here to stay with Camille because I know damned well she's not going home, and she'd be useless there. And then I'm headed out. I've still got a long time till morning and I've got a bargain to strike."

Before she could answer, I turned and hurried back to Camille. I pulled out my cell phone when I realized she hadn't called Trillian yet, and dialed home. Delilah came on the line.

"Camille needs Trillian here. And I think you should come, too. I have to take care of something. Hurry it up. Vanzir will be there to stay with Iris and Maggie. Shade should hang around the house, too. I know we have the guards now, but I just don't trust somebody outside the family to watch over our loved ones."

I quickly filled her in on Morio's condition, and she was off the phone and out the door before I could say another word. I motioned to Chase.

"Can you stay with Camille while I take off? Delilah and Trillian will be here soon, and I have business to attend to. This fucking crap with the ghosts has got to stop. I've got a lead on how to take care of it." Without waiting for his reply, I headed out the door.

As I pulled out of the parking lot, the snow had let up and now a clear patch through the sky was illuminated by stars, glistening down on the silent cover of snow that blanketed the city. I was struck by the intense beauty of the pristine vista, and it occurred to me that Seattle was a city of extremes: beauty and terror, danger and passion, life and death. And we were all just along for the ride.

I stopped at an all-night diner, pulling in to the far edge of their lot, to put in a call to Ivana Krask. Whoever she was, *whatever* she was, no longer mattered. The only thing that I cared about was that Roman said she could help.

On the fourth ring she answered, her voice creaky like bare tree limbs rubbing together on a cold autumn night. "Menolly, so you now call me?"

"Ivana Krask?"

"Yes, my dear. I've been waiting for your call."

"How did you know it was me?"

"Caller ID, my dear. That and I don't get many calls. Not in many years."

"Oh right . . . but you sounded like you were expecting my call." Suspicion was my right-hand man and I wasn't about to let him run away.

Ivana laughed. "Roman called me, dear, and told me to mind my *p*'s and *q*'s with you. So I shall."

But even through the promise of her words, I heard something I hadn't in a long, long time. The sound of Elder Fae blood that hearkened back through thousands of years. The Elder Fae, the Wild Fae, were far more primal than Fae like Bluebell, a dryad now living on Smoky's land, and more feral than Wisteria, the floraed we'd captured and finally managed to kill after she escaped from Queen Asteria.

Just by the tone of her voice I knew she was one of the Elders, the creatures from legend and lore that were so far from human nature they could never assimilate within the modern world: the Bog Man and Black Annis, the Bean Sidhe and Iron Jack. And Horse-Troll and Sleeping Uncle, the Washer Woman and the Flower Maiden . . . all throwbacks to a time in history when my father's people had been living in small villages and humans were just a blip on the map.

The Elder Fae hadn't died out, but they were increasingly relegated to smaller areas, to high mountains and distant swamps and crumbling old castles and streams high in the mountains. But even though they were retreating in the face of the modern world, they were far, far more powerful and terrifying than most FBHs ever dreamed.

And Ivana Krask, whatever she might be, held the energy of the Elder Fae in her voice.

"I want to strike a bargain."

"Roman mentioned you might. I might fancy a plump

child or two to whet my appetite—it's been so long since I've had *bright flesh*, you know." She broke into a weathered laugh. "But to strike the bargain, we must meet. I make no deals over the phone. I will see you first."

Steeling my nerves—I was afraid of few things, but Ivana Krask was apparently one of them—I agreed to meet her. She set the place in Cedar Falls Park, on the edge of Belles-Faire, in an hour. I hung up, wondering what the fuck I was getting myself into.

Cedar Falls Park was a welcome relief from the park in the Greenbelt Park District where I'd found the body. There was no sense, that I could notice, of ghosts or spirits here. Or if there were, they were keeping their mists to themselves. I found the bench that Ivana had indicated and gingerly sat on the edge, brushing the snow away.

As I waited, listening to the soft hoot of an owl calling through the trees, I had the feeling something was watching me. I slowly turned just in time to see a faint shadow on the edge of the tree line. I waited—no way in hell was I headed into the woods to meet one of the Elder Fae. *She* could come to *me*.

And then, the figure began to move. At first, I thought she was hunched over, some old woman beneath a bonnet and shawl and a crazy-ass patterned dress, with a basket on her arm. But the shadow *blinked* and was five feet closer. Only now she stood erect, and I could only see a dark cloak surrounding her shoulders. Another *blink* and a swirl of colors, a sickly green and dark purple, shimmered within the silhouette. *Blink.* She moved twenty feet without me noticing. As if we were in some movie filmed back in the days before the talkies, she jerked toward me.

Blink. She was beside me.

Slowly, I stood and stared at the woman. She was squat. My height at best, but I had the feeling her real height was far taller. I gazed at the bony hand that reached out from the depths of the cloak and merely nodded. Not such a good idea to shake hands. She could claim I'd made a silent deal. The Elder Fae were brilliant about manipulating oaths and vows.

"Ivana Krask?"

"One and the same." She pushed back the hood of the cloak and I gasped. Truly, *Elder Fae*. Her face was distorted—or at least by my view. Terribly wide at the eyes, it narrowed to a sharp point at the chin. Gnarls dotted her face and neck, like old knots on trees, only created from flesh. Her features were almost flat—her nose a pale little bump in the middle of her face. Wide anime eyes reminded me of the Cheshire Cat. Her lips were thin, almost nonexistent, and when she smiled, bone-sharp teeth, like polished arrowheads, gleamed in a long row across her upper and lower gums. The woman could probably chew through metal with that set of choppers.

She cocked her head to one side, so much like an owl that I felt like a mouse hiding in the grass.

"Vampyr?"

She didn't seem to be talking to me but reached out and put one long, jointed finger against my arm, then pushed. Hard. A shot of electricity raced through me—unpleasant, to say the least.

"Vampyr." She seemed satisfied.

"Youch! What did you . . ." I stopped myself. It was not wise to ask unnecessary questions of the Elder Fae, that much I knew from my school days. And why she was shooting energy bolts through me wasn't of particular interest right now, not unless it promised to prove fatal. "Ivana Krask, I presume." No questions, just statements.

"Ivana Krask." She tipped her head to the side again, and the owl I'd heard earlier flew down to land on her shoulder. "I am the Maiden of Karask. What do you want from me?"

Of course! The Maiden of Karask was one of the Elder Fae. She was famous for eating children, luring men to their grisly deaths on the moors, and turning young maids into old hags, but she had one other power that forced its way up from my memory.

The Maiden of Karask was able to vanquish old, powerful spirits. She could move them as well, dislodging them from one dwelling to take them to another distant haunt. In days long past, villages had offered up sacrifices of young children to her when they had a problem due to ghosts and spirits.

Now, I understood why Roman had put me in touch with her, but I'd have to be very, very careful. One wrong slip, one misstep in word choice, could be deadly. And it would be a fight to get her to accept prime rib in place of *bright meat*, as she put it. I also now understood why Roman had warned me never to say *thank you* to her. It would bind me to her—the Elder Fae considered *thank you* to be a pledge of debt, even if the bargain had been struck and met.

I sucked in a deep breath. "I have spirits that need dispelling. I offer you ten pounds of prime beef for one house, twenty pounds if you clear two spots. But there is to be no eating of any bright meat in the area, do you understand? *No capturing, no eating, no maiming, no hurting, no claiming.* Bright meat is off limits. The beef will be tender and sweet, however."

The Maiden of Karask stared at me, her eyes flickering, her irises round and yellow in the wide curved white that glistened under the stars. She hissed, and the owl on her shoulder hissed. "No, I must have bright meat. It has been too long."

"The world has changed, old woman. You cannot steal bright meat from humans or Fae or elves. It is no longer the way, and you must change with it."

"No—change the world may, but not the Maiden of Karask. I am Elder! I am beyond the rules." She straightened her shoulders, and I knew I'd better not argue the point with her or I'd be on her plate.

"Barring discussion. Back to the deal. Ten pounds

of prime beef for one clearing. Twenty pounds of prime beef for a second. Are you willing to strike the bargain?" I crossed my arms and let my fangs descend to remind her she wasn't dealing with any ordinary FBH or Fae.

Her eyes glistened with tears, tears I knew better than to trust. "You are harsh, dead girl. You are cruel. How can I keep my powers without the sweet, succulent meat I love so well? I am ancient past old and you would deny me my sustenance? Cruel you are, and vicious."

"Perhaps I am, but this is my truth: Again, I offer: ten pounds of prime beef for one clearing. Twenty pounds of prime beef for a second. Do we bargain?"

I gazed into those ancient, otherworldly eyes, wondering how long the Elder Fae would continue to accept the modern era. How long before they'd band together and drive their brutal natures through the lands again. They still had their strength, and if they ever chose to work aligned, they could be brilliant and deadly in a way that creatures like my vampire serial killer could only dream of.

But this was not to be the day. Ivana Krask inclined her head, and her owl mirrored the movement. "So will it be. Twenty pounds of raw prime beef for two clearings. Where shall I meet you?"

I gave her the address of the deserted diner. "Here is the first place. I will meet you there within the hour with your beef. Ten pounds to start, ten pounds when you finish clearing the second spot."

She let out another hiss and twisted in a way that reminded me uncomfortably of a bug or a spider attempting to get a better view of me. After a moment she held up one hand, and I gingerly pressed my own against it.

"We have a bargain, *Vampyr*. Now go, and don't be late or I take it in trade. And since I have never tasted vampire flesh before, it would be a new experience to which I would not be averse." And with that, she retreated into the shadows, and I hustled off to QFC—a regional grocery store chain—and soon my shopping cart was filled with twenty

pounds on the nose of prime beef. One pound over and the
Maiden of Karask would be offended. One pound less and
she'd take it out of my skin.

Adding a couple extra pounds, wrapped separately, just
in case they'd measured wrong, I carried the bags back to
my Jag, wondering just what the hell I was thinking. But I
didn't want anybody else in danger, and I wasn't about to
let Delilah or Camille come with me. As I headed toward
the Greenbelt Park District, I realized that my life had
become one freak show event after another.

Strangely, I somehow didn't mind it so much.

CHAPTER 15

I sat in my Jag, across the street from the diner, staring at the darkened building on an even darker block. I really didn't want to go back in there. I didn't want to meet Ivana Krask. I especially didn't want to go meet Ivana Krask *in* the diner. The concept of heading into the dark where we knew there were hostile, hard-to-eradicate ghosts with one of the Elder Fae by my side wasn't my idea of a party. When I saw her scuttling down the street, I pulled out my cell phone and called Roman.

"Listen, I'm headed in to meet Ivana and take care of some of these freak-ass spirits. If I don't check back with you in two hours, call my home and tell them where I went and who I went with."

I was grumpy. I hated feeling nervous, but this was a pretty gruesome situation, which was why I was doing it on my own. Camille and Delilah would have my butt, but they'd be safe from both the ghosts and Ivana. And I wasn't sure which was more dangerous.

I hauled ass out of the car and retrieved the grocery

bags from the backseat. Carrying twenty pounds of beef was like carrying a feather for me as I crossed the street. A light touch on my cheek made me look up, and I saw that the snow had started to fall again—a light dusting that drifted down like powdered sugar on a gingerbread cake.

Ivana was standing in front of the diner, staring at it. As I approached, she held up one hand and I stopped, waiting till she turned her head first one way, then the other. After she'd listened for a few moments, she motioned me over.

"You have my payment?" She swiveled her head, staring at the bags. The tiny bump of a nose on her face twitched.

"Yes, twenty pounds of prime rib here." I set down the bags and stepped back. "You get ten of it now, then the other ten after you finish the work."

Ivana leaned over and lifted the bags, her sharp little teeth nipping at her lips. After a moment she grunted, sounding almost disappointed. "It is here. The bargain is sealed. Show me the spirits, girl."

I held up one hand. "Wait." And ran the second ten pounds back over to my Jag. I didn't trust her, bargain or not. The Elder Fae knew how to twist words in uncannily astute ways.

When I returned, I walked past her to the diner. "Can you clear the spirits from this place? This is the first task." As I yanked the freshly boarded-up door open, a soft yawn echoed from within. The ghosts were waiting. I could feel them circling within.

Ivana gazed at the open mouth of the building, and then with a deep laugh, she motioned for me to follow her. "Come, *Vampyr*. You will perhaps learn a thing or two. Time to earn my meat."

We entered the building and I could have sworn I heard a rumble from deep in the basement. I wished Camille and Morio were here. Or Smoky. Smoky would be good. Not much could affect my dragon brother-in-law, and I could trust *him*. Unlike the freak show in front of me right now.

My feet made no sounds, but Ivana, three steps ahead of me, was stomping across the floor as if she owned the joint. She muttered something under her breath and held out one hand. In the sliver of light from the street, I saw a silver branch appear in her palm, about three feet long and looking for all the world like a tree branch. It glistened, and I realized I was seeing the glow emanating from it, rather than just the sparkle of the metal. Instinctively, I stopped in my tracks. Silver: not so nice for vampires. But my Fae heritage loved it, and I wished, for the hundredth time, that I could still reach out and hold it in my hands.

"What's that?" I cautiously circled away from Ivana.

"Bah. You are *Vampyr.* You do not use silver." She waved me away.

"I used to. I am half-Fae on my father's side. But you're right, I don't use silver anymore." I glanced at the counter as I backed into it.

"This," Ivana continued as if I hadn't spoken, "is my special friend. You do not touch it or you will burn yourself, yes? Because of the fangs and the death? Vampires burn when they touch silver because they are of the undead."

"Yes, we do." I was getting tired of discussing the reason I couldn't touch silver and wanted to change the subject, but she was leading this gig and once again: *Elder Fae.* Anger at your own risk.

"This, my bloodthirsty friend—and what makes you so self-righteous about my eating bright meat when you drink blood?—as I was saying, this will help me rout your unwelcome friends. These spirits are thick and greedy, angry and hateful. They belong in the bogs, not in the city. They are a strong lot and I can put them to use."

Put them to use?

"What do you mean? You *keep* them? What the hell do you do with angry ghosts?" I stared at her, both appalled and oddly impressed. The Maiden of Karask was a piece of work, all right. But then, the Elder Fae never worried about what others thought of them. They didn't need to.

"I harvest them, yes, and fill my swamp. They sing to me at night, of their pain and anger over being trapped by one such as me, and I feed on their angst. While it's not bright meat, it's a sweet dessert." She grinned at me and her mouth reminded me of a shark's, with needle teeth and an almost cartoonish grin—a vacant smile, hungry and searching. I could all too easily see her gnawing on someone's hand, or foot.

I tried not to think about the spirits, already miserable and hateful, trapped in one of the Elder Fae's gardens, used as a feeding source. It occurred to me that I was basically handing them over for enslavement, but then again, it would get them out of the city and I really didn't want Camille coming out here, trying to dispel them. And she would . . . with or without Morio.

Ivana gave me a long look. I just nodded. She seemed to like that, and as she turned toward the end of the diner, she started to grow taller. The ratty hair took on a life of its own and came alive, like serpents, hissing. Her teeth lengthened, now glistening sharp bone blades, and the nubbin of nose vanished. I gazed up at her eyes. The pupils had vanished, and now an abyss of ocean waves crashed against the shore. She rolled her head back and the asps making up her dreadlocks rose up, hissing. Raising her staff, she let out a low growl.

What the fuck? Though I'd heard that the Elder Fae seldom showed their true forms, I wasn't sure just how different they could be. This was on par with Morio's demonic form compared to his human one. *Scary.* Big, and scary.

"Graech wallin ve tarkel. Greach wallin ve merrek. Greach wallin ve sniachlotchke!" Her voice thundered through the room and the staff sparked.

A thousand screams answered in unison, their fury caught in a high-pitched resistance. The rising shriek began to hurt my ears and I began to back toward the door, but before I could, a loud flash of light ripped from the staff and shredded the air as an inky portal opened up, through which I could see vague, vaporous forms entering the room.

They swirled, laughing, dancing, delighting in the pain that emanated from the walls of the building. A wave of anger and betrayal filtered out in concentric rings, energy taking form in a widening gyre, undulating through the room. I was normally headblind, but I could see everything going on.

"Graech wallin ve tarkel. Greach wallin ve merrek. Greach wallin ve sniachlotchke!" Ivana's words echoed, ricocheting from wall to wall, and the spirits who had come through the portal ran crazed, in a dance that spiraled around both of us. I couldn't see their faces, but that they had once been human—or perhaps Fae—was clear.

A rumble from the walls of the building interrupted their play, and they gathered together, focusing on the hallway leading to the basement of the diner. I stiffened as Ivana let out a cackle of delight.

"Come to the Maiden, my pretty ones, my lovely sweet treats." She reached out with one hand, and her jointed fingers curled in toward her wrist, almost touching it. A small flame burst into life in the center of her palm, sickly green with sparkles of purple racing through it. The flame grew, then detached itself and soared into the middle of the swarm of spirits.

"Crap, what the fuck kind of freak show are you running?" I didn't mean to speak aloud, but the words came slipping out.

Ivana snorted, but she did not look back. "What do you care as long as I meet the bargain, dead girl?"

"I guess I don't," I said, but wasn't sure if I really meant it. I'd expected some spell like Morio and Camille might cast, not a full floor show starring Spooks "R" Us.

"Then enjoy the show and be grateful I'm not picking

my teeth with your bones, lovely one. You may be dead meat on the hoof, but when hungry, any source will do." Ivana grinned at me, and I decided it was better when she wasn't looking my way.

"Not a problem. I'm enjoying," I muttered, doing my best to plaster a smile on my face.

The portal ghosts—the ones she'd invited in—were converging at the back of the diner, and I began to notice a sparkling form in their midst. Not good sparkles—there are some shimmers that you just *know* don't have your best interests at heart, and this was one of them. It was one of the diner ghosts, and it was pissed.

Ivana's ghosts spiraled in on it, and I realized they were doing what porpoises do—forming a bubble net around it like the dolphins do around a school of fish they want to eat. The diner ghost let out a loud wail that would have frozen my heart, and there was a flare of sparks as the two forces met. Ivana's spirits tightened their spiral, forcing the ghost into their center until I couldn't see what was happening, but a shriek shook the foundation of the building, echoing from wall to wall, and the ghosts broke apart, again darting in their crazed dance.

I looked for the diner ghost but couldn't see it, and it was then that I noticed a new form among the woo-hoo, party-hearty crowd. The diner ghost was now one of them, and by the intense shimmer around it, I had a feeling it was pissed out of its mind but couldn't do anything about it.

Ivana clapped her hands. *"Nok sillen vog nor taggin!"*

The spirits moved forward toward the basement stairs, and Ivana followed. I didn't want to go back in the basement. I'd had my fill of angry ghosts, of dancing ghosts, of ghosts that absorbed other ghosts. I backed away and leaped on the counter.

"I'll keep watch up here while you go downstairs."

"Stupid *Vampyr*, you don't know fun when you see it." Ivana spit out the words but then ignored me, pressing forward. I watched as she vanished through the doorway.

I might be a stupid vampire, but considering the stake through Morio's side that had been meant for me, I'd rather be stupid and remain intact. And downstairs, where the worst of the from-hell crowd were hanging out, wasn't a safe place for anybody. Except, apparently, the Maiden of Karask and her ghostly cavalcade.

I moved back toward the door, deciding it might be wise to wait outside while Ivana did her stuff, and stepped into the thickening snowstorm. Pulling out my cell phone, I punched in Delilah's number. She answered a moment later.

"Hey, I just wanted to know how Morio's doing. Have they come out of the operating room yet?" I glanced at the time on my cell phone. Ivana and I'd been hanging out together a good two hours now. Lucky me.

"Sharah said they're just finishing up. He was in there so long, Menolly." Delilah sounded like she was trying not to cry. "Camille's a wreck. Sharah put her in one of the rooms and made her lie down. Trillian slipped her a light sedative and although she's not sleeping, she's calmer now."

"Good. Damn it, I wish Smoky were around." I frowned at the snow. This was so not the right time for his family to call on him.

"By the way, where are you and what are you doing?" The sound of chewing told me Delilah was eating something.

"Cheetos or doughnuts? And where I am is none of your business right now." I glanced at the time on my phone. It was almost time to check in with Roman. "I'm taking care of a little matter, so keep your britches on. I'll check in with you in a bit."

Hanging up before she could stop me, I dialed Roman and, when his maid came on, asked to be put through to him.

"Why the fuck didn't you tell me what Ivana is? I so did not expect to be meeting one of the Elder Fae."

"If I'd told you what she is, you might have opted out.

I happen to think your plan is a good one, so I made sure
you'd go through with it. When you are finished with her,
why don't you come over for a visit?"

The low, sultry voice told me just what kind of visit
he was thinking of, and though the thought was appealing, now was not the time. "I'm sorry, but no. Not tonight.
My brother-in-law is in the hospital and we're not sure he's
going to live. My sister will need me after I'm done here."

Roman paused, then said, "Understandable."

"Wade's agreed to withdraw." I realized that in all the
chaos I had forgotten to report back. "So you won't hurt
him, will you?"

"If he abides by his word, he's safe from harm. I'm surprised you managed it without putting the bite on him. He
was hell-bent on the position."

"Yeah . . . I appealed to his desire to preserve his life.
So what about Terrance? What do we do about him?" The
last thing I wanted to do was infiltrate the Fangtabula—
actually, strike that. The last thing I wanted to do was head
downstairs and hang out with Ivana.

"We shall discuss his situation later. Meanwhile, keep
your wits about you. Ivana never forgets a face, nor a bargain. Chances are she will be sniffing at your heels for
more meat in exchange for her services. But be cautious:
You may be half-Fae, but the Elder Fae are a breed unto
themselves. Make too many bargains with them and they
will own your soul."

As I hung up, I thought that Roman conveniently left
important information out of his conversations, and from
now on, I'd ask for more details. I slid my phone back into
my pocket and, glancing at the silent street, headed back
toward the building.

As I reached the front door of the diner, the ground beneath
my feet shook and threw me off balance. I went sprawling

to the ground just as a loud howl echoed like a sonic boom over the diner, and then the building imploded in one massive cloud of dust and debris.

I sat there, dazed, covered with white powder, as a chunk of concrete the size of my fist came hurtling down to hit me on the head. The impact knocked me back but did nowhere the amount of damage it would have caused an FBH or one of my sisters. After a moment, I shook off the *thunk* and jumped up. I started to brush my jeans off, but decided it would be futile.

One glance at the diner told me that nobody would ever be jerking sodas there again. It occurred to me that Ivana might be hurt and I debated going in to find out, but then a figure marched up from the basement stairs. Ivana, in all her freak show glory, leaned on her staff, followed by a glistening swirl of spirits.

A sinking feeling in my gut told me that I'd been secretly hoping the implosion had taken her out with the building. Anybody who could unleash enough force to destroy a diner was somebody I wanted either fully on my side or out of my life totally. I cursed Roman under my breath. If he'd told me who I was dealing with, I would have tried to find another way to deal with this mess.

Ivana marched over to me and gave me a creepy smile. She held up her staff. "I've gathered the spirits and they are here, with me. Second part of the bargain—we go now. I do not wish to be abroad when dawn arrives."

"Neither do I," I muttered. Frowning at her, I decided to see what she'd do if I suggested altering the deal. The thought of her wandering around in Underground Seattle seemed highly dangerous, as in let's-bring-the-city-to-its-knees dangerous. "If you're worried about the time, we can revise the bargain—"

"You are suggesting that I won't honor the deal, *Vampyr*? Offense, I call offense and claim amends!"

Stomping one foot, the Maiden of Karask began to grow

even taller and it occurred to me that I'd fucked up. *Big-time*. But I didn't dare apologize—just like a *thank you*, an *I'm sorry* indicated a situation of debt.

"I believe you will honor the deal. I misspoke." The lump in my stomach was growing. I had to placate her without promising her something that was going to hurt to hand over.

She squinted at me. "You have a quick tongue on you, dead girl." Her lip quivered and I could see the desire in her eyes, the lust over what she might be able to cajole from me, but her eyes darted toward the bag full of beef she carried. She licked her lips. "No offense taken. This time. Second task: Now lead me."

I grimaced, dreading the havoc she could wreak on the tunnel where our vampire serial killer might be hiding, but I had no choice. It was either complete the bargain or dig myself in a lot deeper than I already had.

"I'll meet you a few blocks from here." I gave her the next address and headed for my Jag. No way was I giving the Elder Fae a ride.

Ivana took one look at the second bag of beef and headed down the tunnel while I waited topside. I'd given her instructions, but no way in hell was I following her down there. I wasn't about to get trapped belowground with one of the Elder Fae. So she, her silver staff, and her retinue of spirits vanished down the rabbit hole while I waited in my car, grateful she hadn't ordered me to come with her.

The more I thought about it, the more I decided that having an Elder Fae in my Rolodex was a good thing, though not necessarily safe.

I shifted, wishing I'd brought a book with me, when a movement across the street caught my eye. Quick it was, so quick I knew it couldn't be human. My serial killer? Leaping out of my Jag, I glanced back at the manhole. It would take Ivana some time to work her way through there. Surely I had enough time.

Without a second thought, I raced across the street and gave chase into the park.

CHAPTER 16

As I ran, my feet flying over the snow-clad sidewalk, a thousand thoughts filled my head. Usually my sisters were with me when I was about to face a major foe. Usually we took things on together. Right now, the best I could hope for was that it took Ivana a lot longer in the tunnels than it had taken in the diner. Of course, if she brought the roof down, it might take her out and I'd never have to worry about her again.

My quarry dodged off the sidewalk into a patch of undergrowth, and I followed. I couldn't hear him, but the fleeing blur—the quicksilver movement—spelled *vampire* to me. As I went plowing through a hedgerow, I slowed to a walk. One wrong skewer of a bare branch could act like a stake. Not so good for continued existence. Fighting my way past the last part of the hedge, I stumbled out into a circular clearing. Benches curved around the center fountain, which was turned off for the winter. On the other side stood another figure, but it wasn't the one I'd seen before. No, I was staring at Wade.

"Wade? What the fuck are you doing here?"

"I was out looking for your pervert," he said, as we met by the fountain. "I saw someone come through the hedge, but then . . . I don't know what happened, but he vanished. I know some vampires can turn invisible, but they're rare."

"Rare is right, and that skill usually takes a long time to master. If this was our suspect, he'd have to be a lot older than we think he is." I dropped to the edge of the fountain, sitting on the snowy rim. Wade joined me.

"I talked to Erin at the bar tonight," he said.

Glancing at him, I gave him a weary smile. I wasn't physically tired, but the stress was catching up with me. "And?"

"She'll move into Sassy's mansion once we get it outfitted. Meanwhile, I've asked her to come over and help us turn it into the haven we need. With her experience running a business during life, she could be a damned good project manager. I guess I should have asked your permission first, but it just seemed—"

"Perfect. Which it is. That's fine, I really hated seeing her waste her time cleaning the Wayfarer. You'll send an escort with her to and from work each night? She's still so unaccustomed to being out on her own."

He nodded. "I understand. And yes, in fact, I think she and Brett might get along. Both misfits. He's been a vampire for longer than I have, to be honest, so he'll do just fine on helping her adjust."

"Brett . . . he still on his superhero craze?" Brett was young when he was turned—in his early twenties. He'd been a comic book fan and had always wanted to be a superhero, so now he went around dressed as his alter ego, Vamp-Bat, looking for ways to use his life as a vampire to help people. He'd saved several women from being raped and a handful of citizens from being mugged, and he fed only on blood bank blood except when he couldn't help it.

"Yeah, but it's actually good for him. Keeps him on the straight and narrow. Just like having a job will help keep

Erin focused. I truly believe one of Sassy's problems was that she eschewed any real work. I tried to give her jobs within the VA, but she would get distracted. She never had to hold a job in her life, thanks to her parents' money and then her late husband's inheritance, and a vampire with too much time on his or her hands is a vampire headed for trouble."

"You're right. Erin's smart. She needs to be occupied, and she knows it." I glanced around. "So, no idea where our runner went?"

Wade shook his head. "No, but I'll keep my eyes open on the way out. What are you doing here?"

I quickly ran down the events of the evening.

"Not Morio—he's such a good guy. Crap. Well, I'll see what I can find out about whoever was in the park tonight. I guess I'd better get moving. My thoughts are with your sister and her youkai."

"I'd better get back." Ivana wouldn't wait forever, and I hoped I'd get back so she wouldn't have to wait at all. The last thing I needed was for her to feel like I'd inconvenienced her. I brushed the snow off my shoulders. "Hey, Wade—"

He held up his hand, smiling. "It's good to be talking again."

"Yeah, I've missed it."

"Me, too. Later." And then he was gone.

I took another spin around the area and then headed back to the car. I'd barely reached the Jag when Ivana emerged from the tunnel in a cloud of sparkling dust. Her silver staff glowed like a light saber.

Silently, I handed her the second bag of beef. I didn't have to ask if she'd gathered the spirits. The satisfied look on her face told me what I needed to know. I wanted to ask her if she'd seen anything indicating my serial killer down below, but that would entail yet another bargain. One thing I'd learned in my evening with Ivana was that the Elder Fae do nothing without payment.

I didn't thank her, but instead, slowly backed away toward my Jag. Ivana started down the street, grocery bags in tow. Then, she paused, turning back to me.

"Dead girl!"

"Yeah?"

"You may call upon me again if you wish another bargain. Be cautious with yourself. Not all of the Elders are as discriminating as I am. Not all, as pleasant." And then she vanished into the shadows.

I stared after her, wondering what condition she'd left the tunnel in. I wondered what she was going to do with the spirits and shadow men that she had carted off with her. Most of all, I wondered if the Elder Fae had all stayed Earthside or if some of them had followed to Otherworld during the Great Divide.

About to head below, I paused as my cell phone jangled. A glance at the Caller ID showed me it was Delilah on the other line.

"Yeah? What's up? Any news on Morio?" I waited for her answer.

She spoke slowly. "He's out of surgery. Now it's a matter of time. Sharah thinks he'll make it, but the next twenty-four hours will tell the tale. Camille's a wreck. Trillian's helping her keep it together. Morio's liver was severely damaged, and he lost so much blood."

"Twenty-four hours, huh? He's youkai—demon. He should survive." But the thought that he might not crossed my mind. "Delilah, if he slips . . . do you think Camille would want me to . . ." I couldn't even say the words, but they had to be said. There had to be no recriminations later over what I did or did not do.

Delilah let out a little mew. "I don't know. I'll find out." She hung up.

I paused, then punched in our home number. Iris answered.

"Vanzir there?"

But Iris wasn't going to let me off the hook with being

so abrupt. "Yes, he is, but you can just damned well get your ass back here and tell me what's going on. Nerissa and I've been waiting and waiting for the phone to ring."

Damn. I should have told Delilah to call her when she got the chance. "I'm busy—"

"It's going on four in the morning. You may have a few hours left, but girl, you need to tell me what's happening out there."

I glanced at the tunnel. "Give me twenty minutes and I'll be home. Meanwhile, sit tight." I'd been thinking to ask Vanzir to come help me, but Iris's mood kiboshed that. With one last longing glance, I left the manhole cover and jogged over to my car, speeding off to home.

Iris was waiting up. She looked exhausted but had stubbornly stayed up all night in order to keep watch. Bruce O'Shea, her leprechaun boyfriend, was on vacation visiting his family in Ireland, but Vanzir was sitting with her in the living room, and Shamas, our cousin, was there, too.

"Hey, cuz," he said. "How's Camille? How's Morio doing?" He hadn't fully integrated into our extended family but was doing his best to try.

"Camille will be a whole lot better tomorrow night. *If* Morio lives. Sharah's giving him a sixty percent chance to make it; if he passes the twenty-four-hour mark, he should live."

Iris shook her head. "It boggles my mind how strong some spirits can become. I wonder if there's a way to cleanse them from the area so you can go exploring without worry."

"I . . . well . . . I've taken care of that. At least as far as the diner and the tunnels are concerned." I hadn't meant to say anything—at least not yet—but Iris had a way of making you feel like you were lying if you omitted telling her something.

"And how did you do that?" She gave me a piercing stare.

"I made a bargain with one of the Elder Fae—the Maiden of Karask. She cleared the spirits for twenty pounds of beef."

Iris gasped, and her fingers fluttered to her lips. "Oh no, my girl. You didn't. Please tell me you're joking."

Vanzir looked confused, but Shamas stared at me, his eyes wide. "Are you mad, girl? The Elder Fae? Even the Lords of Fae let them be. They are *our* Titans and—often—our enemies."

I shrugged. "We needed to do something and I didn't want Camille trying to take them on herself, especially with Morio so wounded. You know her—she's going to feel it's her duty to take care of this. I put a stop to that before it could begin."

"But the Maiden of Karask? Girl, her history is terrifying. We have such like her in my own homeland, and the people and Fae give them a wide berth." Iris stood, pacing. "She knows you now; she will study up on you. Once you bargain with the Elder Fae, they never forget you and always come sniffing for what else they can gain from you. You've bound yourself to her as certain as you are bound to the twilight hours. Do you realize what this means?"

I stared at her. "But the bargain was met and paid—"

"The bargain! The bargain *is* the connection. You merely paid the first installment. She has the right to contact you again. She has the right to touch you for more meat—the kind she longs for, not the kind you're willing to pay. She has the right to ask a bargain of *you*, now. Don't you understand? There *are no* bargains when it comes to Elder Fae. Only enslavement on an unwritten level." She was seriously upset, and I began to realize I might have dived in over my head. "For the sake of the gods . . . you did not say 'thank you' or 'I'm sorry' to her at any time?"

"No, that I was mindful of."

"Thank heavens for small favors. But girl, you opened a can of worms. The best we can hope for is that she forgets you. That you slid beneath her notice." With a swish of her robe, Iris returned to the rocking chair and curled up in it.

I didn't want to tell her, but given how grave she felt my error was, I thought I'd better. "When we parted, she said that I could contact her again."

Iris let out a long sigh. "Then it is done. She will remember you. And you will have to deal with her in the future. Pray she's distracted for some time." Iris shook her head. "Don't they teach you anything over in Otherworld? I'm sure some of the Elders crossed over during the Great Divide."

Shamas cleared his throat. "Don't be too hard on Menolly, Iris. We have Elder Fae over in OW, too, but they are usually left to themselves. In the city-states like Y'Elestrial, they are banned and do not have truck with most city folk."

"I wanted to go back down in the tunnel tonight, while the ghosts are gone." I told them what Ivana had done. Iris said nothing but stared at me, a grave expression on her face. Trying to avoid her gaze, I glanced at the clock. "It's nearing five. I have two and a half hours that I could put to good use."

"No." Shamas crossed his arms. "Not unless you take me with you."

"I can come," Vanzir said.

At that moment, a sound caught my attention and I looked up to see Nerissa, rubbing her eyes, enter the room. She was wearing a long pale pink gown and her golden hair trailed down her shoulders. Without her makeup, without the skirt suit, she looked vulnerable, soft, and dewy. Breathless at her beauty, I crossed to her side and gathered her into my arms, pressing my lips to hers, drinking in deep the fragrance of sleep and perfume and the scent of her body. After a moment, I stood back.

"I love you. It's that simple. *I love you.*"

Nerissa stared at me, her mouth curving into a bow. Her eyes glittered. "I love you, too. Now tell me what's going on? I heard some of it on the way in."

"Great, ruin a romantic moment." I sighed. "I apparently screwed up in trying to help out." I explained what I'd done. "Have you ever heard of the Elder Fae?" I wasn't sure if the Weres were aware of the differing flavors of the Fae race.

Nerissa frowned. "I don't know. Venus the Moon Child would have known, but he didn't talk about stuff like that much. Not before you guys opened the portals and came over. We knew the Fae existed, but they were still in the closet. It was hard to mingle when you never knew who your enemies were, or who might out you."

I grinned. "Now you're out in more than one way."

"Check and mate. So are you sure you can get down in those tunnels and out before dawn? You don't want to be caught out of your lair when the sun rises." She ran one hand along my arm, and I caught my breath. Standing next to my half-naked girlfriend who was all softness and bed-headed made me want to forget all about the tunnels and the serial killer and spend some serious time exploring her mysteries.

With a sigh, I tore myself away. "I have to. Camille's going to be out of it for a day or so, and Delilah will be exhausted by tomorrow from sitting up with her. Smoky and Roz are gone. I have Vanzir, Shamas—who also has to get up tomorrow and go to work—and Trillian. And Trillian won't leave Camille's side, not for this."

"I'll go with you." Nerissa leaned down and kissed my lips, but I shook my head.

"No, you will not. You aren't trained for fighting. You have your strengths, but babe, I can't watch out for you and do what I need to do. You stay home with Iris and Shamas. Vanzir, it's us again. I want to get down there before any other haunts take up residence."

We headed for my Jag. I wasn't tired in the least, and

Vanzir looked down, but not out. I promised Iris we'd call her in an hour. Nerissa pouted her way back to bed, but I reluctantly slipped out the door.

"She makes it hard for you," Vanzir said, smiling a little. "You two obviously have it going on. I'm glad you're paying attention and not taking her for granted. It's easy for vamps and demons to forget the niceties."

I thought of Roman. "Not all vampires are like that. At least, not all forget to be generous, even if their emotions are in check."

"Yeah, well, for a living/undead relationship, you two do pretty good." He slid into the passenger seat and fastened his seat belt.

As we veered off, back to the Greenbelt Park District, I thought over the equipment I'd brought. Sometimes I wished I had an arsenal like Roz, but I'd never managed to pull one together. However, in the backseat, I had a bag with several wooden stakes—just in case we met our serial killer—a couple of knives, a pair of handcuffs, and a few other accoutrements.

Vanzir glanced over at me as we sped through the silent streets. "You blame yourself for Morio, don't you?"

I stared at the road, hands on the wheel, not answering for a moment. Of course I did, but I wasn't going to tell him. Instead, I just said, "What happened with Camille?"

It was his turn to press his lips together. Finally, he said, "Touché. Unless you're ordering me to answer, I'd rather she tell you."

I wanted to confront him, to order him to tell, but Camille's privacy was tenuous at best, with three husbands, and I dreaded taking away what she had left. I frowned. "Whatever it is, will it interfere with our quest?"

He shrugged. "It's up to her, and I'll abide by whatever decision she makes. Look, isn't that the turn up there?"

I nodded, silently swinging the car to the left, where I neatly slid into a parking space right near the manhole. Again, the city streets were empty—a few people going to bakery jobs or early-morning diners, but here—in Green-belt Hell—it might as well still be the dead of night.

We hopped out of the car and headed over to the tunnels. Vanzir stopped to shake his head.

"Fuck, woman, what the hell kind of creepshow did you bring here? I can feel her residue. This scares the shit out of me." He shivered and looked around. "She's gone, right?"

"Yeah, she went back to whatever rock she lives under." I tossed the manhole cover aside. "I'm headed down, punk boy. Follow if you dare." And with that, I leaped over the side and floated down to the tunnels below. Vanzir followed, shimmying down the ladder at record speed.

The tunnel felt different as I looked around. It wasn't any brighter, but as I flashed my light around, I realized that the energy had lightened considerably. Thanks to Ivana. Regardless of what the others said, I decided I'd done the right thing. We started through, following our initial direction, but this time nothing jumped out of the woodwork to attack us. Oh, there were a few viro-mortis slimes on the walls, and I saw rats here or there, but the air felt clear and I glanced over at Vanzir.

"Nothing," he said, shaking his head. "There's nothing of what we were fighting left down here. Whatever else the Maiden of Karask might be, she's thorough."

When we came to the side passage, I slid through, Vanzir following. Once in the chamber where we'd fought the shadow men, I glanced at the entrances leading out of the room. Which to pick first?

Vanzir caught my arm. "Are you sure you want to do this? Maybe we should just explore farther up the main tunnel? This seems off the beaten path for your vampire."

"Yes, I'm sure. Now come on." I chose one at random. We still had a serial killer on the loose, and I didn't want to take a chance on getting caught by the creep.

The passage continued for about ten feet before it began to descend, and within moments it had turned into a staircase leading down. I paused, wondering if I should call Iris now. But we'd barely been here twenty minutes, and to call her, I'd have to return to the surface. There was no reception here. I opted to wait.

We approached another opening, through which the stairwell plunged. Vanzir stopped behind me. "Menolly, I don't think this is a good idea. Let's go back—please?"

"What the fuck is your problem?" I stepped through the opening and gasped as the walls fell away.

I gaped at the panorama unfolding before us. A huge system of stairwells covered the gaping chasm below, leading from one lower tunnel to another to another. A neighborhood, entirely belowground. We were no longer in Underground Seattle, but we were truly *under* Seattle. No humans had built this system, unless they were humans no longer mortal.

How far down the cavern went, I do not know. There was no end in sight. I could barely make out figures scurrying along the stairwells. Not many—not like the aboveground sidewalks during daylight hours, but enough to show that the stairwells were well used and active.

I paused, staring at the expanse below me. "What the fuck do you think it is?" I whispered. "The vampire serial killer, he couldn't possibly be responsible for this."

"No." Vanzir drew close behind me, and he placed one steady hand on my shoulder. "Let's go back."

"Hell no, not just yet. Look at this—it's like some city beneath the city. Who knows what's waiting down there in the labyrinth? But our serial killer—if he's down there, we have no chance of finding him." I shook my head. "We'll have to hope he hasn't discovered this place. But what the hell . . . who could have made this?"

Vanzir let out a long sigh. He turned me toward him, as we overlooked the spiraling abyss. "Actually, I know who made it. I suppose I'd better tell you what you've stumbled onto before you start hunting around down here."

"*You* know? Have you been here before?" I tilted my

head, wondering how the hell this could have remained secret for so many years.

"Yeah, but not through this entrance." He shrugged. "Most of the entrances are guarded by magic. I guess they thought the spirits and shadow men would be a strong enough deterrent."

"*Who* thought? What is this place?"

Vanzir let out a low chuckle. "Welcome to the Demon Underground. That's right—we're not just a group, we're an entire suburb below the city."

"You knew this was down here." I gazed at him for a moment, openmouthed, then turned back to the staircases crisscrossing the pit. The Demon Underground. Shaking my head, I took one last glance over the edge and slumped on the steps.

"Okay, tell me everything. And don't hold back."

CHAPTER 17

Vanzir sat beside me. We were in no danger of blocking the way—there was nobody near us. A figure or two that I could see on the lower levels, but here: nada. I waited for him to speak.

"So . . . yeah, this is the Demon Underground."

"I always thought you were referring to a *group* when you called it that," I said. "We all did." The Demon Underground was a network of rogue demons hiding from Shadow Wing, over Earthside. They had formed an alliance to fight against the demon lord, and Vanzir had often consulted them for us when we needed a heads-up on one Big Bad or another.

"It is. A group. But they have to live somewhere, and not all demons can pass for FBHs. I can, to a degree, though most people think I'm one of the Fae, but a good share of the demons look like . . . well . . . demons. Monsters, to the mortals." He shrugged. "Where the hell did you think they were all living? In condos along the waterfront?"

"No, I guess not." But now that he asked the question,

it made sense. It had never occurred to me to ask where all the demons who'd fled the Subterranean Realms had ensconced themselves. Carter, of course, lived in Seattle proper, but he had the ability to mask his appearance, probably because his father was one of the Greek Titans. He wasn't full demon.

I looked up at Vanzir. "I can't believe none of us ever thought about this before. We can be shortsighted at times."

"You can't remember everything while trying to save the world." At first I thought he was mocking me, but then he laughed and I realized he'd attempted a joke. He reached out and hesitantly patted me on the shoulder. "Don't feel bad. We've done a good job of keeping this place under wraps. Karvanak didn't even know. And he beat me senseless."

"Now I see why you tried to veer me off from here. You wanted to keep it secret." Part of me understood why—secret organizations need secret headquarters. Part of me wondered just how far we could trust him.

"Hell, eventually you or your sisters would have come back. Better I'm with you to explain matters than you get yourselves in trouble. The demons here may hate Shadow Wing, but they don't necessarily like humans or Fae. They protect the Underground with a passion. In fact, we'd better go before we're caught. I need to warn them to set up a new guarding system now that the shadow men are gone."

"*You guys* put those fuckers there?" I stood, suddenly understanding what he was saying. "They almost killed me. They almost killed Morio. What do you think Camille's going to do when she finds out you're partially responsible for her husband lying in the hospital? What do you think she'll do if he dies?"

"We didn't put the ghosts there . . . just the shadow men, and they weren't the ones that staked him." He paled. "Menolly, please don't let her think I was the one who did that. I didn't assign them to guard the entrance. I don't run the Underground, I'm just part of it."

"No, but you didn't warn us even though you knew they were there. You let us walk into a deadly situation without warning—"

"You were determined to head down the passage. You knew about the actual ghosts that are there. You knew the area is haunted. What more could you have known that would make it all come out all right? I couldn't fight the shadow men, either. And you'll notice they were coming after me, too. It wasn't my fault Morio got hurt, it was whatever that ghost-thing was that did it." His eyes whirled with anger.

Even though he was right, I pressed my lips together, keeping my thoughts in check as rigidly as I could. It would be so easy to strike him down, but what he said was the truth. Finally, after a few minutes, I managed to regain my equilibrium and nodded abruptly toward the stairs.

"Let's get the fuck out of here."

We silently returned to the tunnels, and I flipped open my cell phone. No bars, but it was time to call Iris. And only ninety minutes before dawn.

"Let's get out of here. I'm not going to find the killer tonight, that's obvious." I hurried ahead, letting him try to keep pace with me. When we reached the exit, I floated up topside and, in a blur of movement, headed toward my Jag. Vanzir struggled behind me.

I slammed my door, popped my seat belt into place and was speed-dialing Iris by the time he climbed in the car. Ignoring him, I waited until Iris answered and then blurted out, "We're on our way home. We're all right."

"Good, but Menolly, I got a call from Chase. We have a problem."

"Morio?" Oh gods, let Morio be all right. None of us could handle losing him, let alone Camille.

"He's still hanging in there, blessed be Undutar. No, Chase called to tell me he got a tip about an hour ago and he's going to have to follow up on it."

"A tip? What tip?"

"That Wade's the serial killer."

I stared at the phone. "You have to be kidding. I'm headed over toward the FH-CSI now."

"Remember: less than ninety minutes until dawn," she warned me.

"I know. Trust me, I know." I put the car in gear and, without a word to Vanzir, sped along the silent snowy streets.

"So, are you just never going to talk to me again?" Vanzir stared out the window as the city streets passed by in a dark blur.

I stared straight ahead, clutching the steering wheel. "Yeah, something like that."

"Going to make it hard to tell me what to do," he said, cajoling me. I gave him a sharp glance and he smiled, faintly, shrugging at my gaze. "What can I say? I could grovel, but you three don't like groveling. But remember: Beyond being your slave, I'm part of the Demon Underground, and we have a loyalty oath there, too."

I was back to staring at the road, but I let out a loud huff. "I know you aren't responsible for Morio's injuries."

"Thank you. But will Camille? She already . . ." He fell silent and stared through the window.

"Already what? What the fuck went on down there while Chase and I were trying to save Morio's life? Why weren't you guys climbing out of the tunnel right after Chase? *What did you do down there?*"

Out of the corner of my eye, I saw him cringe.

"You'd better tell me. Camille's in no shape to, and somehow, as much as I dread hearing whatever it is you have to say, I'm getting the feeling that I'd better know about it."

Vanzir stared at his hands. "I was feeding on whatever that ghost was . . . you remember that?"

I nodded. "Yeah, so what?"

"Do you remember earlier, when I warned her to get out of the way? Her life force is so brilliant when she's running her magic that it's like . . . to be honest, it's like a hard-core turn-on. Why do you think I avoid her more than I do you or Delilah? She runs energy and I'm . . . addicted to feeding on energy."

"Holy crap. You fed on her?" I swerved, barely missing a parked BMW.

"No. Not much." His voice lowered. "Oh, this is all wrong. Why can't I just not give a fuck like the rest of my kind?"

"Because you're not like the rest of them. Just tell me what happened. I'll take responsibility if she finds out. I *order* you to tell me. You can't refuse a direct order." I wanted everything out in the open. Now.

He shuddered. "Crap. You fucking bitch. You would, wouldn't you?" But his voice held no animosity, only resignation. "Fine. There are two ways my addiction comes out. One is to feed, but when I can't feed, and the impetus is still there, then I . . ."

As he paused, I had a flash of memory: what he'd said to her just shortly before that. *If I didn't snag you in with my feeders, I'd end up tearing your clothes off and fucking you raw.*

Oh crap. Was I going to have to kill him myself? "You didn't!"

Head in his hands, he shook it violently. "I didn't mean to. She gave off one last blast at the ghost and I . . . I was so wired and so poised to feed. I broke."

"Oh for the love of . . ." I swerved over to park against the curb and, hands on the wheel, forced myself to stare at the maple tree in the nearest yard. "Go on."

"I started to feed on her and she screamed for me to get the hell out of her head. I was trying to pull back the entire time, trying to stop myself but I couldn't—it was like a feeding frenzy. I think she knew because she grabbed my hands and put them on her waist, then pulled up her skirts."

I didn't want to hear. Didn't want to imagine my sister, desperate to stop the assault on her mind, offering herself up to put an end to it.

Vanzir continued, relentless, his voice cracking. "She was screaming for me to stop feeding on her. I tried to disengage, but the only way I could stop was to . . . was to fuck her. I slammed her up against the wall and . . . she didn't fight. She let me. She was crying and saying that she knew that I couldn't control it. I'd fed too deep on the ghost and was out of control. I know it's no excuse, but I was so caught up in the frenzy that . . ."

Holy Mother Hel. I counted to ten, then twenty, then thirty before speaking. "Camille gave herself to you in order to stop you from feeding on her life force?"

He nodded, tears streaking down his cheeks. "I didn't want to. I didn't want to hurt her. I didn't want to feed on her, but with all the energy flying through the air, with all the fighting, I was so hyped up that . . ."

"That your nature took over, even though you knew she could kill you for it. But she didn't kill you, did she?" As much as I wanted to strike him down right there, I forced myself back from the edge. If Camille hadn't destroyed Vanzir for his actions, then was it my place to finish the job she'd chosen to leave undone?

"There's more." He was whispering now, staring at the floor.

"Oh Great Mother, no. What else?" I didn't know how much *more* I could take.

"While I was . . . while we were . . . while I was fuck-ing her, her eyes turned color—they flashed from violet to silver. And she said something. I'm not even sure she knows that she did. She said, *'If you don't like your nature, demon, then forsake it.'* And that's when it happened."

"What happened?" I was almost scared to hear.

"My feelers, my ability to feed on life force. I think it's gone. When she said that, part of me was stripped away. It was horrible, someone inside me, tearing at me, rooting out

an essential part of myself. And now, I can't feed. I can't
even figure out how I used to. It's like part of me is dead."
He stared at me, a bitter look in his eye. "Your sister did
better than kill me. She destroyed what I am. Now I really
am just a slave. A strong one, but . . . just a slave."

As I gazed into his eyes, I knew he was telling the
truth. There was no way he could lie about it to me. Vanzir
was no longer able to feed. Camille—or someone working through Camille—had destroyed his most powerful
weapon.

There was nothing left to say. I shifted back into gear
and pulled out from the curb, heading toward the FH-CSI
building. This night just kept getting worse. For once, the
thought of daylight and sleep loomed large like a promise
of relief.

Chase was waiting. He glanced at the clock. "Cutting it
thin, aren't you?"

"Yeah, but this night has just made everything twice as
hard as it should be. Any word on Morio?"

"Camille's sleeping in the bed next to him. Trillian and
Delilah are in the waiting room. So far, he's holding his
own. But they've run perilously low on the blood he needs.
Delilah's put out an emergency call to the Supe Community and we've had donors straggling in the past hour or so,
so that's one good thing."

"What the fuck is this about Wade being the serial
killer?"

"I know, I know. It's ridiculous, but I can't just ignore
it. I have to check out any and all leads. The person who
phoned in was male, that's all I know. He claimed that
Wade knew the women and had access to them. I can't
question him now—but on the last ray of sunset, I'll be at
his door. I'd like you to meet me there."

"Sure." I frowned. "Sun is setting at around four twenty.
Meet you there at four fifty?"

"Sounds good. And Menolly, I know you and Wade are on the outs, but I know you don't want to see him go down for—"

"Actually, we're okay. For now, at least. And yeah, I don't want to see him go down unless he actually did something. I'll tell you now, it isn't him. But I know you have to check things out. I'll see you this evening."

I turned to Vanzir. "I'm heading home. Go trade off with Delilah. She's going to need her sleep. Tell her I'm headed home to bed. Make sure she gets her ass out of here. We need to be rested up, with all that's going on."

He nodded, not meeting my eyes.

"Vanzir, listen . . ." I paused, not knowing how to say what I was thinking, so finally I opted for just blurting it out as usual. "Whatever you did, Camille seems to have decided it wasn't worthy of death given the circumstances. She seems to have chosen her own form of punishment, and I'll admit, it was a doozy. So I'll leave it up to her. Obviously I'm pissed as hell, but . . ."

"I understand." He raised one hand, then dropped it quickly and headed to the waiting room.

All the way home, the events of the past twenty-four hours played through my mind. By the time I walked into the house, with thirty minutes to spare before sunrise, I was feeling more exhausted than I had in a long time. Iris had been dozing by the fire, curled up in an armchair. Maggie was in the playpen next to her side. I reached down and planted a soft kiss on the dewy, fuzzy leather of the gargoyle's face. And then, without waking Iris, I slipped down to my lair and crashed into oblivious, dreamless sleep.

When I woke, I jumped into clean clothes and raced up the stairs, waiting impatiently for the kitchen to clear. Finally, I was able to slip out of my lair and into the living room.

"Morio? Is he—"

Iris nodded. She looked tired. I had a feeling it had been

a long day for her. "He's still in critical condition. Sharah said there was something about the ghosts that made it worse. His wounds go deeper than just the stake in the liver. The ghost drained life energy out of him when it attacked."

"*Hungry ghosts*. A variant of the hungry ghosts," I whispered. There were several variations of the creatures. We'd come across one or two before, but these were powerful and angry. The thought of Ivana Krask having control over them was rather frightening, now that I thought about it. But there was nothing to do about it.

"Yes," Iris said. "They fed on him as his pain grew."

Speaking of feeding . . . I looked around for Vanzir, but he was no place in sight. Neither was Delilah, nor Trillian. "Where is everybody?"

"Nerissa headed out to rent an apartment until the condo sale goes through—she said to tell you she'll call later. Delilah and Trillian are back at the hospital with Camille. Smoky and Roz aren't home yet. Shamas is at work. Vanzir took off with some vague excuse. Does he seem different to you, Menolly? I wonder if the soul binder ritual is still working." Iris frowned.

I wasn't sure how to deal with the question. What the hell was I going to tell her? But now that Vanzir's powers were gone, it occurred to me the others would have to know. Next time we went into battle, someone might expect him to be able to feed on the creatures we were facing, and that was no longer possible.

Crap, and *that* meant Smoky, Trillian, and Morio would find out, and that meant . . . Vanzir might as well slit his wrists unless somehow Camille could keep the three of them in check. Trillian she could probably deal with—he was polyamorous by nature, too. And possibly Morio. But Smoky . . . I really didn't want to think about what Smoky was likely to do.

"I'd better tell you something, but, Iris, this is a touchy situation. And hell—it will have to wait. I've got to meet

Chase at Wade's. I'm late as it is. Call down to the bar for me, would you? I'm not sure I'll make it in tonight, either. Ask Chrysandra how Derrick is doing, please. And Erin— tell her I'll see her soon."

I grabbed a bottle of blood from the fridge and drank it without warming it. Normally, the taste would have been pretty bad, but Morio had charmed this bottle into a strawberry shake flavor and it went down easy. Blessing his poor, wounded heart, I tossed the bottle in the sink and raced out the door to my Jag.

As I leaped down the steps, I landed on a patch of ice beneath the layer of fresh snow and went skidding, landing on my chin. I managed to hit a rock, which caused a gash, but it began to heal by the time I was on my feet and in the car.

I rolled my eyes as I felt the scab on my chin. Here I was, *jian-tu*, spy and acrobat extraordinaire, but once again my half-human heritage had knocked me off my feet and into a snowbank.

Speaking of snow—how the hell was Seattle getting so much snow? The city could go for years without it, but the past couple of winters had been overactive in the white-flake department. Of course, last year's deluge had been the result of Loki moving into the area when Dredge came to town. But this year . . . maybe it was El Niño or La Niña or whatever child of the storm was bearing down on us now.

Wet from the fall, I slammed the door on my Jag shut and took off down the driveway. In the growing dusk, I saw two of the elven guards that Queen Asteria had assigned to our land and felt a surge of relief. I'd worry myself sick if Iris and Maggie didn't have any other protection. Shade might be there, but extra hands never hurt.

Chase was impatiently waiting in his car outside Wade's apartment. A couple of landlords in the city had gotten wise and realized how much money they could make by providing security apartments to rent to vampires. The landlords were Supe Community members, mostly Fae and vampire themselves, but there were now two dedicated apartment

complexes where vamps could be guaranteed an apartment
with at least two windowless rooms and a security system
down on the front door to keep vampire hunters at bay.

As I pulled in, I noticed a small group of picketers marching in a circle on the sidewalk in front of the
Shrouded Grove Suites. I hurried over to Chase's vehicle.

"What the fuck do they want?"

"The heart of every vampire in there. Now that I see
this, I'm not sure how safe it is for you to go in there with
me. I can yell and wave my gun around, but somebody
there may have a stake and decide that it's better off used
on you." He looked concerned, and for Chase to be worried
about a group of humans was—in itself—worrisome.

"I can take them on, you know that."

"All it takes is one misplaced stake. We saw that with
Morio." He turned to me, his expression somber. "Seriously, Menolly. I'm not sure what to do anymore. Thanks
to Gambit's paranoia, every religious freak—and I mean
freak, not good upstanding people who live and let live—is
running around trying to play Buffy the Vampire Slayer.
And this latest mess with the vamp serial killer is just making it worse. It's up to me to keep law and order in the city,
and I'm not doing a very good job of it."

I patted him on the shoulder, not used to comforting
people. "Johnson, you're doing a damned fine job. You
can't keep everything under your control. I'm rejoining
the VA, and we'll hammer out some way to help. But to do
that, we need Wade. So I need you to help me prove Wade
didn't do this."

"I hope it won't be too hard," he said, chewing on his lip.

Smacking him lightly with two fingers, I said, "Stop
that. You'll give yourself a canker sore. Now come on. I'm
sure Wade can come up with some alibi. His mother hangs
around his neck like a leech. She's bound to have been with
him on at least one of the nights when the victims were
murdered. By the way, no more bodies so far?"

With a grim shake of the head, he pushed forward to

break through the line. "No. Okay, watch your back and I do mean that. Literally."

As we approached the chanting mob, I glanced at their signs.

STOP THE SUCKERS COLD!
STAKE THE VAMPS!
BLOOD BELONGS TO THE LIVING!
DRIVE THE POINT HOME!

At least that last one was clever, if gruesome. The picture was of a pointy stake aimed at a cartoon vampire.

"Back—get back," Chase said, pulling out his badge.

"We have a right to protest!"

"Vampire-lover! The law's supposed to be on our side— what are you, a vamp wannabe?"

"Look—he's with the half-Fae, half-vampire!"

"Technically, gentlemen, I'm all vampire. I was half-Fae, half-human—" But my attempted correction didn't go over well and the guy lunged at me, aiming the handle of the sign at my chest. Chase pulled out his baton and swung it, catching the sign handle before it came near me.

"Try it and you'll be headed right for jail."

"Killing a vampire isn't against the law." The man eyed me, his gaze glittering and dangerous.

"Maybe not, but I'll guarantee you that I will find enough charges to make you rot in jail for years. *Trust me.*" Chase's voice was an icicle waiting to crash, and the guy stepped back. Once again, I wondered how our detective had gained such a control factor in his timbre. It had to be the Nectar of Life. Question was: How far would it take Chase in his powers?

We wormed our way through without further incident, though the minute we crossed the line, Chase motioned me in front of him so his back was to the picketers and not mine. He showed his credentials to the doorman and we passed through into the spacious lobby.

The building was lit by soft yellow lights. A gleaming chandelier hung from the central lobby, and two very tough-looking guards stood near the elevator. The front desk was manned by an equally formidable-looking woman. If I didn't know better, I'd think they were werewolves. Chances were good they were Were-something. You just didn't get muscle like that on your typical Fae. They could be vampire, I supposed, but that meant they'd had to scour for some super-buff dudes. Although all vampires were strong, few *looked* it.

We halted by the first elevator and once again, Chase showed his credentials. The man nodded us by and we slipped into the car. Chase pressed the button for floor eleven, and we rode in silence as the elevator chugged smoothly up the shaft.

The doors opened with a whisper of a sigh, and we stepped out into a hall carpeted in burgundy. The walls were a pale ivory, and the trim was dark cherry. Rich and lustrous, the building screamed *old money, silent money, money and comfort and tradition.*

As we came to the door marked 1133, I thought that Wade had certainly moved up in the world. Chase glanced at me, and I nodded. He pressed the doorbell and chimes rang from within.

A moment later, Wade answered. He gave me a smile, but it faded as Chase stepped forward.

"Wade Stevens? I'm afraid you're going to have to come down to the station and answer a few questions about the murders of five young women. We've had a tip that you're involved, and we need you to fill us in on where you were the nights of each murder."

Wade blinked, slowly. His smile fading into an accusatory glower, he grabbed his leather jacket and silently followed us back to the elevator.

CHAPTER 18

Wade sullenly got into Chase's car, and I kept a close eye on the dark sedan all the way to the FH-CSI building, but apparently Wade decided not to make any trouble. We pulled into headquarters and I joined them on the way in.

Wade gave me a soft smile. "Chase told me you had nothing to do with this."

"You thought I did?" Great, so that was what the scowl was for.

"I just . . . yeah, it crossed my mind. I was wrong. I'm sorry." The leather of his jacket was still new, and it made a crunching noise as he reached over the top of my head to hold the door open for me.

I slid beneath his arm and in through the door. Wade followed, and Chase brought up the rear. We headed toward Conference Room One. Chase shut the door behind us and flipped on the light. Wade offered me a chair, then took a seat.

"Okay, let's get this out in the open," he said. "You got

a tip that said I'm your serial killer. What do you need to prove I'm not, other than my word?"

"What were you doing in the park last night? I know what you told me, but you'd better tell Chase because if the tipster really wants to frame you up, he might be watching you and it wouldn't be hard to make you look suspicious."

"What? What park?" Chase asked.

"I found Wade in the park last night. In fact, we had a nice long talk about what he was doing there, among other things. I don't believe for a moment that he's our killer. But we should get everything out in the open." I leaned forward. "You said you were looking for the killer?"

"Yeah. I decided you guys could use some extra help. When you told me about him, it rang a bell. I thought I remembered someone from a Vampires Anonymous meeting a few months back. He only came once, and something seemed off about him. I remembered he said he lives around the Greenbelt Park District, so I decided to try to ferret him out."

"Why didn't you call us?" Chase jotted something on his pad of paper.

"I did call the station, but they said you were out on a case, so I decided to take a look-see myself. I was going to tell you anything I found out, but when Menolly told me about Morio and the ghosts, and Ivana Krask, it kind of slipped my mind to call." He shrugged.

"Did you find the guy?" I asked as Chase tossed his pad and pen on the table.

Wade shook his head. "No. I scoured the park and all I found were a bunch of ghosts. They're thick there, and frankly it creeped me out, so I left not long after we talked." He motioned to me. "How is Morio, by the way? Any better?"

"I was just going to walk over to the medic unit and find out. But first, I think Chase has a list of dates that he'd like to check you against."

Chase withdrew a sheet of paper from his pocket and consulted it. "Where were you on December third?"

"That's easy enough. December third was the Vampires Anonymous meeting. I was there setting up for the group from the time I woke up—sunset until the meeting broke up at two A.M. Brett was with me. Then, afterward, a group of us decided to go for some late-night bowling."

Chase and I stared at each other.

"Bowling? You bowl?" Chase was trying to repress a smirk.

I broke out laughing. "Why doesn't that surprise me?"

"I happen to love bowling, thank you. I was on a league when I was still alive." Wade scowled at us. "I'll have you know, I used to bowl in the high two hundreds, and I still do."

Recovering his composure, Chase cleared his throat. "What about after that? Were you there till sunrise?"

"No, but after we left there, Brett and Mandy and I hit a new club that's recently opened up."

"*Mandy?* Who's Mandy?" I gave him a saccharine smile but then winked to let him know I was just teasing him.

He frowned and ducked his head. "Mandy Treat is my new girlfriend." But he didn't sound happy about it. "Well, she's my mother's choice of girlfriends for me. I don't really care for dating her, but you know my mother . . ."

I did, indeed, know his mother. And that was why Wade and I had broken up before we ever really got a relationship started. "Yeah, I do. They broke the mold when they made Belinda."

"What's the name of the club?" Chase asked, pen poised.

Wade tossed a packet of matches over to the detective. It had a black cover with white lettering. I picked it up and examined the logo. A single drop of crimson blood dripped from one fang. The lettering read: *The Jagged Fang.*

"The Jagged Fang? That's a new one to me. Why haven't I heard about it?" I passed the matches to Chase.

"Club just opened last month. One of our VA members

is running it—it's far less dangerous than the Fangtabula or Dominick's. Club is for vamps, but also for humans who want to walk on the dangerous side, yet live. No drinking from unwilling customers allowed, no mesmerizing allowed, no minors allowed. No sex on the premises allowed. In other words, an R-rated club."

Chase flipped back through his date book. "Okay, we have your alibi for that night. I'll need to talk to Mandy and Brett, of course. What about for November twenty-sixth, twenty-eighth? Thirtieth? And December first?"

Wade pulled out his PDA and began flipping through the touch screens. "Busy freak, aren't I? Here we go. Twenty-sixth: another Vampires Anonymous meeting. We meet once a week now. After that was over, I don't have an alibi. I went home, watched TV, read, played video games—oh wait, I can prove it with my online login records. I logged in at midnight and played Superhero City until sunrise. We had a raid going on."

A mama's boy *and* a gamer. Joy, that was one boat ride to romance that I was glad I missed.

"Twenty-eighth, I had a date with Mandy and she spent the night."

At my look, he shrugged. "What? She likes me; I don't dislike her even though I'm not that jazzed on dating her, but she's willing. Friends with benefits."

"Nothing wrong with it, if she knows that's all you want out of her." I grinned again.

"The thirtieth, I don't have a strong alibi. But December first? I stayed in. Hung out at my apartment, read, went shopping at Bartell Drugs for odds and ends. I think I still have the receipt with the time stamp on it. I did laundry down in the laundry room at my apartment building. There was one other woman in there and we talked and she mentioned that she had to get to work by six thirty and she only had forty-five minutes to get there, so it had to be between five and six. I suppose if you went door to door, we could find her. And I had a long conversation with my cousin. He called me at six A.M.—nine his time—and we talked for an hour until sunrise."

Chase leaned back in his chair, a smirk on his face. "Wow, Stevens, you really lead an exciting life for a vampire."

Wade eyed him, a slight tinge of red soaking into the gray of his eyes. "Dude, you are lucky I'm not into testosterone games. I could take you down like a pit bull. I may look like a professional geek, but I could rip apart this room in no time." He shifted, the leather of his pants making a subtle noise, and flashed his fangs. I felt a faint quickening through my body. Wade was becoming a badass, and though he was still learning how to wear it, it made him kind of sexy.

Rein it in, girl, I thought. Between Roman, Nerissa, and a tryst here and there with Rozurial, I had enough on my plate. I'd taken Vanzir off the roster—at least until the whole mess with Camille played itself out. And I *so* did not want to be there when Smoky discovered that Vanzir had thrown Camille against a wall and done her. I fully expected bloodshed and wouldn't be surprised if Vanzir bit the big one, and I—for one—was staying out of the way. Big, bad, angry dragon was nothing to mess with.

"How does that hold up for an alibi?" Wade fiddled with the zippers on the sleeves of his jacket.

Chase shrugged and stuck his notebook back in his pocket. "Good with me. To be honest, I really didn't think you were our guy, but as I said earlier, I have to check out every lead. And this guy sounded pretty convincing. Said the hookers were bloodwhores and that you were overheard saying that the only good bloodwhore is a dead one. I didn't believe it, but I have to check out every lead. But why would someone want to frame *you*?"

I glanced at Chase, then at Wade. "Ten to one it was Terrance. He doesn't know yet that you're stepping down from the race. And so this is just one more way of trying to discredit you within the Supe Community."

"Yeah, well he can suck me dry. Remember"—Wade

held my gaze—"you promised that if I withdraw, Terrance will fall."

"I know—and I promise."

"All right then, if we're done here, I've got shit to do." He slipped out the door, as silently as a whisper. Chase and I watched him go.

"Do I want to know what's going down with Terrance and the Fangtabula?" Chase gazed at me.

"No, not really. I'm going to check on Morio. Meet me over there?"

"Sure. I'll just file this tipster under *L* for *loser.*" He hesitated, then added, "Can I tell you something without you telling Delilah?"

"What is it with all of the secrets people have been shoving my way lately? You can tell me, but I don't promise to keep my mouth shut. Not unless I think whatever it is won't hurt her." I was getting tired of being everybody's confidante. Not my nature.

"She'll find out eventually. I . . . I asked Sharah out on a date. I'm not ready to see anybody on a regular basis. I don't know if I ever will be, but I'm lonely and she was mentioning a movie she wanted to see, and I want to see it and it's not like I'm going to sleep with her or anything—" Flustered, he slid into a chair and shook his head. "Maybe it's a bad idea."

"Whoa, whoa! Slow down, dude. Johnson, listen to me." I reached out and held him by the shoulders. "It's okay. Really. Delilah and Shade—it's like they were meant to be together. I know she won't begrudge you this. You don't have to explain to me, or to anybody. Okay?"

He bit his lip, looking both terrified and relieved. "Okay." Taking a deep breath, he let it whistle out slowly. "I think I'm just scared. I know I'm not ready for dating, but . . . I don't like sitting home alone, and it just seemed natural to ask her. I didn't think she'd really accept."

"Chase . . ." I jumped up to sit on the table, swinging my legs as I sat there. "So much is happening to you right now.

You're smart to recognize that you need time to process it. But that doesn't mean you should be *alone*. It doesn't mean you can't reach out to someone for comfort. Just don't mistake it for love. Don't rush it. Don't push it. Don't let yourself be rushed or pushed, either. Let it be whatever it's meant to be—and maybe it's only going to be a movie and a hot dog with a friend. You know?"

Flashing me a soft smile, Chase let out a soft snicker. "How'd you get to be so smart? You sure you're not Dear Abby in disguise?"

"Heaven forbid. Hell, I can't even manage my own life." I paused, then laughed. "Look at us. We're sitting here talking, like old chums. I kind of miss the days when I scared the shit out of you and used to breathe down your neck just to see you jump."

He broke into a loud laugh with me. "Oh, Fanged One, you still scare the shit out of me and I still jump when you surprise me." He paused, then said, "I kind of miss those days, too. I thought for sure you were going to put the fang on me, and more than once, I wondered . . ." Breaking off, Chase let his voice drift into silence.

I didn't want to follow the thread of his thought, but it was better to get it out in the open. I was *really* tired of secrets. "More than once, you wondered what it would feel like? To let me bite you? Drink from you?"

Silently, he nodded, blushing.

"Listen, Chase . . . it can be sensuous beyond all imagination . . . but it's a dark alley for a human to walk. An FBH—even one with an extended life span and burgeoning powers—isn't cut out to be a bloodwhore for long. And the addiction to letting a vampire feed on you is a one-way street. Yes, it's sexy as hell, if your owner wants it to be, but it's not a good idea. That's why I've never fed on Nerissa, and I never will. She's my girlfriend, not my lunch."

His smile flickered, and then he nodded. "Thanks. I needed to hear that. I knew all that, but . . ."

"But you still wondered. It's natural."

"Yeah, there was always the question in the back of my mind. I don't think I'm cut out to be a bloodwhore. But . . . if anybody made it appealing, you would, with your scary badass braids and the way you don't take any crap from anybody. I've learned a lot from you, Menolly. Thank you for that." Standing, he hit my knee with the file in his hand and headed for the door. "Meet you over in Medical."

I followed him out the door and turned the other way, not sure what to think. Chase had never before admitted any fascination with the vampire culture, and I wondered just how many secrets would crawl out of the woodwork now that he'd drunk the Nectar of Life.

Pushing through the doors into the medical unit, I caught sight of Sharah and motioned to her. "How's—"

She shook her head and pulled me into her office. "He's slipping. Listen . . . I've done some research and there's one thing I can think of that might kick him over into recovery, but I don't know how you'd feel about it."

"What does it matter how I feel?"

"Because . . ." She broke off with a sigh, her gaze darting to the side.

"Just tell me."

"Vampire blood. Not enough to turn him, but I've heard it has healing properties when injected into a mortal."

Holy crap. So not what I wanted to hear. So not something I wanted to even think about. "He's not mortal. He's a demon. There's no way to tell what injecting vampire blood will do to him."

"He's not healing, Menolly. The wound on his side won't coagulate."

I glanced back at the waiting room. Camille wasn't there, but Vanzir and Trillian were. "Do they know? Camille?"

Sharah shook her head. "No. I haven't talked to them yet. I wanted to talk to you first before I approached them. If you say no, I'll let it drop. I think the blood should come from you because you're friends. A strange vampire might gain some hold that could be used against him. I trust you not to do that."

"How much do you need?"

Sharah held up a syringe that ran to a tube holding about four ounces. "Doesn't seem like much, does it, to stand between life and death?"

Gravely, I nodded. "Yeah. You sure this will work?"

"No, but if it doesn't, I'm sure he's going to keep slipping and quite possibly die."

"Fucking ghosts. Why won't the wound heal? What's preventing it?"

Sharah motioned for me to take a seat at her station. "The wound came from one of the hungry ghosts—we think it siphoned enough life force off him to weaken his body, and the stake managed to do far more damage than we first thought. There's no way to give him a transfusion of energy, not unless your friend Vanzir can reverse his feeding technique and give instead of take."

I shook my head, not wanting to mention that Vanzir couldn't even *take* energy from anybody now, let alone give it. "No. Not possible. And there are no magical spells to infuse him with life force? To strengthen his powers?"

She frowned and pointed to a stack of books. "I've been reading all day in hopes of finding something that might work. Camille knows of no spell that will help. We don't have Smoky or Roz here to offer advice. I don't dare ask any of the sorcery shops because of your run-ins with Van and Jaycee—they're still out there and they could easily set it up to poison him as well as help him."

I thought of Wilbur, but dismissed the idea. Wilbur was good but not this good. "So . . . the only option you found was vampire blood."

"Yeah, kind of falls out that way."

She sat silently beside me as I contemplated the idea. It wouldn't turn him into a vampire, but it would create a link—one I didn't know if I wanted. And because he was demon, it might create other problems that we couldn't foresee. But the only other option was to let him die. I couldn't do that, not when my blood might hold the answer to his cure.

Finally, I swallowed my resistance. "Go talk to Camille. If she's willing, I'll do it."

Sharah clapped me on the shoulder. "Thanks, Menolly. I know this isn't easy for you. I know how you feel about sharing blood with others."

My thoughts drifted back to Roman. That hadn't been so bad, but this . . . this was no vampire older than the hills, joining me in ecstasy. Morio was seriously wounded and this might save him, but at what cost? Just as Chase had shifted when he drank the Nectar of Life, this could have serious repercussions on a demon. On a human, it would probably strengthen them for a while, cause euphoria, perhaps even permanently shift their aura. But a youkai . . .

Sharah stood, her scrubs making a scratching sound as she slid past me. I watched as she disappeared down the hall. So many troubles. So much anguish and blood and battle. We were steeped in it. We were all walking under the shadow of death now. Camille had her death magic, Delilah was a Death Maiden, and I was dead. And the shadow was growing as the days progressed.

Sometimes I wished Shadow Wing would just make his move, come through, and that somehow in the mad scheme of life, we'd be able to beat him senseless, slit his throat. But the Unraveller, as he was called, was intent on tearing apart the worlds. All chances were that we'd be toast under his feet.

With a silent plea for a little luck, I slipped out of my seat and followed on Sharah's heels. I ignored Trillian and Vanzir as I strode into Morio's room, where Sharah was talking to Camille.

My sister was pale beyond the moon, pale as morning glory under the moon. She looked up at me, her eyes wide.

"Will you do this thing?"

I held her gaze. She was hoping I'd say yes, but I knew Camille. She would never beg me. She would let me decide even if it cost her one of her loves. We were sisters above all else.

Nodding, I reached out and took her in my arms. "I will, if you want me to. I have no idea how it will affect him, but I'm willing to give it a try."

"Then please, save him if you can." She leaned down and kissed the perspiring brow of the fox demon. His eyes were closed and he had tubes and IVs running out of his body till he looked like a machine man. Sweat drenched his forehead and chest, and I could see the wound—it was a horrid gash, gaping and red and swollen against his side. It was being loosely held together by some sort of thread— probably spidersilk—and was oozing a constant stream of blood and pus that trickled into a basin below.

"Oh gods," I whispered. I hadn't realized just how horrible he looked. I turned to Sharah. "Do it." I sat down on a nearby stool and pulled off my jacket, then rolled up my sleeve while Sharah hurried to fetch a needle and tube.

Sharah gazed at the scars on my arm. "Where . . . I don't know if I can find a vein . . ."

I rolled down my sleeve and pulled my braids back. "My neck. Take it from my neck." I fingered the skin until I found my vein—I could feel the slow blood oozing through my system, no longer driven by heartbeat but by whatever force caused the vampirism.

Camille knelt beside me. "Thank you."

"Thank me if it works."

We watched as Sharah prepared the needle—a good three-inch-long spike attached to a syringe that could hold a large test tube for collecting blood. She rubbed my skin with a splash of rubbing alcohol and then, with Camille watching, she plunged the needle under the skin in the side of my neck, sliding the length into my carotid artery.

I barely felt a twinge as the needle entered my body, but the cool metal nestled against me, oddly at home. I could hear the faint gurgle as Sharah slapped a test tube with a vacuum seal into the syringe and the blood began to rise. Out of the corner of my eye, I could see the level slowly filling, angry crimson blood draining out of my body.

Vampire blood was darker, thicker than normal blood, but it was all life force. I didn't need to have it pumping through my system to survive. I just needed to ingest blood and it changed, working its way through my body, through the veins, a magical river of life keeping me on this side of the veil. I would never die from lack of blood, but I might go dormant or mad, aching with hunger.

Sharah finally eased the syringe out and pressed a bandage over my neck. She removed the test tube from the syringe and slid it into a new one. Then she walked over to Morio, and glanced at Camille and me.

"If you want me to stop, say so now. I can't undo it once I inject it into the wound." She waited.

"Please, help him." Camille sucked in a deep breath and let it out slowly, squeezing her eyes shut.

I nodded. "Now."

Now or never. This could heal him or—or, it might do nothing at all. Or it might backfire or take him on a trip he wouldn't be ready for. Morio was caught too deeply by his fever to tell us what he wanted and had to rely on Camille to make the right choices.

As if she were reading my mind, Camille looked up. "He'd say, *Bring it on, babe.* He respects you, Menolly. He's not afraid of the death magic we work. He's not going to quibble over a little vampire blood in his body."

I hoped she was right. Not that I thought Morio would object, but the way the Nectar of Life had rebounded on Chase left me nervous and wondering about just how far we could go messing about with the essential nature of the body. My sisters and I were mixed bloodline, and it had screwed up our own powers. Images of Frankenstein's monster rolled through my head, and Dr. Jekyll and Mr.

Hyde. What would Morio become? A potential monster? Or . . . or maybe I was just being paranoid.

"All right, then." Sharah slowly inched the needle into the angry flesh surrounding the wound, and the three of us watched as my blood filtered into Morio's system.

CHAPTER 19

The room seemed to darken, and there was a long hush as we watched the wound. I wasn't sure what to expect, but there was a sudden hiss and the gash began to foam, a steady stream of oily white liquid pouring out mingled with the crimson of Morio's blood. It drained steadily into the basin, the stench rising.

Morio began to thrash, pouring sweat. He groaned, and the restraints threatened to break as he began to transform into his full demon self.

"Stop this. We're trying to save your fucking life, babe."

Camille leaned over him, avoiding the long claws that grabbed for her. She was holding it together in a scary way. The last time I'd seen this look on her face was when I burst through the door at home, hell-bent on killing and turning my entire family. Her look of desperation had been replaced with one of sheer will, the will of the damned.

With a loud yip that turned into a scream, Morio began shifting so rapidly it was hard to keep track, first to his human self, then his fox self, then demon, then human . . .

all so fast we could barely keep up with him. The strains of so many rapid transformations were taxing him. Sweat soaked the bed, even as the fluids from his side poured in a deluge, waterfalling out of the gash.

A look of horror on her face, Sharah called for security, but they couldn't get near the flailing youkai. But Camille climbed up on the bed, straddling him, holding him down as best she could while they applied heavier restraints. Sharah gave him a shot of something and within seconds, he stopped fighting.

"What's happening to him?" Camille looked up, her expression bleak.

"I don't know . . . but look!" Sharah pointed to the wound. With a hiss, the pus thinned and then became just a trickle of blood flowing, drop by drop, into the basin. Within another minute, the stream stopped.

Sharah moved the container of blood and infection and washed her hands. I helped Camille down off the bed as Sharah examined Morio's side.

"He's beginning to heal." The flesh was mending before our eyes. Muscle and sinew bound together, weaving new threads, coiling and tightening into scar tissue. Within twenty minutes, the wound was still angry and swollen, but the infection looked to be gone.

"I think he's going to be down for some time, but he should make it," Sharah said, straightening her shoulders. She probed the gash. "The infection is gone, and now it's just going to be a matter of how quickly he can recover from the life energy loss. That's something we can't do anything about. It will take time, but now he *has* that time."

Camille dropped to the floor, weeping softly. "Thank you. Thank you for helping him." She gazed up at both Sharah and me. "Without both of you, he'd be dead."

"Hey, my pleasure." Sharah glanced at me over her head. "But we still don't know just what effect the vampire blood will have in his system. You'll need to watch him closely."

She nodded, wiping her face with the back of her hand. "I will."

As I slowly withdrew from the room, followed by Sharah, I felt a weird pull, like I was stretching a rope between me and . . . oh crap. *Morio.* A connection had been formed. What the hell did that mean?

"You get back in there and make sure he's still alive." I whirled on Sharah. "Something's going on. I feel a bond that's been established between the two of us. He's got my blood in him—he's demon. I'm not sure what that's going to do to us."

Sharah stared at me. "What? What do you mean?"

"I mean, some link was created. When I stepped out of the room, I felt the connection stretch. That's not a good thing."

She blinked, and then without another word, she headed back into the room and leaned over him. Lifting his arm, she felt for a pulse, then listened with her stethoscope, then frowned. Camille gave her a frightened look, but Sharah reassured her before rejoining me in the hall.

"He's alive. I don't know what it is. I told you, I wasn't sure just what kind of effect this was going to have on him. Apparently, it triggered a psychic connection between the two of you. But he's alive. Without your blood, he wouldn't be for much longer. Now, if you'll excuse me, I've got to get in an hour or two of sleep. I've been throwing myself into keeping him alive nonstop since you brought him in."

With a weary sigh, she waved lightly and headed off down the hall. I watched her go, then slowly returned to Morio's room. Camille gave me a curious look, but I wasn't sure just what to say. I didn't know what was going on myself.

As I approached the bed, there it was again—a feeling of familiarity, of inner knowing. Morio . . . his long dark hair was damp from his fever, but the nurses were motioning for us to move back so they could change his sheets.

I slipped over to Camille's side. "I think some side effect happened when she gave him my blood."

"What?"

"I think . . . it feels like there's some connection that's established itself between Morio and me. I don't know what it is, if it will last, or anything about it, though." I decided I'd better warn her so she wouldn't be taken by surprise.

She nodded, pensive. "I suppose we won't know how it's going to play out until he regains consciousness, and then you two have to sort it out."

Not sure how she felt, I put a light hand on her arm. "I didn't mean for it to happen—"

Camille let out a small laugh. "Menolly, you saved his life. That's worth any price. Don't apologize. I hope that whatever it is, it's temporary and easy to live with. But we'll find out, I guess."

I paused, then drew her outside the room. "Listen . . . I know about Vanzir. And I won't say anything until you feel you need to. But you can come to me if things get out of hand. Because I guarantee you, Smoky's going to figure it out. That husband of yours is brilliant, but the temper . . ."

Her mouth formed into an O and she backed up. "I didn't want anybody to know." She paused, looking haunted. "It was bad, Menolly. When you took Morio topside, the ghost attacked us again. Vanzir tried to drain it by feeding on it, and I shot an energy burst. The ghost backed off, but the residue of my magic triggered Vanzir. He . . . he yelled at me to run and I tried to climb up but couldn't find the gloves. My hands—the iron rungs . . ."

Shit. I could see it all too easily. In the darkness, with the ghosts and the worry, no gloves to protect her hands . . . Camille was caught between Vanzir's hunger and the ghost's anger. "What happened?" I knew Vanzir couldn't lie to me but wanted to verify what I'd heard.

"Vanzir was caught in a feeding frenzy. I was hunting

for the gloves but then felt something enter my mind. Vanzir started to drink from me—it was like having tentacles hooked into my thoughts, like being drained off a spark at a time. I remembered what he'd said about the magic being like an aphrodisiac and tried to snap him out of it."

"Did he stop?"

"He tried. He looked so tortured, begging me to run. But there was no place for me to go. I'd have to either run back into the tunnels or burn myself on the iron rungs. So I pulled up my skirts and grabbed his hands . . . pressed them to my waist. If I could get him out of my head, I could handle anything else. I mean . . . it's *just* sex. But feeding on my magic—that was so horrible." She squeezed her eyes shut, and hung her head.

"So . . . he realized what you were offering . . ."

"Yes. Vanzir pushed me against the wall and . . . the minute he touched my body, he withdrew from my mind. It was far easier to have sex with him than let him feed off me."

I nodded, understanding how she could think so. For Camille, sex was sex—but her magic, her spirit was something she shared with very few.

"But while we were . . . the Moon Mother came through. Did he tell you . . . ?"

"Yes. About his powers to feed vanishing?"

"That wasn't me who did it. No, the Moon Mother punished him for attacking me."

"What happened afterward?"

"We just stared at each other. I could have killed him, right there, but I understood him too well to do it. I know what I'm like when I'm caught up in the Hunt. Or you—with your bloodlust, and Delilah when she's under the full moon. This was no different. He was trying to save my life by attacking the ghost, and I was trying to save his."

"Damned if you do, damned if you don't."

"Yeah. What's he going to do now that he doesn't have his power? He may have said he didn't like being a dream-chaser demon, but I think he was lying. And now . . . now he's bare and open like a raw wound. Circumstances fucked us both over."

I nodded. "That's pretty much what he said. I ordered him to tell me, by the way. It wasn't his fault he spilled the beans. I just wanted to . . ."

"To protect me? I can't say that it didn't affect me, but damn it, we were backed into a corner. I'm just afraid that Smoky's not going to understand. And I have to tell him, and Trillian and Morio, because somebody . . . sometime is going to sense that I've been with an outsider. And I'm terrified they'll kill Vanzir."

She shuddered, and a tear streaked down her face. "Things are so bad. This just is . . . so bad . . ."

"I'll help keep the peace. Maybe you should tell Smoky away from the house, and we'll send Vanzir away for a few days to get him out of the way. Trillian might be able to calm the dragon down, too." I hesitated, then whispered, "I'm sorry. I'm sorry it had to be that way."

She flashed me a wan smile. "You know, the irony is—if I weren't happily married, I'd probably jump at the chance to sleep with Vanzir. He's hot. I can't help but admit: I liked it. On one level, I wanted him. But I never would have acted on it, because I'm in love with Morio, with Trillian and Smoky."

Nodding, I led her back to Morio's room. "It's okay, sweetie. It's okay. I know you would have done anything else if you could have. You didn't do anything wrong, and I think you've got remarkable empathy and restraint in not reaching out and killing Vanzir."

"I think the Moon Mother already did worse. Could you get me some water? My eyes are so dry they hurt, I've been crying so hard."

As I moved toward a row of vending machines, she entered the room and took her place by Morio's side again. Once more, I felt the pull to be there, near him. I quickly plugged four quarters into the soda machine and punched the water selection. Pulling the bottle out of the slot, I headed back to find that during our absence, Morio had woken up.

Camille was smiling, and I'd never seen such a look on anyone's face—absolute joy and relief. She laughed at something he whispered and leaned down to give him a long, leisurely kiss. He pulled her into his arms, and with shock, I saw him reach under her skirts, and she was letting him.

"Whoa, you two. I'm pretty sure Sharah would nix any horseplay. Take it easy, dude, you're still recovering—" But then, I stopped. The wound on his side was almost knit through and the gash was a thin red line that oozed clear liquid, free of toxin and pus.

"Wow. You've come a long way in fifteen minutes."

Morio pushed himself to a sitting position—slowly, to be sure, but it was something I hadn't expected to see for some time.

"I'm not ready to get out of bed yet, and you're right. Play of any kind would be a bit much for me right now." He glanced over at me and stopped, his gaze catching my own. "Menolly . . ."

As his voice drifted off, he opened his arms and I walked into his embrace without thinking. It seemed the most natural thing in the world to lean down to kiss him, but, startled, I caught myself before our lips met and pulled away. Camille watched us, eyebrows arched, but she didn't look mad, just confused.

"What the fuck?" Morio let go of me abruptly and pulled back, but his hands lingered along my waist.

"This must be the link," Camille said. "Menolly—do you think the two of you imprinted?"

Morio looked from her to me, then her again. "Link? Imprint? What's going on?" He looked confused. "What the fuck just happened, babe?"

"You . . . uh . . . Menolly?" Camille shot me a pleading look.

I let out a sigh. "To save your life—you were terribly sick with an infection—Sharah injected some of my blood into your wound. You have a little bit of me flowing through your veins. And it appears to have created a link between us."

He let out a sharp yip, but I didn't kid myself. It wasn't a compliment. "I was *that* sick?"

"Yes, love," Camille said quietly. "You were *that* ill. We stood a good chance of losing you."

"But do you know what vampire blood does to my kind?"

"No, that's the point. We didn't. We still don't, though I'm getting the impression it's not a good thing. Not entirely." Camille slid into a nearby chair, and I joined her in the one next to it.

"Tell us," I said. "What do we have to expect now?"

"Vampire blood creates a bond between the giver and receiver, a lot like siring a vampire but without the subservience. It also . . . I'll be a whole lot stronger for a *long, long* time, once I've healed up. And . . ." He glanced at Camille. "Don't worry, my love—I won't forsake you for your sister. But for the next few weeks, it's best if Menolly and I aren't left in the same room alone. My demon nature will be at the forefront a lot . . ."

I didn't want to admit it, but I knew what he was talking about. I wanted to strip down and join him under the covers, to push my sister out of the way and tell her to leave the room. Apparently Morio wasn't feeling quite so possessive, or he wasn't showing it, thank the gods.

"He's right. You're my blood, my sister. And I don't know how long this will last. Morio will be in the hospital for a little while longer . . . I'll just try to keep out of your way," I said. I had no intention of stealing my sister's husband.

As I headed for the door, the bond threatened to snatch me back, to prevent me from leaving. Pushing the feeling away, with an abrupt jolt, I launched myself into the

hallway, ignoring the urge to return to the room where
Morio lay.

This was a fine mess, but my guess was that it would
be temporary. Until it wore off, we'd just be cautious and
avoid being caught alone. Because I knew, were we in the
same room, the pull would be so strong that we'd be in
each other's arms. And the last thing in the world I wanted
to do was interfere in Camille's affairs.

As I hurried out of the medic unit, I didn't know where I
was going. I just knew that I needed to put some distance
between the fox-demon and me. I found myself roaming
down to the Wayfarer, which was open and busy.

Derrick was behind the counter, and the drinks were
flowing. I watched him from the back for a little while, satisfied that he was doing a good job. On a whim, I called
Roman.

"Hey dude, how would you like to see my bar?" I asked
when he smoothly answered the phone.

With a low laugh that set me on edge, he whispered,
"I've seen it before, so no, but I'd like to see *you*. If that's
an invitation, I'm in the car now. I'll be there in five minutes."

As I hung up, a shiver ran up my spine. The pull to
Morio had been strong. I needed to blow off steam and I
didn't trust myself with Nerissa right now. I was too set
on edge. I wanted to feed, even though I wasn't hungry.
Roman was my best choice at this moment.

I wandered over to the jukebox and slipped a few quarters in. "Tainted Love" by Marilyn Manson, "Sister Midnight" by Bowie, "Personal Jesus" by Depeche Mode . . .
all good dance songs. And sometimes dancing was the only
way to get some of the hunger out of my body. I understood
why Camille liked the pounding rhythms she listened to—
ear sex, she called her alternative grunge-goth music.

I began to sway to the music. I might not be curvy, but my hips knew what to do, and the tightness of my jeans accentuated my hunger, making me ache for someone's touch, for the feel of hands on my body. I'd finally accepted my sexuality and it had come through like gangbusters.

A few of the other customers joined me and we rose and fell to the music, letting it move our bodies as it raced from speaker to speaker around the bar. The beat throbbed through the walls and floor, reverberating in my stomach. And then I looked up to see Roman standing at the door.

Everyone fell back as he entered the room. His hair was long and sleek, and he was wearing a pair of leather jeans and a jacket the color of crimson. He took one look at me, and the next second, he took me in his arms. As we danced, weaving and spinning to the music, everything else fell away and I began to transfer the hunger I'd felt for Morio to Roman. Before I knew it, we were kissing, my arms draped over his shoulders, his pelvis pressed against mine, as he wrapped his arms around my waist.

I rolled my head back, fangs extended, and let out a long hiss. He echoed the greeting in return and his eyes flashed as he nuzzled my neck. "We need to fly," he whispered. "We need to run, to own the city."

Without a word, he led me to the door and we raced into the darkening streets. We explored the city via the rooftops, running so fast, so hard that the lights were a long, neon blur, streaks of time-lapse photography. Cars passed by in slow motion, the cacophony of a hundred conversations all blended into one. Building after building fell beneath our feet as the hiss of silent snow fell around us and we claimed the city rooftops for our own.

And still the music echoed from behind me. I could hear it; it had worked its way into my system. Then we were standing atop a rooftop, and his lips were on mine.

I returned the kiss, hungry and fierce. "I need to drink from you."

He stripped the jacket away from his neck. "Please, my sweet. Drink. Drink deep, drink hard."

I sank my fangs into the cream-pale flesh, and a shudder ran through my body as they slid easily into his neck. Blood welled up, sweet liqueur in my mouth, ambrosia of the damned. No longer metallic, but like a fine port, thick and heady. I swallowed, coaxing more into me, and then felt Roman unzip his pants.

Struggling to keep control, I pulled away and stripped out of my jeans and shirt. His gaze followed me, like a cheetah stalking his prey. His cock rose thick and pulsing and I throbbed deep inside, wanting to impale myself on him.

With a shriek, I wrapped my legs around his waist as he cradled my ass and thrust into me. As his delicious length and width spread me wide, I plunged my fangs back into him and he propped my back against a wall for leverage, fucking me hard.

As he drove into me time and again, I coaxed his blood, drawing my tongue along his neck as I sipped on the violent wine. His mother was the Queen of Vampires, Blood Wyne, and the royalty rang in his life force—a dusky, rich, ancient taste of power. He was a god of ice, a god of heat, a god who had witnessed history come and go. He was Roman, and he wanted me.

"Come, Menolly, come, beautiful one." His left hand slid off my butt, around to finger me, driving me further into the blood lust.

"Ivana Krask calls me *dead girl*," I whispered.

"Oh, but you are *my* dead girl. My consort. You may have all the playmates you wish, and you may marry your girlfriend and I will dance at your wedding, but I have chosen you to be my consort. I am the son of Blood Wyne. And at the cocktail party coming up at the Clockwork Club, I will unveil our pairing."

And then he began to thrust in earnest. His lips met my neck as his fangs pierced my flesh, and I lost myself in the haze of blood and passion, sliding into an orgasm from which I did not know if I could extricate myself. At last my mind stilled, with only the sound of the falling snow to sing to us.

CHAPTER 20

"Roman, what did you mean about unveiling our pairing at the Clockwork Club?" The pressure off, I slid back into my clothing, then leaned against the railing that overlooked the street twenty stories below. The lights of the city were soft against the blanket of falling snow. Silent cars trailed slowly through the streets, hesitant ants slipping over the ice.

He hopped up to crouch on the lip of the building. A foot wide, the concrete walkway offered no handholds or supports. A balance beam, a game of Russian roulette, and yet he was rock steady.

"They're having a pre-Solstice party, just a cocktail affair. I want to announce you then."

"What does that mean, exactly?" I wasn't sure what to expect.

"We will attend the party as a couple, and I will announce that you are now my consort. I have a standing in the community—"

"You mean your will *is* the community's will." I was beginning to sort out and understand the nature of Earthside vampire politics and wondered how I'd managed to stay so aloof from them until now. Though, to be fair to myself, we'd been rather busy with Shadow Wing and his retinue.

"Well, yes. I control the vampire community on this continent, for the most part. And once I announce you as my official consort, you will wield far more power than you do now. You will almost be a queen in your own right. And I think you shall need that power during the coming months." He paused. "I have foresight, to some extent. I am aware of your war against the demons."

At my jerk of the head, he laughed. "Oh, Menolly, I'm aware of much more than you think I am. Being my consort means you will have that many more resources to call upon. Should the Demon Lord decide to come through the portal himself, it means the vampire community will rally to help you if you demand it. As my consort, you will wield that power."

I stared at him. "You mean that if you snapped your fingers, the vampires around here would come running? Wade's been trying to establish a communal effort for years with Vampires Anonymous, and he still can't get them to work together. Oh, and speaking of . . . What about Terrance? He tried to frame Wade for the murders our serial killer is responsible for."

"If you become my consort and lend Wade your backing, he will have a much easier time. You think the vampires of the Clockwork Club wield authority? They kneel to me. We who live in power can exert a great deal of influence. *If we choose.* Which is another reason Terrance must die. He refuses to bow to our demands. He would set himself up as a petty general. We . . . *I* . . . am the power behind the public face of the vampire community in North America."

"Who decided to create the Regencies? Wade led me to believe he had a hand in it."

Roman shook his head. "No. Blood Wyne—my mother—decided it was necessary. It cements the family power, while offering a chance for nonroyal vampires to help decide local policies. Each continent will be divided up into several Regencies and the sons and daughters of Blood Wyne will oversee the Regents. The times are changing. As much as I fear my mother, she has finally convinced me of the necessity of an active monarchy."

"So how will this work?" Wade had told me one thing, but when I thought about it, his explanation had never been very clear.

"Blood Wyne will emerge from the shadows for the world to know. However, she will speak through her children, who will speak through the Regents on each continent. And the Regents will form the treaties with the breathers for vampire rights in exchange for certain concessions. The Regency was planned to be an elective office, but that is proving problematic so we are scrapping that plan and choosing the Regents for our mother, making sure they are powerful but balanced, and not terribly bloodthirsty. Neither Terrance nor Wade would do the job right."

"So you will be appointing the Regents?"

"Ostensibly they will be elected, but yes, in truth, the Regents will be vampires from the Old World, who already possess the strength and authority to make policy."

I snorted. "You're rigging the elections."

"If you like, yes. And Terrance's death will be a statement to all vampires living within the Northwest Vampire Dominion. They will know that Blood Wyne and her children are taking control, regardless of whether this be the New World or Europe." He laughed. "Even I knew that my mother would make her move one day. There is no question of her allowing power to be diluted too far from the throne. I may not like her, but she is the queen and I will obey."

It occurred to me that Roman and Wade had something in common there. Only, Belinda Stevens was pretty much relegated to queen bee of her family. "So, when will you take Terrance down?"

Roman laughed again. "Soon. Would you like to be there?"

My fingers itched to see Terrance get his just due. "If possible, yes."

"I'll remember that. Now, in terms of your vampire serial killer, what did Ivana find out for you?"

"Nothing about him, but she helped with the ghosts." I leaned over the railing, staring out into the city. "We have to find him. If he hasn't killed again, he's bound to soon. I don't want to see another woman lose her life to him."

At that moment, my cell phone rang. I pulled it out and gave Roman an apologetic smile. "Sorry, I have to answer. Could be . . . Hello?"

"Menolly, there's been another murder. Get down to the Greenbelt Park District. A back alley near the diner. Follow the lights of the patrol cars." Chase's voice was abrupt, and he sounded tired.

"Fuck! Damn it to hell. Another one." I shoved my cell back in my pocket. "I have to get back to the bar. I need my Jag. What's the quickest way back?"

"Can't you fly?" Roman's brow narrowed. He looked confused.

"Fly? Oh babe, sorry. And I'm no good at doing the bat thing, either. I am vampirically challenged."

He snorted. "Very well. Come here."

Enfolding me in his arms, he pulled me up to stand beside him on the walkway. Before I had the chance to say a word, he had tipped us sideways and we were plunging toward the ground. I was about to scream when we caught up short on the breeze and, like a rocket, blurring through the streets, we flew.

We passed through the blur of concrete and lights faster than I'd thought possible. Within a couple of minutes, we were standing beside the bar, and I was leaning against my Jag.

"You have to teach me that," I said, a faint smile on my face. "You want to come with?"

Roman shook his head. "No, this is not my affair. But go and good hunting. Stop him. I will be in touch." And like a dark shadow, he was gone and within a moment, a dark limo pulled away from the curb up ahead and sped into the night.

I took a moment to recoup and then climbed into my Jag and slammed the door. As I fastened my seat belt and started the car, I couldn't help but wonder where everything was leading me. I'd killed Sassy and reclaimed a friendship I'd thought long gone. My daughter, Erin, was set to work with a group I approved of. Nerissa and I were in love and engaged. Roman had claimed me for his consort. And over everything, Shadow Wing still loomed, dark and ominous.

And here, tonight, murder reigned. Bodies here, bodies there, corpses, bodies, everywhere, and not a killer in sight to catch.

I parked near the first patrol car I found and headed toward the sounds emerging from the alleyway ahead. This time, the girl was still warm. A fresh kill meant that our vampire was probably still in the area. I was looking for Chase when I got a call from Wade.

"Menolly, I think I've got something for you. I was trying to remember what seemed wrong about that one vampire I told you about. Tonight, I was watching TV and it hit me."

"Talk to me, babe. We just found another victim and he might still be in the area." I caught sight of Chase, over by a prone body, and waved to him. Pressing my phone closer to my ear to block out the low buzz of voices coming from the cops, I said, "What have you got?"

"He was wearing a clerical collar."

"Say what?" I leaned against my car, wondering if I'd heard him right.

"I said, he was wearing a clerical collar. That's what struck me as so odd."

"You think he may be a priest?"

"No—I'm thinking he may have *been* one. Or a minister. Or some other member of the clergy." He paused. "If so, being turned into a vampire could very well have messed with his belief system and mind bad enough to make him kill. Remember, I was a psychologist before I was killed. This would be the classic setup for a serial killer of the undead set."

"But why would he kill one type of woman, over and over?"

"Think about it for a minute." Wade let me figure it out for myself.

"Oh, Great Mother." And I knew. I knew exactly why our killer had turned into a serial killer. "He's attacking his sire, over and over."

"There you have it." I couldn't see him through the phone, but I could hear Wade smiling.

"I've got to go. I need to tell Chase what we're dealing with."

"Do you want me down there? Maybe I can help."

I thought. Camille and Trillian were spent. Morio was out of commission. Vanzir was at home protecting Iris and Maggie. Smoky and Roz were gone. Delilah was still recovering from her injury. It was either wait for Shade to get here or . . .

"Yeah." I gave him the address. "Hurry."

"Chase!" I slapped my phone shut and hurried over to the detective. "I know why he's killing them. I know who we're looking for."

"Who is he?" Chase whirled, a look of relief on his face.

"I don't have a name, but I've got his profile. Wade remembered that the guy who seemed odd—that he was wearing a clerical collar."

Chase shook his head. "And?"

"Ten to one our suspect was a priest or other clergy member while alive. We think his sire was posing as a prostitute. This would explain why he's targeting hookers with similar looks. His sire probably has long brown hair and was around that age when she was turned."

Illumination washed over Chase's face. "Crap. And when he was turned . . ."

"Right—he had a psychotic break. His conscience couldn't reconcile his old beliefs with his new state of being. Wade's on his way to help. Now that we know what his motives are, maybe we can track him."

Chase nodded. "Got your drift." He put in a call to Yugi. "Listen, check on any priests or clergy members that have gone missing over the past six months for me, would you?" He glanced at me and added, "Also, any who have died in that time period. I need the info ASAP. Find out the locations of where they died or went missing, too."

As he hung up, we came to the girl. She was splayed out like the others, her skirt ripped away from her, her private areas bloody and maimed. He was getting worse, that much was apparent. I averted my eyes, wanting to give her privacy, though I knew she would never have privacy again until she was in the grave, and then she'd have an eternity of it.

Chase hung his head and let out a long sigh. "He sure hates hookers. Probably women in general."

"I'm so tired of this shit," I whispered, turned away.

"So am I." Chase slid a hand on my shoulder. I glanced at it, considering shaking him off—I really wasn't in the mood to be comforted—but realized he meant well.

"I can tell by the smell, even from here, that we're dealing with the same vampire. The scent of death and mold and . . . mold . . ." *Wait a minute.* "I smell mold."

I hurried to her side and knelt down, sniffing near her neck. "Chase, there's only a residue of the scent, but she's been around viro-mortis slime. And I guarantee you that she hasn't been prowling around in the tunnels. This verifies it, he's using Underground Seattle—the hidden part—as his base. He must have brushed up against a wall. This smells like green viro-mortis slime, so it wouldn't be too dangerous to him."

"You mean we have to go back down there? With those ghosts?" Chase paled.

"No. I mean *I* have to go back down there. You stay topside. I'll wait for Wade, though. Maybe together, he and I can trace our vamp. At least Ivana Krask ate up a lot of the ghosts . . . at that one particular juncture."

Chase's phone rang and he flipped it open. "Yes? What?" He shifted to pull out his pen and notebook, jotting something down as he listened. "Right. Where was he last seen? . . . Good work."

After he hung up, Chase scribbled on another sheet and tore it off, handing it to me. "We have our man. A priest named Charles Shalimar disappeared two months ago. Guess where he disappeared from?"

"The Greenbelt Park District?"

"Bingo. There's a Catholic church near the park—Our Lady of Mercy—and several priests live at the rectory. Charles didn't come home from a late-night visit to the hospital where one of his parishioners had asked for him. From what Yugi said, someone looked into the disappearance but nothing was found, and for some reason, nothing more was ever done or said."

"Where was he last seen?"

"He said good-bye to the night nurse after his charge died and mentioned something about walking home. The hospital is about ten blocks from the church and the quickest route would have taken him right through the park."

Chase held up his phone. Yugi had e-mailed him a picture of the priest. He looked to be in good shape for his age and physically fit. But not fit enough to fight off a vampire.

"The park . . . where we've found most of the victims."

"Yeah. Apparently he's returning to the scene of his own murder."

I pulled out my cell. "Can you e-mail me that picture, so I know who I'm looking for?"

"Sure thing." He punched in my number. "One other thing, Menolly."

"What?"

"Be careful. Yugi mentioned that we've been getting reports tonight of vampires around the city being attacked. It looks like the Earthborn brotherhood's up in arms and taking action. Two members of the cult have shown up dead with vampire punctures. I'm going to have to go on TV with a press conference here in a bit."

Great, one more thing to worry about. I nodded, and as soon as Yugi beamed me a picture of the good priest, I jogged back to the manhole cover to wait for Wade. I was tempted to head down without him, to rampage through every tunnel and opening, but I knew better. Dealing with a psychotic vampire wasn't going to be easy, even with my strength. Psychosis made for strength.

While I waited, I thought over the situation. There were far-reaching consequences that I really didn't want to see happen. The fallout onto the vampire rights movement was going to be deadly. For one thing, the church was not going to be forgiving of a vampire turning one of their priests.

They'd been relatively quiet on the whole issue, only issuing a statement that once a mortal died, his or her soul moved on so whatever was left could not be considered the same person as they were before. Thank heavens, the law ignored their moral imperative, because they were wrong. All vampires retained their souls—we were stuck in our bodies, unable to break free until the sun, a stake through the heart, or in some cases extreme fire put an end to us.

But although the church had not been our friend, neither had it been our enemy. No, it had been the fringe cults that had sprung up. When the portals opened and we came over from Otherworld, the cults had taken root. They'd grown when the Earthside Supes came out of the closet. The fringe faction were reactionary. They didn't have much to lose, unlike the government and religious institutions, so they could afford to become extremists.

But with this, would the truly religious take up the crusade against vampires? Would they join the ranks of the Earthborn Brethren? And what would they do once they found out about the demons?

All of this was running through my head as I waited for Wade. Half a block away, Chase and his men worked over the crime scene. To pass the time, I pulled out my phone and punched speed dial for home. Iris answered.

"Iris, hey . . ." I stopped. How the fuck could I tell her everything that had passed so far this evening? Luckily, she'd already heard some of it.

"Menolly! Where are you? Camille called, so worried about you. She told me what happened at the hospital."

I could hear the question behind her words. "I'm all right. I had to get out of there. The pull to Morio was too strong. I spent some time with Roman to take the edge off. But I've got news about our vampire serial killer—he was a priest, and he's targeting women who remind him of his sire, who posed as a hooker. I'm waiting for Wade. We're going back in the tunnels to find him."

"What about the ghosts?" Her voice was soft, a tremor of fear behind it.

"Ivana dealt with most of them. And hey, two vampires are better than one, right?"

"Just you be careful, missy. Maggie needs you. We all need you." She hesitated, then added, "You know none of this is your fault, right?"

"Morio is. I know people are saying no, he just was in the wrong place at the wrong time, but the fact is he pushed me out of the way to save my life, and he almost died for it. I'll never forget it. I'll never look at him without remembering that."

"Menolly, do you think Chase feels that way about Zachary? Zach did the same thing, and Karvanak paralyzed him. He's forever maimed for performing a selfless act. But Chase doesn't blame himself, does he?"

"I don't know. Maybe he should. Maybe not, but *I* can't forget it. The look on Camille's face, and what happened to her afterward—"

"What are you talking about?"

Crap. I almost blurted out Camille and Vanzir's secret. "Nothing. Never mind and please, don't ask." With relief, I saw Wade pull up in his black Beamer. "Wade's here. I have to go. I'll call you as soon as I'm able. But please, don't worry. We'll be okay. We should be fine, especially now that we know who we're looking for."

She didn't answer, but I could hear the sprite's soft breathing. Feeling under the gun, I sought for something else to soothe her worry. "I have to do this. We can't let any more women die—and there was another murder tonight."

"I know," Iris finally said. "I just don't want you going down there feeling guilty over Morio. I don't want your subconscious doing anything to get you hurt. Sometimes you have more conscience than I think is good for you, girl."

"I have to. Otherwise, I'd just be another monster." Hanging up, I slid my phone in my pocket, watching as Wade hustled over to my side. "Yo. We've got to get moving. He could be long gone by now."

"Do you really think he is?"

I shook my head. "No. Actually, I think his lair is near here."

"If things end up playing out the way we think they are, I wouldn't worry about him disappearing. He's pulled to this area. I worked up a quick profile based on everything we talked about. He's probably feeling so much guilt over either fucking a hooker, or even thinking about it, that he's compelled to stay here. He's constantly searching out his sire, and—in his mind—killing her over and over again. But because she's a vampire, she can't die and his subconscious knows that. So he has to strike again and again. In a sense, he's trying to cope with a feeling of impotence since he can't seem to strike her dead."

I stared at Wade. "We really need to talk more often. Crap, that's good. And we *are* dealing with a priest." I told him what Chase and I had found out about Charles Shalimar.

"That adds a whole new layer of guilt. I guess we're good to go."

I brought out several wooden stakes, handing him a couple of them, fixing several in my own belt. Then I handed him a cross.

"What the . . . ? Religious objects don't work on us." He took the wooden T and frowned at it. "What should I do with this?"

"Ah, it won't work on you or me, but remember—he was a priest. He's had a psychotic break. The cross may very well carry some impact with him since he is a believer and he sees himself. . . . well, hell . . . I don't know exactly what he thinks he's thinking, but it can't hurt to try. The crosses won't actually hurt him, but he might *think* they will. And that could buy us valuable time."

"Brilliant. So, shall we?" He motioned to the gaping hole.

I flipped open my phone and called Chase. He might be only a block or so away, but it was easier to call than run over there. He answered. "Chase, Wade and I are headed down. I suggest you keep some of your men in the area for a while."

"I'll stay myself. We'll be over in a few. And, Menolly—"

"Yes?"

"Be careful."

I slid my phone back in my pocket and looked at Wade. "Time to go hunting, babe." And I jumped into the hole, floating down, hoping that this time we'd successfully bag our quarry.

CHAPTER 21

The tunnels were becoming all too familiar. Old friends, almost, or rather—frenemies. They were comforting in their darkness, and I felt at home in the dusky passages, but they were also fraught with danger and my common sense kept me alert.

"I smell something," Wade said. "Blood."

I inhaled deeply and the coppery scent spread through my body. "Blood. Of course—he has to be covered with her blood. You didn't see . . ." Visions of her mutilated body raced through my mind and I tried to shake them away. "He has to be covered in her blood. Follow the scent and we follow him."

And so, silent, we tracked him through the tunnels. We headed in the direction of the passage where we'd found the shadow men, but fifty feet or so before the fork, the scent led us to the left wall of the passage. It was brick and seemingly solid. I frowned, running my hands over the aged tablets. And then I felt it—a thin line, running vertically.

"I think I found it," I whispered, keeping my voice so

low that only another Supe could hear me. Wade nodded
as I traced my hand along the crack. It was in the shape of
a door, and there must be a trigger stone. But as I felt for
some indentation, protrusion, or other anomaly, a shriek
behind us caught me off guard.

I whirled to find myself staring at a wispy cloud, tendrils emerging from a vaporous cloud that coiled like a
serpent in front of me. Wade slowly turned, and I could
feel him stiffen, staring at the creature. The tentacles of fog
danced, serpentine in the darkness, glowing with a faint
incandescence. They spiraled, reaching out to brush my
face. I steeled myself, forcing myself not to move. Until we
knew what it wanted, whether it would be friend or foe, I
didn't want to startle it.

The form stretched, writhing in the air, as if in slow
motion, and brought one slow tendril around to hook
over my shoulder. I didn't want it to encircle my neck and
quickly stepped back from the wisps of fog.

As I moved, there was a sudden hiss from the creature
and the tendril that had been trying to loop around my
neck lashed back, then whipped across my face, leaving a
stinging slash.

Crap. Not good! I suddenly realized that, vampire or
not, Wade didn't have any formal training in how to fight.
I'd have to protect him as well as take care of myself.

But he surprised me. He did a quick cartwheel out of
the way and came up in a crouch, reaching into his jacket
for something. I didn't have time to see what, but I decided
that if the spirit could materialize long enough to touch me,
I could touch it. I whirled, kicking toward the center, and
was pleasantly surprised when my heel made contact. The
cloud form moved back, just a little, but enough to tell me
that we could fight it.

It was materializing even more as we watched. The
vaporous shape was condensing, congealing into a creature right out of Lovecraftian nightmare. Hideous olive-
green tendrils streamed out from every side—there must

have been fifty of them. Visions of the Karsetii demon flashed through my mind, but this was no Karsetii. Ghost or demon—I did not know, but it was after us and that was enough for me.

As I tried to aim for the center, Wade darted in, a Taser in hand, and he managed to make contact. For a moment, the creature blinked in and out, then two of the tentacles snapped at him, knocking him back against the wall with a resounding thud.

I did a running flip, aiming straight for the center, feet wheeling over my head. A two-footed landing, right into the core of the monster, knocking it back as the impact of my weight slammed into it. The moment I felt it whip back, I broke my jump, landing in a crouch in front of it. As I raised my head, with my fangs fully descended, the creature came racing back for me. I screamed and grabbed the nearest tentacle, attempting to use it like the chain of a mace to whirl the monster through the air.

The thing was both heavy as hell and unwieldy, but I managed to gain momentum and sent it slamming into the wall. At that moment, Wade blurred by, landing on top of the thing. He sank his fangs into the materialized spirit, and an ear-piercing shriek filled the tunnel.

I scrambled on top of it next to him, adding my fangs to the fray. The monster writhed beneath us, tendrils attempting to dislodge us, but we were no ordinary mortals, and it couldn't pull us off. One tentacle coiled around my waist, attempting to squeeze me, but I just bit harder and the shriek continued.

Wade clasped his hands together and brought them down in a double-handed blow that thundered into the core of the monster. It shuddered. Taking my cue from him, I followed suit and we pounded the living crap out of it.

A moment later, the creature began to dematerialize, and within seconds it vanished, leaving us to fall to the floor. I scrambled to my feet and glanced around. No sign of it.

Wade picked himself up and shook his head. "Crap. Is this what you guys do for fun?"

"Mostly," I said, wondering if it would be back—and would it bring friends?

"No wonder you stay in such good shape. Or your sisters, rather."

I snorted, but I knew what he meant. I'd never change shape. Not now. Once you were a vampire, you stayed the way you were when you'd died. In a perverse, vanity-induced way, I was glad that—if I had to be a vampire—I looked good and was young enough to retain my beauty. I didn't admit that much, although I knew Camille would understand me, but it was true when I really let myself think about it.

"Come on. We have to get hold of him before that motherfucker comes back with its brothers. Or Mommy. I have no idea what it was." That was actually a lie. Though I didn't know what it was, I'd figured out that it was some sort of demon, probably another guardian sent by the Demon Underground to replace the shadow men.

I went back to the door and Wade joined me. We searched in vain for a trigger to open it. "So if the catch isn't here, then maybe . . ." I turned to the opposite wall. "Let's look over here. There has to be something to open this mother."

Wade took one section of the wall and I took another. After a few minutes, he whistled. "Menolly, look—what do you think?" He pointed to a small metal plate against one of the bricks, three rows up from the bottom. It was directly opposite the outline of the door.

"Go for it." I readied myself, making certain the stakes on my belt were easy access.

Wade pressed against the catch and I heard a faint click. The door shivered and popped an inch. We could push it open now, and I reached out and gave it a quick shove. It slowly opened, leading into a dimly lit passage.

"Come on. The scent of blood is stronger here." I ducked

in, Wade following me. The tunnel was brick and the floor of the passage was lined with cobblestones. I glanced around, looking for the light source, then saw it up ahead. A lantern, hanging from a hook on the side of the wall. There were several doors off this passage, and I had the feeling we were within reach of our prey.

I took the lead, running lightly to the first door, which was off to the right. I peeked in—the door had long been broken in—but it was only a musty, empty chamber. I was about to move forward when Wade stopped me.

"The scent—it leads in here. Can't you smell it?"

I forced myself to take another breath and yes, there it was. "You think another secret passage?"

"I wouldn't be surprised. We've found one . . . why not another?"

As we paused by the entrance, I examined the floor. "Look." Footprints in the dust—and they led right to the opposite wall. I followed them, coming up against another brick front. I scanned the area for a metal plate. And bingo, like clockwork, there it was, this time off to the side. I motioned for Wade to give it a press and when the door opened, we sprang inside, hoping to get a heads-up on our quarry if he were there.

Surprise. The chamber into which we entered was a natural cave, not another room. It looked to be about twenty feet high and was rounded, narrowing at the other end. But still, a dim light shone through the inky darkness, and lanterns lined the walls in strategic places, lighting a curving trail through a mass of boulders and cavern formations.

"Notice anything odd about the lanterns?" Wade whispered.

I frowned, staring at them for a moment. Then I saw it. "No flame. They aren't fire-based. But he was an FBH—he doesn't have magic. What's going on?"

We approached the nearest lamp and examined it closely. I realized it was sealed—a sealed glass case—and as I pressed my face to the glass, a face in the glowing light stared back at me. Inhuman, with slanted eyes and a pursed mouth. The creature had no nose and no real form other than an amorphous shimmer of light. It reminded me, vaguely, of the tentacle monster we'd just fought.

"Crap—I think this is a young version of what we fought out there—captured inside some sort of glass. But mere glass couldn't hold this thing. So it must be some sort of magical trap."

Wade shook his head. "Something's going on here. No normal vampire would have access to anything like this. Especially a newly minted one. *Especially* a psychotic one. I have the feeling we're on the edge of something bigger here—bigger than you, me . . ."

I thought of the Demon Underground. Could they have made a deal with the killer? Why would they? If he posed a threat, they'd just stake him and be done with it. No, there was something going on that eluded our grasp. I thought about smashing the container, letting the creature out, but there was no guarantee that it wouldn't turn and attack us. After all, it had been imprisoned, and it wasn't going to be happy with vampires. Or maybe—

"Maybe this isn't the work of Charles. Maybe he's just taking advantage of it? He might have stumbled on this—and I think I know who did this. Or at least, I have a general idea. I doubt they even know he exists."

"They who?"

I stared over at Wade. We hadn't told him about Shadow Wing; we hadn't told him about any aspect of the demon war. So he wouldn't know about the Demon Underground, either. Debating whether to say anything without first talking to Delilah and Camille, I opted for caution's sake. Wade and I were friends again, but he'd have to prove himself before I could trust him again.

"I can't tell you that right now . . . you'll have to wait for later and trust me, you'll understand why. But I am going to tell you this: Be very careful down here. Go after Charles only. Forget everything else you see—it's in your own best interests. There are powers far, far greater than you or me at work, and though I can't talk about them, I need you to obey me on this."

He considered my words. Finally, he nodded. "Very well. I'll take your word for it now, but I want to know everything when we get out of this. *If* we get out of this."

"Leave the lanterns . . . we are not freeing these creatures. Now, let's go." And off we went again, weaving our way through the cavern.

The cave dropped off to the right into a darkened abyss, and we skirted the edge with care, working our way back to the center.

Limestone flowed down from the ceiling, forming a thick column of stalagmites and stalactites, a statuary of twisted flowstone. In the center of the falls, an opening allowed dripping water from the ceiling to trickle down, falling into the hollowed-out rimstone pool, where the mineralized liquid slowly ate away at the floor, creating the basin. Fortified by the continual drip, the walls had slowly built up over the centuries; now they were ornamented with amorphous, bulging pillows, looking for all the world like fossilized cauliflower.

As we worked our way through the cave, skirting delicate stalactites and stalagmites, we followed the trail that Charles had worn in the dust. Vampires were light on their feet, but he was still new and hadn't learned to lessen his presence.

The light from the demon lamps reverberated from wall to wall, creating flickering shadows that looked like creatures creeping alongside us, and now that I knew the lights were imprisoned spirits, my stomach twisted. What if they got out? What if their caretakers were near? What if we were caught down here without Carter or Vanzir to vouch for us?

We skirted the central sculpture and found ourselves on the other side of the cavern. To our left was another drop-off; to our right, another passage. I edged my way up to the overlook and peeked over the edge. A sheer black drop. I held the flashlight over the edge but the light barely penetrated ten feet down.

Wade crouched beside me. He picked up a small pebble and dropped it and we listened, waiting to hear it bounce against the bottom, but there was no sound—not even a faint *thunk*—and I glanced up at him.

"We do not want to go over. Not without some damned good ropes and lights." I slowly backed away and Wade followed me. We wended our way through the narrow passage to the back of the cavern. The scent of blood led us, and as we slipped through the tunnel, I noticed patches of green viro-mortis slime dappling the limestone walls. I motioned to them.

"Do not let them touch you. We're vampires, so they can't hurt us too bad, but they're fucking nasty and you don't want to get them on anybody who's still alive. And if you see a purple variety, avoid them at all costs. Those *can* hurt us."

He nodded, turning sideways to slip along behind me.

The passage ran along for about fifteen feet before ending at a fork. Wade, who was hungrier than I was, could smell the blood more easily. He motioned to the right and we turned. Another five feet found us standing at another opening. Peeking through, we could see the standard old-school setup.

A coffin sat in the corner—and it was a nice one. There was a recliner next to it, a battery-powered light, and a small bookcase overflowing with books. Then I noticed that the walls of the chamber were brick. We were looking into another section of Underground Seattle, also adjacent to the hidden cavern. It looked like someone had broken through the brick to get into the cavern. I had no idea whether Charles Shalimar or the Demon Underground had been responsible for discovering the connection.

As I entered, slowly, I could see that the coffin was empty. Shit. Were we going to be chasing him to the ends of the Earth? What the fuck was he doing running around? He couldn't have *that* many errands. Then I saw the bloody clothes on the floor and motioned for Wade to stay where he was.

I slipped over to the opposite door and peeked out.

Bingo. Another chamber, with yet another exit leading out into what was doubtless one of the Underground tunnels. This room was lit by more of the demon lamps. And in the center of the chamber, a tub, filled with steaming water. Nearby, what looked like a jury-rigged pipe led down to the bath. Charles had been siphoning off somebody's water system, it looked like.

In the tub was our man. Charles was washing—totally focused on scrubbing the blood off him. He was an older man, in his sixties, it looked, but he was well built and he would have his vampire strength.

I decided that it was better to ask questions later, and slowly slid one of the stakes out of my belt. As I crept closer—I didn't want to chance throwing it and missing, warning him in the process—Wade eased his pack down. But we weren't dealing with just any ordinary killer.

Charles was a vampire and he had the same acute hearing we did. He leaped up, out of the tub, his body wet and slick from the water. Although he was naked, I felt an icy chill race through me. He was a psychopath, he was a vampire, and he had no remorse for what he was doing.

"Charles—listen to me. Give it up. Now. You let us take you in and we'll make sure you get help." I was lying, of course—I fully intended to take him out. This wasn't any ordinary murderer whom you could toss in jail and forget, letting him rot. A vampire serial killer was far too dangerous. We had to take him out, to dust him.

Charles glanced at me, looking mildly confused. "You know my name."

"We know all about you. We know you were a priest, and that you were turned into a vampire."

Another shift of the head, another start of surprise.

"Go away." He raised his hand, as if shielding his eyes from my gaze. I could see the conflicting emotions race across his face. Guilt, anger, rage, hunger, all tied together. Oh yeah, Charles wasn't playing with a full deck, that was for sure. In the blink of an eye, he'd grabbed his jeans and slid into them. I winced. They were covered with dried blood. Apparently he washed his body to remove the sin of his actions, but he conveniently forgot to clean his garments.

"Charles. You have no choice. You can't run because we'll hunt you down. Come quietly and we can get you some help." Wade entered the room behind me. "You know you feel bad about those women—"

"No! They were whores, Jezebels. They were evil, tempting women and the only way I could save their souls was to cleanse them." His voice was querulous and tinged with argument.

"Charles, you are aware you're a vampire now?" I didn't want to overlook the obvious. Since some ghosts weren't aware they'd died, maybe in the break that happened to his psyche, he'd lost track of the fact that he was a vamp.

"I am their savior. I am here to wipe the world clean of harlots and sinners. I am the sword of blood and justice. My God has forsaken me, but I will find myself in his graces again when I have cleansed the Earth for him."

Oh, delightful. Not only was he a psychopath, but he had a martyr complex, too. Just what we needed.

"Charles, please—if you are the sword of justice, then hear us out."

"You are spawn of the devil. I know what you are! You are like Jezebel, the beauty who would have tempted me. I fell . . . my God, I fell." Tears began to streak down his cheeks. "I wanted to touch her—it was so hard, so very hard. I tried to resist, but she lured me in and I couldn't stay away from her."

His sire had used her glamour to reel the priest in. No wonder he was so guilt-ridden. He must have been true to his post, but no FBH could withstand the lure of a vampire. Especially if she was older.

Charles took a step back and reached for something. I gauged whether I had a clear shot of his chest, but he was aware enough to keep his body turned just so that if I threw my stake, it would lodge in his arm. And that wouldn't slow him down.

I motioned for Wade to begin edging toward the other door. We didn't want him escaping again. Wade nodded and Charles glared at him as he clasped whatever it was he had picked up. I prayed it wasn't a stake-shooting gun that some FBH fanatic had worked up. We'd heard tales of a few lately, using the same technology as a spear gun to shoot wooden stakes.

But when he opened his hand to show me what he was holding, my fear factor jumped off the scale.

"Charles—put that down. We can talk. If you are the new savior, then you really don't want to use that."

"It won't hurt me. I'm *immortal*. I'm *invincible*. I cannot be killed." And every word he said was filled with self-confidence. Charles really didn't think he could be killed. And he was holding what looked to be a live grenade.

CHAPTER 22

"He's got a grenade!" I frantically motioned for Wade to stop. He quickly took in the situation and changed course.

Grenades and explosions, though not a guaranteed death, could do a great deal of damage. Some, if powerful enough, could put an end to a vampire. This was a small space, enclosed, and the explosion would be devastating. Not to mention that it might bring down the entire tunnel system around here.

"You don't want to do that." Wade's voice was even. He steadily moved toward the vampire, one small step at a time. "Put the grenade down and we can talk. If you are the new savior, then maybe we can help you."

Charles slowly shook his head. "You want to stop me— the spirits told me. They told me you're the spawn of the devil, that you're not anointed by the blood of the Lamb."

I stared at him. He'd lost it and there was no coming back. The only thing we could hope for was to get the grenade away from him intact, because no matter what, we couldn't let him escape again. A vampire with a martyr complex on the loose: *Not Good*. A vampire with a martyr complex on the loose with a live grenade: *Very Bad*. With a glance at Wade, I slowly began to move in. Playing along wasn't working. It was time to be straight.

"Charles, listen to me. You aren't a savior. You aren't the sword of God. You're a vampire—you were a priest and a vampire killed you and turned you. She should not have done that. She was wrong and I'm so sorry. But now, you're killing innocent women to get back at her. Can't you see how twisted your logic is—" I stopped. Wade was frantically shaking his head at me.

"You're wrong. I'll prove you are. *I am immortal!*" And Charles pulled the pin.

"Run!" Wade dashed toward the cavern and I followed suit. We managed to clear our way through the short passage into the one leading back into the cavern when the explosion rocked the area. Smoke billowed from behind us as the Earth shook and the sound of rocks crashing to the ground echoed around us. *Living surround sound*. I covered my head and suddenly Wade was leaning over me, trying to protect me from the falling debris.

The passage we were in reverberated with heavy rock fall as dust filled the air. Grateful neither of us needed to breathe, I waited until only a trickle of pebbles echoed through the passage.

As Wade slowly crawled off me, another slide of rocks echoed from somewhere up ahead. I gingerly pushed myself to my feet and felt for my flashlight, which I'd hooked to my belt loop.

I flipped it on to find a cloud of dust flickering in the thin yellow beam. Squinting, I tried to see through the settling debris. *Damn*. Our way back into the cavern was blocked by thousands of pounds of debris. The tunnel had broken down near the entrance, and even as I pressed against the rocks, I knew it was futile. We might manage to clear our way out—after all, we could go a long time without blood and we didn't need air—but it would take an awfully long time to get out from this direction.

Wade examined the tunnel on the other side.

"How is it?" I asked, coughing as the dust filled my mouth. "We're fucked over here."

"I think we can manage to squeeze through there." He flickered his light up to show a crawl space between the roof and the top of the rocks. It looked narrow but possible. We were strong enough to move some of the rocks to give ourselves more space, but we'd have to be careful not to start another rock slide.

"Shit, this is so beyond fucked. Here, let me crawl up there. I'm lighter and will have less of a chance of setting off another avalanche."

Holding my penlight between my teeth, I slowly inched my way up the precarious mountain of loose rubble. The rocks were mixed with bricks on this side—the side leading back into Charles's lair—and a layer of dried, powdered mortar seemed to cover everything.

Twice, my footing slipped and a cascade of debris rained down toward Wade. He didn't flinch, merely held his flashlight steady to give me extra light to see by. I managed to reach the top after about ten minutes of cautious maneuvering. I would have used my ability to hover, but I would have still had to scramble over rock and ruin to reach the crawl space.

Gingerly, I probed the space, testing how steady it was. Another trickle of rubble and then one large boulder went rebounding down, crashing to the floor below, taking a stream of debris with it. Wade lightly jumped back, out of its way.

"Sorry, I barely touched it. Better it went now than later when we're trying to crawl through here." I flashed my light into the narrow gap and was pleased to see that the rock slide was only about five feet wide. "I think we can do it. I'm going through, then you join me when I call from the other side."

"Okay. But be careful." Wade kept his light aimed in my direction.

I flattened out onto my back and began to wiggle through the gap. The stones were sharp and rough, abrading my hands as I clawed my way through. I went in, face toward the ceiling, to avoid poking an eye out or any such nasty business. Extending my arms above my head, I used my fingers to claw a hold into the ceiling and pulled myself along with my hands as I pushed with my feet. The going was rough and rocks jabbed me in the back, but finally my head broke through and I birthed myself out of the channel, only to find that no floor was in sight—just an endless pile of rocks extending to fill the tunnel halfway to the ceiling.

I cautiously inched my way onto the swath of rubble. I had just passed the fork and was back in the five-foot section of tunnel right before Charles's lair. It must have been better reinforced than the section leading back into the cavern, since the rubble didn't reach the ceiling here. I could see the top third of the entrance leading into his chamber—which was relatively clear. That was some strong brickwork in there. Of course it had survived several earthquakes, so what was a hand grenade?

"We're fielding more rubble over here, but we can make it back into his chamber. Come on."

"On my way," Wade shouted back.

Cautiously, while Wade made his way through the cleft in the rocks, I inched my way toward the chamber where Charles had exploded the grenade. I reached the arch leading into his lair and slid through the opening. The room was still illuminated by the demon lamps—three of them had survived, but a fourth had been crushed under the weight of rocks falling down from one side of the wall.

I hurried over to where Charles had been standing, and

there was nothing to see. If he'd been killed, he would have turned to dust. But suppose . . . suppose he'd survived?

No, my mind answered. That wasn't possible. He'd been holding the grenade . . . or had he? Had he lobbed it at us when we ran? Could he have possibly escaped?

"Any sign of him?"

Wade's voice startled me, and I jumped. He was at my side in the blink of an eye. "Sorry, didn't mean to scare you. So, any clue as to—"

A sound alerted both of us, and we turned just in time to see some of the rocks moving from the mini-slide over against the wall. And then I saw a foot kick away a boulder the size of my head, and then another.

"Charles—that has to be him." I glanced around, looking for a stake. The ones on my belt had splintered in the chaos.

Wade grabbed up a board and smashed it over his knee, so one long sliver stuck out from the end. He tossed me the other piece and, though not a perfect point, it was pointed enough to use as a stake.

Charles rose from the bed of rock, a triumphant glimmer in his eye. "I told you. I am immortal."

"You were lucky," I said, hissing as my fangs descended and I began to circle him. Wade took the other side, and we hedged him in, trying our best to keep him from escaping.

"I am the sword of justice." Charles started in my direction, his face awash with the joy only a martyr can feel. "I will cleanse Earth of the abominations of the flesh and all the world will know of my coming and tremble."

I ducked in then, as he raised his hands in triumph, joyous and feral. He'd left his chest open to attack and I raced directly into him, ramming him with the piece of wood, feeling the rip as it tore through his chest and into his heart. Charles stared at me, disbelief replacing the joy, and then—with one last shriek—he was gone. Dust floated to the ground where he'd been standing.

"Martyrs usually don't have a lot of common sense,"

Wade said, putting down his own makeshift stake. He knelt by the lingering wisps of dust and ashes that were the only remains signifying Charles's existence. "He was a tormented soul. Even if we'd caught him before he turned murderous, I don't think we could have done anything for him."

"Neither do I." I looked around the room. Religious icons littered the walls, but Charles had spread blood on them—no doubt the blood of innocents. "I'll never get over the fact that religion can be such a boon, a salve to some, and a license to murder for others. Extremists from any faith scare me."

"Now our question is, can we get out of here?"

We examined the door opposite the tunnels and found that they led directly to a manhole tunnel. I floated up, dislodging the cover to peek out. We were in the park. Only two blocks away from where we'd gone in. There was a crowd down near the original manhole, and Chase's car was there.

Wade and I jogged down the street. I could see Chase standing there, Iris beside him.

I couldn't resist sauntering up to them, about to ask *What's up?* when my question died on my lips. There was a sinkhole in the street, in the center of the intersection, about twenty yards from the manhole. Dust billowed up from the hole as a group of firemen and FH-CSI officers stared down into it.

Iris saw me first, and raced over to throw her arms around my waist. "Menolly! You're safe!"

Chase whirled. "Menolly! Wade! Thank God you're okay. What happened? We were waiting for you, and then after a while there was this loud explosion and part of the street caved in."

"We got him." I looked at Chase, shaking my head. "He was too far gone. There was no chance to stop him other than to kill him. He's dust. It was Charles Shalimar. He thought he was some sort of martyr, called himself the sword of justice. He also managed to find himself a live hand grenade, and that's what happened to your street."

"You guys lived through a grenade?" Chase stared at us, his eyes wide. "Shit. Are you okay?"

I nodded. "We're hardier than you think. Charles survived it, too, but he couldn't survive a stake through the heart. The killing spree is over, Chase, but now we have to put out the aftermath. You might want to spend a little time in your news conference mentioning that a couple of vampires took care of the problem."

He caught my intentions. "Yeah, if we show that you guys willingly went after one of your own, that might be enough to appease the recent spate of hate crimes against vampires."

Maybe, but I wasn't so sure. I had a nasty feeling things were going to explode pretty soon, unless some clear and definite lines were drawn. But I wasn't going to dampen his optimism. He'd seen too much horror over the past week or two, too many bodies. At least we'd caught our man and taken him down.

"Yeah, maybe you're right." I walked over to Iris, who had moved back to stare down into the hole, next to Wade.

"You need to get home. Morning's not far off." She glanced up at me—I was barely five one but I was still more than a foot taller than she was. "Menolly, things are shifting, aren't they? Something is on the move . . ."

"Yeah, I can feel it, too." I stared into the chasm, wondering what we were talking about. But instinctively, I knew. Something big was coming, something big and something bad, and it felt like things were growing more and more chaotic. "Let's go home."

Wade gave me a quick hug and headed out for his apartment. I waved to Chase and headed back to my Jag, Iris beside me.

"How did you get down here?" I asked, after a moment.

"I made Vanzir drive me down, then told him to go

home. What the hell happened with him? He seems mute, almost . . . docile."

"You don't want to know," I whispered. "But you will. Soon, Iris. It's not up to me to tell you."

And with that, we climbed in my car and headed for home, the silent streets passing by in a blur of snow and concrete.

When we got home, I silently went in to pick up Maggie. She was dead to the world but the minute I lifted her, she woke and gave me a sleepy yawn, then a giggle, and yanked on my braids. I held her close, sitting on the end of Iris's bed, kissing her downy head and ruffling the calico fur that covered her body. Her wings folded and unfolded with delight, and she wrapped her arms around my neck and went to sleep against my shoulder.

For some reason, my heart felt like it was breaking, and for the first time in a long while, I wanted to cry. I pressed my lips to her head, then her nose, and then rubbed my cheek against the top of her head.

Iris came in, watching me closely. After a few minutes, I felt like I was back in control of my emotions and I softly slid Maggie back into her crib and followed Iris out into the kitchen. Shade and Delilah were there, both wearing pajamas. Vanzir was straddling a chair, leaning his arms on the back of it.

"We have a lot to talk about," I said, sitting down next to Iris. "Can we do tea? I may not be able to drink it, but damn it, I need some feeling of continuity."

Iris nodded, bustling over to the sink to fill the kettle. Shade offered me a bottle of blood from the fridge, but I wasn't hungry. I'd drunk deep from Roman and still felt sated from feeding on him.

Delilah pulled out Camille's steno pad. "Okay, where are we at? And if we're going to do this, I need cookies."

"You just want cookies because you have a sweet tooth that won't quit," Shade said, grinning as he brushed his fingers down the side of her face.

"And what are you going to do about it?"

"Nothing, because it's part of you." He bent to kiss her full on the lips, and I tried to repress a grin.

"Get a room, you two. Come on, let's please get a handle on what's going down." I waited till Delilah was finished smooching with Shade and paying attention, then said, "Wade and I killed the vampire who was murdering hookers. In doing so, we blasted a hole in the middle of the intersection. Or rather, our killer did. He had a grenade. Grenades go boom when you pull the pin. Which he did."

Delilah blinked. "Say what? He was carrying around a grenade?"

"No, he had one in his bedroom down in the tunnels. By the way, there are several things we need to get on the table. Vanzir—I have to tell them. They have to know." I was talking about the Demon Underground, but apparently he misunderstood.

"Fine, so tell them. Camille would have to sooner or later. I've lost my powers thanks to a big-ass mistake." He stared at them, and before I could stop him, he added, "I . . . I overpowered your sister in the tunnels when Morio was attacked, and the Moon Mother stripped me of my powers."

Delilah jumped up, her eyes wide. "You did *what*?"

"Stop—before you think a single thing." I stood up and crossed between their line of sight. "Delilah, stop. Camille and I had a long talk. She's dealing with this—and there were extenuating circumstances that forced Vanzir's hand. It was a bad situation, no matter how you looked at it, and neither one had much say in the matter. Vanzir's feeding got away from him and Camille made a choice."

Delilah was shaking—I could see the tremors in her hand. She slowly took her seat, glowering at Vanzir. "What did Trillian and Morio say?" Then a look of stark terror filled her face. "Oh Great Mother, what the hell do you think Smoky's going to do? This isn't something that you can keep from him."

"We kind of figured that out, and hell . . . I don't know. I'm thinking we should send Vanzir away for a little while until Camille has a chance to talk to Smoky and smooth things over. We could send him to Otherworld for a little while, or to stay with Grandmother Coyote."

Vanzir shook his head. "I can't stay with her, she scares the crap out of me. I could stay with a friend in the Demon Underground."

"Speaking of the Demon Underground, I've seen it." Again, with Vanzir's help, I outlined what we'd found below the surface. Once again, Delilah looked like she was seriously thinking of throttling Vanzir.

"You didn't think to *tell* us about it? You didn't tell them that the shadow men were guardians? You put everybody at risk—" She hung her head, and when she raised it, I could see Panther staring through her eyes.

"Pull it in, babe. Pull it in—Vanzir has reasons. Maybe not the best, but he does have reasons. Remember, we watch every thought about him. You don't want to do something that cannot be undone." The soul binder around Vanzir's neck allowed us to kill him with a single directed and prolonged thought. I waited until her breathing softened.

Iris frowned. "You know . . . let me check something." She stood and crossed to Vanzir, placing her hands on his shoulders and closing her eyes. After a few moments, she stood back, staring at him. "It's gone. *The soul binder is gone.*"

He hung his head again and crossed his arms. "Yeah, I know. It vanished when my powers vanished. I'm free of your Subjugation spell."

"Why didn't you tell me? I've been trying to defend you, to keep Delilah from killing you with her anger." I pushed to my feet, staring at him from across the table. "Vanzir, what the fuck's going on?"

"And what would you have done if I'd told you?" He stood and leaned across the table. A smug look clouded his face, but beneath it, I could see the hints of worry. "When your sister's goddess stripped away my powers, the soul binder went with it. I'm free. But I'm still here. After what happened with Camille, I know it's going to be hard to trust me again, but I'm still here and I'm willing to stay and play by your rules."

I gazed into his eyes. The whirling kaleidoscope flickered by, a never-ending parade of indescribable colors. "You're still willing to fight with us, even without your powers? Even though you aren't bound to us?"

He nodded. "Even more so now. This is my choice. I owe it to Camille for what I did to her. I owe it to you for the fact that you spared me. I may have kept the Demon Underground secret, but they're all against Shadow Wing, so really, did it harm you? Does it have anything to do with your war against the Unraveller?"

Delilah answered for me. "No. No, it doesn't . . . but from now on, you be straight with us. We may not be able to put you under a death threat about it, but we can certainly kill you with our hands rather than our minds."

Vanzir smiled then, dropping back into his chair and crossing one leg. "Puddy-tat, I would expect nothing less than that. I'm in, if the big lizard doesn't tear me to shreds. Camille . . ." A pained look crossed his face. "I'll always regret what I did, but some things cannot be undone. She and I knew that . . . at the end."

The room was silent for a moment, then I slowly told them about everything that had happened with Morio and my blood, and how Wade and I had chased Charles through the tunnel and the explosion. By the time I was done, we were all exhausted.

"Camille said she'll be home later today," Iris said, clearing the teacups and saucers from the table. "Let's hope things look up from here out."

"Yeah," I said, heading toward my lair. Delilah and

Shade had retired to their rooms upstairs. Vanzir was gone, out to the shed. "Iris, does it feel like things are falling apart to you?"

She shook her head, slowly. "No, dear, things are simply evolving. Rest. Let go of the day. Tomorrow night things may seem brighter. Go now and sleep."

And, taking her words as gospel, because I couldn't afford not to, I obeyed.

CHAPTER 23

When I woke, I could hear the commotion all the way down in my lair. I threw back my covers, slipped into jeans and a blue turtleneck, pulled on my boots, and headed upstairs. The noise didn't sound like it was coming from the kitchen, so I took a chance and slipped through the hidden entrance to my nest. I was right. Whatever was going on was confined to the living room.

I raced in to find that Smoky had returned. For a moment I thought he was going after Vanzir, but the dream-chaser demon was nowhere in sight. Smoky was ranting, and Camille and Trillian were trying to calm him down.

"Hey, bro, good to see you. What the fuck's all the commotion about? Where's Roz?"

"Rozurial is resting." The six-four dragon turned to me, and his eyes could have frozen my heart if it had been still beating. "My father, that's what the commotion is about."

Camille looked petrified. She gave me a slow shake of the head. "Hyto . . . he tried to kill Smoky's mother and when the guards caught him and put a spell of banishment on him, the last thing he said was that he's coming to punish the one responsible."

"Meaning Camille." Smoky's hair was up in arms, too, it seemed, the ankle-length tendrils coiling and snapping through the air like wild silver whips. His arms were around her shoulders, holding her to him. He wouldn't even let Trillian near her.

"My father will die before he ever puts a single finger on my wife," he said with a growl.

I'd never seen such a horrific look on his face, not even when Camille was in danger from our enemies. His dragon energy swirled around him, a mist of white with silver sparkles, and he looked ten seconds away from transforming. Which would totally trash the house, if he did.

"He tried to kill my mother, and for that alone, he must die. But if he thinks he can touch my wife, I will rip his throat out, I will emasculate and eviscerate him, and then toss him over the highest mountain in the land."

I blinked. He wasn't kidding.

"Is your mother okay?"

Smoky gazed at me, his face a frozen sculpture. "She is. She is more powerful than Hyto, and she cast him down. My brothers and sisters wing-strapped him until help could arrive. Ever since she denied him in front of the Council, he's apparently been planning her death. If he sets foot in the Dragon Reaches again, he will be tortured and put to death."

I glanced at Camille, who was looking absolutely petrified. Nothing like being on a dragon's shit list, that was for sure.

The thought of fighting dragons was certainly enough to cow me. "It must be a terrible sight, dragon against dragon."

Smoky gave me a subtle nod. "It is a terrifying spectacle. An actual fight between dragons can ravage the country for miles around. Some young males who do not want to accept their place in the hierarchy bear scorch scars across their bellies and backs for life." He let out a long breath. "But we will address this later. What's going on? Where's Morio?"

"Fox Boy almost got himself killed," Trillian said softly. "We've had one hell of a time the past couple of days."

"Sharah says he can come home tomorrow, but he'll be out of the action for a couple of months. Delilah, just as you're coming off bed rest, he's going on it. Menolly's blood saved his life, but he's not going to be doing much of anything for a while." Camille glanced up at Smoky anxiously. "Please, treat him with care—we almost lost him to a hungry ghost."

Smoky gave her a kiss on the head. "Understood, my love."

"At least the killer's gone," I started to say, but my cell phone jangled. I glanced at the ID. *Roman.* "Excuse me, I need to take this."

Moving to one side, I answered.

"You still want in on taking Terrance down?"

"Yes."

"Then be ready. My limo will pick you up in ten minutes. My driver is on the way. Dress for speed and action."

"Need any other help?"

Roman laughed. "No, my dear. This is for you and me. Alone." And he hung up. I stared at the phone. Once again, I had to go into battle without my sisters, and it felt odd. Lonely, even. But this was not my call to make, so I decided to make the best of it.

"I have to go. Vampire business with Roman."

"You sure you don't need help?" Camille gave me the soft doe eyes that usually cajoled me into letting her take part in whatever I was doing. But this time . . .

"I wish you could—I've missed having you with me. But you stay and help Iris get ready for Morio's return. He'll need a bed set up and everything else . . . and you and Smoky may want to . . ."

Smoky let out a loud guffaw. "That we do."

Camille cleared her throat. "I'm actually pretty tired. Let's get Morio's bed ready, and then we'll see about anything else."

As I headed toward the door, it occurred to me that our lives were slowly peeling off. We were still united, still had each others' backs, but we were finding our own ways in the world, as well. Someday, perhaps we wouldn't be living together like this. What then? Where would we go? Unaccountably saddened, I headed out the door to wait on the porch.

A moment later, the door opened and Camille slipped out on the porch. She shivered under Smoky's heavy white trench, which dragged on the floor, and pulled it around her shoulders as she sat on the porch swing beside me.

She glanced at the fine white mist of snow leisurely drifting down. "Winters are getting harder here."

"Yeah, they are."

"Why are you upset? I know things have been rough lately, but they'll work out." She slid one hand over to hold my own. "I promise, I won't let Smoky kill Vanzir."

"Isn't that Delilah's job? To bring on the ridiculous optimism?" But even as I said it, I felt a little lift. Camille's hand felt warm and alive, and thoroughly welcome in the cold night. The chill didn't bother me—I was as cold as the frozen snow—but sometimes even the pretense of warmth brought bloom to the spirit.

"What's wrong?"

I ducked my head. "Everything is changing. So much flies in at us. Delilah and Shade watch *Jerry Springer* together. He's bored by it, but he does it because he loves her. That . . ." I was almost ashamed to admit I was jealous of him.

"Was your job until he showed up?" She grinned.

Nodding, I didn't answer. It was embarrassing to be jealous of her boyfriend. But Kitten and I didn't get much time to spend together, and it seemed she'd been so thoroughly caught up in her new romance that she'd barely had the chance to hang out with me lately.

"The sparks will fade to a passionate ember, and she will come up for air again. Look at me—three men. I must have been unbearable for the longest time." She cleared her throat. "What else?"

I gazed into the sky. The colors of silver and white merged on the skyline and it was difficult to tell where the cloud cover ended and the ground began. "We're moving apart, aren't we? Look—I'm waiting to go out with Roman to trounce Terrance. And you and Delilah aren't coming with me. Wade and Chase and I took care of Charles."

"Silly girl!" Camille stood up and the coat slid off her shoulders to the floor. Hands on her hips, she shook her head. "Listen to me and listen good. I couldn't be there— not with Morio in the hospital. And Delilah's not allowed to fight again yet. You think we would have missed the action if there hadn't been a good reason? I'd love to go out with you tonight but I'm exhausted, and with Smoky just home . . . besides . . ." She sat down with a thud. "I need to make sure nobody tells him about Vanzir and me yet. You and I both know Smoky would kill him, and I'm not sure what he'd do to me."

"To you? It wasn't your choice."

"Technically, it was. I could have let him feed on my magic. But I think Smoky would decide either sin was worth killing for. I have to impress on him first just how traumatic and horrifying the event was—for *both* of us, not just me. Then, he might understand." She shrugged. "And if not, then Vanzir can at least run without the soul binder killing him. And he'd have to run long and hard to get away from Smoky's wrath."

I turned to her and took her hands. "What do you think about that? Vanzir is no longer under our control. I'm not sure what to think about that."

"Me either, but he's in pretty deep with the Demon

Underground and I think that may come in handy. He seems to want to stay." She hung her head. "If I could have it to do all over again, I'd come up those rungs, iron or not."

I didn't know how to ask the next question but finally decided just to blurt it out. "Was he . . . was it painful? Did he hurt you?"

Camille's eyes were wide as she shook her head. "No, in fact it was . . . exhilarating. I've been avoiding Vanzir since we first bound him through the Ritual of Subjugation, and now I know why. When he was feeding on my energy, it was like he was a crazed monster—gobbling up every speck of light and brilliance in my soul."

I winced, not wanting to hear but feeling like I had to. I had to understand what had gone on if I was going to help hold things together when Smoky found out. "That bad . . ."

"Yes. And then, when I forced his attention to my body, then he was overwhelming in a passionate way. I love sex, but he was . . . the attention, the focus and drive were almost too much. It was as if he owned me in a way that I've never given anyone permission to own me before. He was . . . more than a part of me. I don't know how to explain it—but I don't think I ever want to experience it again, even though the actual sex was incredible."

"He's demon—that probably has some play into it. But Morio, he's a demon, too. Isn't it like that with him?"

"He's a youkai—not the kind of demon that Vanzir is. There's a difference." She fell silent. After a moment, she added, "I feel like I've betrayed all three of them. Menolly, I enjoyed it." She glanced at me out of the side of her eyes. "I don't want to admit it, but the fear and the worry—I was so high-strung, and then Vanzir began to feed on me and I panicked."

"I'd be surprised if some part of you *didn't* enjoy fucking him. Camille, look at who you are." I bit my lip, trying to find a way to make her see what I could see. "You're a highly sexual woman, and you are our father's daughter. The Fae in our blood drives you. And any time you're running an adrenaline rush, of course that side of you is going to be on high alert."

She let out a shudder that was almost a sob. "I don't want to tell them, but I have to. I know Trillian will understand, but Morio—how will he feel knowing that he was lying there dying while I had my legs wrapped around Vanzir?"

I couldn't answer. But I *could* tell her what she needed to hear. "It will all be okay. Just wait for the right time. The rest of us won't say a word. Just think before you speak. Don't let your guilt eat at you. You have nothing to feel guilty about."

Roman's limousine appeared in the driveway. I pressed her hand, then stood. "I have to go. What we're doing tonight is important, not just for the vampires of Seattle, but for the FBHs, too. Because vamps like Terrance feed on the innocent. Wish me luck. I'll be home before morning."

And as I headed down the steps, leaving them to sort out the mishmash of things that had happened, I knew Camille was right. She and Delilah would be at my back always. We might grow our own separate ways, but we wouldn't grow apart. I just wished I could have made her feel better the way she had me. But that was my sister: always the rock of the family.

Roman was dressed in black jeans and a tight black sweater, and his hair was caught back in a French braid. I gazed at him.

"I should tell you, I'm going through with a pledging ceremony with my girlfriend come spring. I can be your official consort, but I can never be your wife." Camille's words about betrayal were ringing in my ears, and though I'd already talked to Nerissa about Roman, I wanted to make my stance perfectly clear.

He inclined his head. "And as I said, I have no problem with that. I will place your intended under my protection, as well. I assume she is not vampire?"

"No, she's a werepuma." I paused, staring out the tinted windows. "We caught the serial killer. He's dead." I gave him a quick wrap-up of what happened. "Do you think we should look for his sire?"

"Why would we do that?"

"I don't know . . . she's siring innocent victims. Look what her actions cost—five lives. Six, if you count Charles."

"No need. If she continues to be a problem, we'll take action, but for now, let it be." He gazed at me with his frost-ridden eyes. "Once the Regency is secure, she won't be welcome in the city."

After a moment, I looked ahead through the dividing glass at the driver. "Who is your driver? He a vampire, too?"

"Yes. His name is Hans, and he's been with me for three hundred years, as a horseman, a buggy driver, and now, my chauffeur. He was turned in the year 1210, on a raiding party."

Old. These were old vampires. "How old is Terrance? I don't know much about him. Delilah tried to ferret out information but couldn't find more than a scrap or two on him."

Roman shifted. "Terrance is not so old—younger than Hans, even. He was born into his second life in the year 1815. He was a petty thief, a con man, and a murderer in his former life. He lived in the Southwest—was born and bred there. Died young, around twenty-five. He had aspirations, shall we say, to become a famous card player. He didn't play well enough to keep from getting run out of every town he drifted into. The last one, he was forcibly evicted by the sheriff late one night and fell into the hands of a vampire."

"How did he become so . . . so . . ."

"So worldly? So educated?"

"I was going to say *so popular*, but that works, too." The Terrance I'd met seemed older than a scant two hundred years, minus a few. He came across as smooth, suave, and sophisticated, not like some two-bit con man traveling from city to city, trying to make a buck.

"A man may become educated through school, he may learn manners through a tutor, but he will never develop class unless it is in his nature and heart. And Terrance has no class. He's greedy, grasping, and though he's not an actual threat to the throne, he's an impediment."

Roman shifted, crossing one leg over the other. "My mother is harsh, but she has a regal air that lends itself well to her position. She is never crass or boorish. Terrance is a poor specimen to represent our kind, and that is why he must die. For, unlike your young friend, he will never step down if asked."

"What's the plan?"

"The plan is, we meet my associates at the club, walk in, and take out Terrance."

"I've been in the Fangtabula before. There's a lot of security there."

"You were not there with me, or my guards."

"True." Actually, he'd piqued my curiosity. Just how big was his army, and who was in it? Before I could ask anything, we pulled to a stop.

The Fangtabula was down in the Industrial District—in south Seattle. This was an area of town you didn't want to go strolling through at midnight. Although there was talk of expanding the district to include more residential areas, it hadn't happened so far, but if people kept moving to the city, no doubt the high-rise condo buildings would find their way down into the grungy concrete jungle that was a maze of train tracks and old warehouses. In fact, the Fangtabula was in what had once been a meatpacking plant.

As we pulled into the parking lot, the club stood out as it always had, with bright red doors against walls patterned with black-and-white stripes. Three stories tall, the Fangtabula did a lot of business, even though it was on Chase's to-close-down list. A number of underage girls and boys were rumored to hang out there, and though Chase had managed to call a couple raids on the place, Terrance was always two steps ahead and nobody carded ever came up as a minor.

"It looks like we're here. Come, my dear. We've got work to do." Roman stepped out of the limo and held out his hand. I took it and allowed him to help me out of the car. "Stay by my side, whatever you do. This is going to be bloody."

As I stood up and looked around the parking lot, I saw four other cars pull up—all black sedans—and out of each car stepped four vampires. Mostly men, but a few women in the mix, and they were all dressed in the same black jeans and turtlenecks as Roman, with a signature crest woven in white on their shirts. They wore black sunglasses—Ray-Bans, by my guess—and fell into two lines, standing at attention, arms crossed.

Roman turned and I saw the same crest splashed across his back, and it was easier to make out what the picture was. A pair of crossed white swords in the center of a circle. The circle rested atop the back of a mighty lion, with a chalice clasped in its paws.

"Your family crest?"

He nodded. "*My* crest, but the chalice indicates my lineage—that I'm a child of Blood Wyne. And all of these"—he stopped to nod at the vampires gathering around us—"all of these are my children; I've sired every one of them."

As I looked from face to face, I saw only one commonality—an unquestioning loyalty. Roman's children were his, and his alone, and they would live or die for him depending on his whim.

The vamps fell into two lines behind us, and we headed toward the club. Security saw us—the two vamps guarding the door suddenly stood and one disappeared inside. We weren't making a secret entrance, that was for sure.

Roman pulled out a pair of glasses like those of his children and slid them on. "I believe we are ready."

We paused, waiting for Roman to give the order. I was used to leading the charge when it came to fights, but I gave over to him. This was his battle—more so than mine—and it would affect every vampire in the region and would cement Roman's authority.

Roman glanced around. "Remember, guests of the club will be allowed to leave. If they side with Terrance, they are fair game. No mortal is to be harmed unless you have no recourse. Stun them, charm them, knock them out, but do not kill them and absolutely *no drinking* from anybody! We're here to make a statement, not have a party. Understood?"

As one voice they answered. "Understood, *Liege!*"

"Forward—and do not flinch."

As Roman and I led the columns of vampires toward the building, people began spilling out of it, running every which way. Half-dressed, some drunk, they were making sure they were out of the way. Word of our coming had spread. Relieved, I steeled myself for battle. It was good that my sisters weren't with me, after all. Vampire against vampire caused some of the bloodiest battles around.

In the parking lot, the snow had turned to slush from the number of cars driving through, and the ridiculous image of Terrance and Roman lobbing snowballs at one another raced through my mind. I tried to brush it away, but it kept teasing me until I let out a short laugh. Roman glanced at me. I shrugged, pressing my lips together. I wasn't even going to bother trying to explain.

The crimson doors slammed open as we approached, and four burly vampires stepped out to block the way.

Roman straightened his shoulders, removed his glasses, and unleashed his full glamour. He was power incarnate, glorious and godlike. His aura preceded him, weaving a spell as he stood, magnetic and alluring, commanding countless armies. He stared at the vampires standing in his way, his stature shouldering the millennia he'd seen. I fell under his gaze, caught in the hoarfrost and silver waves that crashed against his face.

"On behalf of the Throne of Blood, I, Roman, son of Blood Wyne, Queen of the Crimson Veil, order you to stand back and let us enter unimpeded. I give you one chance to obey."

Two of the vampires immediately dropped to their knees, crouching as they scuttled away from the door. The other two looked terrified, but held their posts. Roman put his glasses back on and started walking toward them, and I fell into place beside him. His children had our backs.

As we came to the door, the two vamps who had not deserted their posts quivered as the son of Blood Wyne moved within arm's reach. Roman gazed at them but did not issue another warning. Instead, he reached out with one hand and pressed it against the nearest guard's chest. The vampire did not move, so petrified was the look on his face.

Roman smiled, faintly, and then quick as lightning he was holding the man's heart in his hand and the vampire stared down at his gaping chest, as if surprised to find he was no longer whole, and then a roil of smoke rose up and he turned to dust, as did the heart in Roman's hand. The guard's partner took one look at us and ran.

"Let him go," Roman said. "It's time for bigger game."

And we entered the Fangtabula, ready to raise hell.

CHAPTER 24

When we broke through the doors, all the memories of the last time we'd been here came flooding back. The red and black and silver color scheme, the gigantic chamber with a staircase descending to the main floor, tiled in a checkerboard of black and white. The twenty-foot ceiling still stretched overhead, an awesome vista, but the cloth panels that had draped down to produce a labyrinth of billowing walls were gone.

Two stairwells led to an upper level on either side of the room, and in the center, a three-sided railing overlooked the open area below, where a long staircase descended to the underground levels.

The bar against the left wall was empty, as were the tables and booths. A glance at the grotto on the right side of the chamber, however, still showed a few bloodwhores who hadn't escaped yet. We'd have to be careful around them.

As we spread out, Roman's children forming two rows of eight in a semicircle in back of us, we could see Terrance ascending the staircase from the underground levels, and behind him, his retinue. One I recognized from our last attack on the Fangtabula. Amazon Bitch was back, only the bodybuilder vamp had gotten rid of the fringed white pants. Now she wore a black catsuit, her muscles rippling beneath the stretch lamé material. But I didn't recognize the rest of them.

Terrance was a dark vampire—swarthy, with curly hair that grazed the top of his shoulders. He had a sneer that seemed perpetually ingrained on his face.

"Cease. Give over, Terrance. You can't win and you know it." Roman stepped forward. "Blood Wyne sent me."

"I don't care what your mama wants. I don't recognize the power of the Crimson Veil." Terrance was eyeing Roman cautiously. He was no fool; he knew how old and powerful a vamp he was facing.

Roman let out a slow hiss. "Then you are signing your death warrant."

"It was signed the day you decided I was a threat. Now, you just have to make good on it." And Terrance attacked.

He flew toward Roman, a blur of movement, as his henchmen spread out to take on our guards. I found myself up against the Amazon Bitch again. She grinned when she saw me, her fangs sharp and glittering.

"I remember you, D'Artigo. You might want to rethink your company, you know, considering how ethical you consider yourself. Your companion has killed more humans by his own hand than all of us combined." She jostled, her breasts bouncing lightly beneath the lamé suit. She must have just gotten implants before her death, because gravity was no threat to her and never again would be.

I circled her, aware that Roman and Terrance were engaging one another.

"I remember you, too. Decided that leather chaps weren't the way to go, finally?"

As we sidestepped around each other, two cautious rhythms keeping pace, I zoned out the rest. Fight your own battle, I'd learned early. Fight your own battle, and keep up your shields so you know if someone else is incoming on the side or at your back. A shriek echoed behind me, but I didn't turn. Somebody was getting munched on.

Letting my fangs descend, I gauged her strength. If I remembered right, she and I were fairly matched, though I'd recently drunk Roman's blood and that would give me an edge. Even now, I could feel his essence drifting through my body, his energy infusing my own, and I focused on that, calling it to the forefront, encouraging it like I might encourage a shy cat or a reluctant child.

My opponent arched her eyebrows and licked her lips. "You're delicious, Menolly. I can hardly wait to sink my teeth in you and drink you dry."

And then she flew at me, and we engaged. I dodged to the side, whirling to land a kick on her lower back as she stumbled past. She lurched but was quick to rebound. She turned, running to leap into a cartwheel, flipping once, twice, and then right over my head. When I saw what she was doing, I launched myself into the air to catch her mid-flip, and we both went crashing to the ground.

Over to my left, Roman and Terrance were grappling. Terrance might not have been an old vampire, but he was strong and Roman had his work cut out for him. They rolled on the ground, seeking purchase with their fangs.

And out of the corner of my eye, I saw that the children were engaged in battle—a blur of cloth and skin as they danced with death and fought against Terrance's guards. The scent of blood hung in the air, driving everyone into a stronger frenzy.

I tried to ignore it, tried to focus on my enemy. We were rolling now, with my hands around her throat and her fingers scrabbling for my eyes. I launched a kick, bringing my knee up to land against her stomach. She moaned and lost purchase, and I rolled her over onto her back, pressing my fingers against her throat. She didn't need to breathe, but if

I could break her neck, I'd have the advantage and be able to kill her before she healed.

I straddled her, squeezing my knees against her. Bringing my hands up over my head, I clasped them together, then swung them whistling down toward her face. She struggled, trying to get her hands free from where my legs had pinned them against her side, but she couldn't, and my fists made contact, crushing her nose, breaking through the cartilage and bone. Even then, she'd heal if I didn't do something to prevent it. I looked up and saw one of Roman's sons staring at me. He tossed me a stake and I caught it firmly in my hand and brought it down into her chest.

The Amazon shuddered once, turned to dust, and was gone. I grabbed up the stake and pushed myself to my feet, turning to see that my weapons benefactor had been watching me, not interfering, but standing guard.

I grinned at him. "Thanks!" And then turned to see what was going on.

Terrance and Roman were still fighting, but most of the other vamps had been dispatched. Roman's children were well trained, although when I counted them up, I saw only fourteen. Two lost.

Just then, Terrance managed to break free and came racing my way. His face was a bloody mess of fang wounds and his clothes were ripped to shreds. Instinctively, I leaped into his path to stop him, holding out the stake that I'd killed his girl Friday with. He careened out of the way just in time and caught the railing overlooking the lower levels. As he dropped to the floor below, I didn't even think twice. I went racing up and launched myself over the side after him.

As I hit the floor, Terrance disappeared from sight, but I'd seen the direction in which he'd gone. The lower levels of the Fangtabula were a labyrinthine maze. I came out of my crouch and hit the ground running. Behind me, I could hear others following. Roman was right behind me, and several of his children behind him.

I raced forward, my feet skimming the floor. Up ahead, down a long dark corridor that was painted black with the same checkerboard floor, I saw Terrance disappear into one of the rooms. When I came to the door, I didn't think twice but slammed it open with my foot and dove through the opening.

Terrance was on the opposite side, holding a young girl to his chest, his nails conveniently placed at her jugular.

"Come one step closer and I'll kill her."

I stopped, putting the brakes on. I could not endanger the child, even to kill Terrance. But Roman continued forward. I grabbed his arm.

"No—that's a little girl. Look at her—she's terrified!"

"Collateral damage."

I couldn't believe that Roman was willing to put her life in danger. "No! I won't be a part of it."

"Leave me be, woman!" Roman shook me off.

Terrance laughed. "And that is what makes you weak, girl." He neared the opposite door. Roman continued toward him and I strode to his side, determined to stop him. But then something caught my attention. The girl. She didn't look so much terrified as triumphant. And then, she smiled, just enough, and I saw the fangs descending.

"Fuck, she's a vampire!"

"Don't ever question my methods again," Roman said as he fell on the pair. I joined him, yanking the girl out of Terrance's arms. Terrance tried to get away—he was so close to the door he could almost touch it—but then Roman caught hold of his head and yanked it back by the hair. Terrance fought, but Roman sank his teeth into the albino flesh and drank deep.

At first, Terrance moaned, but then, as Roman drank deeper and deeper, Terrance screamed, thrashing to get away.

The girl I was holding struggled, but her strength was spare against my own. She looked up at me and a mixture of feelings washed through her eyes. She looked back at Terrance, and a slow smile spread across her face.

"Who is he, to you?" I whispered to her.

"He sired me. He raped me, sodomized me, and then he turned me—a hundred years ago. And he's kept me prisoner ever since. He said he always had wanted a little girl." She blinked, and I saw the same hatred in her face that I'd felt for Dredge. My heart broke and I found myself crying bloody tears. I pulled her into my arms and held her tight, even though she struggled against me.

"Stop. Stop and listen to me," I whispered. "I was tortured, raped, and turned, too. I know what it's like, though thank the gods I was older than you. But I understand the hatred you have inside you. I want to help you."

She paused, her eyes guardedly meeting my own. As we matched gazes, I felt her probing, searching my look, trying to decide if I was on the up-and-up. I opened up, lifted the veil, and rolled up my sleeves to show her my scars.

As she hesitantly reached out to run her fingers over them, I said, "My sire did this to me, all over my body."

"Is he still . . ." She glanced up at me, wanting to ask but afraid to.

"No, I killed him. I destroyed him and he's gone forever. I'm learning how to live a happy life, even as a vampire, without being anybody's slave." I smiled, and she hesitantly smiled back.

"My name is Serena," she said.

And just then, Roman finished draining Terrance and, as the nightclub owner collapsed, he held out a stake.

"Wait," I said, stopping him. I looked at Serena. "Do you want to do it? There's nothing quite like the feeling when you've freed yourself from a tormentor."

She looked at Roman. He nodded, holding out the stake. She took it and, with me bracing her shoulders, she plunged it through Terrance's heart. One cloud of dust later, the Fangtabula was closed.

On our way out, Roman turned back. "Clean it out and lock up," he told his children. They nodded and we headed to the limo. A group of bedraggled vampires and blood-whores huddled in the parking lot, and as the guards took a step in their direction, they scattered into the night.

Serena came with us. I wasn't sure what the hell to do with her, but Roman solved that. He made a quick call, stepping to the side so we couldn't hear him, then returned. "I have a female friend you can stay with for a few nights till we make provisions for you. Will that be all right?"

She nodded. Ever since she'd dusted Terrance, the girl had fallen mute, seeming weary beyond belief. On the way home, we stopped at another mansion, where Roman sent Serena to the door with the driver, and within moments, she vanished into the palatial estate.

"Who's she staying with?"

"My ex."

I stared at him. "You were married?"

"Thirty-five times. Either they died—they were mortal—or they grew bored and wandered off. This most current, she's a vampire, too, and we were married during the fifties. But she grew restless. We kept in touch, however, and she can be trusted. She runs several women's charities—behind the scenes, of course—and a safe house for abused women."

I shook my head. There were so many layers to this man, and I had the feeling it would take several lifetimes to discover them all. "So . . . what now?"

"Now, we rest. And at the Winter Solstice ball, I unveil you as my consort. I will also be introducing the new Regent. By the way, your friend Wade will receive an invitation to the ball, too. He is *not* to bring his mother. I've heard enough about her. But he will be expected to attend. Vampires Anonymous will be playing a bigger part in the community these coming months."

I nodded, wondering just what Wade would say about that. But Roman silenced my thoughts as he pulled me to him. My lips met his, and we slid down onto the seat, rocking the limousine in the silent and deadly night.

CHAPTER 25

Camille, Delilah, and Iris were waiting up when I came back through the door. They took one look at my bloody clothing and Iris pointed to her bedroom. I quickly stripped, tossed my clothes in the hamper, and took a shower. She'd fetched my robe from my room and it lay waiting on her bed. I wrapped myself in the warm terrycloth and joined them again in the kitchen.

"So . . . Terrance is dead." I took my place at the table and told them about the evening, including Serena. "I plan on handing her over to Wade, unless Roman's ex-wife wants to take over the case."

"So much blood the past few days. So much death." Delilah shook her head. "But that's what we're here for, it seems."

"Yeah, it seems so, doesn't it?" I glanced at Camille. "You ready for Morio to come home?"

She nodded. "More than ready. I've managed to avoid Smoky knowing anything about Vanzir yet. But it's going to come up soon and I dread it."

"Changes, changes everywhere," Iris said. "Speaking of which, I know we're nearing midwinter, but can you and Smoky and Rozurial leave with me in a week or so? We'll be back before your induction into Aeval's Court on the solstice."

Iris was off to search for a way to break a curse that had been laid on her centuries back, when she was in line to become high priestess of the temple to Undutar. She had been given the highest of titles: Ar'jant d'tel—Chosen of the Gods—but it had been stripped away when she was suspected of torturing and killing her fiancé. She had no memory of what happened, but until she broke the curse, she would be forever barren. And for a Finnish Talon-haltija, or house sprite, in her childbearing years, that was one of the most devastating things that could be done to her.

Now Iris had to venture to the Northlands, in search of the spirit of her lover, to find out the truth, and she'd extracted a promise from Camille and Smoky to go with her. Rozurial had volunteered, too, having spent many years in the icy northern wastes.

Camille nodded. "Yeah, we will. And that in itself should prove to be an adventure." She turned to me. "So, big vampire party coming up in a couple weeks?"

"Yeah . . . and a cocktail party before then. And hand-fasting to plan." I thought of Nerissa, who was tucked warmly away in Delilah's playroom upstairs. She'd come over, waiting for me, while I'd been gone. "This is going to be one hell of an interesting ride."

"We're living in interesting times. The old Chinese curse, playing out in our lives. But at least I'll be off bed rest as of next week," Delilah said. "And that is a good thing."

"A good thing indeed," I said, thinking about all the things that were going on. We'd seen good and bad together, and my fears about us splitting up were at rest. I'd fought my battle tonight without them, but they'd still been there—in spirit—in my heart.

No matter whether we stood on the front line together, or whether Camille was hunting with the Moon Mother, or Delilah prowling with the Death Maidens, or even me—skimming the rooftops with Roman and dancing under the stars with Nerissa—we still had each other. And that would forever be enough.

ONE WEEK LATER

The Clockwork Club was old money, rich leather as smooth as silk, blood in Waterford crystal, warmed gently, from willing young donors who kept their bodies clean and free of toxins.

As we entered the sepia-toned ballroom, I felt giddy. My hand was resting on his arm, and I couldn't help but be delighted with my gown that rustled every time I walked. Roman had ordered a special showing at a local gallery, allowing me to shop at night so I wouldn't have to rely on Camille and Nerissa. I'd found a form-fitting cerulean blue cocktail dress, mermaid design with chiffon ruffles that gathered in at my knees, to blossom out in a muff of fluttery wings around my calves. The dress was beaded with clear Swarovski crystals and had cost—well, I didn't want to think what it had cost. Roman had paid for it without blinking.

Nerissa had delighted in playing hairdresser, and my hair was loose—falling around my shoulders, a blistering tangle of curls. A silk wrap covered the worst of my scars, and satin heels completed the ensemble. She'd also laid me back, made love to me, and sated me so well that, as she put it, "If you sleep with Roman tonight, you'll remember that I was here first." I'd laughingly reassured her that I always remembered she came first.

Now, we came down the staircase into the ballroom and paused near the bottom.

"Lord Roman, Son of Blood Wyne, and his consort,

Menolly te Maria D'Artigo." The announcer called out our names, and a hush fell over the crowd.

We mingled, with me trying to put faces to names, until Roman led me toward the front of the chamber where what looked like an official retinue had gathered.

"See him," Roman whispered, nodding at one of the men. "The one in black tails next to the plump lady, who would be his wife, I believe?"

The woman was lovely, if yes—plump. The man was straight shouldered and looked rather fierce.

"Yes, who are they?"

"Frederick Corvax and his wife. The new Regent sent by my mother. This weekend will be the official swearing in, and they'll formally present at the Winter Solstice Ball. You are still expected to attend with me." Roman tucked his hand over mine.

"Of course, no doubt." It was going to take some getting used to—these official functions—but they were kind of fun, in a stuffy, awkward way. My thoughts drifted to home, wondering how Camille and Iris were doing. They had left yesterday, along with Smoky and Roz, for the Northlands, and I hoped they were okay. So far, Smoky hadn't figured out what was going down with Vanzir, and that was a good thing.

Delilah and Shade were at home watching Maggie. Nerissa was there, keeping them company, and our cousin Shamas. Chase and Sharah were out on their second date tonight, and I mentally wished the detective well. We'd been through a lot the past few weeks, and I felt like I'd gotten to know him a lot better. And I—I was here, in the winter wonderland of a room that was dripping with crystal and silver decorations.

The lights went out and heavy drapes opened to show a snow-studded vignette from outside—fir trees dripping with white diamonds. Inside, a thousand Christmas lights in clear white and blue flashed on. The area cleared of those just mingling as the first song of the evening began. It was "Without You," by David Bowie, and Roman drew me out, swirling me onto the dance floor.

If this was the pre-gala cocktail party, what the hell was in store for the actual dance?

"I think I was lying." Roman softly spun me around the floor.

"About what?" I tensed, knowing what he was going to say, praying he wouldn't say it. But he did.

"I think I'm growing to love you." He reached down to nuzzle my neck, and I closed my eyes. His touch felt so good, and I liked him so much, but . . .

"Don't get hooked on me, Roman. Please, don't make me hurt you. You know I love Nerissa."

He nodded, pressing his lips against my skin. "I know, I know."

"I hope so," I whispered, "because Nerissa owns my heart." In the depths of my soul, every word I said rang as true as crystal. Nerissa was my chosen mate. As my thoughts drifted toward our promise ceremony, I fingered my promise ring, and my love for my beautiful Were swelled.

But Roman's words sliced through my thoughts. "There's no reason you can't share your love, you know. Your sister Camille does."

And then, before I could protest, we sped up, and the music flowed as we danced away blood and murder and the ever-present darkness in which we lived.

CAST OF MAJOR CHARACTERS

The D'Artigo Family

Sephreh ob Tanu: The D'Artigo sisters' father. Full Fae.

Maria D'Artigo: The D'Artigo sisters' mother. Human.

Camille Sepharial te Maria, aka Camille D'Artigo: The oldest sister; a Moon Witch. Half-Fae, half-human.

Delilah Maria te Maria, aka Delilah D'Artigo: The middle sister; a werecat.

Arial Lianan te Maria: Delilah's twin who died at birth. Half-Fae, half-human.

Menolly Rosabelle te Maria, aka Menolly D'Artigo: The youngest sister; a vampire and *jian-tu*: extraordinary acrobat. Half-Fae, half-human.

Shamas ob Olanda: The D'Artigo girls' cousin. Full Fae.

The D'Artigo Sisters' Lovers and Close Friends

Bruce O'Shea: Iris's boyfriend. Leprechaun.

Carter: Leader of the Demonica Vacana Society, a group that watches and records the interactions of Demonkin and humans through the ages. Carter is half demon and half Titan—his father was Hyperion, one of the Greek Titans.

Chase Garden Johnson: Detective, director of the Faerie-Human Crime Scene Investigation (FH-CSI) team. Human who has taken the Nectar of Life, which extends his life span beyond that of any ordinary mortal, and which has opened up his own psychic abilities.

Chrysandra: Waitress at the Wayfarer Bar & Grill. Human.

Erin Mathews: Former president of the Faerie Watchers Club and former owner of the Scarlet Harlot Boutique. Turned into a vampire by Menolly, her sire, moments before her death. Human.

Greta: Leader of the Death Maidens; Delilah's tutor.

Iris Kuusi: Friend and companion of the girls. Priestess of Undutar. Talon-haltija (Finnish house sprite).

Lindsey Katharine Cartridge: Director of the Green Goddess Women's Shelter. Pagan and witch. Human.

Luke: Former bartender at the Wayfarer Bar & Grill. Werewolf. Lone wolf—packless.

Marion: Coyote shifter; owner of the Supe-Urban Café.

Morio Kuroyama: One of Camille's lovers and husbands. Essentially the grandson of Grandmother Coyote. Youkai-kitsune (roughly translated: Japanese fox demon).

Nerissa Shale: Menolly's lover. Worked for DSHS. Now working for Chase Johnson as a victims-rights counselor for the FH-CSI. Werepuma and member of the Rainier Puma Pride.

Roman: Ancient vampire; son of Blood Wyne, Queen of the Crimson Veil.

Rozurial, aka Roz: Mercenary. Menolly's secondary lover. Incubus who used to be Fae before Zeus and Hera destroyed his marriage.

Sassy Branson: Socialite. Philanthropist. Vampire (human).

Shade: New ally. Delilah's lover. Part Stradolan, part black (shadow) dragon.

Siobhan Morgan: One of the girls' friends. Selkie (wereseal); member of the Puget Sound Harbor Seal Pod.

Smoky: One of Camille's lovers and husbands. Half-white, half-silver dragon.

Tavah: Guardian of the portal at the Wayfarer Bar & Grill. Vampire (full Fae).

Tim Winthrop, aka Cleo Blanco: Computer student/genius, female impersonator. Human.

Trillian: Mercenary. Camille's alpha lover and third husband. Svartan (one of the Charming Fae).

Vanzir: Indentured slave to the sisters, by his own choice.
    Dream-chaser demon.
Venus the Moon Child: Shaman of the Rainier Puma
    Pride. Werepuma. One of the Keraastar Knights.
Wade Stevens: President of Vampires Anonymous.
    Vampire (human).
Zachary Lyonnesse: Junior member of the Rainier Puma
    Pride Council of Elders. Werepuma.

GLOSSARY

Black Unicorn/Black Beast: Father of the Dahns unicorns, a magical unicorn that is reborn like the phoenix and lives in Darkynwyrd and Thistlewyd Deep. Raven Mother is his consort, and he is more a force of nature than a unicorn.

Calouk: The rough, common dialect used by a number of Otherworld inhabitants.

Court and Crown: "Crown" refers to the Queen of Y'Elestrial. "Court" refers to the nobility and military personnel that surround the Queen. "Court and Crown" together refer to the entire government of Y'Elestrial.

Court of the Three Queens: The newly risen Court of the three Earthside Fae Queens: Titania, the Fae Queen of Light and Morning; Morgaine, the half-Fae Queen of Dusk; and Aeval, the Fae Queen of Shadow and Night.

Crypto: One of the Cryptozoid races. Cryptos include creatures out of legend that are not technically of the Fae races: gargoyles, unicorns, gryphons, chimeras, and so on. Most primarily inhabit Otherworld, but some have Earthside cousins.

Demon Gate: A gate through which demons may be summoned by a powerful sorcerer or necromancer.

Earthside: Everything that exists on the Earth side of the portals.

Elqaneve: The Elfin lands in Otherworld.

Elemental Lords: The elemental beings—both male and female—who, along with the Hags of Fate and the Harvestmen, are the only true Immortals. They are avatars of various elements and energies, and they inhabit all realms. They do as they will and seldom concern themselves with humankind or Fae unless summoned. If asked for help, they often exact steep prices in return. The Elemental Lords are not concerned with balance like the Hags of Fate.

FBH: Full-blooded human (usually refers to Earthside humans).

FH-CSI: The Faerie-Human Crime Scene Investigation team. The brainchild of Detective Chase Johnson, it was first formed as a collaboration between the OIA and the Seattle police department. Other FH-CSI units have been created around the country, based on the Seattle prototype. The FH-CSI takes care of both medical and criminal emergencies involving visitors from Otherworld.

Great Divide: A time of immense turmoil when the Elemental Lords and some of the High Court of Fae decided to rip apart the worlds. Until then, the Fae existed primarily on Earth, their lives and worlds mingling with those of humans. The Great Divide tore everything asunder, splitting off another dimension, which became Otherworld. At that time, the Twin Courts of Fae were disbanded and their queens stripped of power. This was the time during which the Spirit Seal was formed and broken in order to seal off the realms from each other. Some Fae chose to stay Earthside, others moved to the realm of Otherworld, and the demons were—for the most part—sealed in the Subterranean Realms.

Guard Des'Estar: The military of Y'Elestrial.

Hags of Fate: The women of destiny who keep the balance righted. Neither good nor evil, they observe the flow of destiny. When events get too far out of balance, they step in and take action, usually using humans, Fae, Supes, and other creatures as pawns to bring the path of destiny back into line.

Harvestmen: The lords of death—a few cross over and are also Elemental Lords. The Harvestmen, along with their followers (the Valkyries and the Death Maidens, for example) reap the souls of the dead.

Haseofon: The abode of the Death Maidens—where they stay and where they train.

Ionyc Lands: The astral, etheric, and spirit realms, along with several other lesser-known noncorporeal dimensions, form the Ionyc Lands. These realms are separated by the Ionyc Sea, a current of energy that prevents the Ionyc Lands from colliding, thereby sparking off an explosion of universal proportions.

Ionyc Sea: The currents of energy that separate the Ionyc Lands. Certain creatures, especially those connected with the elemental energies of ice, snow, and wind, can travel through the Ionyc Sea without protection.

Koyanni: The coyote shifters who took an evil path away from the Great Coyote; followers of Nukpana.

Melosealfôr: A rare Crypto dialect learned by powerful Cryptos and all Moon Witches.

The Nectar of Life: An elixir that can extend the life span of humans to nearly the length of a Fae's years. Highly prized and cautiously used. Can drive someone insane if he or she doesn't have the emotional capacity to handle the changes incurred.

OIA: The Otherworld Intelligence Agency; the "brains" behind the Guard Des'Estar.

Otherworld/OW: The human term for the "United Nations" of Faerie Land. A dimension apart from ours that contains creatures from legend and lore, pathways to the gods, and various other places, such as Olympus. Otherworld's actual name varies among the differing dialects of the many races of Cryptos and Fae.

Portal, Portals: The interdimensional gates that connect the different realms. Some were created during the Great Divide; others open up randomly.

Seelie Court: The Earthside Fae Court of Light and Summer, disbanded during the Great Divide. Titania was the Seelie Queen.

Soul Statues: In Otherworld, small figurines created for the Fae of certain races and magically linked with a baby. These figurines reside in family shrines and when one of the Fae dies, his or her soul statue shatters. In Menolly's case, when she was reborn as a vampire, her soul statue reformed, although twisted. If a family member disappears, his or her family can always tell if their loved one is alive or dead if they have access to the soul statue.

Spirit Seals: A magical crystal artifact, the Spirit Seal was created during the Great Divide. When the portals were sealed, the Spirit Seal was broken into nine gems and each piece was given to an Elemental Lord or Lady. These gems each have varying powers. Even possessing one of the spirit seals can allow the wielder to weaken the portals that divide Otherworld, Earthside, and the Subterranean Realms. If the all of the seals are joined together again, then all of the portals will open.

Stradolan: A being who can walk between worlds, who can walk through the shadows, using them as a method of transportation.

Supe/Supes: Short for Supernaturals. Refers to Earthside supernatural beings who are not of Fae nature. Refers to Weres, especially.

Triple Threat: Camille's nickname for the newly risen three Earthside Queens of Fae.

Unseelie Court: The Earthside Fae Court of Shadow and Winter, disbanded during the Great Divide. Aeval was the Unseelie Queen.

VA/Vampires Anonymous: The Earthside group started by Wade Stevens, a vampire who was a psychologist during life. The group is focused on helping newly born vampires adjust to their new state of existence, and to encourage vampires to avoid harming the innocent as much as possible. The VA is vying for control. Their goal is to rule the vampires of the United States and to set up an internal policing agency.

Whispering Mirror: A magical communications device that links Otherworld and Earth. Think magical video phone.

Y'Eírialiastar: The Sidhe/Fae name for Otherworld.

Y'Elestrial: The city-state in Otherworld where the D'Artigo girls were born and raised. A Fae city, recently embroiled in a civil war between the drug-crazed tyrannical Queen Lethesanar and her more level-headed sister Tanaquar, who managed to claim the throne for herself. The civil war has ended and Tanaquar is restoring order to the land.

Youkai: Loosely (very loosely) translated as Japanese demon/nature spirit. For the purposes of this series, the youkai have three shapes: the animal, the human form, and the true demon form. Unlike the demons of the Subterranean Realms, youkai are not necessarily evil by nature.

PLAYLIST FOR *BLOOD WYNE*

I listen to a lot of music when I write, and when I talk about it online, my readers always want to know what I'm listening to for each book. So, in addition to adding the playlists to my website, I thought I'd add them in the back of each book so you can create your own if you want to hear my "soundtrack" for the books. —Yasmine Galenorn

AC/DC:
"Back in Black"

Air:
"Napalm Love"
"Playground Love"
"Cherry Blossom Girl"
"Venus"
"Ghost Song"
"Surfing on a Rocket"

Beck:
"Farewell Ride"
"Nausea"
"Mixed Bizness"

Blue Oyster Cult:
"Godzilla"

Bob Seger:
"Turn the Page"

Bravery, The:
"Believe"

Cat Power:
"I Don't Blame You"
"Werewolf"

Cher:
"The Beat Goes On"

Chester Bennington:
"System"

Chris Isaak:
"Wicked Game"

David Bowie:
"I'm Afraid of Americans"
"Let's Dance"
"Sister Midnight"
"Without You"

Deftones:
"Change (In the House of Flies)"

Depeche Mode:
"Personal Jesus"
"Stripped"
"Dream On"

Don Henley:
"In the Garden of Allah"

Eddy Grant:
"Electric Avenue"

Everlast:
"I Can't Move"

Faith No More:
"Epic"

Gabrielle Roth:
"Rest Your Tears Here"
"The Calling"
"Raven"

Gary Numan:
"Down in the Park"
"Hybrid"
"Prophecy"
"Tread Careful"
"Are Friends Electric?"
"Soul Protection"
"My Breathing"
"Hybrid"
"Cars (Hybrid Remix)"
"The Sleeproom"
"Survivor"
"I Can't Stop"
"Call Out the Dogs"
"Strange Charm"

Gorillaz:
"Hongkongaton"

Hives, The:
"Tick Tick Boom"

Jay Gordon:
"Slept So Long"

Kraftwerk:
"Pocket Calculator"

Lady Gaga:
"Telephone"
"Poker Face"
"Paparazzi"

Ladytron:
"Ghosts"
"Burning Up"
"Black Cat"
"Predict the Day"
"I'm Not Scared"
"High Rise"
"Destroy Everything You Touch"

Lenny Kravitz:
"American Woman"
"Fly Away"

Lindstrøm and Christabelle:
"Lovesick"

Little Big Town:
"Bones"

Low:
"Half Light"

Madonna:
"Vogue"

Marilyn Manson:
"Tainted Love"
"Personal Jesus"

Metallica:
"Enter Sandman"

NIN:
"Closer"
"Sin"
"Get Down, Make Love"

Nirvana:
"You Know You're Right"

No Doubt:
"Hella Good"

Oingo Boingo:
"Elevator Man"
"Dead Man's Party"

Pussycat Dolls:
"Buttons"

Ricky Martin:
"She Bangs"

Rob Zombie:
"Living Dead Girl"
"Never Gonna Stop"

Róisín Murphy:
"Ramalama Bang Bang"

Saliva:
"Ladies and Gentlemen"

Seether:
"Remedy"

Shriekback:
"Over the Wire"
"New Man"

Susan Enan:
"Bring on the Wonder"

Talking Heads:
"Life During Wartime"
"I Zimbra"

Tears for Fears:
"Mad World"

Toadies:
"Possum Kingdom"

Tool:
"Schism"

Zero 7:
"In the Waiting Line"

Dear Reader:

I'm thrilled so many of you have taken my Otherworld series to heart. As many of you know, I have started a second series: the Indigo Court Series. Here, in the back of *Blood Wyne*, you will find a sneak peek at the first chapter of *Night Veil*, the second Indigo Court book (Summer 2011).

But rest assured: I am *not* done with the Otherworld series. I love writing about the Sisters and have plenty of adventures planned for them. You'll be able to read a novella about Iris in an anthology titled *Hexed* (Summer 2011). Find out just what dark secrets the Talon-haltija has been hiding all these years.

Come Fall 2011, *Courting Darkness* will be released (Camille's fourth book). Watch out—Smoky's daddy is back and he's on the rampage, out for revenge. And yes—there are more books planned after that.

So between the Indigo Court series and the Otherworld series, I hope to keep you in reading material for the coming year. Again, thank you for supporting the series and taking the Sisters to heart. You can find plenty of Otherworld perks on my website: www.galenorn.com.

> Bright Blessings,
> The Painted Panther,
> Yasmine Galenorn

And now . . .
a special excerpt from the second book
in the Indigo Court series

Night Veil

by Yasmine Galenorn
Coming Summer 2011 from Berkley!

Myst led her people into the shadows and ice, and there they hid, sheltered in the depths of lore. Considered pariah, the Vampiric Fae were a dirty secret, Shadow Hunters that debased the entire realm of Faerie.

And so in furtive silence, the host fed and drank deep and they did rend the flesh of their victims and feast. But their thirst was unquenchable, and it was then that Myst discovered one of their newfound powers: Members of the Indigo Court could drink from the souls of the magic-born . . . With this discovery, a vision for the future began to evolve, and the foundation of terror began . . .

—FROM *THE RISE OF THE INDIGO COURT*

The great horned owl sat in the oak.

I could see the bird from my window, huddling in the sparse branches, trying to protect itself from the snow. I longed to join it, to strip off my clothes and turn into my owl self, to fly free under the haunting winter moon, but the weather was harsh and cold. And Myst was out there, hiding in the forest with her people, waiting.

And somewhere, hidden in her mists and shadows, Grieve is there, captive, caught in Myst's web. Can he still possibly love me? Can he still be saved from the blood that now flows through his veins? How can I let him go now that we've found each other again?

I opened the window and leaned out, glancing down at the yard below. The snow gleamed under the nearly full moon, a crystal blanket of white flooding the lawn. The Golden Wood—or Spider's Wood, as I called it—was aglow as usual, with a sickly green light that I'd seen every night since returning home to New Forest. A thousand miles and years seemed to separate me from my former existence, although it had only been a couple of weeks since I arrived back in town. But in that short time, my life had turned upside down, in every possible way.

The wind called to me to come and play and I closed my eyes, reveling in the feel of the breezes lashing against my skin. My owls—a pair of blackwork tattooed owls flying over a silver moon impaled on a dagger banded both arms—shifted, urging me to fly.

Slipping on my leather jacket and gloves, I cautiously climbed out on the shingles, making sure that the snow that had built up didn't send me sliding to the ground, but it had turned to ice. I scooted until my back rested against the window, then brought my knees up, circling them with my arms, and huddled.

As I stared up into the oak, the great horned owl let out a soft hoot, stirring my blood. Over the past month, he'd taught me to shake off the fear of falling, to soar through the unending night turning on a wing, catching mice in the yard, while always, *always,* keeping an eye on the forest.

You are Uwilahsidhe. You are magic-born. You must keep watch for Myst, he constantly reminded me. *The queen of the Indigo Court seeks to destroy you.*

I raised one hand in salute, the snowflakes softly kissing my skin, and he hooted again, a warning in his tone.

"What is it?" I whispered. "What are you trying to tell me?"

Ulean, my Wind Elemental, swept around me like a cloak, answering for him. *He fears for you. There are ghosts riding the wind tonight, and the Shadow Hunters are out and about. There will be death before the morning.*

More death. More blood. My stomach churned as I thought about the four deaths reported over the past two days. One of those had been a child. All had been mortal, torn to bits, eaten to the bone.

I gazed at the forest. What were Myst and her people up to tonight? Who were they hunting? The bitch-queen was ravenous and without mercy.

There has been so much death over the past few days. They are terrorizing the town and now everyone fears them, even though they don't know who it is they run from. I leaned against the gentle current that signaled Ulean was leaning against me. She had been my guardian since I was six years old, bonded to me through ritual, a gift from Lainule, the Queen of Rushes and Rivers.

And they should fear. Myst will not just go away. She is here to make her mark and conquer. She is here to destroy. Ulean caught up a skiff of snow and sent it into the air, spiraling around me.

I glanced back inside at the clock. Seven P.M. Another two hours before we were to meet with Geoffrey. Finally, after five days of silence, the Northwest Regent for the Vampire Nation had summoned us. Five days after we had rescued our friend Peyton from Myst. Five days after I'd lost Grieve to her. Five days in which the Indigo Court had rained hell on the town and killed eight people.

The owl hooted again and as I glanced in his direction, a shadow of movement caught my eye from below, over near the herb gardens.

Crap—something was rooting around down there. Not an animal, so what was it? Another glance over at the Spider's Wood showed nothing, but we couldn't take any chances.

Ulean, do you know what that thing is?

A moment passed and then she drifted gently around me again. *Not one of the Shadow Hunters, but I have no doubt it belongs to the Indigo Court. Myst is attracting the sinister Fae.*

I leaned forward, trying to keep it within my sight. *I need to know what it is. We can't take a chance on letting it prowl around our land.* I scrambled back through the window just long enough to slip on my wrist sheath and make sure my switchblade was firmly affixed. Grabbing my fan from the dresser, I slipped back out on the roof and slid to the edge.

The two-story drop was problematic, but a couple of days ago I'd installed a roll-up ladder to provide easy access. I'd been out flying and landed back on the roof, only to discover that somebody in the house had thought I was off shopping and had shut my window and locked it. I'd been stuck out in the snow, naked, too tired to change back into owl form to fly down to the ground and come through the front door. Now, I had the option of climbing down, which was a whole lot easier than shapeshifting when I was exhausted.

I rolled the ladder over the edge, and was about to swing onto the rungs when Kaylin stuck his head through the window.

"What are you doing?"

"Goblin dog or something of the sort in the backyard. I was going to check it out."

"Give me ten secs and I'll come with you." He ducked back through the window as I headed down the ladder. A moment later, Kaylin was shimmying down the ladder to land next to me. The dreamwalker was far older than his looks suggested, and he was far more skilled in fighting than I was. Having him at my back made me feel much more secure.

"Where are the others?" I hadn't seen my cousin Rhiannon all day.

"Rhiannon is out running errands, and Leo is doing a last-minute run for Geoffrey."

Leo was a day-runner for the vampires. More specifically, he worked for the Regent, doing his errands that Geoffrey and his wife could not do during the daylight hours.

"What about Chatter?"

"He's in the basement, working on charms against the Indigo Court."

"I thought the house seemed quiet." I moved forward, cautiously.

The backyard of the Veil House was more like the back-forty. Filled with herb gardens, stone circles, and fruit trees, it lay blanketed in a thick layer of snow, and the rising moon set off a bluish tinge to everything around. We stopped, listening to the owl as he hooted again, his warnings echoing through the yard.

We were as quiet as possible, but at one point I stepped on a fallen branch that had been buried in the snow and it snapped in two. The creature, which had apparently been working its way toward the house, heard us and froze.

"This way," Kaylin mouthed, circling around it.

I followed his lead, edging closer to whatever it was. We managed to slip behind a nearby bush before it could back away. There didn't appear to be more than one, and we were able to get a good look at it.

The creature was about four feet tall, with long, bony arms that dragged along the ground and a bloated stomach. Its head was distorted, elongated and elliptical, with longish ears. The eyes were wide set and cunning. Drawing back its lips into a grimace, it dripped drool from between its needle-sharp teeth.

"Have any idea what it is?" I whispered to Kaylin, wishing he could talk on the slipstream. It was much easier to avoid being overheard when sending messages along with the currents of air.

Kaylin cocked his head, his ponytail shifting slightly. "Yes, it's a goblin. One of Myst's toadies, no doubt. If we let it live, I guarantee it will bring others. Somehow they can get through our wards where Myst's Shadow Hunters can't, so she's probably testing how far she can push into our land."

"Kill, or wound as a message?"

"Go in for the kill. If we just wound it, we'll have yet another nasty enemy on our hands."

I gave him a short nod, saving my breath as we burst out of the bushes and poured on the speed. As we caught up to the thing—the goblin was terribly quick—I pulled out my fan and whispered, *"Strong Gust,"* and snapped the fan open, waving it twice.

A quick blast of air slammed against us—and the goblin. Startled, the creature skidded to a halt at the edge of the forest, looking confused. Kaylin dove forward, rolling to come up in fighting stance. He kicked it in the chin. As the goblin lurched back, I slipped through on the left side and brought my switchblade down on its arm, stabbing it deeply.

Kaylin fumbled for his shurikens as an icy gust of wind came whistling from the direction of the forest, and a shadow figure loomed at the border dividing the woods from the magical barrier we'd constructed. A glimpse of pale skin with a cerulean cast to it told us all we needed to know. One of the Vampiric Fae. *A Shadow Hunter.*

"Shit," I muttered, steeling myself as the goblin launched itself at me.

The Shadow Hunter raised a bow. He might not be able to set foot on our land, but his weaponry could. I shouted at Kaylin and managed to wave my fan in the direction of the Vampiric Fae, whispering, *"Strong Gust."* The arrow came zinging toward Kaylin, but missed him by inches.

The goblin landed on me and we both went down, rolling into the snow. I couldn't use my fan in such close quarters so I struggled to catch the creature by the throat. I was bigger than the goblin, but not as tough. After struggling against leathery skin, I finally managed to get one hand on its neck.

Gnashing its teeth, the goblin lashed out at my hand and I pulled away just in time. Even if I didn't lose any fingers, chances were good it had some nasty bacteria in that mouth and I wanted no part of any infection it might be carrying. We wrestled, me trying to force back its hands as it scrabbled to reach my face. One swipe of those claw-like nails could take out an eye. The stench of the creature was putrid, like a combination of gas and vomit, and its eyes were round and lidless.

I sucked in a deep breath and heaved, pushing with both hands and feet, and managed to roll on top, trapping it between my knees. I squeezed my thighs together, trying to keep the goblin from slipping away from me. At that moment, Kaylin let out a shout and I jerked around. A muscle pulled in my neck.

"*Fuck!*" The Shadow Hunter's second arrow had grazed his arm.

The bolt had penetrated the heavy leather he was wearing, but looked like it hadn't gone too deep. Kaylin yanked the arrow out, tossing it to the ground, and dashed over the boundary line. The Shadow Hunter hadn't been prepared for his assault and went down, Kaylin atop him in the snow, a flurry of fists flying.

I turned my attention back to the goblin. If I let this thing get away, it would be back, with reinforcements. I flipped the blade on my switchblade and paused. Killing creatures—even our enemies—was still new, and did not come easy to me. I sucked in a deep breath.

You can do it. Steady. Aim for the forehead. Goblins are vulnerable in the third eye area. Ulean flurried around me, trying to keep the snow from blinding my vision.

With a surge in the pit of my stomach, I brought the blade down, wincing as it slid through the goblin's head. New Forest had become a town of kill or be killed. We no longer had the luxury of allowing our enemies to live in peace.

I drove the blade all the way through to the ground below. The goblin screeched, loud and jagged through the twilight, and then fell limp as a fountain of blood stained the snow red, diluting into petal pink. The scent of the creature lingered, joined by that of blood. I withdrew my blade.

Another shout. I looked up to realize that—in my

fight—I'd also passed the boundary line and the Shadow Hunter was on the run, aiming directly for me. I froze, but he merely shoved me aside and fell to the side of the goblin's body, his face pressed against the creature's wound.

As I backed away, horrified, he lapped at the blood, and then began to transform, his mouth unhinging like that of a snake as he shifted into a dog-like monster, his jaws lined with spiny teeth. With ravenous fury, he bit off the head, chewing it, spattering bits of brain matter every which way.

Kaylin brushed his fingers to his lips and slowly edged up on the Shadow Hunter. He brought out a short dagger, serrated and coated in a magical oil. As he plunged the knife into the side of the Vampiric Fae, aiming for the heart, the oil encouraged the blood to flow and it stained the snow still further.

The Shadow Hunter turned, but I was quicker, stabbing its haunch with my blade and dragging it along the side. Then Kaylin and I lightly danced backward, out of reach of those deadly teeth.

A voice echoed from behind us and I turned to see my cousin Rhiannon, panting as she stretched out her hands, a small red charm in the palm of her right. She whispered, just loud enough for us to hear, "Flame to flame, bolt to bolt, fire to fire, jolt to jolt. Lightning, let me be thy rod."

All hell broke loose as a bolt of snow lighting came forking out of the gathering clouds, ripping to the ground to shatter the Shadow Hunter into a thousand pieces, as if he were a glass dish smashed on concrete.

As soon as the spell sang out of her body, Rhiannon collapsed and Kaylin raced over to catch her. I stared at the remains of the Shadow Hunter and the goblin. Not much left. Nothing to take home with us, except two more notches on our belt, and the hope that we'd be able to sleep soundly, knowing there was one less member of Myst's court in the world. One less toady of hers to slip onto our land.

Kaylin shivered. He was bleeding through the rent in

his jacket from the arrow. And I noticed a trickle running down my shoulder. I glanced down. A puncture wound had penetrated my jacket. I slipped it off to see blood saturating my top. The goblin must have stabbed me with its claw. I hadn't even noticed.

"We're growing numb to our pain," I said as we turned away from the carnage we'd just inflicted.

"We have to," Kaylin said. "We have to learn to weather the battles because there will be far more to come before things get back to normal. If there even *is* such a thing as 'normal' anymore."

I nodded, and looked at Rhiannon. "You saved the day." She knew the thank-you was implied.

She slipped her arm around my waist and leaned down to kiss my forehead. "I just got home and saw the commotion from the car. Leo's still in town and I don't know where Chatter is."

"In the basement, working with the charms."

"Ah. Good. We'll need them."

"I guess we'd better get back on our land, before anything else comes out of the woods. We need to tend to our wounds and make sure they don't get infected." I wearily turned back to the house.

As we crossed the demarcation line that magically divided the Golden Wood from the Veil House, I couldn't help but shudder. Like it or not, we were pawns in a war between two powerful enemies, and we were doing our best just to stay alive.

**FROM THE *NEW YORK TIMES*
BESTSELLING AUTHOR OF THE
OTHERWORLD SERIES**

YASMINE GALENORN

Harvest Hunting

The D'Artigo sisters are sexy supernatural opera-
tives for the Otherworld Intelligence Agency. It's
Samhain, and the Autumn Lord calls Delilah to
begin her training with the Death Maidens. . . .
And she finds that she likes it. But the sisters have
problems: Werewolves are going missing and a new
magical drug, Wolf Briar, is being used as a weapon.
But most dangerous of all: Stacia Bonecrusher has
put a bounty on their heads. Now it's a race to take
out the demon general before she realizes the sixth
spirit seal is within her reach. . . .

PRAISE FOR YASMINE GALENORN

"Yasmine Galenorn is a sheer force of
nature. . . . The magic Galenorn weaves with the
written word is irresistible."
—Maggie Shayne, *New York Times*
bestselling author

penguin.com

M777T0910

Don't miss the new series from
New York Times bestselling author

YASMINE GALENORN

NIGHT MYST
An Indigo Court Novel

Eons ago, vampires tried to turn the Dark Fae in order to harness their magic, only to create a demonic enemy more powerful than they imagined. Now Myst, the queen of the Indigo Court, has enough power to begin a long-prophesied supernatural war.

Cicely Waters, a witch who can control the wind, may be the only one who can stop her—and save her beloved Fae prince from the queen's enslavement.

M714T0510

NEW FROM *NEW YORK TIMES*
BESTSELLING AUTHOR

Yasmine Galenorn

BONE
MAGIC

**"Galenorn's kick-butt Fae ramp up the
action in a wyrd world gone awry!"**
—PATRICIA RICE

Another equinox is here and life's getting more
tumultuous for the D'Artigo sisters. Smoky, the
dragon of Camille's dreams, must choose between his
family and her. Plus, the sisters can't locate the new
demon general in town. And Camille is summoned to
Otherworld, thinking she'll reunite with her long-lost
soul mate, Trillian. But once there, she must undergo
a drastic ritual that will forever change her and those
she loves.

penguin.com

M551T0809

Don't miss a word from the "erotic and darkly
bewitching"* series featuring the D'Artigo sisters,
half-human, half-Fae supernatural agents.

By *New York Times* Bestselling Author

Yasmine Galenorn

WITCHLING

CHANGELING

DARKLING

DRAGON WYTCH

NIGHT HUNTRESS

DEMON MISTRESS

BONE MAGIC

HARVEST HUNTING

BLOOD WYNE

Praise for the Otherworld series:

"Pure delight."
—MaryJanice Davidson, *New York Times*
bestselling author

"Vivid, sexy, and mesmerizing."
—*Romantic Times*

penguin.com

*Jeaniene Frost, *New York Times* bestselling author

M192AS0910

8675

Enter the tantalizing world
of
paranormal romance

Christine Feehan

Lora Leigh

Nalini Singh

Angela Knight

Yasmine Galenorn

MaryJanice Davidson

Berkley authors
take you to a whole new realm

penguin.com

M4G0610